Serving Up
LOVE

A
Four-in-One
Harvey House
Brides Collection

Serving Up
LOVE

A Flood of Love · TRACIE PETERSON

More Than a Pretty Face · KAREN WITEMEYER

Intrigue a la Mode · REGINA JENNINGS

Grand Encounters · JEN TURANO

BETHANYHOUSE
a division of Baker Publishing Group
Minneapolis, Minnesota

A Flood of Love © 2019 by Peterson Ink, Inc.
More Than a Pretty Face © 2019 by Karen Witemeyer
Intrigue a la Mode © 2019 by Regina Jennings
Grand Encounters © 2019 by Jennifer L. Turano

Published by Bethany House Publishers
11400 Hampshire Avenue South
Bloomington, Minnesota 55438
www.bethanyhouse.com

Bethany House Publishers is a division of
Baker Publishing Group, Grand Rapids, Michigan

Printed in the United States of America

Library of Congress Cataloging-in-Publication Data
Names: Peterson, Tracie. A flood of love author. | Witemeyer, Karen. More than a
    pretty face author. | Jennings, Regina (Regina Lea). Intrigue a la mode author. |
    Turano, Jen. Grand encounters author.
Title: Serving up love : a four-in-one Harvey House brides collection / Tracie
    Peterson, Karen Witemeyer, Regina Jennings, Jen Turano.
Description: Minneapolis, Minnesota : Bethany House, a division of Baker
    Publishing Group, [2019]
Identifiers: LCCN 2019024673 | ISBN 9780764232695 (trade paperback) | ISBN
    9781493420452 (ebook) | ISBN 9780764234811 (cloth)
Subjects: LCSH: Romance fiction, American. | Waitresses—Fiction. | Fred Harvey
    (Firm)—Employees—Fiction. | Christian fiction, American.
Classification: LCC PS648.L6 S465 2019 | DDC 813/.08508—dc23
LC record available at https://lccn.loc.gov/2019024673

Scripture quotations are from the King James Version of the Bible.

Cover design by Koechel Peterson & Associates, Inc., Minneapolis, Minnesota/Jon Godfredson

Karen Witemeyer is represented by Books & Such Literary Agency.
Jen Turano is represented by the Natasha Kern Agency.

19 20 21 22 23 24 25   7 6 5 4 3 2 1

Contents

A Flood
of Love

—

Tracie Peterson

Chapter One

Gretchen Gottsacker stepped from the train and looked around at the tiny town of San Marcial, New Mexico—pronounced *Mar-see-al* by those of Spanish descent and *Mar-shall* by the white settlers. Despite being named for a French saint, the town hugged the Rio Grande in the midst of arid sands and tamarisk brush. It was some of the most desolate land America had to offer, but amazingly there were small farms and a bustling economy here. The latter came courtesy of the Santa Fe Railway, which had built shops where extensive repair work could be done on just about any engine. There was also a roundhouse to turn the engines and, of course, the Harvey House—Gretchen's destination.

At twenty-eight, she had worked for the Fred Harvey Company for ten years. It had never been a goal or ambition of hers to work as a waitress, serving alongside the Santa Fe. However, it gave her ample money to support herself, and promotions had lifted her to a status above that of a mere waitress. For a single woman, the money was too good to give up, even if the lifestyle was taxing at times.

She walked the short distance from the train station to the

two-story Harvey House along with the other passengers hoping to be served one of Fred Harvey's famous lunches. Since she wasn't expected until the evening train, Gretchen decided to eat before she made her presence known to the house manager.

Like all Harvey Houses, the tables were set impeccably with china, linen, and silver in the dining room, while the lunch counter offered simpler fare. In the dining room a man had to wear a jacket, but at the counter a fella—or lady—could take their meal as they were.

Although Gretchen's original destination had been the counter, a group of ladies from the train invited her to join their table. "We gals need to stick together," one overly painted matron declared. Gretchen nodded and claimed the chair beside her.

As the waitresses took their orders, coffee cups were arranged in a variety of poses to signal what beverages had been selected. It was yet another detail of the intricate system Fred Harvey had designed to keep passengers on the Santa Fe dining in style.

Gretchen asked for iced tea and placed her order for a ham sandwich before leaning back to observe the handling of the dining room. The Harvey Girls were good at their jobs. Their intense training saw to that, but often they got lazy if not firmly supervised. The girls at San Marcial apparently were proud of what they did and continued to uphold the high standards.

Gretchen had finished her sandwich and started on a piece of pie when the train's first warning gong sounded. Several passengers looked panicked until their waitress assured them they would not be left behind. By the time the second gong rang, many of the passengers had already headed back to the train. As the dining room emptied out, a couple of boys came in to start clearing the tables.

Gretchen left her huge slice of pie only half eaten and motioned one of the girls to her table. "Would you mind calling the manager for me?"

The redhead paled. "Is there a problem, miss?"

Gretchen smiled and shook her head. "No. I'm here to fill in for your house mother."

The girl's mouth dropped open, but she quickly regained her composure. "Oh, of course. I'll fetch him right away, Miss Gottsacker."

Gretchen smiled again. Apparently the staff was aware of her impending arrival.

It wasn't but a moment before the manager appeared. "I understand you're Miss Gottsacker." He smiled. "I'm so glad to meet you. Did you have a pleasant lunch?"

"I did. I thought it best to come in early, unannounced, and observe the girls at work."

"And did we pass inspection?"

Gretchen thought he actually looked a little anxious. "Yes. They are good at what they do, and they made the customers feel welcome. In fact, when one of the men dropped his bread on the floor, there was a Harvey Girl there immediately to clean up the mess while another filled his plate with more bread. He scarcely had time to notice anything had happened."

"Wonderful. I'm glad to hear it. I'm actually delighted you've come early. Not only are we missing the house mother, but we've lost two girls. Both had family emergencies and had to leave town this morning. I know it's asking a lot, but do you suppose you could fill in as waitress too?"

"Of course." Gretchen dabbed her mouth with her napkin. "We do what we must. I'll be ready for the evening passenger line."

He smiled. "Thank you so much. Now, if you're finished with your lunch, why don't you let me show you around? I have your room ready."

Gretchen folded her napkin. "Thank you."

After an hour of touring the two-story building, the manager ended the tour on the long veranda. "We have four trains a day but also get plenty of business because of the shops," he told her. "Most of the men in this town work for Santa Fe, and they work hard. This is the Horney Toad Division, and everything that has ever happened to a railroad has happened here."

The Santa Fe line between Albuquerque and El Paso was known as the Horney Toad Line, and its workers were Horney Toad men. They made it very clear that the spelling included the "e" because there were no other "e's," or *ease*, to be had on that rail line. When the corporate leaders wanted to grow a man and prove his worth, the Horney Toad Line was the training ground they sent him to. There was no stretch of railroad meaner, harder, or uglier. Gretchen had ridden the train from Albuquerque to El Paso, and she had to agree. The land was desolate, with miles of nothing stretching out on all sides. Despite the hardship, the Santa Fe line was one of the most important in the country.

The manager was well aware of this fact. "We are one of the premier shops for the railroad. We also have a large team of office workers, which means a good number of the Santa Fe management comes visiting. We never know who will show up."

"I'm quite familiar with the line and the town," Gretchen assured him. "In fact, I used to live here. And, in keeping with Mr. Harvey's original standards, I shall treat each man, woman, and child as if they were the most important person in the world."

He smiled. "What a relief to have not only a well-trained member of the company, but also someone already familiar with our town."

That evening after the rush of the passenger train and cleanup, Gretchen decided to take a walk to reacquaint herself with the area and allow the stream of memories she had so long buried to run free. She had grown up in San Marcial, which was one of the reasons she'd been picked for this job. It certainly hadn't been her desire. She hadn't wanted to come back—not ever—yet here she was.

She walked down Main Street in what they called New Town and smiled at the greetings of several cowboys. There were quite a few people out enjoying the evening now that the sun had set. Someone had mentioned a bingo game at the Catholic church, but most of the men seemed bound for the pool hall. The heat during the day had been overwhelming, just as Gretchen remembered. But, as she also remembered, the evenings were pleasant and cooled off fast.

The town was larger now. There were far more businesses and places of entertainment than when she'd lived here. The Santa Fe drew in many who saw it as an opportunity to make their pot of gold off the workers. With Prohibition wearing on the nerves of hard-drinking men, Gretchen felt confident there were also plenty of adventuring sorts who were happy to bring in liquor from Mexico. No doubt more than one gathering place had a hidden room where a drink could be had.

Walking a faintly familiar path to La Plaza Vieja, or Old Town, Gretchen enjoyed the heady scent of chilies and spices. Someone was charring large peppers on an outdoor grill, and the aroma reminded her of her grandmother. Grandmother—or Oma, as Gretchen had called the old German woman—had lived in Old Town. She'd come to San Marcial with her husband in the early days of the railroad. The little adobe dwelling they called home had been a haven of love for Gretchen. Her father had brought her here after Mama died. Not long after that, he died too, and Gretchen was left to be raised by her grandparents. Life with Oma and Opa had been full of love and happiness, but then her grandfather had been killed in a train accident, and now Oma was gone as well. They were all gone.

She passed the Protestant church and Gonzales Grocery Store and continued through Old Town to the little cemetery.

It was quiet here. Finding her parents' graves, Gretchen knelt and swept the debris and sand from the top of the stone marker. They'd both been gone for so long—most of her life. In fact, she didn't even have memories of her mother, who had died from a fever when Gretchen was barely three. Her father had been killed ten years later in an accident working on the railroad. Railroading was a deadly business.

She left her parents' graves and went to the far side of the cemetery, where her grandparents had been buried side by side. Again, she cleaned off the shared, hand-carved stone.

"Whatcha doin'?" came a child's question.

Gretchen straightened to find a precocious-looking girl watching her. "Hello. Who are you?"

The child beamed and did a little twirl. "I'm Katiann, and I'm nine years old, but I'll be ten in December."

"Well, very nice to meet you, Katiann. I'm Gretchen."

The nine-year-old danced over and tilted her head to one side. "Whatcha doin' here?"

"I came to visit the graves."

"Why?" She bobbed her head the other direction, and her brown curls bounced up and down.

"Well, I suppose because I haven't been here in a very long time, and it seemed to be the thing to do." The child was a pretty little thing. Gretchen glanced around for her mother or father. "Are you here alone?"

"Yep. I ran off. My nanny, Mrs. Escalante, was *muy enojada*."

"Why was she very angry?"

Katiann's brown eyes lit up. "You speak Spanish?"

"I do. I grew up here."

Katiann came closer and looked down at the gravestone. "What kind of a name is Gottsacker?"

"It's German. My family were of German descent."

"Do you speak German too?"

Gretchen laughed. "*Ja, mache ich.*"

The child frowned. "I've never heard anyone speak German. We were in a war against the Germans. They were the enemy. I learned that at school."

"There were a lot of Germans who didn't like the war and came to America. My family came to America long before the war, but they were very sad when the fighting started. They didn't like it at all."

Katiann considered this for a moment, then nodded. "There's a lot of things I don't like. Like when Mrs. Escalante tries to make me stay in my room until Daddy comes home. He works for Santa Fe."

Gretchen smiled. "A lot of people do. Where's your mother?"

"She died when I was born." Katiann started dancing around again, careful not to step on the gravestones. "I don't like that that happened either."

"Is she buried here?" Gretchen looked around, thinking perhaps that was why the child had come.

"No. She died far away from here. Daddy came back here to live 'cause he said it's the only place he's ever been truly happy."

What a strange contrast to Gretchen's own heart. Yet at one time she'd been happy here as well. "Where do you live?"

"We live in a house by the school and the Methodist church. It's close to the railroad so Daddy isn't far away from his work."

"Well, perhaps we should make our way back to town so your father doesn't worry about you, Katiann." Gretchen started for the gate, and the little girl fell in step beside her.

"I watched you come up here," Katiann offered. "I think you're very pretty. There aren't many people here who have yellow hair."

Gretchen laughed. "No, there have never been a lot of blonds here. Thank you for the compliment. I think you are very pretty too."

Katiann nodded. "I am. Everybody says so." She gave a little sigh, like it was a burden.

"The proper response would be to say 'thank you.'" Gretchen hoped Katiann wouldn't feel bad being corrected.

"I know, that's what Mrs. Escalante says. She wants me to say 'thank you' all the time."

"It is what polite people do, and you do want to be polite, don't you?"

They stepped out of the cemetery and back onto the sandy dirt road. Katiann gave a twirl and then surprised Gretchen by doing a cartwheel in spite of wearing a frilly pink dress.

"I don't know if being polite is all that important," Katiann replied, remaining in constant motion. "I heard a man say 'thank you' once to another man just before he punched him in the mouth. Sometimes I think words and rules mean too much to folks. Like my friend Kimberley. She has a rule for every word, and she hates *l-y* words. She hates them so much, she won't even spell her name with *l-y*. She has to have it be *l-e-y*. She's always getting after me when I say 'amazingly' or 'wonderfully' or even when I tell her she looks lovely."

Gretchen couldn't fault her conclusion and smiled. "It sounds like Kimberley would make a wonderful editor for books or magazines. You know, there's an important reason for rules."

Katiann sighed. "Yes, Mrs. Escalante says it keeps order in society and the household. But I don't think using *l-y* words is going to cause a revolution. Oh, look. J.B. is going to play."

Gone was her concern about the English language and rules of society as she ran over to a collection of old men who'd gathered at the corner of the grocery store with their guitars. A dark-skinned man was picking out a tune while the others strummed along.

Katiann went right up to them. They all seemed to be old friends. "Hi, J.B.," she said to the old black man.

He smiled and pulled a harmonica from his pocket. "Howdy, Miss Katiann. You bring a friend to hear us play?" His three Mexican companions began to pick out a tune on their guitars.

"That's Gretchen," she told the men, pointing Gretchen's direction. They nodded and smiled, but none stopped playing. "We gotta go, but we'll come again." Katiann began walking with Gretchen again. "They always play there, every night. Sometimes there are a whole bunch of people, and sometimes they dance." She glanced back and shook her head. "I don't think anybody will dance tonight 'cause there's a bingo game."

They had no sooner reached the Catholic church than an older Mexican woman came barreling around the corner. She shook her finger at Katiann and berated her in rapid-fire Spanish.

"Mrs. Escalante, this is Gretchen Gottsacker," Katiann said. "She speaks German . . . and Spanish."

Gretchen noted the amusement in Katiann's voice. Her statement silenced the older woman, who looked momentarily embarrassed. From some of the things she had said to the child, Gretchen wasn't surprised.

"Forgive me. It's just that I've been looking all over for this child. She was supposed to be in her room. Her papa will be home soon and expect her to be there for supper."

"I understand." Gretchen gave Katiann a wave. "It was nice to meet you, Katiann. You'll have to come see me sometime at the Harvey House. That's where I'm staying and working for the next few weeks."

"I'll come see you soon," the child promised.

Gretchen chuckled as she made her way back to the Harvey House. "No doubt you will."

Chapter Two

Katiann was true to her word. She not only came to see Gretchen the next day, but every day after that. Gretchen found her company charming. Katiann said what she thought and asked what she wanted to know. There were no barriers between them. Katiann was simply . . . Katiann.

After a week of working and gaining a better understanding of the staff, Gretchen felt almost at home. Fred Harvey had a rule about his many lunchrooms and restaurants being identical in service whether in Topeka, Kansas, or Winslow, Arizona. San Marcial was no exception. The silver service gleamed, and the floors were clean enough to eat off of—at least for a full minute after they were scoured and polished.

But the summer days were hot. Unbearably so. Another town along the Rio Grande might be a veritable oasis, but not San Marcial. Here, it was said that the only things that grew well were sin and horned toads, and the latter weren't doing so well thanks to their encounters with trains.

Gretchen could bear the heat no longer. As a child she had often gone swimming in the river, and she intended to repeat that pleasure, since it was her day off. She'd heard many of the girls talk about swimming in the river at a particular location just west of the city where there was more privacy, and she wanted to give it a try. She had learned to swim in the river when she was very young. Her father had begun her lessons, and she'd followed the examples of others after he was gone. Most of the time she had been content to sit in the water at the edge of the river and dream of a happy future.

Katiann had caught wind of Gretchen's plans and, with Mrs. Escalante's permission, had come to join her. She even brought cookies, compliments of her nanny.

"Mrs. Escalante makes really good cookies. She calls them *hojarascos*. It means 'crumbled up leaves' or something like that. But they don't really have leaves in them. They're amazingly good. I didn't know if you'd ever had them."

"I have, and I'm very fond of them," Gretchen admitted.

They reached the river and set up a little camp under the cottonwood trees, where they put their extra things. Gretchen, grateful for the loan of a bathing suit from one of the Harvey Girls, began stripping off her clothes. It had to be at least one hundred degrees, even in the shade.

Katiann wore nothing but a loose Mexican dress. She pulled it over her head to reveal her own suit. It was charming, resembling a smaller version of the suit Gretchen wore. Sleeveless, the top was like a shortened dress that fell to just above her knees. Beneath that were bloomers that tied at the knee. It was made from several different colors of material and suited Katiann's rambunctious personality. On the other hand, Gretchen's suit was a simple navy color. The bloomers worn beneath the sleeveless top were straight-legged and cut just above the knee.

"Do you use a swimming hat?" Katiann asked as Gretchen opened her large bag.

"No, I just keep my hair pinned up and worry about it later."

"I thought maybe you were looking for your hat. What are you doing?"

Gretchen smiled. "I'm putting my clothes away so they don't

get wet or filled with bugs." She put her things inside the bag along with her shoes, then pulled the drawstrings. Then she found a branch to hang the bag from. "I grew up here, remember? I know all about scorpions and spiders and snakes. I don't want any of them trying on my clothes."

Katiann giggled. "If they try on my dress, I'll just shake them out. Besides, I use my dress to sit on when I'm done swimming." And with that, she hurried into the water and splashed handfuls back at Gretchen. "It feels wonderfully cool."

Gretchen joined her, remembering when she'd come here with her grandmother or other friends. San Marcial—like many riverside towns—had a complicated relationship with the Rio Grande, which was known as "the Nile of the Southwest" because of its propensity to overflow its banks when the rains came. Yet the many times she had swum here as a child were some of the happiest memories Gretchen had.

As they enjoyed the water, several other people arrived to join them. Katiann had to speak with each person as if she were the town's welcoming committee. Everyone seemed to know her. One woman with several children even handed Katiann a bottle of soda.

The hot sun beat down on Gretchen's fair skin, reminding her that if she wasn't careful, she'd be burnt to a crisp. Oma had always had Gretchen soak in a soda bath after getting sunburned and afterward had smeared her arms with the gooey contents of snapped aloe vera leaves. She wondered if anyone in town had a plant or two to share. She thought of her friend Nellie. She hadn't had time yet to look her up. She would make that a priority and use the aloe vera as an excuse. They had once been so close, but over the years they had communicated less and less.

After a while, Gretchen made her way back to the sparse gathering of cottonwoods. She spread a towel on the ground and leaned back against the rough bark of a tree, grateful for the shade. Katiann continued to splash and play with her friends. It was clear this was nothing new to her.

Dozing off, Gretchen thought about the last time she'd been in San Marcial. It had been ten years ago. The funeral services for her grandmother had been the day before, and Gretchen was left with the responsibility of packing up the final bits of their life together. It wasn't like they'd had much. Oma earned what little money they had by doing laundry for the railroad men. Gretchen could still see the clotheslines out behind their little adobe house. There were four lines and always, rain or shine, they hung with rows of work shirts, denim overalls, and a variety of undergarments and socks. When Gretchen wasn't in school, she was helping her grandmother. The workmen were always generous when paying for their clothes and often brought additional treats as well. Gretchen remembered them fondly.

A scream split the air, and Gretchen awoke with a start. She straightened and looked for Katiann just as the girl screamed again. A man had lifted her out of the water and was preparing to throw her back into the river.

Gretchen jumped to her feet. "Stop that! Unhand that child!" She raced to Katiann's defense, but it was too late. The man had already tossed her into the water.

Katiann quickly resurfaced, and once Gretchen was sure she was all right, she turned to rebuke the man. "Just who do you think you are?"

But then their eyes met, and Gretchen knew exactly who he was.

⁓

Dirk Martinez was stunned when a shapely blond woman demanded he unhand his own child. He made sure Katiann was safely back to the surface of the water before turning to see who the woman was. Her familiar blue eyes bore into him for only a moment before her expression changed from anger to shock.

"Gretchen." His voice was barely a whisper. Here was the woman he had left behind ten years ago. The woman he had come back hoping to find. The only woman he had ever loved.

She shook her head and gazed at Katiann, then reluctantly turned back to Dirk. "She's yours?"

He nodded, still not certain he could speak. Gretchen was just as beautiful as the last time he'd seen her. The emergency that had forced him to leave town without telling her had turned into a life-changing decision. A part of him had always regretted that choice, while another told him he would have regretted it more if he hadn't followed through.

Gretchen said nothing. Katiann joined them, all smiles. "Daddy, this is Gretchen. She's my friend, and she works at the Harvey House. Gretchen, this is my daddy. His name is Dirk."

Dirk could see the same confusion on Gretchen's face that he felt. He'd thought he'd lost her forever. Thought he'd never see her again. "You've moved back?"

She turned, walked back to the grove of cottonwoods, and began collecting her things. It was clear she wasn't happy about the encounter.

Katiann, bless her, went to Gretchen and took her hand. "What's wrong, Gretchen? Why are you leaving? Don't you want to swim some more? Are you sick?"

Gretchen took a bag down from the tree. "I'm fine. I have things to do." She opened the bag and pulled out shoes and clothes.

Before Dirk could think of something to say, she was dressed. He could hardly believe that after all this time, she was here. For years he had looked for her without any luck, even writing to her old friends, but no one knew where she had gone.

Katiann looked at her father. "Gretchen is so much fun. I think she should come eat supper at our house. She always eats at the Harvey House, but I told her sometime she could come eat with us."

"That would be fine," Dirk murmured.

Gretchen slipped into her shoes and straightened, her bag in her hand. "I have to go, Katiann. I'll see you later." She walked toward the Harvey House without another word.

"Daddy, you look sad. Are you sad?"

Dirk sighed and hoisted Katiann onto his shoulder. "I'm not sad. I'm just thinking."

"About Gretchen?" she asked innocently.

He nodded. "Yes. About Gretchen."

"I think she's pretty. Don't you?"

Dirk wasn't sure how much to say. He wanted to explain to Katiann that they had once been close—but if he did, his daughter would just want to know why that was no longer the case.

"Daddy?" She leaned down to put her face beside his. "Don't you think she's pretty?"

"I think she's the most beautiful woman in the world."

⁓

Gretchen's heart was nearly pounding out of her chest by the time she made it to her second-floor bedroom at the Harvey House. She quickly cleaned up and dressed, then turned on a fan and sat down in front of it.

Dirk Martinez in the flesh.

She had believed she'd never see him again. When he'd left her all those years ago, he'd gone without a word of explanation. Just disappeared. The next thing she'd heard was that he had married some woman in Kansas City. Not even a week after she'd been certain he was about to propose to her.

She let the memory of their last evening surface. All these

years she had kept it carefully stuffed down in the deepest well of her mind. But now it was once again at the front of her thoughts, perfectly preserved—still able to wound.

"You are the most beautiful woman here," Dirk had told her as he held her in his arms. "The most beautiful woman in the world."

Gretchen had basked in the warmth of his attention that chilly night. He had just walked her and Oma back from evening church services. Oma had gone into the house, but Dirk and Gretchen lingered under the starlight.

She was just eighteen, hardly more than a girl. Dirk was twenty-five and already held an impressive management position with the Santa Fe Railway. His Hispanic father and American mother gave him dark eyes and an exotic presence that caused most women to take a second look. He was also fluent in Spanish, which helped with his job amid the heavily Mexican population.

They were in love—at least she'd thought they were. She knew she was. And she had been so certain of his feelings for her that she anticipated his proposal any day.

"I have to go," he told her. His face was lit by the warm glow of lamplight from the house. "But tomorrow I want to see you again. I want to take you to supper and then, well . . ." He grinned. "I want to discuss something very important."

Gretchen felt as if she might faint. The anticipation of what he wanted to say was almost more than she could stand. She'd had other fellas ask her to marry them, but none that she had ever wanted to say yes to. Until now.

Before he left, Dirk kissed her. It was a gentle, almost chaste kiss, but it held the promise of so much more. Gretchen had started to put her arms around his neck, but Dirk pulled away and took hold of them instead. He kissed each hand, then let her go.

"Tomorrow," he whispered and then disappeared into the night.

She never saw him again. Not until today.

A tear trickled down her cheek. "Why did you have to come back now, Dirk? Why?"

Chapter Three

With the train rush gone, the Harvey House girls still found plenty to do. There were railroad men and townsfolk to feed, as well as tables to set and other jobs to be tended. Gretchen had her hands full making sure the girls stayed on task, but her biggest job had been avoiding Dirk. She didn't know how to deal with him. Her heart told her that she was still very much in love with him, while her mind reminded her that ten years had passed between them without a word of explanation.

"Why, Miss Katiann, what are you doing here?" one of the local cowboys asked as the child made her way to one of the counter seats.

"I came to see Gretchen. How are you?" She arranged her cotton dress.

"Oh, you know, busy. Hot and busy."

Katiann nodded and leaned her elbows on the polished mahogany counter, then put her chin in her hands. "Where's Bubba D.? You guys are always together."

"Had to see to a pool game."

"He's pretty good."

Felix laughed. "He's the best, and you know it."

Gretchen decided to interrupt. "Katiann, what brings you to the Harvey House?"

The girl turned to her with a heartwarming smile. "I haven't seen you for a long time." She turned to Felix. "Do you know Felix? He has horses that swim."

Gretchen smiled at the cowboy. "Don't most horses swim?"

"Sure, but his like to swim. They swim all the time in the river. He's got a couple that are so strong, they can swim against the current."

Felix nodded. "It's true."

It had been nearly a week, and Gretchen had known she wouldn't be able to avoid Katiann forever. Thankfully, Gretchen only had to be in San Marcial for another week or two. "Well, I think that's wonderful, but you didn't answer my question. Why are you here?"

Katiann cocked her head to one side as her eyes narrowed. "I did answer. I said I hadn't seen you in a long time. That's why I'm here. I was worried you were sick. You left so fast when we were at the river, I figured you had a stomachache or something."

"I'm just fine, but I have a job to do and not a lot of free time."

Katiann shrugged. "Well, you don't have to work at night. I asked my daddy, and he said you could come have supper with us."

Gretchen felt her cheeks warm. That was the trouble with having a fair complexion. Every moment of embarrassment was a public announcement. "I, ah, we'll see."

The door flew open, and a tall skinny young man bounded inside. He had dark hair and piercing eyes that took in the entire room as if assessing for danger. "Felix, aren't you done eating yet?"

Katiann leaned forward. "That's Bubba D. He works on the ranch with Felix, but he plays pool and makes more money slickerin' the other fellas out of their wages."

"Now, Katiann," Bubba D. began, "it ain't slickerin' when a fella is just playin' better than everybody else. Ain't my fault they can't play as good as me." He tousled her curls, then took a seat beside her and picked up the menu. "Guess I don't have much time for lunch. Just pack me up five ham sandwiches. I'll eat 'em on the ride back."

"Five sandwiches?" Gretchen asked, looking at the skinny kid. "Are you sure that's all you want?" She tried not to sound sarcastic. It was hard to believe this young man was going to eat five of Harvey's big ham sandwiches. Why, the ham alone was sliced half an inch thick.

Bubba D. grinned. "I'd get some pie too, but it's too messy to take with me."

Katiann nodded. "Bubba D. eats a lot."

"Yep, and then I work it right back off. You ever try breakin' horses, Katiann? It's hard work." He pulled a bottle of soda from his back pocket.

The child shrugged and looked at Gretchen. "All the boys work hard around here. J.B. says if a fella sits for more than a minute and isn't workin', the devil himself will show up to find him a job."

Gretchen smiled. She remembered some of the old men in town imparting similar proverbs when she was Katiann's age. Some things never changed.

She got Bubba D.'s sandwiches for him while he finished off his soda. He and Felix paid, then headed out just as a group of men entered. They wore business suits and looked like railroad officials. The last man to come through the door was Dirk.

"Daddy!" Gretchen moved away from the counter as Katiann jumped from the stool. She ran to her father but waved to one of the other men. "Hey, Mr. West."

Gretchen recognized the San Marcial railroad superintendent, B.A. West, but the other men were strangers. That wasn't unusual. Men were always coming to visit from offices elsewhere. The men took a seat in the dining room, and Gretchen breathed a sigh of relief when Molly, one of the other Harvey Girls, jumped into action, taking drink orders.

Gretchen finished her duties at the counter and hoped to slip away, but it wasn't to be. Molly came toward her, looking concerned. "Those men are from Kansas City. There's some sort of inspection and audit going on. Can you help me?"

"Of course. What do you need me to do?"

"Would you go take their orders while I get the drinks? I'll serve them, but they're in a hurry."

Gretchen nodded. "I'll take care of it." She made her way to the table, avoiding Dirk's gaze.

Katiann was having an animated conversation with Mr. West. "Why can't a girl be a hogger?" she asked.

Mr. West chuckled. "Why would you want to be an engineer on a train? It's hot and sweaty in the summer and will freeze your bones in the winter."

"Yeah, but I think it would be fun to stick my head out the window and feel the wind in my face as the world flies by." She swished her curls back from her face to demonstrate. The men all laughed at this.

Gretchen smiled. Leave it to Katiann to put everyone at ease. "Welcome to the Harvey House, gentlemen. What can I have prepared for you today?"

The men gave Gretchen their orders one by one. They were used to the fare offered at the Harvey Houses. By the time she worked her way around the table to Dirk, she could hardly breathe. He'd been watching her the entire time.

"And what would you like, Mr. Martinez?" She tried to look over the top of his head rather than meet his eyes, but it was no use. Dirk had always had a power over her that made ignoring him impossible.

As their gazes met, Dirk gave her his lopsided grin. His brows rose in challenge. "There's a lot of things I'd like, but I used to come here with the prettiest lady. It was about ten years ago. We always ordered the same thing." He looked at the men seated around the table. "We were creatures of habit, I guess."

The men laughed. Gretchen knew exactly what they'd ordered but gave him a completely blank look as he returned his gaze to her.

"I'll have what I had then."

"And that would be what?" she asked in a sweet tone. She wasn't going to admit that she knew he wanted meatloaf and mashed potatoes.

He roared with laughter, which only further unnerved her. She thought about leaving, but with these important railroad men here, she didn't dare. Unfortunately, Katiann chose that moment to leap out of her chair in order to look out the window at a wagon passing by. Gretchen startled and whirled around. She knew the minute she lost her balance exactly where she'd end up.

Dirk easily caught her as she hit his lap, but when he tightened his grip on her arms, Gretchen knew he wasn't in any hurry to let her back up. "Are you all right?" he asked with mock concern.

She nodded, knowing that if she dared to turn her face, their lips would be only inches apart. "I'm fine. I'm very sorry, sir." She tried to emphasize the formality.

"That was a good catch, Dirk," Mr. West declared.

"I'm sorry, Gretchen." Thankfully, Katiann took Gretchen's hands and pulled. Dirk no doubt wished to avoid any more of a scene and let her go. "I didn't mean to make you fall."

"I'm fine." Gretchen smiled at Katiann. "I tell you what. You get your daddy's order while I go put in the rest. You'll be my Harvey Girl in training. It won't be as exciting as being a hogger, but you'll work every bit as hard."

The men loved this and laughed heartily while Gretchen made a hasty retreat. She could still feel Dirk's arms around her. Smell the scent of the same cologne he'd worn on the last night they'd been together. It was as if ten years had never passed.

Later that day, after her work at the Harvey House was completed, Gretchen couldn't get Dirk out of her head. She knew it would be best to confront him and hear what he had to say, but she wasn't sure she could bear to have his reasons for rejecting her put into words.

After bathing and changing into a lightweight cotton blouse and skirt, Gretchen made her way from the Harvey House, not really knowing what to do. After wandering for a while, she decided to search out one of her childhood friends. She'd asked around and learned that Nellie Harper had married her long-time love interest, Mark Campbell. They had moved up and down the Santa Fe while Mark did various jobs, but two years ago they had settled in San Marcial once again.

Their house was on the other side of New Town, but not at all far. Nothing was that far in San Marcial. Gretchen found the adobe house quite pleasing from the outside. Nellie had always been artistically blessed, and she'd made a beautiful arrangement of colorful clay pots to line the walk to their door. Flowers had a hard time growing here, so she'd arranged ceramic figurines in each pot to add additional color and interest.

Gretchen knocked on the screen door. A dark-haired boy of about eight or nine answered. "Hello," Gretchen said. "Is your mother at home?"

"Nope. She and Pa are out visitin'."

Disappointed, Gretchen gave a nod. "Would you tell her that Gretchen Gottsacker stopped by and that I'm working at the Harvey House? If she has time to visit, I'd love to see her."

"Gretchen who?"

"Just tell her Gretchen, her friend when she was little. She'll know."

The boy scratched his chest and nodded. "I'll tell her."

Gretchen thanked him and made her way back toward the center of town. There were a lot of people out. It was Friday night, and no doubt there were dances and parties to be had, just as there were in the big city. She tried not to think about how lonely the evenings were, but when she saw happy couples arm in arm, those feelings couldn't be avoided.

Lord, I don't know what to do. I didn't know he'd be here. I didn't know I'd still care.

Well, that wasn't exactly true. Gretchen knew she still cared. She'd tried for nearly ten years to convince herself otherwise—to tell herself that her romance with Dirk had been nothing more than childish love—but it wasn't true. From the first time they'd met, Gretchen had known he was someone special. She'd felt certain they belonged together.

"So why do I feel that way, God, if that isn't how You arranged it?"

She remembered so many times when she and Oma had prayed for her future husband. Oma had started when Gretchen was a little girl. Every night before bed, they would pray together, and her grandmother always asked God to save Gretchen's heart for just the right man—a godly man who would love her for the rest of her life. When Gretchen met Dirk just after she turned seventeen, she thought God had answered all those prayers.

Like most people, Dirk had come to San Marcial with the railroad. Having grown up here, it seemed only natural that Gretchen should find work with the railroad too. Almost as soon as Oma died, Gretchen made her way to Albuquerque and then on to Kansas City, where she trained to work in the Harvey

Houses. She'd always anticipated returning to New Mexico, even if she hadn't wanted to return to San Marcial. She loved the arid land and scenic mountains. She had worked in various locations along the line but had enjoyed the city of Santa Fe the most. And now she was back in San Marcial. She'd come full circle in more ways than one, and still she had no idea what to do.

Without looking where she was going, Gretchen picked up her pace and stepped from the boardwalk in the fading light, only to plow headlong into a man coming from the opposite direction. The minute his arms went around her, however, Gretchen knew it was Dirk. As their eyes met, Gretchen realized she was in trouble. He gave her that grin—the one she could never resist—then kissed her soundly on the mouth. For a moment Gretchen thought she might be able to resist his touch, but a second later her arms went around his neck.

When he pulled away, the grin was gone and a serious expression had settled on his face. "I've wanted to do that since I first saw you."

Gretchen opened her mouth to speak, but the words stuck in her throat. She swallowed. "I have to go." She turned on her heel and all but ran the rest of the way to the Harvey House. It was only after she was safely behind the door of her room that she let herself think about what she'd just done.

Now he'd know she'd never stopped loving him. Now he could hurt her all over again.

Chapter Four

Gretchen cherished her days off under normal circumstances, but with Dirk Martinez in town, circumstances weren't normal no matter how she looked at it. Before she realized he had returned, Gretchen thought nothing of wandering the town. Now, however, she feared running into him and stayed mostly to her room at the Harvey House.

Today, however, she'd been asked by the manager to drop off some papers at the Santa Fe offices, and since he was tied up with other duties, Gretchen didn't feel she could refuse. Even if it was her day off. She decided it was foolish to be afraid of Dirk. If he tried to rekindle their relationship, she would just refuse him. She was a strong woman. She'd learned over the years how to manage things on her own, and she wasn't going to let Dirk take that away from her. Not when he was the reason she'd had to become this way in the first place.

After leaving the papers with a rather stout, matronly clerk, Gretchen decided to take a walk up to the cemetery and think. If things went well, she'd be leaving in less than a week, and then she'd never have to see Dirk again. But was that really what she wanted? It was clear he had some feelings for her. Unfortunately, he could be sure by the way she'd responded to his kiss that she had feelings for him.

Why couldn't I have just punched him in the mouth? She smiled as she remembered Katiann's story about a man telling another *thank you* before hitting him. "I could have said, 'Thank you for the kiss,' and then hit him." The thought made her laugh.

"I like hearing you laugh."

She froze and turned to find Dirk trailing after her some ten feet behind. "Where did you come from?"

"I saw you at the office and followed you. I need to talk to you."

Gretchen looked around for any sign of Katiann or anyone else who might keep her from having to be alone with Dirk.

"If you're looking for Katiann," he said as if reading her mind, "she's playing with friends."

Gretchen sighed and tried not to notice how handsome he was in his double-breasted navy suit. "Aren't you sweltering in that?"

He nodded. "So maybe we could sit on the porch at the Harvey House. Unless you'd like to go swimming."

She felt her cheeks grow hot. "The porch is fine, although I don't see any reason for us to talk."

"You don't? I left town on the eve of proposing we spend the rest of our lives together, and then you disappeared completely for ten years, and you don't think we should talk about it?"

Gretchen started walking toward the Harvey House. "No. It'll just hurt too much." She hadn't meant to say that aloud.

"It doesn't have to," he said, catching up to her. "I never meant to hurt you. I never meant to leave without telling you what had happened. I sent a letter. I know I didn't do it right away . . . I couldn't. But I sent it after Katiann was born, and it came back to me not even opened."

She glanced at him. "I never got a letter. I left San Marcial after Oma died. Six months after you left."

"Katiann was born seven months after I left."

35

They had reached the porch, and Gretchen claimed a rocker to avoid having to sit side by side. Unfortunately, Dirk grabbed a chair and pulled it up in front of her, and there was no escape even if she wanted it.

"That last night I was here, after I left you, I went home, and there was a message from my folks. My brother, David, had been in a car accident. I caught the first train out of here—a freighter—and made my way to Kansas City."

Gretchen listened but tried not to care about anything he had to say. She refused to look him in the eye and instead turned her face downward and stared at her hands.

"My brother was so severely injured that his death was inevitable. By the time I got there, he was barely hanging on. My folks were devastated, and David's fiancée, Catherine, was so upset that the doctor had sedated her and put her to bed in a room down the hall."

He paused a moment, and Gretchen couldn't help but glance up. She saw the pain in his face. She remembered how close he and his brother had been. Dirk had always shared stories of their childhood. They were barely a year apart and had done almost everything together.

"David had told everyone that he wanted to see me alone, and when I went in to talk to him, he asked something of me that would forever change my life—and our future."

He now had Gretchen's full attention. She watched as emotions seemed to battle within him. It hurt to see him so pained.

"My brother told me that Catherine was with child. They were to have eloped—he was on his way to pick her up when the accident took place. You must understand that our family is extremely bound by our religious beliefs. What he and Catherine had done would have been condemned, which was why they were in a hurry to marry quietly and right the wrong. It was a matter of honor between brothers."

"What was?"

"David asked me to marry her. To give his child his name."

The truth suddenly dawned on Gretchen. "Katiann."

"Yes." Dirk leaned forward with his elbows on his knees. "You must understand, David and I . . . we were like one. I would have done anything for him, and he for me. He was so grieved over what had happened—not for himself, but for Catherine. She had no family—no one but him. He knew she would be shamed, ostracized, and perhaps even abandoned by the few friends she had if they found out about the baby. He knew nothing about my love for you, my plans to propose. He begged me to marry her, and I promised him I would before I could even consider the consequences. Then he died."

Gretchen was still trying to process the truth about Katiann. She wasn't Dirk's child. She was his niece. "Does Katiann know?"

"No." He shook his head. "Catherine and I ran off the day after the funeral. We married, and she gave birth seven months later and died from complications. We never pretended to love each other. But we let others believe we were a regular man and wife—that the baby was mine—that we had married out of grief over David. Thankfully, Katiann was tiny, and no one questioned her being born earlier than normal, but I think my folks always knew the truth.

"I wanted to write and tell you what had happened, but while Catherine lived, I couldn't bring myself to do it. I knew I had betrayed you. And I knew if I put pen to paper, I would betray my promise to David. I hated myself for being relieved when Catherine died. She was so unhappy after David's death, and even expecting a baby didn't help her with her grief. She would spend hour after hour crying and mourning his loss. I used to fear what it would do to Katiann, but as you can see, she's a happy little thing."

"She is. I would never have guessed her to have experienced anything but pure joy in her life."

"I've tried to make her life a good one, but it hasn't been easy. While my folks were still alive, we lived with them in Kansas City, but then I lost them as well, and Katiann and I were on our own. After that, I hired nannies to help me, and that worked fairly well until the last year or so."

"Then what happened?"

"Katiann just seemed to outgrow them. She's gone through a dozen in the last year, and I have my doubts that Mrs. Escalante will be with us much longer—although I have bribed her with more pay."

Gretchen didn't know what to say or even think. Dirk's story was full of tragedy and hardship, as well as love and loyalty. How could she condemn or hate him for being so noble? Yet all those years and not one word . . .

"I still think you could have written me a short note to explain what happened."

"I wanted to. And after Catherine passed away, I did. I wrote you a long letter, but as I mentioned, it came back to me. You had moved and left no forwarding address."

"Yes. Before Oma died, I had already thought of becoming a Harvey Girl. I knew Oma wouldn't be long for this world, and I didn't want to settle for one of the railroad men begging me to marry them, so I knew I'd have to support myself. I left San Marcial shortly after the funeral, and I haven't been back since."

"Why now?"

"Why, indeed. I keep asking myself that very question." She shook her head. "The official answer is that the house mother for the Harvey House needed a vacation. I was asked to fill in for her. I do that a lot because of my vast experience with the company."

"I'm surprised we haven't run into each other before now," Dirk said, offering her a smile.

She looked away. "It's so hard to remember those days— those years."

"I need you to forgive me." The words were barely audible, but Gretchen heard them clearly.

"Forgive you?" She sighed. "I don't even know what to think about all of this. For ten years I convinced myself that you were a master of deception and had played me for a fool. Now you tell me a story that, if true, makes you an admirable hero."

"I'm not a hero or a deceiver. I left you on that night fully planning to marry you. Instead I found myself in a hopeless situation, torn between my loyalty to David and my love for you. I wanted so much to come back to you. I never stopped loving you, Gretchen. You're the only woman I've ever loved. I never even touched Catherine. I couldn't, because you're the one I would have been thinking of."

She realized what he was saying. He hadn't been unfaithful to her in any way. To withhold forgiveness would not only go against everything her faith had taught her but would also be cruel. How could she hate him for what he'd done? Katiann might be dead now if not for him.

A light rain began to fall. Rain in the desert was always a mixed blessing, just like Dirk's confession. On one hand, Gretchen was grateful for knowing the truth, but at the same time it had opened up painful wounds.

Dirk got to his feet. "I know I don't deserve your forgiveness, but I'm hoping you'll at least think about it. Because I still love you, and God must have a reason for bringing us here together. It can't just be coincidence, because I don't believe in them."

She met his pleading gaze and tried to speak, but the words wouldn't come. Dirk seemed to understand that she needed time and, without another word, he left the porch and walked away. Gretchen stepped into the rain as if to follow him but stopped.

The rain came a little heavier, and Gretchen watched as the drops hit the parched earth and disappeared. It was like tears from heaven. Tears from the depth of her soul. It wasn't until she reached up to push back a loose strand of hair that she realized she was crying. It wasn't just the rain that fell.

⁓

"And then what happened?" Nellie Campbell asked as she nursed her infant son.

Unable to think of what else to do, Gretchen had shown up on her friend's doorstep, rain-drenched and confused. Fortunately, Nellie had been home this time, and after a long, tearful hug of reunion, they were settled in Nellie's kitchen. "He walked away, and I didn't do anything to stop him."

"What a terrible and sad story."

"But you can't say anything to anyone. I'm sorry now that I even told you, because it's critical that Katiann not find out. At least not until Dirk is ready to tell her the truth."

"Gretchen, you know you can trust me to remain silent. After all, I knew where you'd gone all those years ago, and I said nothing to anyone, just like you asked. Not even to Dirk." The petite brunette reached over and squeezed Gretchen's hand. "I won't betray your trust."

"I know that. I'm just so overwhelmed. I don't know what to think, much less do."

Nellie raised the baby to her shoulder and began to gently burp him. "Do you still love him?"

"Yes." There was no sense in pretending otherwise. "Ever since I learned he was here, he's been all I can think about."

"Then maybe that's your answer."

"My answer? I don't even know for sure what the question

is," Gretchen countered. She got to her feet and paced in Nellie's large kitchen. "I feel completely confused by all of this."

"Then maybe you need to spend some time in prayer. Do you remember when your grandmother would tell you that confusion and chaos were the Devil's tools? She always made me smile when she told us to pray about something, because she believed fervently that prayer was the most powerful of all tools given to Christians."

Gretchen nodded. "I remember."

"It's seen me through many dark nights when my children were sick or when I was uncertain about something."

The baby boy fell asleep to the rhythm of his mother's gentle pats, and Gretchen envied the look of complete peace on his face. "I wish I had Baby Gene's ability to sleep through it all." She paused by Nellie's chair and ran her finger down the infant's cheek. "So soft and sweet."

"You'll have one of your own one day. I believe that." Nellie smiled up at her. "Maybe sooner than you think."

Chapter Five

Katiann came into the Harvey House as she often did, but this time she plopped down at the lunch counter and gave a heavy sigh. "I'm in a snit."

Gretchen raised a brow. "A snit?" She forced back a smile. "Why are you in a snit?"

"Mrs. Escalante quit." The child planted her elbows on the counter. "And for no good reason."

Knowing Katiann's rambunctiousness and ability to try the patience of everyone around her, Gretchen could imagine many good reasons for the old woman to give her notice.

"Why don't I get you a piece of pie, and you can tell me about it?" Gretchen went to the pie case and chose Katiann's favorite custard pie. She put the huge Harvey House-sized slice in front of the child, then grabbed two forks. Since no one else was in the dining room, she decided to break the rules and eat with Katiann before the next train filled the house with hungry passengers.

Katiann picked up the fork. "It's just not fair. Daddy is going to be so mad. He made me promise not to aggravate this one." She took a bite of the pie and shook her head.

"Well, sometimes the things we think are acceptable . . . aren't. You know that Mrs. Escalante likes to know where you are at all times, and still you run off. Like right now, I bet she doesn't know you're here."

"She doesn't care 'cause she quit," Katiann said around a mouthful of pie.

Gretchen ate a bite and tried to figure out how to soften the consequences for the child. She hated to think of Dirk punishing her.

"The worst of it is that Daddy is going to come home from work, and there'll be no supper. He hates that. He likes to clean up and then have supper right away. I think it's 'cause he doesn't always stop for lunch. But now Mrs. Escalante is gone, and there's no supper. Just chicken sitting in the icebox."

"Well, how about this? I complete my work in about an hour. Then I can come over to your house and fix supper."

Katiann's entire face lit up. "Do you know how to cook chicken?"

"I do. In fact, I can make quite a few dishes using chicken. So, finish what you want of this pie." Gretchen grabbed another quick bite for herself. "The train is due any minute, so it would be best if you took it to the kitchen and ate there."

Katiann nodded, picking up the plate. "Thanks, Gretchen. You saved my bacon."

Gretchen felt her lips twitch. "'Saved your bacon'? Where'd you learn to talk like that?"

Katiann shrugged. "The Horney Toad men, of course."

"Well, I wouldn't get your hopes up completely. Your father will still have something to say about all of this. After all, who's going to fix supper tomorrow?"

"Why can't you? I mean, if you can really cook."

Gretchen rolled her eyes. "I can really cook, but I have a job here, and your father will need someone to care for you."

"I'm old enough to take care of myself. I can do just about anything if I have to."

"I have no doubt, Katiann. No doubt at all."

⁓⟋⟍⟋⟍⟋⟍⟋⟍⟋⟍⟋⟍⟋⟍⟋⟍⟋∽

Dirk wrote out Mrs. Escalante's last paycheck. "I do wish you'd stay. It's going to be almost impossible for me to find someone to take care of Katiann, especially on short notice."

"Especially if they know her reputation," the older woman muttered.

Realizing he wasn't going to convince her to change her mind, Dirk signed the check and handed it over. "Well, thank you for coming to tell me in person. The last three just left me a letter with their forwarding address."

Mrs. Escalante took the check and hurried to his office door. "I must go. The train leaves in ten minutes."

He stared after her a moment, then put his checkbook away. What in the world was he supposed to do now? He knew Katiann could fend for herself well enough, and it wasn't like he was that far away. She often stopped by the office, and he supposed he could just make it a rule that she had to come by at certain times each day to check in. They could take all their meals at the Harvey House for a time.

"Lose another nanny?" his clerk asked, bringing Dirk a stack of papers for his signature.

"I'm afraid so. I didn't even hear why. She was so bent on catching the train that she didn't want to discuss it." Dirk shook his head. "It's going to be a long August. Maybe I could talk them into starting school early."

The younger man chuckled. "Doubtful."

"Especially knowing Katiann will be there."

Dirk's clerk smiled.

The rest of the afternoon passed quickly. It was raining again, and from the sounds of it, there were concerns about flooding. This area was notorious for flooding. Deluges of water often came crashing downstream to drive the river out of its banks.

Given that the railroad tracks ran right along the Rio Grande, this often spelled trouble for the Santa Fe.

The government had seen the problem and had even begun to rectify it by building dams. Elephant Butte Dam had been completed in 1921, but even as it was finished, a horrible flood had inundated the San Marcial area, destroying homes and railroad facilities alike. Some folks said it was the river's last showdown, but everyone knew that probably wasn't the case. Even the state officials were leery and sent workers to bolster the levees along the river. This new fortification appeared to be working, but there were always concerns.

Despite needing to get home to see what sort of trouble Katiann had gotten into, Dirk stopped at the railroad shops to hear the gossip from the men who had been up Socorro way. If anyone knew what the real threat was, it would be the old-timers.

"It's raining to beat all," one of the old engineers said. "Gonna flood for sure."

"Even though they have the new levees in place?" Dirk asked.

The old man nodded. "That's the only reason it ain't flooded yet. That and the dam. But the dam is full, as I hear tell."

"I heard it too," one of the other men replied. "They told me when I was up there yesterday to be ready to get as much equipment as possible loaded up and shipped north to wait out the situation."

If Santa Fe was already quietly telling the workers to do that, Dirk knew they figured a flood was coming. He made his way home, wondering what he should do about Katiann. He didn't want her in danger, but without a nanny, he could hardly send her away.

As he approached their small house, Dirk heard laughter coming from within. It wasn't just Katiann's either. He recognized Gretchen's lyrical laugh as well. He paused under the kitchen window. Apparently they were making supper. The aroma of grilled peppers and onions wafted on the air.

"Okay, it's your turn. Ask me a really hard question," Katiann declared.

"Very well. Earlier, when we were cutting the chicken, you said you thought I was God's answer to your prayer. What did you pray for?"

"That's not hard. That's the easiest question in the world." Exasperation lined Katiann's reply, but Dirk had to admit he wanted to hear the answer. "I prayed for a mama, and God sent you."

"Wait a minute, Katiann, you don't know that," Gretchen protested.

"Sure I do. I prayed for a mama, and God answered me. You like me and I like you, right?"

"Yes, that's true."

"Don't you like my daddy?"

Dirk held his breath as he waited for the answer.

"Of course I like your daddy. He's a very nice man."

"I know you knew him a long time ago. Last week Daddy told me all about how you were together and that he planned to marry you."

Dirk wondered what Gretchen would think of his openness with Katiann. He hadn't intended to use his child in wooing Gretchen back, but now that she was in the thick of things, very few people could resist Katiann's charms.

"I figure since you two were going to get married anyway, you could get married now. Wouldn't that be great?"

"It's not a matter of whether or not it's great, Katiann. Marriage is a very important thing. Two people should never just jump into it without thinking it through."

"Yeah, that's what Daddy did when he married my mama."

Dirk frowned. Where had that come from? He didn't have long to wait for an answer.

"My grandma told me that he and Mama weren't supposed to get married. That they both were in love with someone else."

Why had his mother told Katiann that? His mother had died just after Katiann's seventh birthday. What would have prompted such a conversation?

"Grandma said they got married because they were so sad about my uncle David dying that they needed each other."

"I'm sure they did, Katiann. Losing someone you love hurts a lot. You must have felt really sad when your grandma died. I know when mine died, I cried for days."

Dirk hated to think of Gretchen mourning her loss without him at her side. He knew how much she had cherished her grandmother.

"I do miss her sometimes. Grandma was always fun to be with, and she smelled like vanilla."

Gretchen chuckled. "Mine smelled like cinnamon. Oh, speaking of which, would you please get the cinnamon for me?"

Dirk heard movement in the house and figured the conversation would turn toward food. He started to leave, but Katiann's next comment made him pause again.

"That wasn't a hard question at all, but now it's my turn to ask you one."

"All right. What's your question, Katiann?"

"Do you think you might still like to marry my daddy?"

Chapter Six

Dirk didn't wait to hear Gretchen's reply. "Katiann!" he called as he came through the back door.

"Oh great," he heard his daughter mutter. "Now I have to explain about Mrs. Escalante."

He came into the kitchen and found Gretchen wearing a colorful pinafore apron over a peasant blouse and cotton skirt. "I didn't know you'd be here," he said, hoping to put her at ease.

"Katiann was concerned that you wouldn't have a hot meal for supper. Wasn't that thoughtful of her?"

Katiann beamed up at him as if she'd just saved trapped puppies from a fire. "I know you like to have supper when you get home from work."

"Yes, but why couldn't Mrs. Escalante fix my supper?" He looked down at the child with a knowing glance.

Katiann held her hands in the air. "It wasn't my fault. Well, it was, but Mrs. Escalante just worries too much. You know how she is."

Dirk sat on one of the kitchen chairs. "What did you do, Katiann?"

She pursed her lips and cocked her head, then gave a little shrug. "I climbed out of my window onto the roof."

"I see. And why would you do that in the rain?"

This time she gave a more exaggerated shrug. "Because I'd never done that before." She made it sound as if it were the most logical thing in the world.

"Weren't you afraid of being up so high on the slick roof?" Gretchen asked.

"No. It wasn't that high, and it wasn't slick. I thought it was really nice. I'd like to sleep out there some night."

"You might roll right off, and then you'd get hurt. You might even break your arm or leg," Gretchen countered before turning back to the stove.

"Katiann, Mrs. Escalante quit, and now you have no one. What am I supposed to do?" Dirk asked.

"Daddy, don't worry." Katiann crawled up onto his lap and put her arms around his neck. She knew how to worm her way into his good graces. "Gretchen and I have been talking about it. She'll come over and cook supper every night so you don't have to be hungry."

"That's not the part I'm worried about. We can eat at the Harvey House or even at Mama Rosita's café. I'm worried about *you*, Katiann. The rain is causing flooding, and you know how bad that can be. I can't have you here by yourself. If the river floods, you could get trapped."

"I'd just crawl out on the roof. See, it's a good thing I already know how!"

An exasperated sigh escaped Dirk's lips. He glanced at Gretchen, who seemed to be gauging his response. Shaking his head, he turned his attention back to Katiann. "You don't understand how much you mean to me. If something happened to you, it would break my heart."

Katiann put her hand against his cheek. "I'm sorry, Daddy. What can I do? I got Gretchen to cook so that you wouldn't miss supper. I promise I'll be good. I love you, Daddy."

"I need your obedience. That's how you can show me love.

In the Bible, Jesus tells His disciples that if they love Him, they should keep His commandments."

The child's expression grew sorrowful, and tears came to her eyes. "I know. And Ephesians says, 'Children, obey your parents in the Lord: for this is right.' I'm sorry, Daddy. I try to obey. But you never said I couldn't climb out on the roof."

"No, I didn't, but I did say that you weren't to do anything that would cause Mrs. Escalante extra worry." He gave her a smile. "Look, it seems supper is nearly ready. Why don't you go wash up and dry your tears? We can talk about this later after Gretchen goes home."

Katiann kissed his cheek, then jumped off his lap. "I promise I'll do better." She scurried away, leaving Dirk to shake his head.

"She's got a good heart," Gretchen said.

"I know. She's a good kid but way too curious for her own good." He looked up at Gretchen and smiled. "It was good to come home and find you here."

She flushed and turned back to the stove. "Supper is ready. If you want to wash up, now would be the time."

Dirk got to his feet. "What I'd really like to know is how you answered Katiann's question."

Gretchen whirled around. "What question?"

"I overheard her ask if you had any interest in marrying me." The kitchen seemed to grow smaller around them. "But maybe more important is to know whether or not you can forgive me for what I did to you—to us—all those years ago."

"Of course I can forgive what happened. What you did . . . well, that was quite honorable. I know how much your brother meant to you."

"Still, I shouldn't have married Katiann's mother. I didn't love her. I loved you. I've only ever loved you."

Gretchen bowed her head. "I never loved anyone but you."

"I'm back!" Katiann declared. "I'll set the table now, Gretchen."

Dirk fixed his gaze on Gretchen's face and smiled. "I'm still interested in your answer."

Gretchen felt like she was all thumbs as they shared supper. It was almost as if they were a real family. Dirk told them about his day at work and concerns about the river flooding, while Katiann and Gretchen threw out the details of their day.

"This is the best meal I've had in years," Dirk told Gretchen. "Who knew chicken, rice, and black beans could taste so good together?"

"It's my oma's recipe. Nobody cooked like she could." Gretchen smiled. "And she taught me everything I know about cooking."

"Can you make flan pie?" Katiann asked.

"I can. Have you ever had pumpkin flan pie? Oma used to make it and pile lots of whipped cream on top."

Katiann's eyes grew wide. "Can you make that for us?"

Gretchen chuckled. "Of course. I wouldn't have mentioned it if I couldn't." She got to her feet. "I should get back to the house. The girls may need me or have questions about tomorrow. And . . . the house mother is due back in another day or two. I need to make sure everything is ready for her."

Katiann frowned. "Are you going away?"

Gretchen didn't like to think of leaving. "Well, I was only supposed to be here for a couple of weeks. I'm sure the Harvey House back in Santa Fe needs me."

Katiann wrapped her arms around Gretchen's waist. "I don't want you to go. I want you to stay here and be my mama."

Gretchen hadn't expected this outburst. Embarrassment washed over her. She wondered what Dirk was thinking. She gave Katiann a hug, then pulled away. "We can talk about this tomorrow, Katiann. Right now you need to help me gather the dishes so we can get everything cleaned up."

"Katiann can handle it herself, since she's the cause of Mrs. Escalante leaving so abruptly," Dirk said. "Maybe she'll appreciate having someone more if she has to manage the work for a while."

"But I want—"

Dirk's expression turned stern. "Katiann, you need to obey me."

"Yes, Daddy." She sighed and left Gretchen's side to start collecting plates.

"I'm sure I'll see you both for breakfast at the Harvey House. I'll save you a nice spot," Gretchen promised.

She headed for the front door, still feeling overwhelmed by all the evening's talk about marriage. She loved Dirk and had come to love Katiann. Marrying into this ready-made family would suit her just fine. But was that what God wanted for her?

"I want to thank you again for supper," Dirk said, following her to the door. "It made the unpleasantness of losing Mrs. Escalante much easier to bear."

"I hope you won't be too hard on Katiann." Gretchen paused and glanced out the screen door. "It's still raining."

"Gretchen, do you think—"

"Mr. Martinez!" An overall-clad man rushed up the walk. "You're needed at the shops. Telegraph came, and the Rio Grande's flooding. Superintendent said you needed to come immediately."

Dirk frowned and looked at Gretchen. "Katiann."

"She'll come with me. I'll take her back to the Harvey House after we clean up."

"Forget about that, ma'am," the older rail worker declared. "The women and children are to get to high ground."

Gretchen caught the worry in Dirk's eyes. "I'll take her with me. I need to check in at the Harvey House and see what's to be done. Is there anything here that we should move to the second floor?"

"I can't think clearly. I suppose pack a bag for Katiann and one for me. I'll come get it when I pick her up."

Gretchen nodded. "I'll see to it."

"What's going on?" Katiann asked, joining them.

Dirk knelt down. "Darling, this is one of those times when absolute obedience is required. Can you give me your word that you'll do what Gretchen tells you?"

"Sure, Daddy, but what's wrong?" She looked from face to face of the adults standing around her.

"The river is going to flood, and we need to get to safety. I have to go help with the railroad's things. Gretchen is going to take care of you. You stay with her and do exactly what she says. Understand?"

"Yes, Daddy. I promise." Katiann hugged him tight. "You won't get hurt, will you?"

Dirk glanced over his daughter's shoulder at Gretchen. "No. I'll be just fine." But the worry in his expression belied his words.

"Don't worry about a thing, Dirk," Gretchen said, trying to reassure him. "We'll head up to San Geronimo rather than leave on the train. You can find us there. I'll keep her safe."

He straightened and surprised her by pulling her into his arms. "Keep yourself safe too. I have plans for you." He kissed her hard and much too briefly. Then he was gone.

Katiann put her arm around Gretchen's waist. "I'm scared."

Gretchen looked down at the child and nodded. "Then we should probably pray."

Chapter Seven

"We need to move everything possible to the second floor," the Harvey House manager declared. "The tables and chairs, the dishes, whatever equipment we can move, and of course all the linens and food. Once that's done, I want everyone on the train north."

Gretchen organized her girls in a line so that no one had to make numerous trips up the steps. The men brought things to the stairs, and the girls moved them along in assembly-line fashion until the downstairs was empty of everything but the heavy stoves, iceboxes, and freezers. It was amazing the strength the girls had when pressed to perform. Gretchen was very proud of each one and told them so.

An hour earlier, Gretchen had put Katiann to bed in her own room. That room was now stacked to the ceiling with food and glassware, but they were able to leave the bed free. The sweet girl had helped all evening until even Gretchen could see she was asleep on her feet.

One of the men decided it would be best to board up the windows and even the doors in hopes of keeping out the flood-waters. They had the benefit of not being built right on the ground, as so many of the residences and businesses were, but already water was starting to pool on the main floor.

"What's the word on the river?" Gretchen heard the house manager ask the sheriff as he passed by.

"It's out of the banks to the north. We need to get everybody out of here and on the train, or at least up to high ground. They've set up some tents, and folks are offering shelter to those in need up at San Geronimo. There are several wagons transporting people up. You should get the ladies up there if they're determined to stay in the area. The men we need to help with sandbagging."

The house manager nodded. "We'll see to it right away." He turned to Gretchen. "Tell the girls to get out on the train. Tell them to hurry. If they don't want to leave, send them up to San Geronimo. Then get up there yourself after you're sure everyone else is out."

"Yes, sir."

Gretchen had barely reached the steps, however, when one of the men who'd been boarding the windows rushed inside. "The levee gave way. It's too late! The town's flooding."

"Everyone to the second floor," the house manager declared.

Gretchen could hear a horrible rumble outside. Was that the river? She hurried upstairs just as several other girls were start-ing down with their belongings. She waved them back. "The levee broke." She could see the terror in their eyes.

The house manager appeared behind her. "It's too late to leave. There's a heavy current out there, and I'm afraid it would pull us under. Back up so the men can get up here too."

The look of horror on each woman's face left Gretchen little doubt that they were just as fearful as she was. She made her way to each room to announce what had happened. Everyone hurried to the windows to see out into the darkness. The streetlamps revealed water steadily rising.

"How deep will it get?" one of the girls whispered.

"I've seen it flood as high as the porch overhang," one of the men muttered.

A shiver went up Gretchen's spine. The porch overhang was at least ten feet off the ground.

Gretchen went to her room, where Katiann slept, oblivious to the disaster. She stroked the child's dark curls and whispered a prayer for their safety.

Out in the streets, debris began crashing against the Harvey House, filling the air with booms and the sound of splintering wood. Gretchen had endured other floods in San Marcial when she was a girl. It had always been terrifying when the river turned from friend to foe. At least they usually had plenty of warning. These rains had come in a deceptive manner, and with the government's promises that the new dam and levees would prevent flooding, people had relaxed their guard. Now they would once again pay the price for living on the river's edge.

With Katiann sleeping comfortably, Gretchen went to soothe those Harvey Girls who'd never experienced anything so frightening. Several of them huddled in one room, weeping.

"Come now, ladies, it's not the end of the world." She smiled. "I used to live here, and the river flooded often. We just have to wait it out. The worst should be known by morning."

"Will it tear the building apart?" a petite blonde asked.

"I doubt it. The men reinforced what they could, and the Harvey House was built well. I think we'll be just fine." They seemed to relax a bit. "Now, don't forget we still have some guests here. We'll want to figure out a way to offer breakfast of some sort when daylight comes. Why don't you find Cook and see what he recommends?" She knew the cook would already have a plan in mind for feeding those gathered in the Harvey House.

"I remember my grandfather talking about a bad flood here years ago. Some men were working at the shops and got swept away. What if that happens tonight?" one of the girls asked. "I have a beau working there."

Gretchen's thoughts immediately went to Dirk. What if he were swept away? What if he died? What would happen to Katiann? Gretchen knew if the worst did happen, she wouldn't let Katiann out of her sight. She would do whatever was necessary to take the girl as her own.

I've got to stop thinking about the worst. It does nobody any good if I sit here supposing the future.

Gretchen curled up beside Katiann. She had to smile when the child nestled in close and gave a sigh. No matter what, she wanted to be this girl's mother and she wanted to be Dirk's wife. She whispered a prayer that somehow God would do whatever needed to be done to make that happen.

Dirk found himself praying that Gretchen and Katiann had made it to safety. He knew Gretchen was obligated to help with the Harvey House until the last minute, but he felt confident she would keep Katiann safe. Earlier in the evening, the railroad had train cars, both freight and passenger, waiting to get people and supplies out of the flood zone. As soon as a train came in, the engine was turned in the roundhouse, attached to the loaded cars, and sent back out again. As long as possible, the railroad men had worked to do what they could to get people and equipment evacuated. The huge machinery of the roundhouse and shops, millions of dollars of equipment needed for everyday production, would be lost to the river's havoc. Many floods over the decades had settled several feet of silt in the town's buildings, and the shops had been no exception. It discouraged many a man to realize just how bad it was going to get before it got better.

One of the railroad men came toward them at a run. "We're clearing out of here, boys. The bridge collapsed at San Acacia, and the levee just broke. The water is rising too fast. Last train is pulling north as we speak. I suggest you get yourselves on it or at least make a mad dash for the hills."

"Have they got the Harvey House people up to San Geronimo?" Dirk asked.

"I guess so," the man replied. "I haven't had time to check on them. I had some of the secretaries load up the office papers earlier this evening, and the Harvey House was still lit up and folks were working there. I know some of the girls were on an earlier train out of here."

Dirk nodded. Folks were doing well to keep track of their own responsibilities, much less other people's.

"You'd be wise to finish up here and get to higher ground. We're already up to three feet, and the current is strong. It's going to get much higher. Don't be fooled."

"I won't be." Dirk glanced toward the door. He knew Gretchen was a wise person, but whether she had the ability to leave was another matter entirely. If she thought she could escape and get Katiann to safety, she would do it. If not, she wouldn't risk it.

The loud crash of something smashing against the building caused silence to fall across the room.

"Let's go!"

Everyone scrambled for the side of the building farthest from the river, where they hoped the water would be easier to manage. It wasn't by much. Dirk and the other men formed a line and handed a rope down.

"Hold on tight, fellas. We'll see each other through."

They stepped into the rapidly rising water. It immediately came up to Dirk's hip. The men inched their way through the water, fighting the constant attempts to pull them off their feet.

"Watch out!" one of the men ahead of Dirk called. "There's some debris coming our way."

In the darkness it was difficult to make out what the debris was at first, but as it came upon them, it became clear it was a wagon bed. The men in front of Dirk pulled forward and raised the rope high, while Dirk and those behind pulled back. The wagon passed through without entangling them.

"Move out and pick up the pace, otherwise we might not get out of here alive."

That was all the incentive they needed. By the time they reached the cemetery in Old Town, the water was less volatile and not nearly so deep. They coiled the rope and made their way on their own. Dirk wished someone had thought to bring a lantern, as there were no streetlamps here. They finally managed to find the road to San Geronimo by using landmarks, and as they climbed the hillside, the water was less and less a threat. Down below, however, the eerie glow of the remaining few streetlamps glistened off the newly expanded Rio Grande. It now engulfed the entire town.

The second floor of the Harvey House was brightly lit, and from the shadows, it was clear there were still people inside.

"Dear Lord," he murmured, feeling suddenly sick. They hadn't all gotten out.

Chapter Eight

Dirk searched through the camps at San Geronimo but already knew in his heart that Gretchen and Katiann wouldn't be among them. When he happened upon Felix and Bubba D., he sank to the ground where they were playing cards.

"You doin' all right, Mr. Martinez?" Felix asked.

"No. I think Katiann and Gretchen are trapped in the Harvey House."

"What? There are still folks down there?" Bubba D. asked, straightening. "We gotta get 'em out of there. I heard the flood is tearing through buildings and rippin' 'em to shreds."

"I heard the same," Dirk said, "and believe me, I wouldn't be stopping to talk to you about it unless I thought you might be willing to help me."

"Of course we'll help," Felix said. "Shouldn't be that difficult."

Dirk raised a brow. "In case you haven't noticed, the Rio Grande is now a raging lake."

"My Chapo can swim that." Felix folded his hand of cards.

"My horse can swim it too," Bubba D. offered. "We can get 'em out of there."

Dirk perked up at this thought. It was well known that the boys often swam the river with their horses. People marveled at their strength against the current. "Do you really think you could?"

"Of course," Felix said with a casual shrug. He grinned. "I think it'll be fun."

"That water is probably ten feet deep by now," Dirk said. "You'll have to get them off the second floor."

"They can climb out on top of the porch and then slip right onto Chapo's back. I know we can do it." Felix stood and stretched. "Come on, Bubba. Let's go rescue us some folks."

Dirk got to his feet as Bubba D. did likewise. "What can I do?"

"I guess we'll need a wagon to pick them up when we get the people to dry ground. We'll get 'em to the San Geronimo Road, and then you can take 'em from there."

They headed down the road back to Old Town. Dirk glanced toward several wagons still hitched with teams. Torches had been erected to offer light. "I'll talk to the men who've already been freighting folks up here." He walked to where two of the men were talking conspiratorially with the sheriff. "Hey, fellas, I need a favor."

They looked up and gave him a nod. "What can we do?" one of the men asked.

"My two friends over there are going down into town to rescue the folks trapped at the Harvey House."

"I'm afraid I can't let them do that," the sheriff said, turning toward Felix and Bubba D., who were already saddling their horses. "Boys, come over here."

They left the blankets on the horses' backs and joined Dirk. "What is it, Sheriff?" Felix asked.

"I can't have you going into town. Not yet. We don't know how bad things are, and we can't see to keep out of the way of debris. Those folks are just fine where they're sitting, and I promise you that at first light we'll see what we can do. One of the brakemen said something about getting a raft or boat down from up north."

"Ah, we don't need a boat or a raft," Felix declared. "My Chapo can manage just fine. I'll swim up with him and take folks one at a time off the roof. Bubba D.'s horse can do nearly as well as mine."

"We don't know how many people are down there, Felix. Those horses are going to wear out just swimming the current, much less transporting two people at a time."

"Well, we can't just wait around for Noah's Ark to show up either." Dirk hadn't meant to sound so sarcastic, but he was ready to swim the current himself to see Gretchen and Katiann to safety.

"I understand you want to help those folks, Mr. Martinez."

"My daughter and future wife are trapped there. You aren't going to keep me from trying to save them."

The sheriff put his hand on Dirk's shoulder. "I wouldn't dream of it. I'm just asking you to wait until light. If Felix and Bubba want to try it then, I'll do whatever I can to help."

Dirk knew it was the best he could hope for. If he tried to sneak off down the road now, the sheriff would only have his deputies stop him. He could hardly help with the rescue if he was forced to spend the night in the San Geronimo jail.

Throughout the night, reports filtered in, and none of them were good. The water was tearing the town apart at an alarming rate. By first light, even the sheriff was anxious to get involved in the rescue. It was a good thing too, because Dirk had considered binding and gagging the lawman so he could rescue his family.

He wondered if Gretchen was afraid. Katiann no doubt considered it a great adventure. At least until she grew bored with being cooped up. Dirk smiled as he imagined her racing around the Harvey House as she decided her best course of action. But

Gretchen was a mystery. Would she know that he would come for her? Would she understand that he couldn't stop thinking about her, wanting her safely at his side . . . in his arms?

"All right," the sheriff said, gathering a team of about twenty men. "This is what my scouts tell me. A great many buildings have been destroyed and now float freely. That, along with all sorts of other debris, makes safety a questionable issue. Last night the last of the railroad workers who made it in told us the roundhouse is buried in silt and water. However, Felix and Bubba D. are willing and able to help with rescuing the folks at the Harvey House."

"You bet we are," Felix declared, nudging Bubba D. with his elbow. "We've even got a challenge between us to see who can rescue more people."

"What's important is safety," the sheriff chided with a smile. "They're going to be scared and uncertain of what you have in mind. We don't know for sure how many are there, but it shouldn't be too many. Most of them got out early."

Dirk wished Gretchen had been less devoted to her job so she and Katiann might already be safely sleeping in San Geronimo.

"If you men are ready to stand by with the wagons, and Felix and Bubba D. are ready to ride into the flood, we'll do what we can to bring those folks out."

There were nods and murmurs. Dirk walked down to where the water started. He stared off toward the Harvey House, wondering and watching for any sign of life. Whispering a prayer, he folded his arms and waited.

"Don't worry, Mr. Martinez. I'll have 'em back here before you can say *horny toad*," Felix declared.

"They're going to be terrified. Well, at least Gretchen will be. She's afraid of heights, and climbing out on the roof isn't going to set well with her." Dirk frowned at the thought of her refusing to go. Then a smile crossed his face. "Say, Felix, I've got something you can tell her that will give her some incentive to take the risk."

Felix looked down from his horse and smiled. "What's that, Mr. M.?"

"Look, Gretchen! It's Felix and Bubba D.," Katiann shouted from the open window. "They're coming to get us. I knew they would." She danced around in a circle. "This is going to be so much fun."

"Hardly that." Gretchen frowned as she stuck her head out the second-story window to see what was going on. Several of the Harvey House men were already out on the porch roof, shouting encouragement to the boys.

"I wish Daddy had come." Katiann frowned. "You do think he's okay, don't you?"

Gretchen pulled back inside. She turned to see Katiann's concerned expression. "I'm sure he's fine. Your daddy is a smart man."

Katiann's worry faded. "Yes, he is. He knows all sorts of stuff."

"You ladies want some cold ham and bread for breakfast?" Cook asked, popping his head into the room. "I got lots of fresh fruit too."

"We're going to get rescued," Katiann declared. "We don't have time to eat."

Cook gave her a scolding look. "Everybody has time to eat. It will give you extra strength for the rescue."

"He's right, Katiann. We don't know how long this procedure is going to take, so why don't you have some food, and I'll see what I can do to make sure you are one of the first ones out of here."

"I won't go without you," Katiann replied. She surprised

Gretchen by hugging her tightly around the waist. "I won't. You're too important now. I prayed for a mama, and God sent you. You have to come with me. You have to stay with me."

Gretchen was touched by her insistence. "I'll stay with you, Katiann." She pulled the child away and knelt down. "I love you, Katiann. I love you very much."

The little girl nodded. Her mussed brown curls bounced on her shoulders, and her eyes brightened. "And you love my daddy too." It was more statement than question.

Gretchen was taken aback by her declaration but didn't see the need to deny it. "Yes. I love your daddy too."

Chapter Nine

"All right, Katiann, I need you to come down to the edge of the roof," Felix called while trying to keep Chapo in place by the eaves. "Then just climb into my arms. I'll put you right here in front of me."

"This is so much fun." Katiann didn't hesitate, and before Gretchen could warn her to be careful, she was safely deposited in front of Felix.

The young man looked up at Gretchen. "Come on. You don't weigh much more than she does, and Chapo can handle all three of us."

Gretchen had managed to climb out of the window. She stood looking down at the swirling brown water. From time to time a branch or piece of broken furniture rushed by. She tried to tell herself that it wasn't so high up and if she fell, she would simply fall into the water and be swept away. Surely she could swim long enough to get to a place of safety.

But what if she couldn't?

"I . . ." She moved a little closer to the edge, slipping on the wet surface. "I'm not sure I can do this, Felix. Why don't you get Katiann to safety and come back for me?"

"Because Chapo's tiring out. Come on, Miss Gottsacker. We got to go."

Gretchen nodded and sat down on the roof to slide the rest of the way. She felt a sensation of vertigo wash over her and closed her eyes.

"Mr. M. said you might be hesitant, so he told me to tell you something."

She opened her eyes to Felix's grinning face. "And what was that?"

"Well, it's not so much something to tell you as to ask you." Felix laughed and glanced over to where Bubba D. was helping a man onto the back of his horse. "If you don't hurry up, Bubba D.'s going to beat me back to the wagons. We got some money on who's gonna haul off more folks, so you can't let me down."

Gretchen shook her head. "What did Dirk tell you to ask me?"

Felix fixed her with a stare and sobered. "He wanted to know if you'd marry him."

Katiann gave a cheer. "Of course she will. Come on, Gretchen! I want to see my daddy and tell him you said yes."

"But I haven't said anything yet."

Gretchen knew as well as Katiann, however, that she would most assuredly say yes. The question did give her motivation, though, just as Dirk had supposed it would. She knew the danger was building, and if she didn't hurry, Chapo would be too tired to take any of them back to safety.

"Just grab my shoulders, Miss Gottsacker. Grab and hold tight while you throw your leg over Chapo's back. Do it now!"

The horse worked madly to keep afloat, and Felix was starting to have trouble controlling him. Fearing the worst, Gretchen took a deep breath and pushed off from the roof. For just a moment she felt as if she were flying, as the short distance seemed to take forever. Then she slapped hard against Felix's high cantle. She reached for his arm and missed but managed to grab his neck before slipping too far to the side. Chapo's body dipped farther into the water with her weight, but Felix wasted no time in giving the horse free rein.

"Hold tight, now. Chapo will have us to dry ground soon enough."

Gretchen did as instructed. "Are you all right, Katiann?"

"I'm great. This is so much fun. I'm going to ask Daddy to get me a horse I can teach to swim. When we get to go back to our house, I can teach him to rescue me off the roof."

"I don't think there is going to be much left of your house, Katiann," Felix said, shaking his head. "I think this is pretty much the end of things for San Marcial."

Gretchen glanced over her shoulder at what was left of the town. No doubt he was right. She couldn't remember any of the floods ever being this bad. If it was as destructive as it looked, then there was a very real possibility the Santa Fe Railway would never risk rebuilding the shops. They'd probably just move everyone farther up the line. It would spell the death of the town she'd known. The town where most of her childhood memories resided. The town where she'd fallen in love.

She thought of her parents' and grandparents' graves. Would they survive the flood, or would the ground give up the dead and force families to find new accommodations? The thought made her shiver. What a horrible thing.

But you won't ever have to face it alone.

She had a family now, and she had God. Her relationship with Him had seen her through the last lonely ten years and would no doubt be her comfort in the years to come, no matter what happened.

As the water receded and the horse began to pick his way through the mud and sand to reach the road, Gretchen could see Dirk standing near one of the wagons. He gave a wave, and Katiann all but jumped up onto the back of Chapo.

"We made it, Daddy! We made it on Chapo!"

"Indeed you did," he called back to them.

Felix stopped the weary horse and handed Katiann down to Dirk. Gretchen slid off the side of the horse and collapsed to the muddy ground.

"You gonna kiss the dirt?" Dirk asked.

She laughed and slowly stood. "Not exactly. I was just a little weak in the knees."

Dirk grinned. "I have that effect on some women."

Gretchen cocked her head and gave him a stern look. "You'd do best to have that effect on only one woman."

"Did she answer my question?" Dirk asked, looking at Katiann.

His daughter shook her head before Gretchen could speak a word. "She didn't answer at all, Daddy, but I think she will say yes."

Dirk looked at Gretchen. "You didn't answer?"

"I've waited ten years for this proposal. I'm not going to do it by proxy. Not even via the man who saved my life. I want a proper asking from you, Mr. Martinez."

Dirk wasted no time. He sank to one knee and took her hand. "Gretchen Gottsacker, would you do me the honor of being my wife?" When she didn't immediately answer, he gave her his endearing boyish grin. "Would you please marry me?"

Katiann threw herself down beside him and took Gretchen's other hand. "Will you marry us?"

Gretchen couldn't help but laugh. "Of course I will. I will happily marry the both of you."

⸻

That evening, despite the smell of muddy, putrid water and campfires, the town of San Geronimo hosted a wedding feast like no other. The people needed a reason to celebrate, and the Gottsacker-Martinez wedding was just the thing.

Gretchen borrowed a flowery skirt and white embroidered blouse for her wedding clothes, while Dirk stood beside her in a light cotton Mexican wedding shirt he'd borrowed. Katiann had found someone to lend her a beautiful communion dress of white satin. She looked every bit the proper bridal attendant, even if the bride and groom were understated.

"Gretchen, will you have this man to be your lawfully wedded husband?" the Methodist preacher asked.

"I will." She looked into Dirk's eyes, letting all the years and pain melt away.

"And, Dirk, will you have this woman to be your lawfully wedded wife?"

"I will."

The preacher looked down at Katiann. "And what about you, little miss? Will you take Gretchen to be your mama?"

Katiann looked up at Gretchen and nodded. "Of course I will. She was always mine, 'cause God gave her to me."

"That's good enough for me," the preacher said, laughing along with anyone else within hearing range. "I pronounce you man and wife. Let's *fiesta*!"

Cheers rang out around them. Dirk pulled Gretchen into his arms and gave her a long, passionate kiss that left her nearly unable to stand. She could scarcely believe all that had happened in just a few short weeks. When she'd come to San Marcial, she had dreaded the memories and sorrow that had haunted her for the last decade, but now that was all behind her. She had found what she had lost, what she had come home to find.

"Come on over to the schoolhouse, folks," someone called out. "We've got a whole passel of food—hot tamales, enchiladas, and, of course, wedding cake."

Even more cheers went up around the newly married couple, and Katiann took their hands. "Come on, Daddy . . . Mama. It's time to celebrate!"

Chapter Ten

MARCH 1931—ALBUQUERQUE, NEW MEXICO

"I hope you don't care, but I taught William to walk," Katiann announced out of the blue.

Gretchen looked up from preparing supper. "Oh really? You taught your nine-month-old brother to walk when he just started pulling up last week?"

"Will is really smart. I can't help that," Katiann said with a shrug.

Gretchen laughed and threw a questioning look at her husband. "What are your thoughts on the matter?"

Dirk put down the Albuquerque paper. "I have a feeling if he wants to walk, he's going to walk. He's been headstrong in just about everything else. Besides, I was walking at eight months."

Gretchen rolled her eyes. "You're absolutely no help."

Katiann gave another shrug. "Well, it doesn't matter, 'cause he's doing it."

"Maybe you just were lucky and he took a few steps," Gretchen said, turning her attention back to the onions.

"You just wait here, and we'll show you."

Gretchen wiped her hands on her apron. "Very well." She stepped away from the counter. It had been a year and a half

71

since the floodwaters had devastated San Marcial. The Santa Fe had relocated Dirk to Albuquerque, and Gretchen had resigned from the Harvey House in order to be a full-time mother to Katiann. Within a month, she found out they were going to add a baby to their family, and everyone was over the moon. Around that same time, San Marcial had another flood, and this one sealed its fate. The town was no more.

Katiann returned to the kitchen with the baby in her arms. William's cherub-like expression broke into a big smile at the sight of his mother. The little cotton dress he wore was hiked up to reveal chubby legs that pumped back and forth in perpetual motion.

"There's my big boy!" Gretchen cooed.

Dirk got up from the table and stood beside his wife. "All right, let's see this feat."

Katiann nodded and placed William on the ground. Next she took hold of his arms and helped him stand. Holding on tight, she walked him forward. "See, he's really good, and in a minute, he'll just do it by himself. I just have to remind him of what he already knows."

And true to her word, that was exactly what happened. Gretchen watched in awe as her son took off across the tiled floor, arms flailing at his side and a squeal rising up from his throat.

"Well, I'll be. She really did teach him," Dirk said, shaking his head.

William plopped down on his backside and looked up with a grin. Gretchen clapped for him, then scooped him up. "That was wonderful. What a brilliant boy." She smoothed down a cowlick of his sandy brown hair.

"That was pretty amazing," Dirk admitted. "Katiann, you're a great teacher."

"I know." She danced in a circle.

"Katiann, what have we said about that?" Gretchen deposited William in her husband's arms.

"To say 'thank you.'" Katiann gave an exasperated sigh. She put her hands on her hips. "Thank you. Now I'm going to go help my friend Rachel. She wants to teach her baby brother to walk."

Gretchen started to laugh, then remembered the baby in question was only six months old. "Katiann, he's a little too young to be walking. You should probably wait a few weeks."

Katiann nodded. "I know. I tried to tell Rachel that, but she said it shouldn't matter. He's got two legs." She raised her arms and shrugged. "You can't convince some people, no matter what you tell them."

Gretchen stared after her as Katiann trudged from the room as if going on an expedition into the desert.

Dirk waited until she was gone to break into laughter. "You know, we had that postcard from Bubba D. the other day—the one from the army."

"I remember."

"Well, Katiann declared that she thought girls should be able to join the army too. She said she figured she could run just as fast for just as long as any of those boys. I reminded her that they had to carry heavy packs and shoot guns, and she just shrugged and told me that Harvey Girls had to work just as hard."

"Did you remind her that nobody is shooting at Harvey Girls while they're working?" Gretchen threw him a smile.

"I did, but then she reminded me of the time we were at the Harvey House in Belen and some drunken cowboys shot up the place. She told me every job could be dangerous—it was just a matter of learning to deal with it."

"That girl is something else." Gretchen went to the stove and began to stir the concoction of simmering vegetables.

Dirk left William on the floor with one of his toys and came to put his arms around Gretchen. "So are you."

Gretchen set down her wooden spoon and turned to face him. "And why would you say that?" She never tired of his praise and words of love.

"Because it's true. But like Katiann said, sometimes you do have to remind people what they already know."

Gretchen wrapped her arms around her husband's neck. "I'm glad you reminded me of just how much I love you."

Dirk grinned. "My pleasure." He kissed her, then pulled back to gaze into her eyes. "My very great pleasure."

Note to Readers

The San Marcial flood of August 1929 destroyed a great deal of the town. The story about Felix and Chapo is a true one and was spoken about for years after the event.

In September of that same year, monsoonal rains crossed the state and brought even more flooding, and on the twenty-ninth, the Rio Grande again flooded San Marcial. This time it left complete devastation, and the town never rebuilt. The following month, the great stock market crash took place, Santa Fe relocated their shops and people, and the death of San Marcial was assured.

Today there's nothing left. It's not even noted on most maps. But the spirit of the Horney Toad Division and the Harvey House lives on in the resilient people who still tell stories of Felix and Chapo and the men and women of the Santa Fe Railway.

More Than
a Pretty Face

Karen Witemeyer

To Bonnie and Sherryl

The details of this story would not have been possible without your help. The tour of Gainesville's Santa Fe Depot and Harvey House that you arranged allowed me to step back in time and into my heroine's shoes. Sherryl—you were a font of local historic knowledge, and the numerous photos and documents you provided made research a breeze. Bonnie—without you, this trip wouldn't have happened. From our time at the museum, to the lunch we shared, to the wonderful driving tour of the area's historic homes, I couldn't have had a better day.

Thank you both.

Stand fast therefore in the liberty wherewith Christ hath made us free, and be not entangled again with the yoke of bondage.

—Galatians 5:1

Chapter One

"I'm not going to marry her, Mother."

Caleb Durrington bit the inside of his cheek to keep the rest of the words piling up on his tongue from escaping. She meant well. He knew that. But his mother's constant harping irritated him worse than a stone in his shoe.

Estella Durrington frowned at her son in a way that managed to convey both disappointment and determination in the same expression. She was formidable. An essential trait for putting up with an ornery cuss like his father for thirty years. Caleb should have known she wouldn't let a little thing like his personal wishes keep her from arranging his happiness.

"Roberta Fletcher is a lovely young woman," his mother insisted, eyeing him over her teacup as they sat in the fancy parlor she'd recently had redesigned in shades of peacock blue and cream. Caleb hadn't even known the color *peacock blue* existed. And cream should be whipped and served on pie, as far as he was concerned.

Dad never would have sat in a chair covered in flowers and squiggly paisley shapes, crotchety cowboy that he'd been even after making his fortune during the cattle boom. But then, he'd never have lived in a house in town either. No, Mother's purchase of this Queen Anne-style abode had been the fulfillment of a desire long held in check by a no-frills man who'd insisted on utility over ornamentation. That, and an escape from all the memories of the man she'd loved. They might not have seen eye-to-eye on much, but they had agreed on what mattered most—loving each other and loving the son they'd brought into the world.

"Are you listening to me, Caleb?" The needling question jabbed through his wandering thoughts.

"Yes, Mother."

She raised a doubt-filled brow but advanced with her campaign anyway. "Roberta comes from a good family and possesses a sweet disposition. She's lovely to look at and, from what I hear, is adored by the children she teaches in Sunday school. She'd make a wonderful mother."

Caleb shot her a warning glance. Pushing prospective brides at him was one thing, but manufacturing children for him to sire was going too far.

A fact she must have realized, for she gave up a couple inches of ground and reconfigured her troops, setting her teacup in its saucer and shifting her legs to the other side of her chair before returning to the offensive. "For heaven's sake, Caleb. You and Bobbie grew up together. You're friends." She wagged a finger at him before he could even think about opening his mouth. "Don't deny it."

He held up his palms. "I'm not."

That soothed a few of the ruffles in her feathers. "Good. So we agree. She's perfect for you."

Caleb refrained from sighing. Barely. He also refrained from growling, which was the bigger accomplishment, since he felt like a cougar backed onto a narrow rock ledge. "We agree that she is the perfect friend for me," he conceded, praying his mother would accept that as sufficient.

Her cup and saucer jerked all the way down to the tabletop. "You need more than a friend. You need a wife." Her eyes measured him, making him feel like a kid being asked if he'd washed behind his ears. "You're twenty-eight, Caleb. Your father and I had already been married for a full year by the time he was that age. What are you waiting for?"

The right woman.

"School is behind you, your law practice is on solid footing. Nothing stands in the way of matrimony except your stubbornness. Roberta Fletcher would make a lovely bride and a supportive helpmeet. There is no one better suited to you."

He could think of someone . . . but his mother's shrill tone cut off that thought as if she'd seen it materializing inside his head.

"What could you possibly find unacceptable about Roberta?"

"Nothing!" He lurched to his feet. "Nothing's wrong with Bobbie. She's everything you said. But she's like a little sister to me. There's no spark between us."

"Successful marriages need more than sparks, Caleb." Mother slowly rose to her feet, her gaze never leaving his face. "Passion won't get you through the hard times. You need mutual respect, commitment, and love. There is no better basis for love than a strong friendship. Your father might have goaded my temper more than any man alive, but he was also my dearest, most trusted friend. Don't discount friendship because it seems less exciting than the flash of infatuation."

Caleb stilled his pacing. She wasn't wrong. He'd seen the relationship his parents shared. A lasting bond had held them together, one based on something much deeper than physical attraction. But he also knew where they had started. It had been one of his father's favorite stories.

"You're right, Mother. Love and friendship do go hand in hand. But friendship by itself is not enough. Dad always said lightning struck him when he saw you at that church social back in '71. And even with your uppity ways, he knew no other woman would do."

A blush rose to his mother's cheeks. "I was never *uppity*."

"Not where it counted." Caleb grinned. "After all, a truly uppity woman never would have married a land-poor cowhand with nothing to offer but dreams of a brighter future and a heart that beat for her alone."

A wistful look softened his mother's face.

"Did you know that he credited his ranching success to you?"

"Me?" Her chin jerked up. "Heavens, what did I do? That man earned every penny he made by the sweat of his brow. I've never met a man who worked harder."

Caleb set a gentle hand on his mother's shoulder. "He told me once that it was your belief he could better himself that gave him the courage to face hardship head-on. He told me to find a woman who challenged me in the same way." His arm fell back to his side. "Bobbie's a sweetheart, but there's no lightning when she looks my way, and no challenge stirs within me when we talk." Unlike another lady of his more recent acquaintance. "It's not enough. I want what you had with Dad. And I'll find it in my own time and in my own way."

His mother blinked at him once before the softness in her features hardened with purpose once again. "If your father trusted me to shape his future, Caleb, you should too."

Not wanting to argue with her anymore—there was no point, since neither of them was going to change their mind—he sketched a small bow. "Thanks for the tea, Mother. I'll see you tomorrow."

"But you barely took more than a sip. And you didn't even touch the cookies I set out. They're your favorite. Oatmeal."

A twinge of guilt plucked his heart, but he ignored it. He'd visited just as he'd promised. And while he did love a well-baked oatmeal cookie, he was in the mood for something sweeter. Something served by a woman who'd presented him with a constant challenge since the day he'd met her at the Harvey House lunchroom two months ago.

"I'm going to stop by the depot and grab a piece of pie." Avoiding meal times and train stops had proven an effective strategy for gathering intelligence. When the dining room wasn't overflowing with hungry rail passengers on a tight timetable, a fellow could actually exchange conversation with the lady serving him that went beyond elucidating his order. Which was why Caleb had memorized the train schedules three weeks ago.

The next train wasn't due to pull into the station until 5:33, which left him nearly a full hour and a half to continue his efforts to solve his new favorite puzzle—Miss Rosalind Kemp.

"You better not be thinking about taking up with one of those . . . *waitresses*." The scorn lacing his mother's words brought a frown to Caleb's face.

"The girls working at the lunchroom are properly bred young ladies, Mother. They are polite and prim and possess impeccable manners."

Estella Durrington waved a dismissive hand in the air. "Nothing but window dressing. Those Harvey Girls serve men food and drink downstairs and have *rooms upstairs*. Everyone knows what that means." She eyed him with raised brows. "I wish Fred Harvey had never brought his fancy food and fancy ladies to Gainesville. We've worked too hard to eradicate the rowdy reputation of this town, what with all the cowboys stopping over after their trail drives, drinking themselves stupid, and causing trouble. Those Harvey Houses are simply saloons dressed up in courting clothes to deceive good people into believing they are fit for decent society, when in truth they should be hidden away in Silver City with the rest of the brothels."

"Mother!" He knew he should reprimand her for her incredibly prejudicial statement, but at the moment he couldn't get past the shock of hearing the word *brothel* pass her lips.

No proper lady—or gentleman, for that matter—spoke about the seedier side of Gainesville. It was an unwritten understanding that one was supposed to pretend Silver City didn't exist. But it did. And apparently his mother not only knew its name but also the trades plied there. It made a fellow wonder exactly what she and her friends talked about during those church missionary meetings.

As the shock dissipated, Caleb's indignation rose. "You've taken Sunday lunch in the Harvey House. You've seen the ladies who work there. Not an inch of skin is exposed beyond their faces and hands. They wear no flashy colors, just modest black dresses with high-neck white aprons. No jewelry. No cosmetics. There's nothing immoral or improper in their behavior. They conduct themselves with courtesy and professionalism. Equating them with soiled doves"—if she wanted to speak plainly, he'd oblige her—"is like equating a . . . a . . ." He fumbled for an adequate comparison until his skittering gaze locked on his mother's china tea service. "It's like equating a teapot with a whisky jug simply because they both hold liquid."

Estella Durrington's eyes narrowed. "Don't you use your barrister arguments on me."

Which meant she didn't have an adequate reply to his logic yet refused to admit any flaw in her own theory.

She sighed, her gaze softening. "I'm simply looking out for your best interests, Caleb. Don't think it has escaped my notice how often you frequent that establishment. It's obvious you're taken with one of those girls. But you know nothing of her past nor her moral character. A pretty face might be pleasant to gaze upon over coffee, but don't be taken in by appearances, son. 'Favour is deceitful, and beauty is vain: but a woman that feareth the Lord, she shall be praised.'"

"Yes, but just as all plain women aren't necessarily devout, all fair women aren't necessarily immoral. Look at Esther. God used her beauty to save a nation. And look at you, Mother. Still as lovely today as you were twenty years ago."

A touch of pink colored her cheeks. "Flattering an old woman just to win an argument—shame on you."

Caleb grinned, his ire fading as the mother he'd always adored emerged from the overprotective dragon she'd been hiding in. "What old woman?" he said as he crossed to her side. "All I see is the vibrant Estella Durrington, a lady in the prime of life." He bent down and kissed her cheek.

"Scoundrel." She batted at his arm, but a grin curved her lips. "You get your charm from your father."

Caleb winked at her, playing up the compliment and taking advantage of the lessening tension between them to make his escape.

He might have inherited his charisma from his father, but he'd inherited his stubbornness, his love of a good debate, and his ability to scheme from his mother. She could play dragon all she wanted, but he'd be making his own selection when it came time to choose a bride.

And since the lady currently at the top of the list seemed immune to charisma, it was time to deploy a new tactic. One his mother would approve of if the young lady in his sights was someone other than a Harvey Girl. After all, how many times had she insisted that a woman's mind was equal to any man's? That a woman's intelligence should be prized above her figure? He'd seen the truth acted out before him all his life. His father might have run the ranch, but his mother ran the business. She kept the books, managed the budget, and kept the buyers happy.

If he couldn't gain Rosalind Kemp's attention through friendly chatter and heartfelt smiles, he'd follow his mother's advice and appeal to her mind.

Chapter Two

Rosalind Kemp approached the new Santa Fe Depot from the west, making use of the exterior door that led directly into the kitchen. Thankful for an architect who'd crafted convenient entrances and exits for each section of the building, she slipped into the Harvey House kitchen without disturbing any of the guests in the neighboring lunchroom.

Their heavyset French chef looked up from rolling out pastry crust for the English-style baked veal pie that always seemed to be in demand during the dinner service. "How is Mrs. Williams faring today?"

Savory aromas from meat pies already in the oven tickled Rosalind's nose as she closed the door behind her. The clanking cadence of boys washing dishes mixed with the rhythmic tattoo of the assistant's knife as he prepped the vegetables. The music of a Harvey House kitchen. An orchestration that Felix Dupont directed to perfection.

Rosalind smiled as she tucked the white linen napkin she'd borrowed into the laundry basket under the shelf nearest the door. "She ate one of the tea cakes you sent."

Monsieur Dupont winked at her, the movement twitching his carefully waxed mustache. "*Très bon.* She is far too thin and far too sad. I am glad you asked me to bake for her. We will get her smiling yet, *oui*?"

"That's my goal." Rosalind grinned, feeling better than she had in ages.

She'd balked when she'd received the notice that she'd been reassigned to the new lunch counter in Gainesville. She'd grown quite content with Kansas. After completing her training in Topeka, she'd taken a position in Emporia followed by one in Wellington. As one of the few girls who'd managed to avoid matrimony within her first year of employment, she'd built up an impressive five years of seniority and had earned not only the opportunity to travel at the end of each contract period, but also the privilege of requesting transfers to other stations. She'd dreamed of putting in for a new post in California, some-place so far removed from Texas that the mistakes of her past wouldn't find her. Unfortunately, before her current contract expired, she had been reassigned to the very place she'd gone to such lengths to avoid.

No doubt the Fred Harvey company thought they were doing her a kindness by moving her to a station so close to her home-town of Honey Grove—and in truth, she had been grateful for the chance to spend a few days with her sister, brother-in-law, and her adorable two-year-old nephew, Pierce, before starting work in Gainesville—but Texas was the last place she wanted to be. Not with the increased risk of a cowhand or railroad worker having a Prairie Rose tucked into his billfold.

Be that as it may, when the Fred Harvey Company asked one of its girls to take a position somewhere, she took it. With a smile. So here she was, determined to make the best of things. Focusing on someone other than herself helped. Everyone had troubles and regrets. If she could ease the burden of one such person while she was stationed here, then her return to Texas would have been worth all the worry and stress.

"I don't know why you two bother with the crazy train lady," one of the dishwashers said as he moseyed closer, a freshly washed cake tin in his dish towel-clad hands. "Ya'll are new here, but everyone in these parts knows Widow Williams's got an attic full of cobwebs, if ya know what I mean." The lanky youth tapped a finger to his temple as if she might need the clue to decipher his oh-so-subtle insult.

Rosalind glowered at him through the clear-glass spectacles she'd taken to wearing since returning to Texas. "Constance Williams deserves our pity, not our scorn. She's all alone in this world and misses her son. Can you blame her for hoping for his return?"

"I can when the feller cocked up his toes seven years ago. He ain't a-comin' back, Miss Kemp. Not by train or wagon or three-legged mule. And his mama visitin' the depot ever' Tuesday to look for 'im among the passengers ain't gonna change that fact."

"Enough, Henry." Chef Dupont jabbed his rolling pin in the direction of the sink. "Get back to work."

"Name's Hank," the boy groused, but he turned to obey. Jobs that paid as well as a dishwasher in the Fred Harvey system were few and far between for a lad of his years. Plenty of locals would line up to replace him if he lost the position.

After ensuring the boy returned to his station and resumed his work with sufficient vigor, Chef Dupont turned his gaze to Rosalind. "I feared that might be the case with Mrs. Williams. Losing a child"—his gaze dropped to the floor, then lifted slowly, as if the effort required for the simple movement was almost too much for him—"is a difficult storm to weather. Some . . . lose their way."

Had *he* lost his way? Or perhaps someone he loved had suffered that fate? Rosalind had heard him speak of a wife once or twice, but always in the past tense. And never in relation to a child. Rosalind placed a hand on his arm, the ache in her chest growing as she tried to fathom the depth of such pain.

Her touch seemed to rouse the older man from his melancholy, for he straightened his posture and twitched his curled mustache upward with the force of a quickly manufactured smile.

"We will be her compass in the storm." He nodded to underscore his words. "I will bake her sweets to remind her that living can still bring joy, and you will bring her company to remind her that she is not alone."

"Yes." Rosalind's voice cracked slightly, but she didn't care. This man with his tender heart and skilled hands was the epitome of the father she'd always wanted.

Her own father had been a skilled baker, a trade he'd begrudgingly passed down to Rosalind's older sister, Abigail, when he'd failed to sire a son to succeed him, but his heart had been far from tender. Rosalind had fared better under his sharp tongue than Abby had, with his penchant for constantly finding fault. However, the favor Rosalind had enjoyed had nothing to do with her skill with a needle or her nursing abilities when he took ill. He had valued her strictly for her face, planning to trade her looks for a suitable son-in-law who could run the family bakery in Abigail's place.

Rosalind smiled as she considered the son-in-law her father had acquired after his death. Edward Kemp would not have cared for Zacharias Hamilton one bit, seeing as how Zach had a knack for putting bullies in their place. Zach would have told him to his face that he was a bigoted fool to think any man could run the Taste of Heaven bakery better than Abigail. And he'd have been right.

Allowing Chef Dupont to get back to his veal pie, Rosalind crossed to the silver cabinet to see about polishing away any water stains that might mar the shine of the utensils scheduled for the dinner service. No Harvey Girl was ever to sit idle, after all. There was always silver to polish and china to inspect for cracks or chips. Nothing but the best would be placed before a customer. Fred Harvey might have passed away last year, but his standards for quality lived on in each of his establishments.

Rosalind had just started rubbing out a small smudge on the handle of a butter knife when the door connecting the lunchroom to the kitchen pushed inward.

"Is Rosalind back from her break yet? Oh, there you are. Perfect!" Callie Sanderson skittered to the back of the kitchen, neatly dodging worktables, stoves, and splattering dishwater, successfully keeping her white apron as bright as her smile.

The petite brunette with glowing eyes and pink cheeks exuded joy wherever she went. It was no wonder she had already collected a half-dozen marriage proposals from besotted rail workers and cowhands alike. The only proposal that mattered to her, though, had come last week, when Mr. Flint Halbert stopped over for an extra day on his monthly business trip from Topeka to Denver. Callie hadn't stopped smiling since. She'd met the young businessman during her training in Topeka a year ago, and the two had kept in touch via letters. They planned to wed as soon as Callie finished her current contract. Gainesville would need a new Harvey Girl by Christmas.

Callie grabbed the knife from Rosalind's hand, heedless of the fingerprints she left in her wake, and pushed the empty water pitcher she held toward Rosalind's chest in exchange. "Trade with me."

Rosalind grabbed the pitcher out of reflex. "Why?"

"Because *he's* here." Callie's eyes danced.

"He, who?"

"Listen to you. 'He, who?' Who do you think, silly?" Callie circled Rosalind and gave her a little shove from behind. "Only the handsomest lawyer in Gainesville. The one who asks for you

93

every time he comes in. The one with the warm brown eyes that would make even me swoon if I weren't already so enamored with Flint's baby blues."

Rosalind's belly clenched, and her pulse quickened. *Mr. Durrington.* She squashed the urge to smile.

None of that, now. He was a customer, and Fred Harvey had strict policies against romantic activity between employees and customers. Which was a good thing, because she needed to steer clear of anything even hinting of romance. She was a Harvey Girl. Dedicated to the system. Determined to earn her way into a California position. The West equaled freedom. An escape from her past. Julius's photography business was based out of Austin, after all. The chance of his work touching her in California was extremely slim. Once there, she could finally be her true self again, stop looking over her shoulder, and maybe even find love.

Stumbling across love in Texas would be a disaster. For her as well as for anyone who cared for her. Better for all involved to stick to the California plan. Caleb Durrington would tire of her soon enough. Heaven knew she did all she could to discourage his interest while maintaining the gracious demeanor required of all Harvey Girls. He was persistent, though, and she couldn't deny that his tenacity gave her a secret thrill. But she'd managed to resist his charm this long. She'd manage a bit longer.

A second shove sent Rosalind careening toward the large water barrel stored near the door to the restaurant.

"I wish you'd let me do something different with your hair," Callie lamented as Rosalind placed the empty pitcher beneath the spigot and removed the cork plug. Local water was used for cooking and cleaning, but Harvey had deemed it unfit for their famous coffee, so they shipped in barrels of drinking water from Fort Worth. "I've seen your hair after you wash it. It's so pretty, all those gorgeous golden waves. I don't understand why you pull it back so tightly and wrap it in that rigid braid. Why scrape it into such an unattractive style?"

To make myself unattractive. But that was not the answer Rosalind voiced. "To keep it tidy. You know how Mr. Ledbetter is about hair escaping its pins. My curls can run amok." They didn't usually, but they *could* if she, say, got caught in a windstorm or had a bird alight on her head.

"Yes, but the rest of us manage to stay tidy with our looser styles," Callie bemoaned as Rosalind stoppered the spigot and turned to face her well-meaning friend. "Doesn't it make your head ache?" She pulled a face. "Mine hurts just looking at you."

"I've gotten used to it." Mostly. Although the first thing she did every night when she reached the privacy of her upstairs room was pull out every last pin and massage her scalp.

"Well, at least Mr. Durrington doesn't seem to mind." Callie's face cleared, and the twinkle returned to her eyes. "He asked for you specifically, you know. Better quit dawdling and get out there."

For a moment Rosalind considered sloshing the water from the pitcher onto her dress so she'd be forced to go upstairs and change, but such clumsiness would do her no favors in proving to Mr. Ledbetter that she was worthy of promotion.

"I'm sure one of the other girls can take his order," she tried instead. Not that she expected such a weak ploy to work. Ever since Callie had gotten herself engaged, she'd been on a mission to help her compatriots find husbands as well. Whether or not they wanted one.

Callie grinned mischievously. "Not if I gave them the hands-off signal."

Harvey Girls were not allowed to chat with each other while in the restaurant, but they found ways to communicate without words. Hands gathered behind the back with fingers displayed to enumerate section and seat numbers, for instance, staked a claim on a particular customer. All other girls would keep their distance.

"Why would you do that?" Rosalind frowned even as her heart thumped a little faster. "I've got no interest in him."

"Ha! And I've got no interest in Monsieur Dupont's petit fours." Callie ate at least two each evening after the final dinner service. "Either way, Mr. Durrington certainly has an interest in *you*. He asked for you by name, Rosalind, so the hands-off signal was really his doing, not mine."

"You're a meddler of the worst sort, Callie Sanderson." Rosalind rolled her eyes, but a smile crept onto her face despite her attempt to remain exasperated.

"You'll thank me someday."

I doubt it.

Nevertheless, having been given no choice in the matter, Rosalind gripped the water pitcher's handle in her right hand, straightened her posture, and pushed through the door leading to the lunchroom.

Chapter Three

Customers were sparse at three in the afternoon, which made it impossible for Rosalind to enter the restaurant without being spotted by the other two girls on duty. Fern smirked at her from the coffee station behind the large horseshoe-shaped counter that could seat up to forty guests. Rosalind ignored her, set the water pitcher at the cold beverage station, and continued moving forward. Dottie winked at her as she approached the front sideboard and paused in her collection of fresh linen napkins in order to signal a seat number. Four fingers extended from her left hand above the open linen drawer, while her right hand circled into a fist. Seat number forty.

Of course he'd be sitting there. He always sat there, in the very last chair in the northeast corner. The corner opposite the kitchen and farthest from the depot. The seat that afforded the nearest thing to privacy that could be found in the Harvey lunchroom. Which was why Rosalind had kept her gaze firmly directed toward the south when she'd entered. Yet she couldn't avoid him forever. Customers must be served in a timely manner, after all.

Steeling her resolve not to be charmed, Rosalind grabbed a menu card, circled the sideboard, and headed down the east side of the counter. Grace and efficiency. Those were a Harvey

Girl's trademarks. She'd focus on efficiency today. The faster she took Caleb Durrington's order, the faster she could escape his warm smile and affable manner.

As she approached, however, the oddest thing happened. He didn't look up. He always looked up. Smiled. Greeted her by name. But not today. Even when she halted directly in front of him, he ignored her. Why would he ask for her by name only to ignore her? And why did his lack of attention rankle? He seemed far more interested in the letter lying on the counter than in her.

Good. She *wanted* him to lose interest in her. And she'd just keep reminding herself of that fact until the ache in her chest resolved itself.

"What can I get you to drink today, sir?"

He chuckled softly at something, *still* keeping his head bent over that letter. It must be quite something to hold him so enraptured that he failed to hear her ask for his order. She knew she shouldn't peek but stole a quick glance at the paper anyway. He was making no effort to hide it, after all.

But what she saw when her gaze darted over the paper made it impossible to look away.

Squares and dots. Well, not really squares. Not all of them. Some were shaped like *L*'s, though they turned every which way. A few were angled. Other figures had three sides. About half had dots inside. The rest were empty.

No wonder he made no effort to hide his correspondence. It was written in hieroglyphs. Yet Mr. Durrington seemed to have no trouble deciphering the shapes. His finger followed the lines of symbols just as one would keep one's place on a page filled with actual words.

Intrigued, she longed to ask him about it, but to do so would be highly improper, so she asked him the only question she could. "Do you care for coffee today, Mr. Durrington? Or something else?"

Finally he looked up, the remains of his quiet chuckle leaving a smile upon his face. Heavens, that smile did strange things to her equilibrium. And Callie was certainly right about his eyes. Rich brown, like the tea Rosalind preferred, sweetened with honey. It wasn't as if she hadn't noticed his eyes before. She had, but she usually avoided extended eye contact with male customers. Especially Mr. Durrington. She'd taken to mentally rehearsing menu options in her mind when serving him to stay focused on company business, but that crazy letter had distracted her, and now that she was caught in his gaze, she couldn't seem to look away.

"It's a pigpen cipher," he said.

She blinked. "Excuse me?"

He pointed to the letter. "A pigpen cipher." He turned his head as if considering the symbols for the first time. "I'm guessing it got its name from the opened and closed 'pens' with the occasional pig-like dot inside, though I'm not really sure. What I do know is that Freemasons used it a hundred years ago to keep their records and correspondence private."

"Like a secret code?" Rosalind pressed her lips together. What was she doing? This was veering dangerously close to the edge of professional and dipping into the realm of personal. Yet before she could apologize and ask again for his drink order, he answered her question.

"Exactly."

Why did he have to smile like that, like he found her exceedingly clever? A woman could come to crave such a smile.

"Here, let me show you." He reached into the satchel that sat on the vacant seat beside him and pulled out a writing tablet.

He scooted his carefully arranged place setting aside and set the pad of paper directly between them. He drew a three-by-three grid in the top left corner, another in the right corner, then beneath those, he fashioned two large X's. He added dots to the interior corners or lines of each square section of the second grid, then did the same at the inner angles formed by the crisscrossed lines of the second X. Then he put a letter of the alphabet in every grid square and triangle.

"I had a friend in law school who shared my love of puzzles. We ran across this cipher while researching a case that took place following the War Between the States. Union soldiers who were imprisoned in Confederate camps used this code to communicate."

"Fascinating." The whispered word fell from her lips without her consent.

"David and I memorized the figures and started utilizing the code with each other in short notes until we became proficient enough for longer items. It wasn't of much use for note-taking in class, since drawing the figures takes considerably more time than regular penmanship, but it's perfect for using in date books or anything else one wants to keep private. When we graduated, we agreed to carry on the tradition in our personal correspondence. We wouldn't want our code skills to grow rusty." He turned the tablet around so that the cipher key faced her. Then he placed the letter his friend had written beside it. "Give it a try," he urged.

Rosalind's gaze darted from the papers up to Mr. Durrington's face. "I couldn't. That's your private correspondence."

"David won't mind. It's mostly dry details about a property case he's working on. Nothing personal." He pushed the two papers to the far edge of the counter, directly under her nose. "Just the first line. Here." He handed her the pencil he'd been using. "You can make notes at the bottom of the cipher page."

She hesitated, then glanced over her shoulder. No one was paying her any mind. No new customers had arrived in her area. Maybe she'd have time to do a couple words. She'd already noticed a pattern in the symbols—a three-item block that appeared several times over the page. A common word. No repeated symbols, so each of the letters was distinct. Probably *the* or *and*. She checked the key. The first symbol was an angle pointing right. *T*. It must be *the*. But it didn't appear in the first sentence.

Rosalind knew she shouldn't engage with the challenge—it wasn't proper Harvey Girl procedure—but her fingers picked up the pencil anyway. The puzzle was simply too intriguing to resist. A five-letter word sat at the top of the page. Most likely *Caleb*, Mr. Durrington's given name. The L-shaped first symbol confirmed the word started with C. She wrote out the name, then moved on to the sentence beneath. She didn't have time to verify each letter. Mr. Ledbetter could inspect the dining room at any moment. If he caught her . . .

She'd just have to be fast.

First word in the first sentence. Three letters. A mountain with a dot at its peak: *Y*. A box open on the left with a dot: *O*. *You*. Next word. Four letters, the end two were the same, and the first was the mirror image of the symbol for *Y*. *Will*. Square with dot: *N*. She recognized the next two symbols. *Not*. The next word was longer, started with *B*. Rosalind jumped to what she hoped was a logical conclusion. *Believe*. Another *W* word but with a table-shaped second letter: *H*. *What*. Next word had five letters, started with a backward *L* with a dot in the corner: *J*. This was a lawyer friend, right? *Judge*. The next grouping was probably the judge's name. She couldn't guess that and didn't want to take the time to translate the long string, so she skipped it and called him *X*. The last three words were short and had familiar shapes. She jotted down the remainder, dropped the pencil, and scooted the paper back toward her customer.

You will not believe what Judge X has done now.

Her heart thumped as if she'd just run to the courthouse square and back. Partly due to the anxiety tied to the possibility of getting caught fraternizing with a customer, and partly due to the pride swelling in her chest over her accomplishment. Caleb Durrington was a highly educated man—a lawyer. Rosalind might work in an eatery, but she was no dullard. She'd been piecing her own clothing designs together for years, a craft that required mathematical precision, geometric arrangement, and an eye for detail. What were those, if not puzzle-solving skills?

Mr. Durrington stared at the paper for a moment, then slowly wagged his head from side to side. Rosalind's heart raced faster, worried she'd done it wrong and made a fool of herself. But when he glanced up, it wasn't disappointment she read in his features. Not charm or flirtation either. It was awe.

"And here I thought David and I were the clever ones. But you . . . you're a natural. Your speed was astonishing!"

Rosalind felt a blush heat her cheeks. She offered a shrug, embarrassed by his praise even as his compliment slid into a secret, thirsty part of her soul that slurped it up like a cat lapping cream. "Well, I'm on duty, so I had to hurry. I guessed at most of it."

"Intelligent, insightful guesses. You've surprised me, Miss Kemp." He flashed one of those heart-stopping grins, the ones she'd been doing her best to avoid these past few months because they set off a riot of unwanted fluttering in her midsection. "I knew you to be a woman of many fine qualities, but you've been hiding more than pretty blue eyes behind those spectacles."

Hiding. If he ever discovered how much she was hiding, all the puzzle-solving in the world wouldn't preserve his good opinion.

Rosalind dropped her gaze and took a step back. She pasted on a bright, patently false smile and retreated behind her Harvey apron. "What can I get you to drink, Mr. Durrington?"

Her abrupt change in demeanor didn't have the desired effect, however. Instead of resuming the light, professional relationship of customer and server as she'd signaled him to do, Caleb Durrington peered at her even more closely, as if he'd caught the scent of secrets lurking beneath her surface and decided to keep digging. Without a word, he picked up his cup from his saucer, turned it upside down, then set it back on the counter, tilting the mouth of the cup against the saucer.

Rosalind jerked her gaze from his hands to his face. He'd made the effort to figure out the Harvey cup code? Right side up meant coffee. Upside down inside the saucer meant hot tea. Upside down outside the saucer meant milk, and tilted meant . . .

"Iced tea, please." No cheeky grin. No smug look of victory. He simply exuded a calm confidence that made her feel . . . safe.

Odd. A man with such an obvious propensity for solving puzzles should deepen her anxiety, not ease it. Yet here she stood, the knots in her belly loosening and the starch in her spine relaxing.

Then he smiled, his eyes going warm and gooey like cookies fresh from the oven. "And a piece of blackberry pie."

Pie?

"Everything all right over here, Miss Kemp?"

Rosalind blinked as Mr. Ledbetter's voice cut through the haze that had dulled her wits.

She smiled at her manager, who was striding over from his position at the cashier's counter. "Absolutely, sir." Drat. She'd lingered too long and roused his suspicion. Mr. Ledbetter harbored a kind soul, but he was a stickler for the rules. "Mr. Durrington has decided on blackberry pie."

The manager drew to a halt and gave her a nod before casting a warning glance at Caleb.

Rosalind scurried off to fetch the pie and iced tea her customer had ordered, but her feet stuttered. When had she started thinking of him as *Caleb*?

Pull yourself together, Rosie. Just deliver the order, then you can keep your distance.

And that was what she did. Poured his tea without a word, delivered his pie with the most platonic of courtesy, then retreated to the west side of the horseshoe until Caleb Durrington took his leave.

She knew the precise moment he swiveled out of his chair and gained his feet. She might be across the lunchroom, but she was still acutely aware of every move he made. Including his long, slightly bowlegged stride that more closely resembled a cowhand than a man of letters. She released a breath when the door closed behind him. Hopefully, with him out of sight, she'd be able to get her mind back where it belonged.

Returning to his seat to clear away his dishes and redo the place setting, she snatched up his empty pie plate and fork, then reached for the napkin sporting a small purple smear of blackberry filling. The moment she lifted the napkin, however, she realized the truth. She wasn't going to be able to put this man out of her mind as easily as she had hoped.

For on the counter, beside the generous monetary tip he'd left her, lay a folded sheet of paper, the top of which opened slightly when the weight of the cloth napkin was removed. Even before she reached for it, she could see the boxes and angles of the cipher symbols he'd taught her.

How on earth was she supposed to resist a man who left her a note penned in secret code?

Chapter Four

Hands shoved in his trouser pockets, Caleb paced the street in front of the two-story limestone courthouse and glanced up at the clock tower. Again.

Would she come? Had she even read his note, or did she deposit it straight in the trash bin after he left the depot yesterday? Reaching the corner of California and Dixon, he peered east down California Street, scanning the handful of pedestrians bustling about for an overly prim blond woman in spectacles. He didn't see her. At least not in the first block. She could be farther down, closer to the railroad.

He probably should have left the code key for her. He'd debated but decided to respect her intelligence. She'd watched him make the grids. They were simple enough to duplicate, and her memory had proven more than capable. It still amazed him how fast she'd translated that line. She had a keen mind.

Would she enjoy spirited debates? Most of his friends avoided engaging in political or religious discussions with him, not sharing his passion for a good argument. After being accused once too often of playing devil's advocate just to be a bur under someone's saddle, he'd moderated his conversation practices. But he missed it. Missed the challenge. Missed the way it made his mind come alive. He and David used to go back and forth for hours while in school, but discussing by letter lacked the excitement of being in the heat of battle. His mother sometimes proved an adequate sparring partner, but lately the only point she wanted to argue pertained to Roberta Fletcher, and Caleb had grown weary of that particular fight.

He glanced up at the clock tower again. Prayer meeting started in ten minutes. If he waited much longer, he'd be late. He set his jaw. Rosalind Kemp was worth being tardy for. Even if it earned him a scolding from his mother.

Surely Miss Kemp would consider his offer to escort her to a church service a harmless social outing. Although, she was fairly skittish. She never flirted. Never made extended eye contact with male customers. Avoided interacting with the rail workers who brought in supplies.

At least according to his source, one Hank Lowry, Harvey House dishwasher and prime informant. The enterprising kid had recognized Caleb's interest in Miss Kemp early on and offered to feed him information in exchange for legal advice regarding extricating his mother from an abusive marriage. Caleb would have advised the kid for free, but the boy seemed determined to pay his way. Caleb respected that. He also respected the kid's desire to protect his mother. Caleb was fairly certain Hank had taken on the dishwashing job to save up enough funds to help her run away from his father, but Caleb feared she would never leave. She refused to press charges against her husband or even admit any abuse had occurred.

Caleb had worried Hank would cease seeking him out after depleting his legal advice, but the boy kept visiting Caleb's office and reporting on Miss Kemp's activities. The kid probably just didn't want to go home, but Caleb gladly welcomed his company. He'd been praying that he might exert some positive influence in the boy's life.

Hank had been the one to remind Caleb that Miss Kemp

always arranged her schedule to attend Sunday service and Wednesday prayer meeting at the Christian Church, and had pointed out that, "If the two o' yous are gonna be in the same place anyhow, might as well go together." Hank had a definite knack for matchmaking. After he'd inspired that idea, Caleb had hired him on the spot as his courtship consultant. Fifty cents a week.

Which probably explained why the kid was herding Miss Kemp down California Street this very minute. He might figure he'd get a bonus if he led her down the chute. Caleb fought a grin as he yanked his hands out of his pockets and moved to intercept them. Hank would get his bonus. Maybe even a raise.

"Mr. Durrington," the kid called. "Fancy meetin' you here."

Caleb had to give the little schemer credit, as he actually sounded surprised to see him. "Hank." He nodded to the boy, then lifted his hand to tug on the brim of his hat. "Miss Kemp."

Her cheeks glowed pink, and her blue eyes shone behind her spectacles. Her black uniform and white apron had been traded in for something with a bit more color and style. The dark blue skirt was covered in tiny white polka dots, and the shirtwaist she wore had a pleated front and a ruffled collar that added a touch of softness to her that was rarely in evidence. The simple straw hat on her head would be swallowed whole by the monstrosities his mother favored, but the blue ribbon around the crown matched her skirt and proved a nice backdrop for the little white fabric rose placed jauntily at the side.

"You look quite fetching."

She frowned. Not the reaction he'd expected. But then, she wasn't the type to be won over with charm. What else could he offer?

He mentally scrambled until he came up with, "I'm glad you were able to decipher my note."

Her brows arched as if she were unsure if he'd intended to insult her intelligence with that clumsy comment.

Caleb fought down a growl. He was a lawyer, for Pete's sake. He was supposed to be good with words, with thinking on his feet. Apparently not when Rosalind Kemp was involved.

Giving up on witty conversation, he offered his arm. "May I escort you to services?"

She didn't take his arm. Instead, she unfastened the clasp on her small handbag and extracted a folded piece of paper. Still not saying a word, she handed it to him.

His stomach cramping, Caleb reached for it as Hank backed away.

"I'll save ya a spot on the back pew, Miss Kemp," the kid said as he created some distance between himself and the adults who had yet to settle anything between them.

A smile born of fondness bloomed on her face, banishing the wariness that had dominated her features since Caleb approached. "Thank you, Henry." So her voice *did* work. "I'll be there soon."

They would be there soon. Together. Hopefully.

"I don't remember the last time I saw him in church," Caleb said absently as he watched the boy jog off.

"He asked me to embroider a handkerchief for his mother's birthday next month and offered to barter in return for the service." Miss Kemp's eyes danced as she turned her attention from Hank to Caleb. "I told him that a month of church attendance would cover the bill."

"Why, Miss Kemp, how divinely devious of you."

She laughed, and the sound filtered through him like warm bathwater soaking into tired muscles. It relaxed away the nervous tension that had him so tightly coiled and left him at ease.

She didn't hold his gaze for long before her chin dipped, but it was enough to fill him with hope. If the note she handed him didn't tell him to scram, he just might have a chance.

Slipping his finger into the folded paper, he flipped open the note and grinned.

She'd written him back in code.

A chuckle rumbled from his chest. He'd suspected for the last few months that Rosalind Kemp was special, that she might very well be the woman God intended for him. And this confirmed it. Lightning might not have struck him as it had his father, but there had definitely been a spark—a spark that grew more electric with every encounter, every puzzle and challenge she presented.

Caleb scanned the carefully penned code, his elation dimming the longer he read. She was accepting his escort on the condition that he acknowledge that nothing more than friendship could exist between them. Apparently she had plans to take a position at a Harvey House in California in the near future.

He closed the note and bent in a small bow. "I will gladly accept your friendship, Miss Kemp, and look forward to learning more about your western aspirations." He extended his arm to her again.

She lifted her hand but let it hover in the air. "So we understand one another, Mr. Durrington?"

"I understand you perfectly."

Whether she understood *him* was another story. But as far as he was concerned, delayed understanding on her part was completely acceptable. After all, any lawyer worth his salt knew one needed time to present compelling arguments to sway a jury's opinion. He might be presenting to a jury of one, but this could be the most important case of his life. He'd use every advantage at his disposal.

As her hand settled into the crook of his arm, he grinned and immediately began his campaign.

"If we're to be friends, I think you should call me Caleb."

A smile blossomed on her face, but she immediately ironed out that wrinkle by pressing her lips together. "We'll see, Mr. Durrington," she said once she managed to get the rebellious smile contained. "We'll see."

Yes, they would.

When they reached the church, everyone had already taken their seats. He escorted Rosalind to the back pew where Hank sat slouched in the corner, handed her into the seat, then slid in beside her.

Halfway up the aisle on the opposite side, his mother sat in her usual place in the family pew, the plumage of her wide-brimmed hat twitching as she shifted in her seat. She had scooted in far enough to allow her son to take his rightful place beside her. When he failed to do so by the time the service started, she turned to scan the crowd. Her gaze eventually found him, then found the woman at his side. Her mouth puckered in disapproval, and her eyes shot dragon fire at him.

He'd mentally prepared himself for her displeasure, so the flames did no damage. As he removed his hat and hung it on his bent knee, he smiled and nodded to her. She'd come around eventually. As would the woman at his side.

It was ironic that the two women actually had similar goals at the moment—obstructing his romantic interest in Rosalind Kemp.

Caleb settled back against the wooden bench and grinned, making his mother's scowl even darker before she whipped her head back around and faced forward. It was a good thing no one sat too close. They could have lost an eye to that pirouetting plumage.

"Your mother doesn't seem to approve of your seating arrangement." Rosalind whispered the observation as she leaned forward to retrieve a hymnal from the rack on the back of the pew in front of them.

Caleb searched her face, suddenly worried that his mother might succeed in scaring her off before he had the chance to woo her away from California. *He'd* been prepared for dragon fire, after all, but his companion had not. Yet there was nothing timid about the glance Rosalind aimed across the aisle. She might not be ready to accept courtship, but she wouldn't be accepting disparagement, either.

"Don't let her bother you," he murmured. "She tends to contract dyspepsia whenever my decisions fail to line up with her wishes. It'll pass with time."

A gurgle that sounded suspiciously like suppressed laughter echoed between them before Rosalind schooled her features and dutifully turned her attention to the song leader who'd just called out the number of the first hymn.

The more Caleb learned about Rosalind, the more he found to admire. Intelligence, backbone, *and* a sense of humor. She was obviously a woman of faith and, according to a disgruntled Hank, kind to lonely old ladies who might or might not be in possession of all their faculties. If he had a list of ideal qualities to seek in a wife, she'd check all the boxes. Even the one at the bottom: fair of face and form. Spectacles and severe hairstyle aside, Rosalind had lovely features and pleasing proportions, attributes she curiously made a point to minimize.

The hymn began, and Caleb joined in, the words and tune memorized years ago so that they did nothing to impede the thoughts still rioting in his brain. His attention floated from the notes and words on the page before him to the woman sitting beside him.

What was she hiding from? Why did she frown when he complimented her appearance? Had she been raised to feel guilty for being beautiful? He'd known some rather dour Christians who seemed to believe that anything too pleasing had to be sinful. Rosalind didn't strike him as particularly prudish, though, just excessively modest, as if determined to deflect all attention away from herself. Like a shield. A defense. Against what? Overeager men?

Caleb's jaw clenched, cutting off his singing voice. Had she been hurt by some man who thought her beauty was his for the taking?

It was surely a sin to think violent thoughts against another in the middle of a prayer meeting, but Caleb couldn't help himself. The idea of someone harming Rosalind made his fist ache to mete out western justice.

Good thing the Lord knew what he needed before he could ask, because Caleb was certain that the hymn announced next was intended specifically for him. Loosening his jaw, he sang the words his heart needed to pray.

"Dear Lord and Father of mankind, forgive our foolish ways; reclothe us in our rightful mind, in purer lives Thy service find, in deeper reverence, praise."

Thank you for reminding me where I am and what I need to be about. You are in control of the past, present, and future and are worthy of my trust. Help me be worthy of Rosalind's trust. To be a friend to her, and if it be thy will, perhaps something more. I leave her past and my future in your hands and give you my present.

Worship came easier after that, though having Rosalind at his side was a distraction that proved difficult to banish completely.

Good thing they closed the service with "Amazing Grace."

Chapter Five

"Where is he taking you tonight?" Callie asked as she sauntered into Rosalind's bedchamber and met her gaze in the small mirror above the washstand.

Rosalind quirked a brow. "Most people knock, you know."

Callie shrugged. "Most people aren't your best friend." She grabbed the iron bedstead with one hand and flopped onto the corner of the mattress.

Nibbling on her lip as she added another pin to ensure all her hair stayed in place, Rosalind held her answer ransom a little longer. No sense in rewarding snoopiness. Even if it was well-intentioned.

"Your hair is much prettier like that," Callie said. "You should let your curls show more often."

Rosalind frowned at her reflection. Had she let vanity override good sense? She hadn't styled her hair in the tall pompadours that ladies of fashion currently preferred, but she had eliminated the overly tight braided coil she usually hid behind and bundled her waves into a loose knot at her nape, securing the mass with a pink sash that matched her dress.

She reached for the ribbon and started to pull it down, but Callie shot to her feet and stopped her.

"Don't you dare!" Her friend snatched Rosalind's hands

away from her coiffure, then deftly repaired the damage with a few quick tucks and turns. "I don't understand you, Rosie. There's nothing wrong with wanting to look your best. Mr. Durrington is obviously taking you someplace special, or you wouldn't be all gussied up in this gorgeous pink confection I've never seen before. Did you have this hidden away in your trunk all this time? Because I've riffled through your wardrobe, and this wasn't in there."

"Callie!" Rosalind spun around. "You went through my things?" What if she had found the Prairie Rose photo card? Rosalind kept it hidden in a box in the bottom of her trunk, and she was careful to keep her trunk locked, but she could have forgotten or been in a hurry or—

"Not when you weren't present, silly," Callie teased, though her smile dimmed beneath growing shadows of concern. "Remember? Two weeks ago? You loaned me that cute little black hat of yours when Flint came to town. You were busy embroidering Henry's handkerchief and told me to fetch it from the top of your wardrobe. That's when I snooped at your clothes. You're not mad, are you?"

"Of course I'm not mad." Rosalind wrapped her friend in a hug. Good grief. She was becoming paranoid. "You can riffle through my wardrobe whenever you like." She released Callie and stepped back. "Yes, I stored this one in my trunk. It's still a bit wrinkled in places, I'm afraid." She frowned at the creases she hoped would get lost in the folds of the bell-shaped skirt. "I didn't expect to have occasion to wear it. But when Caleb invited me to the opera house, I figured I should dig it out."

"The opera house?" Callie's cheerful demeanor fully restored, she clasped Rosalind's hands, swinging her arms out and back until the lacy sleeves at Rosalind's elbows started to itch against her forearms. "Flint's promised to take me there one day, but he never seems to come to town on a weekend when there's a production scheduled. What are you going to see?"

"I'm not sure." Rosalind brightened, her worries shrinking beneath the flood of Callie's enthusiasm. "A vaudeville-type show, I think. A collection of different acts."

"Ooh. I hope there are acrobats. Those are my favorite. Or one of those fellows who can juggle swords." Callie ceased her arm-swinging and gave Rosalind a serious look. "If there's anything even the slightest bit scary or surprising, be sure to grab your man's arm and lean into him. A darkened theater is the perfect place to get close." She giggled, and Rosalind couldn't help but smile.

"You're terrible."

Callie's eyes widened in mock innocence. "Not me. Men are natural protectors, you know. It boosts their confidence to feel needed. We're doing them a kindness."

Rosalind shook her head, grinning. "Caleb's confidence doesn't require any boosting. It's plenty strong all on its own."

She didn't think she'd ever met a more self-assured man who managed to be humble at the same time. Her brother-in-law came close, but Zach bore too many scars from past battles with his demons to be completely confident in all situations. It was one of the things she loved best about him, though. He understood what it was like to live with the consequences of poor choices and to try to build something new from the leftover pieces.

Caleb, on the other hand, exuded goodness. As if he had no secrets hiding in his past, no shameful misdeeds waiting to pounce on his happiness at the worst possible moment. Yet there was a compassion in him, as well, that never seemed to pass judgment on the struggles of others. When she'd told him about Constance Williams, he offered to check in on the widow once a week and then had actually done so. Constance had told her all about it last Tuesday, chattering for a good ten minutes about a young man other than her son, going on and on about how polite Caleb was and bragging about how he'd unclogged her stovepipe for her when he noticed it smoking into the kitchen.

Oh, he was no saint. Caleb hated to lose an argument and tended to press his point further than what was considered polite. He was stubborn, a little sneaky, and it was nearly impossible to change his mind once it was set, but when Rosalind was with him, she felt safe. And she hadn't felt that way in a very long time.

"Hellooooo?"

Rosalind blinked to find Callie waving a hand in front of Rosalind's face. "Sorry." Heat warmed her neck. "Did you say something?"

Callie smirked as she lowered her hand. "I think I have my answer."

"To what?"

"Oh, nothing. Just an observation that you and Caleb are becoming quite a pair. I imagine Mr. Ledbetter will have openings for *two* Harvey Girls soon."

Rosalind's belly tightened. "No. Caleb and I are just friends. I made that clear from the outset. Mr. Ledbetter *will* be short two girls, but not because marriage is in my future. I'm transferring to California."

Callie shook her head and winked at her friend. "You're not going anywhere, Rosie. That man's been wearing you down for five weeks now. Escorting you to church, taking you on scenic buggy rides, leaving notes for you with us other girls so you can't be accused of fraternizing with a customer, and now the opera house. If you're not in love with him already, you soon will be." She waltzed toward the door that led into the hall, shooting a warning glare over her shoulder as she went. "And if you think California will bring you more happiness than a man who obviously adores you, then you're not half as clever as I thought you were."

Rosalind had walked by the Gainesville Opera House on several occasions—it was situated right off the courthouse square, after all—but she'd never been inside. It had to be the most luxurious theater she'd ever seen. Chandeliers hanging from the ceiling, carpeted floors, sculptures and framed art throughout the lobby, and finely upholstered seating arranged so everyone had a clear view of the stage. Even the electric sconces along the aisles sported decorative flourishes.

When the curtain came down at intermission following a particularly delightful song-and-dance duo, Rosalind turned to her escort, heart brimming with appreciation.

"This place is marvelous! I can't remember ever enjoying an evening more. Thank you for bringing me here."

Caleb smiled, the expression in his brown eyes soft and warm and completely focused on her. "My pleasure. I'm finding the experience tonight rather remarkable myself, but I think that has more to do with the company than the production."

The resistance she'd been so keen to hang on to after her disturbing conversation with Callie began to disintegrate like sugar dissolving into freshly brewed tea. Would opening herself to this man really be so bad? Maybe God had brought her to Gainesville, and Fred Harvey had only been his instrument. Maybe meeting Caleb had been God's will for her all along.

Or maybe courtship with Caleb had been *her* secret desire all along, and God had nothing to do with it. Rosalind ducked her head to hide from Caleb's regard, too many warring emotions swirling in her breast.

Then his hand touched hers, and she could no more look

away from him than she could ignore the Harvey gong when it announced a train's arrival. Her gaze found his, and her pulse throbbed. He looked at her the way Zach looked at Abigail, as if she was the answer to his prayer.

But she wasn't the woman he thought her to be. She was a fraud hiding behind fake spectacles with a trunk full of secrets that would bring him shame should they ever come to light.

Rosalind lurched to her feet. "I . . . I need to visit the ladies' retiring room."

Caleb rose as well, a puzzled expression etching his brow before he smoothed it away with a polite smile. "Of course. I'll show you the way."

Ever capable, Caleb steered her around mingling patrons, the buzz of conversation growing louder and louder in her ears. She knew they weren't talking about her, about the scandalous past she lied about every time she signed a new Harvey House contract. Yes, she agreed to exhibit high moral character at all times and had done so and would continue to do so, but the contract required that there be no blemish on her character, and that was simply not the case.

They reached the lobby, and Caleb pointed to a doorway near some potted plants. "Right through there, I believe."

She nodded. "Thank you. I won't be long." She released his arm and stepped away.

"I'll wait for you." Something about his tone had her glancing behind her and intertwining her gaze with his.

I'll wait for you. I'll wait until you're ready to love me the way I love you.

Surely not. Rosalind broke his gaze and scurried through the doorway in front of her. Surely he simply meant he'd wait for her in the lobby until she finished refreshing herself. Nothing more.

Yet what if he *had* intended more?

Zach had overlooked Abby's past, and she'd forgiven his.

Their love had overcome. Could Rosalind and Caleb do the same? Would their love be strong enough to grow in rocky soil, or would her past slash down like a hoe, tearing the tender shoot to bits before it could reach maturity?

"It's Miss Kemp, isn't it?"

Rosalind startled out of her thoughts to discover a brunette in a gorgeous bronze silk gown approaching. The woman could have been a magazine fashion plate in that ensemble, yet she put on no airs. Her smile simply exuded an abundance of friendliness.

Rosalind nodded. "Yes. Rosalind Kemp."

"I'm Roberta Fletcher, but you can call me Bobbie. All my friends do." Her genuine warmth charmed Rosalind into a small smile. And since she was in desperate need of a distraction at the moment, she flung herself into some harmless female chatter.

"Please. Call me Rosalind."

"Delighted to finally meet you, Rosalind." Bobbie took Rosalind's elbow and steered her to a private corner away from the door. "Caleb's told me all about you."

"He has?" So much for harmless female chatter.

"Sure. We've been friends for ages. Grew up on neighboring ranches. Our mothers even thought we might marry one day."

She chuckled softly, as if the idea were ridiculous, but Rosalind saw nothing humorous about the statement.

Something must have shown on her face, for Bobbie immediately sobered and reached out to clasp her arm. "Don't worry. Neither of us entertained that notion for even a moment. We're practically siblings. Besides, I have my eye on a handsome cattleman from Abilene." She gave Rosalind's arm a little pat. "Caleb's great, but far too bookish for the likes of me. I'm a ranch girl at heart, and he'd rather argue law than rope a steer these days. He hires out all the work on his father's ranch and only rides out a couple times a month to check on things." She recited the charge as if listing a mortal sin. Then her eyes brightened. "Oh! You should get him to take you to the Bar D sometime. There's a real pretty spot by the creek that would be perfect for a picnic." She released Rosalind's arm and took a step toward the doorway. "I'll go pester him about it right now before intermission's over so you can take care of whatever personal business I've been keeping you from." As if changing her mind about leaving, she retreated back to Rosalind's side. "Sorry for waylaying you. I just had to introduce myself to the woman who captured Caleb Durrington's heart."

"Oh no, I—"

But the whirlwind that was Roberta Fletcher spun away with a wave and a smile before Rosalind could correct the misunderstanding. If there was a misunderstanding. Maybe she really *had* captured Caleb's affection.

Before she could recover from that disturbing revelation, however, a shadow fell across her path. A woman in a black gown dripping in crystal beads separated herself from the crowd that milled around several large mirrors, patting coiffures and checking hems. She approached, a black feathered plume jutting straight up from the back of her sleek silver hair to an impressive height. The already statuesque woman gained at least six inches with her strategic accessory.

Recognizing the older woman from church, Rosalind lifted her chin and stiffened her spine. Maybe she and Caleb had a future together. Maybe not. But that was for the two of them to decide. She wouldn't allow Caleb's disapproving mother to make the decision for them.

"Mrs. Durrington." Rosalind bobbed a tiny curtsy. This was Caleb's mother, after all, and even if she wasn't the most delightful of women, she still deserved to be treated with respect.

Estella Durrington smiled, but the gesture failed to soften

the steel in her eyes. "Miss Kemp. I'm glad I bumped into you. I hoped we might have a word."

"Of course." Rosalind made room for Caleb's mother in the relatively secluded corner. "Are you enjoying the show? I can't remember when I've enjoyed an evening's entertainment so well."

"I imagine the *evening entertainment* you're accustomed to is much more . . . rudimentary."

Rosalind blinked. What was that supposed to mean? Mrs. Durrington's tone hinted at a hidden meaning in her words, but deciphering it was more difficult than decoding one of Caleb's secret messages. "Yes, well, most of my evenings consist of little more than needlework and reading, so I suppose you're right."

Mrs. Durrington's lips tightened slightly, but then her face cleared, and she reached out to touch Rosalind's arm. "You and Caleb have been spending a great deal of time together of late."

Rosalind nodded, though her intuition warned her to step carefully. "Yes, ma'am. I suppose you could call us friends."

"Oh, I'm so relieved to hear it." Mrs. Durrington sighed dramatically as she patted Rosalind's wrist. "I'm glad you are a sensible girl. I worried that Caleb's attention would lead you to believe there might be a chance for a romantic association between the two of you. My son possesses a keen mind, but his soft heart often leads him astray. I'm glad to know that you are clever enough to recognize that he deserves a woman of higher, shall we say . . . standards. Someone who will aid him in building a law career, not be a hindrance." The words might have been spoken in smooth, cultured tones, but they pierced Rosalind's heart like tiny darts, quiet yet painfully barbed.

Mrs. Durrington obviously held her son in great esteem. And why shouldn't she? Caleb was everything that was noble, honorable, and good. It was what drew Rosalind to him. She saw in him what she wanted in her own life, what she might have been if she hadn't muddied herself so thoroughly that the stain wouldn't wash clean.

"Caleb is indeed a fine man." Because what else could she say? "I certainly understand you wanting what is best for him."

"That I do." Mrs. Durrington smiled that pointed smile of hers again, and Rosalind's stomach churned. "I'm so glad we understand each other, dear. That will make it easier for you to refuse Caleb's next offer of escort."

Rosalind bristled. "Why would I do that?" She could guess, but she wanted to see if Mrs. Durrington would actually say it.

"Because as his friend, you want what is best for Caleb, just as I do. And we both know that Caleb deserves better than to have his name tied to a *waitress*."

She pronounced the word *waitress* as if it were a synonym for *trollop*.

Perhaps Rosalind had made shameful errors in her past that might, in fact, deem her unworthy to be Caleb's wife, but *no one* insulted the employer who had given her dignity and purpose.

"You have obviously been misinformed, madam." She drew back her shoulders and stepped toward Caleb's mother, her toes nearly bumping the front of the other woman's evening slippers. "The Harvey company only engages women of upstanding character to work in their establishments. Think what you will of me, but I will not allow you to disparage my esteemed compatriots with such a slanderous implication. We are not *waitresses*, Mrs. Durrington. We are *Harvey Girls*."

With that, she pivoted and made her exit before the sputtering woman could utter a response.

Caleb appeared at her side almost instantly, casting a slightly apprehensive glance past her to the retiring room. "Feeling better?" he asked.

"Quite." Nothing like getting one's dander up to enliven a wilting spirit.

Mrs. Durrington might have intended to drive Rosalind away, but their little confrontation had sparked the opposite reaction. It crystalized the myriad conflicting thoughts in Rosalind's mind into a single truth—Caleb was a man worth fighting for, a man worth the risk of heartbreak.

No more sitting on the sidelines. Time to open her heart and enter the battlefield.

Chapter Six

The following afternoon, Caleb's hands trembled as he steered the buggy team down the drive that led to the house he'd grown up in. He hadn't felt this on edge since presenting his first trial case before a judge. In a way, that was what he was doing today, presenting his case to the lovely woman at his side, his future happiness hanging in the balance.

Something had changed last night. He couldn't define it or explain it, but he recognized the difference. Rosalind had lowered her guard. Maybe not completely, but enough to give him hope that he might find a way past her defenses. A way to her heart.

Bobbie's urging last night for him to show Rosalind around the Bar D had provided the perfect opening. A bribe of opera house tickets for Callie and her fiancé to enjoy the next time Flint came to town secured a trade in shifts, providing Rosalind with the opportunity to escape for a couple hours this afternoon. He'd promised to return her to the depot in plenty of time for the dinner rush and had prepared to argue away any other protests she might offer. But none came. She'd accepted his invitation with a solicitude that bordered on eagerness. That was when he knew—today was the day.

The gentle sway of the open buggy pressed Rosalind's hip and shoulder against his side, leaving his pulse as unsteady as his hands. He watched her from the corner of his eye as she absorbed the simple country scenery as if it were fine art stretched across a museum canvas.

"Look!" She pointed at a jackrabbit scampering across the road in front of them, her laughter bringing a smile to his face.

"Wait until you see our new foal. Born just last week." Caleb twisted to meet Rosalind's gaze, her blue eyes so filled with delight that he found it impossible to look away. "She's a beauty." As was the woman before him.

"I can't wait to meet her."

Meet who? He'd completely lost his conversational bearings. Staring at her smile had that effect. Made a man forget where he was and what he was doing.

"Didn't expect to see ya today, Mr. D." A dark-skinned man exited the barn, a wide grin splitting his face as Caleb quickly adjusted his hold on the reins to keep the horses from walking straight through the barn door. "And you brought a lady friend too." The wrangler moseyed over to Rosalind's side of the buggy once Caleb had the conveyance fully halted, and tipped his hat to her. "Lincoln Sanderson, ma'am."

Rosalind, who had bitten her lip to hold back what was surely a chuckle at Caleb's driving blunder, unleashed a bright smile on Linc. "A pleasure to meet you, Mr. Sanderson." She held her hand out to him, and the middle-aged wrangler blinked at her, either undone by the force of her smile or immobilized by shock that a white woman unknown to him was inviting his touch.

He managed to shake off his stupor, though, and jumped forward to help her descend. Taking her hand and elbow, he ensured her balance as she found the buggy's step and finally the ground.

A little disappointed that he hadn't been awarded the pleasure of helping her alight, Caleb snuffed out the jealousy flaring in his midsection and circled the rear of the buggy to regain his position at Rosalind's side.

"Linc here's the best wrangler for miles around. There's not a horse he can't train, an ailment he can't cure, or tack he can't repair. The Bar D's lucky to have him."

Linc dipped his chin, then aimed a wink at Rosalind. "Don't let him bamboozle you, ma'am. I'm just an old cowhand who's picked up a few things over the years, is all."

"I believe they call that wisdom," Rosalind said. "A rare and valuable asset."

Linc stood a little straighter. "Thank ya, ma'am." He nodded to Rosalind, then moved closer to Caleb. "You done well for yourself with this'un, Mr. D."

Not wanting to unsettle Rosalind with a claim that wasn't yet his to make, Caleb dodged back to a safer topic. "I'd like to show Miss Kemp Penelope's foal. She in the paddock?"

"Yessir." Linc gestured with a tip of his head at the barn's alleyway. "Straight back. Go on and take yer lady through. I'll see to your rig." Linc moved to the team, his hand floating over the nearest horse's side as he strolled up to their heads.

"Thanks." Caleb held an arm out to Rosalind. "Shall we?"

She nodded and fit her hand into the crook of his arm. Satisfaction flooded him at a level completely out of proportion for such a platonic gesture. Yet there was nothing platonic about the feelings stirring in his chest as he drew her forward. He wanted this woman by his side—not just today, but forever.

As they cleared the shade of the barn, sunlight made Caleb squint as he sought out mother and babe. "Ah, there they are."

A chestnut mare to his right raised her head from where she'd been grazing. She eyed the newcomers, then nickered softly.

Caleb had known Penelope from the time she was a filly herself. She'd been one of his favorite mounts, her gait smooth and her temperament spirited, until she'd been set aside for breeding last year.

He approached slowly, hand outstretched. "Hey, Penny. How's my girl today?"

She tossed her head, sending her mane flying, then stepped forward and nosed his hand. Caleb ran his palm up over her cheek and patted her neck as he eased closer. Glancing over his shoulder, he urged Rosalind to follow him with a wave.

"It's all right," he said, trying to reassure both of his ladies.

Rosalind stepped closer, holding her hand out in front of her. Caleb fit his cupped palm beneath her outstretched hand and guided it to Penelope's nose, letting the horse familiarize herself with Rosalind's scent. Then he gently tugged Rosalind even closer, positioning her in front of him and showing her how to stroke the mare's coat. She'd told him that she hadn't spent much time around horses, having grown up in a town where she could walk everywhere she needed to go. Yet it wasn't purely a desire to instruct her that motivated Caleb. Holding her hand was pure pleasure, and standing close enough to catch the floral scent of her hair and feel the brush of her skirt against his legs was about as near to heaven as he'd ever come.

He should let her pet the horse on her own—it wasn't a complicated task, after all—but he didn't. He just kept stroking the mare with Rosalind's hand cupped in his, inwardly exulting when she made no effort to pull away. They stood like that for several minutes, arms spooned together, breathing melding into a single pattern, until Penelope grew restless and stomped a back hoof. The mare sidestepped and turned her attention back to her foal.

Lashes lowered, Rosalind dropped her arm and pivoted to

face him. The physical connection might have ended, but Caleb swore a metaphysical one still linked them. Her lashes lifted. Their gazes met and held. And for the first time, she made no effort to hide herself from him. She exposed doubt, a touch of fear, and a lingering sadness he'd never perceived before. Yet hope and longing glimmered above the rest, making his breath catch in his throat.

"Rosalind." He reached for her, but before his fingers could find the curve of her cheek, she twisted sideways and focused her attention on the foal walking on wobbly legs beside her mother. Penelope had grown weary of humans who were more interested in each other than in her, and had decided to take her offspring on a lap around the paddock.

"What's the baby's name?" Rosalind held her hands together in front of her as if physically restraining herself. From what? Reaching for him? Caleb prayed it was so, for that might actually mean that her feelings for him mimicked his for her. She refused to look at him, though. Instead, she followed the horses' movements with her eyes, as mare and foal meandered along the paddock fence.

Caleb slid in beside her. He kept his hands to himself and made a show of watching the horses, but all of his attention focused on Rosalind. "We haven't named her yet." He twisted his head in her direction. "Would you like the honor?"

That brought her face around. "Me?" Her blue eyes brightened as if he'd just offered her a box of diamonds.

His chest tightened. This was what he wanted. The chance to make her happy, to see her eyes light up, to share little moments like this with her for the rest of their days. "I don't see why not." He wanted to touch her, to clasp her hand or stroke her cheek, but he settled for holding her gaze, not wanting to jeopardize the fragile closeness blooming between them. "Go ahead," he urged, his voice almost a whisper. "Name her."

She turned back toward the foal, its spindly legs braced wide as the pair halted and the filly stretched her neck up to nuzzle her mama's face.

"Jennie." Rosalind's soft voice filtered through the air like a child's prayer. "My mother's name." She dipped her head and stared down at her feet. "She died when I was eleven. Childbed fever."

Empathy rose inside him. "I'm sorry. I lost my father last year. Influenza. It was hard to watch him fade. He'd always been so strong. Indomitable, really." A smile tugged Caleb's mouth as he recalled the man he'd respected more than any other. "He built this place up from a spread of thirty head to one of thirty thousand. I didn't think anything could take him down, but I guess death conquers all of us eventually."

Rosalind finally unclenched her hands and reached out to touch his arm. "My father was a self-made man too. A baker with his own shop. He passed when I was seventeen. Heart failure." She paused, her hand slipping away from his arm. "He was never particularly kind to my sister or me—he always wished he'd had a son instead of daughters—but he wasn't cruel. And he softened toward the end. I'm not sure Abby ever saw that side of him. She was so busy running the bakery and keeping the business afloat. But I noticed the change as I tended him during his illness. I'd sit with him for hours. Reading to him, feeding him, making sure he was comfortable. And he'd tell me stories. Stories of how he met my mother, how much he'd loved her, how he missed her. He saw her in me, he'd say. My looks. My personality. Abby took after him—driven and determined. It was probably why they butted heads so often. But I was more like his beloved Jennie, content to let others lead while I nurtured from the sidelines."

Caleb could hear her love for her father in her voice. The loss that still impacted her heart. Saying good-bye to his father was the hardest thing he'd ever done, but he'd been a grown man out of school and well on his way to establishing his own path in life when he'd been faced with that task. He couldn't imagine losing both parents at such a tender age.

"Is losing your father what led you to become a Harvey Girl?" he asked.

She kicked at a clump of grass with her shoe, not meeting his gaze. "In a roundabout way, I suppose. My sister and her husband would have preferred that I stay with them, but once I knew Abby would be well taken care of, I chose to leave. To find my own way in the world and see new places. Fred Harvey allowed me to do that."

His gut told him there was more to the story, but he wasn't going to press for answers. Not yet. He'd learned more about her past in the last fifteen minutes than he had in the last five weeks. Yet while he was willing to forgo the mysteries of her past, the direction of her future was a different matter entirely.

"Are you still set on transferring to California?" He shifted his stance until he stood directly in front of her, then gave in to the desire to touch her and lightly traced the outline of her face with his finger, diverting over her left ear to tuck away a tendril of hair that the breeze had tugged free.

Her blue eyes widened as his finger skimmed along her jawline and paused beneath her chin. "M-maybe."

Her uncertainty fell on his ears like the finest Mozart sonata.

"I think you should consider staying in Gainesville." His finger fell away from her chin as he fit his palm to the side of her neck and curled his fingers around her nape. "With me."

A breathless sound escaped her lips, parting them ever so slightly. He tugged her face close, his mouth hovering inches above hers. But he couldn't kiss her. Not yet. Not until he pled his case with the most compelling testimony at his disposal.

Lifting his gaze from her mouth to her eyes, he opened his heart to her with a prayer that this jury of one would find in his favor.

"I'm in love with you, Rosalind, and I want to spend the rest of my days at your side."

Chapter Seven

I'm in love with you.

How could such small words capsize her so completely? Rosalind felt herself falling, losing her grip on the raft that had kept her afloat the last five years. The control she'd clung to slipped from her grasp, plunging her into a river that flooded her with warmth and begged her to cease fighting against the current and simply let go.

Let go and let herself love this man. This godly, intelligent, kindhearted man whose hand on her nape made her knees weak and her pulse hum.

That hand drew her closer, making her forget all the reasons she should resist loving Caleb Durrington. And when his lips met hers, she nearly wept from the tenderness of his touch. The brush of his mouth was gentle, almost reverent, and she could no more hold back the tide of love welling within her than she could rein in the Texas wind. So she ceased trying. She raised her palms to his chest, anchoring herself in his solidity, and gave herself over to his kiss.

The beating of his heart quickened beneath her hand. He deepened the kiss, and Rosalind matched his passion with her own. This was love—sharing, giving, joining with someone you trusted completely, someone whose needs you'd gladly place before your own.

But could trust truly exist in the presence of secrets?

Rosalind pulled away from the kiss. "Caleb, I . . ."

I love you too. That seemed the most important truth at the moment. Surely the rest could wait.

His face hovered a few scant inches above hers, his brown eyes peering into her with an intensity that made her feel cherished yet exposed at the same time.

Rosalind swallowed and lowered her lashes. "There are complications, Caleb. Complications that might change the way you feel." She shook her head slightly, having said more than she'd intended. Then, straightening her shoulders, she took the plunge and admitted her feelings to herself as well as to him. "You snuck up on me. Luring my heart little by little with your ciphers and outings, your kindnesses to old ladies and adolescent dishwashers, until it became fully yours." A tentative smile wobbled onto her face as she gave in to the current. "My heart belongs to you for as long as you desire it."

He stroked the pad of his thumb along her jawline, a crooked grin turning up his mouth at one end. "Then it will belong to me forever, for my feelings will never change."

She leaned into his touch even as her heart squeezed. *Please, God, let it be so.*

But as the prayer left her soul, Rosalind braced for the pain that would come should her petition be denied.

Caleb could not recall a time in his life when he'd been so blissfully happy or so certain of his future. The woman he loved loved him in return. That one staggering fact completely altered his ordinary existence. The sun seemed brighter, the sky bluer. Work invigorated him—*all* of his work, even the minutiae of property law and will preparation. Nothing could dull his senses or drag down his spirit.

It had been three days since their visit to the Bar D. He'd only seen Rosalind a couple times since then—escorting her to church on Sunday and stopping at the Harvey House lunchroom for a quick bite yesterday. He'd carved out time this afternoon, though. Tuesday was the day Rosalind met Constance Williams at the depot. The perfect opportunity to orchestrate a rendezvous away from the restaurant, where she wasn't permitted to fraternize with customers. Of course, he didn't just have fraternizing in mind. He planned to do some full-on wooing.

First, though, he needed to pay a call on his mother. Not a pleasant prospect, knowing how the news he was about to impart would be received, but his mother needed to come to terms with his decision. Rosalind was his choice of bride, and nothing would change that.

His mother welcomed him into the front parlor with her customary clasping of hands and kiss on the cheek. "Caleb, my darling. You're looking well. Shall I ring for tea?"

He shook his head as he allowed her to lead him to the wing chair he preferred. "No, thank you. I won't be staying long. I have some news to share, and I wanted you to be the first to know."

She alit on the edge of the settee across from his chair and smiled. She loved to be the purveyor of information in her circle of friends. "Is this about taking on the Fentons as clients? I recommended your services to Annabelle when she mentioned that she and Timothy wanted to set up a trust for their grandchildren."

"This has nothing to do with my law practice, though I do thank you for the recommendation."

She leaned forward and patted his knee. "One easily given, as you're the best young attorney in town." Her smile dimmed a bit as a serious light came into her eyes. "You know how much I care about you, Caleb. About your future. I want only the best for you, and I'll do anything I can to ensure you get it."

"I know that, Mother, and I appreciate the love that prompts your concern, but I'm a grown man." He paused, gathering his courage and every ounce of diplomacy he'd learned in school for dealing with a hostile witness or a disgruntled judge. "My future is my responsibility. While I value your opinion, I will make my own decisions and ask you to respect them."

Her mouth pinched. "Even if they're wrong?"

Caleb nodded. "Even if they're wrong."

A niggling doubt rose along with the memory of Rosalind's prediction of complications. He brushed it aside. He didn't know what she'd been referring to, but it didn't matter. Whatever they had to face, they'd face it together and be stronger for it.

Estella Durrington lurched from the sofa and paced the length of the rug that outlined the seating area. Caleb stood, as gallantry demanded, but he opted for a stationary position in front of his chair.

"You can't expect a mother to do nothing while the child she loves races headlong for a cliff!" She spread her arms wide as she turned to face him. "It's my job to protect you, to open your eyes to the dangers you're too blind to see, and to divert your path to one less likely to lead to your destruction."

Caleb raised a brow. "Laying on the melodrama a bit thick, aren't you?" He stepped forward and placed a hand on her shoulder. "Have a little faith. You raised me to think logically and to look at a situation from all possible angles. I know what I'm about."

She stiffened. "You know nothing. And that's the problem. You see a pretty face and a sweet veneer, but you know nothing about what lies beneath the surface. That waitress is manipulating you,

Caleb. She's a shiny trinket glimmering atop the water, luring you in. She's no fool. You have money, position, education. You're the perfect catch. If she gets you on her hook, she'll have everything she needs to secure her future. And you? You'll be left flopping around in the boat, suffocating, as you realize that the love you thought you'd found has no basis in reality. I want better for you!"

Caleb removed his hand from her shoulder before his rising temper reached his fingertips. He curled his digits into a fist and slowly lowered his arm. "You say *I'm* blind, but you're the one who is so distracted by fear that you can't see the truth. You judge Rosalind based solely on the fact that she is employed in an eatery, but you have made no effort to get to know her as a person. Her labor is honorable, her character admirable, and her heart is soft toward others. She's clever, kind, and when I spend time with her, I never want it to end." His fist relaxed as the indignation drained from him. "I love her, Mother. And I'm going to marry her."

"Then you're a fool. Just like your uncle Edgar."

Uncle Edgar? Caleb frowned. He hadn't heard that name in years. He had a vague recollection of a laughing man who used to carry him around on his shoulders, but Edgar's visits to the ranch had stopped sometime before Caleb started school. "What does Uncle Edgar have to do with anything?"

"He was taken in by a pretty face too, and it destroyed him. I warned him that Fiona Murphy was only after his money, but, like you, he refused to listen. Too blinded by her beauty and her lies. Edgar accused me of being a hypocrite. I'd married a poor cowhand for love, so he should be able to marry for love too. Only, I knew his love was one-sided. I'd seen Fiona flirting with other men. Richer men. Ready to toss Edgar over in an instant if a fatter goose came along. I couldn't support his choice."

His mother moved behind the sofa and gripped its back. Her knuckles whitened. "It tore a rift between us," she said, her voice quivering slightly. "The younger brother I adored would have nothing to do with me. He and Fiona eventually eloped, and within a year the wife he'd thought so admirable had drained his bank account and left him in order to be the mistress of a silver tycoon from Nevada who'd promised to keep her swimming in jewels.

"It broke him. The shame. The humiliation. But he loved her still. Last we heard, he'd followed her to Nevada, hoping to win her back."

Caleb ached for his mother's grief and for the uncle he barely knew. "Maybe he did."

His mother stiffened, the softness of her sorrow hardening into cold determination. "Even if Fiona came crawling back to him, it fixed nothing." She came around the sofa and jabbed a finger in the air. "Not one letter from him in twenty-five years. Not to Mother. Not to me. I don't even know if he's still alive. Fiona Murphy stole my brother from his family, shamed him, and broke his heart. I won't allow my son to suffer the same fate."

"But Rosalind is nothing like Fiona."

His mother flung her arms up in exasperation. "That's exactly what Edgar would have said! Don't you see? This *waitress* has you hoodwinked. You'd be better off with a girl you've grown up with. If not Roberta, then another local lady. Someone we can trust. Someone we know."

Caleb's sympathy hardened. "I trust Rosalind." He trusted her character, her heart. She might be hiding something about her past, but that didn't change the woman she was today. "I trust Rosalind, and I'm asking you to trust me."

His mother started to speak, but Caleb cut her off.

"I'm sorry about what happened with Uncle Edgar. You have my word that I will never turn my back on you. Ever." He looked at her, willing her to hear the solemn promise in his words, praying it would ease her fear. "So the question comes to you, Mother. If I marry Rosalind, will you turn your back on *me*?"

She gasped, then covered her mouth with her hand and shook her head, more in disbelief that he'd asked the question than in answer to it.

Caleb pressed forward. "All I ask is that you give her a chance. Set aside your animosity and look at Rosalind with new eyes. I'm sure you'll come to love her as much as I do."

Estella Durrington paled. Her head wagged back and forth in denial. "You can't marry her." She barely croaked out the words. "I forbid it."

Caleb slumped, his heart heavy. "As I said, I'll never fully turn my back on you, but don't force me to choose between the two of you, Mama. Please. You won't like the choice I make."

Her eyes widened, and tears shimmered. The sight cut him to the quick. His tough-as-nails mother never cried. But Caleb held his ground. Her argument was flawed, based on circumstantial evidence and innuendo. It couldn't be allowed to win the day.

He knew Rosalind. Maybe not every detail of her past, but he knew what mattered. He knew her heart. He'd build his case on that and let the rest fall where it may.

───────◦───────

Having spent longer at his mother's than he'd intended, Caleb didn't reach the Santa Fe Depot platform until after the mid-afternoon train passengers had disembarked. He spotted Constance Williams sitting on a bench alone. Had he missed Rosalind?

He hurried to the frail woman's side only to notice that she didn't appear quite as frail as she had a month ago. The air of sadness that had hung over her like a low fog seemed to have lifted a bit. The hollows of her cheeks were not nearly so sunken, and they even sported a touch of pink as she glanced up at his approach.

Rosalind had done this. Brought this woman back from the grave. His chest swelled with pride in his beloved. A woman who befriended a hurting widow most folks either ignored or scorned was not a woman who cared only for money and security.

"Caleb!" Mrs. Williams grinned at him and held up a napkin. "Come see what treats Monsieur Dupont has baked up for me. Tiny white cakes with raspberry filling. They taste like heaven. Here." She extended her napkin-draped hand toward him. "I was saving these for my Gordon to try, but he wasn't on the train, and I fear they won't last until next week. Please." Her eyes implored him with a hunger that had nothing to do with cake and everything to do with human interaction. "Try one."

Unable to resist the plea in her gaze, Caleb reached for a petit four. He ate half of it with one bite and had to admit that she was right. The cake was moist and sweet, with just a touch of tart from the raspberry. The Harvey House chef had outdone himself.

"Delicious." Caleb tossed the remainder in his mouth as he took a seat on the bench. As he chewed, he scoured the area for signs of the female uppermost on his mind.

Mrs. Williams beamed a smile at him as he settled beside her, and patted his knee. "Rosalind should be back soon."

Caleb jerked his attention back to the widow, abashed to have his motives so clearly discerned.

The older woman chuckled. "Don't fret." She gave his knee another pat, then busied herself with wrapping up the rest of her cakes. "I might be past my prime, but I remember what it felt like to be in love. All your energy centered on one person. It can be a mite distracting." She grinned again, but then her expression grew more serious. "That girl's special, Caleb. Hold on to her tight. You never know when life will turn on you and take away the ones you love."

Like her husband and son. Like his father.

Caleb nodded. "I will."

The thought of losing Rosalind left his breath shallow and shaky, but he inhaled methodically until it passed. He had Rosalind now, and while being reminded of the brevity of life might help him appreciate each moment they were together, he couldn't allow the fear of losing her to taint his joy. Even so, a sense of urgency grew inside him as he scanned the thinning crowd and found no sign of her.

"Where did she go?" he asked.

Mrs. Williams's brow wrinkled. "A couple of the railway workers recognized her uniform and asked her to help them sort out a delivery for the Harvey House. She didn't think it would take very long."

But it was taking longer than Caleb found comfortable. After five more minutes without spying her, he pushed to his feet. "I'm going to check on her."

Mrs. Williams nodded, the concern on her face setting his senses on alert.

Lengthening his stride, Caleb strode down the platform to the end of the depot building, then dropped down to the ground and marched along the line of freight cars where railroad workers unloaded supplies onto wheeled carts. Usually Fred Harvey's goods came in on refrigerated boxcars designed to keep produce fresh, but this train carried no such cars. Just simple freight and a few stock cars near the end that were being unloaded into cattle pens.

Except the cattle seemed to be meandering on their own. The two cowhands at the top of the chute had their attention focused elsewhere. At a spot behind the last cattle car.

Caleb's instincts flared, and he broke into a jog. When he reached the end of the cattle car, the two hands manning the chute startled and immediately turned back to the herd, waving their hats and hollering as if it were the cows' stubbornness and not their lack of management that had caused the slowdown.

Ignoring them, Caleb rounded the end of the last train car and took in a scene that so stunned him, his feet staggered to a halt.

Rosalind shoved the heel of her hand directly into one man's nose. As he howled and grabbed at his face, she brought her knee up into his groin, then turned to run. Another man moved to stop her. She dropped into a deep crouch, causing his grabbing arms to find only air. Taking advantage of his momentary surprise, she braced her hands on the ground and kicked out like a mule, her foot connecting with his knee. He cursed and made another awkward grab for her, but she was too fast. She brought her hands up from the ground and flung fistfuls of dirt directly into his eyes. While her opponent staggered blindly, she ran.

Caleb sprinted after her, two thoughts charging through his mind.

Who had taught her to fight like that? And, more importantly, why?

Chapter Eight

Footsteps echoed behind her. Rosalind ran faster along the length of the train. Her vision zeroed in on the locomotive. If she could just get to the front, she could cross the tracks and dash inside the depot. She'd be safe there.

The steps pounded louder. Closer.

God, don't let them catch me! Her breaths heaved as she tried to outdistance her pursuer. She'd managed to take them by surprise the first time, but she'd lost that advantage. She'd be at their mercy now.

"Rosalind! Wait!"

Run. Faster.

But she felt herself slowing. Cramps attacked her side. Her legs ached. Her lungs burned.

Just a few more cars. *Please, Lord!*

"Rosalind!"

A hand grabbed her arm. Yanked her to a stop. She struggled. Tried to break free. But he captured her other arm, his grip tight. She tried to bring up her knee, but he clutched her against his chest, making the maneuver impossible. She slammed her head forward, hoping to connect with his nose, but he was too tall. The blow merely glanced off his chin.

He grunted. "Rosalind. It's me—Caleb. It's all right, sweet-heart. You're safe."

Caleb?

The name burned a hole through the haze of blinding panic. Her frantic movements slowed. She lifted her gaze and drank in the blessedly familiar features of the man she loved.

"Oh, Caleb!" She collapsed against him. He released his hold on her arms and wrapped her in a warm, protective embrace.

Safe. She was safe. With Caleb. Strong, wonderful Caleb.

Relief overwhelmed her, and she nearly buckled. Her hands trembled as she clutched his shirtfront. Tears coursed down her face.

"Shh. It's all right. I'm here now." His hand stroked her back. So gentle. So loving.

She wanted to stay in his arms forever. Letting him soothe and reassure her. Letting him hold the ugliness at bay. Believing that everything really *was* all right.

But it wasn't.

She wasn't. And she couldn't pretend anymore. Caleb's mother had been right. Her son deserved better than a woman who would bring scandal to his doorstep. A woman who would hamper his career. He was still growing his practice. He needed clients with clout, with the social connections to open doors. Tying himself to her would slam those doors in his face. She couldn't do that to him. Couldn't stay in this town and watch his love for her wither as the truth came out. For it would. Despite how careful she'd been or how adamantly she'd denied their claims, those cowhands had recognized the truth. The Prairie Rose and the Harvey Girl were one and the same.

Steeling herself for the pain that would come when she stripped the dream of Caleb from her heart, Rosalind straightened away from the comfort of his embrace and forced herself to meet his gaze.

"I'm sorry, Caleb. So sorry." The tears he'd just soothed away rose again, but she blinked them back. "I thought I could make this work, but I can't. It's not fair to you."

His brow furrowed. "What's not fair? Sweetheart, you aren't making any sense." He wrapped an arm around her shoulders and started steering her toward the front of the train. "Let me get you back to Mrs. Williams. You can sit with her while I round up the marshal."

"No!" Rosalind jerked from his hold and refused to take another step.

Caleb frowned. "Those men accosted you. I might not have seen it with my own eyes, but I saw a terrified woman defending herself—with admirable skill, I might add—and I'll testify to that. You can explain the rest. What they did was a crime. They need to be held accountable."

She shook her head. If those men were brought before the marshal, they'd expose her, expose the photo card. She couldn't let that happen. Not if there was any chance remaining of her escaping with her reputation intact.

"Leave it alone, Caleb. *Please.* Bringing in the law will only make matters worse."

"I don't understand."

Rosalind's heart shriveled. "I know. But it doesn't matter anymore. I have to leave. I still have several months left on my contract, but I'll do my best to persuade Mr. Ledbetter to transfer me. I'll volunteer to go anywhere they need me outside of Texas."

"Whoa. You can't just leave."

Caleb stepped close—so close that all she wanted to do was lean into him, but she had to stay strong. For both of them.

"I love you, Rosalind." His gaze scoured her face. "I want to marry you. Whatever trouble you're in, we can face it together."

One tear slipped free and trailed slowly down her cheek. "I

love you too, Caleb." He needed to know that. "So much. I don't want to leave. I want to stay with you. But that's not possible."

"Why not?" Hurt lit his eyes, and the sight of it made her heart bleed. "Just tell me what you're running from. Let me help you."

Rosalind took his hand in both of hers and brought it to her lips. She pressed a kiss to his knuckles, squeezing her eyes closed as she savored the moment for as long as she dared before facing him again. "You're a good man, Caleb Durrington. So upright and just. I don't doubt for a moment that you would stand by my side and do your best to slay my dragons. But I won't risk you being scorched by their fire when I have the power to lure them away."

"Then take me with you." He yanked his hand from hers and cupped both her shoulders in his grip. "If you're set on leaving, then we'll go together. I'm sure people in California need lawyers too. We can make it work."

Heavens, how she loved this man. Yet others loved him too. Others with a prior claim. "And who will oversee your father's ranch?"

"I can hire—"

"What about your mother? You're the only family she has left. What happens when her health starts to fail? You can't just abandon her, Caleb. She needs you."

"But I need *you*."

"No. You *want* me. Just as I want you. But we are young. Resilient. We'll survive. The pain will be agonizing at first, but it will fade over time. Perhaps leave a few scars to help us remember." Gently, she peeled his hands from her shoulders and stepped away, her lips curving into a sad smile. "Trust me, Caleb. It's the right thing to do."

"I don't believe that."

His voice echoed dully between them, yet he made no move to

follow her as she turned to go. It was for the best. Still, her heart broke a little. The first of many cracks that were sure to come.

She glanced over her shoulder, allowing herself one last look at the man who would forever own her heart. The man who would learn the truth soon enough, for she wasn't so foolish as to think it wouldn't come out after what had happened today.

"I *can't* believe that," he insisted, a hint of fire returning to his eyes as he fisted his hands at his sides.

Rosalind turned away. "You will."

Caleb followed Rosalind from a distance, ensuring she reached Mrs. Williams without further incident. The whole time he trailed her, his mind spun with questions, arguments, and pleas to God for wisdom as he tried to figure out his next move. She'd begged him to let the issue with the cowhands go, but it wasn't in his nature to give up without a fight, and when life with the woman he loved hung in the balance, he'd keep swinging until the last breath was driven from his body, whether she wanted him to or not.

Rosalind might think she was protecting him, but between her and his mother, Caleb was fed up with women trying to do what was best for him—even if it was out of love.

Love.

Caleb's step stuttered. Rosalind had professed her love for him. Admitted she wanted him, respected him, and cared about what was best for him and his family. Not even her threat to leave could spoil the gift she'd given him. She loved him, and there was no way he was letting her go.

The thought goaded him to pick up his pace. He jogged up the courthouse stairwell to his small office on the second floor. He yanked the shade down over the one window in the room, then opened the cabinet where he kept a few personal items, including a change of clothes for when he needed to ride out to the Bar D.

Rosalind might not be willing to explain what had spooked her into trying to run away from him, but she wasn't the first reluctant witness he'd encountered. When a witness didn't offer the whole story, it was the attorney's job to investigate until he uncovered the truth. A proper defense could only be devised when one had all the facts. And as far as he could tell, there were at least two other witnesses who had testimony to offer—the pair of cowhands who'd attacked Rosalind. They possessed knowledge he needed, and he intended to get it.

Caleb fastened his worn trousers, did up the buttons on the plaid shirt that would match any other cowhand's attire, and slid his feet into a pair of beaten-up boots that still carried a layer of ranch dust. As the final piece of his disguise, he slapped on the sweat-stained hat that always made his mother grimace and pulled the brim low over his eyes. He'd sprinted around the train so fast in his pursuit of Rosalind, he doubted any of the cowhands delivering cattle to the stockyards would recognize him, but they'd probably recall the lines of his suitcoat and the silver band on his black felt hat. Besides, they'd be more likely to talk freely with one of their own.

Fifteen minutes later, Caleb entered the stockyards and spotted a group of men gathered by the main holding pen. He approached, keeping to the periphery. He recognized the two men Rosalind had tangled with. Both looked rather grumpy, no doubt having been subjected to a fair amount of ribbing over being bested by a girl.

"I told ya that was no genteel female. She might have them Harvey House folks fooled, but I seen through her disguise the minute I saw her." The fellow who'd been the recipient of Rosalind's well-aimed knee turned to spit an arc of tobacco juice at the base of the nearest fence post. His expectoration fell short of the mark, much like his opinion of the female in question.

"Only 'cause you've been moonin' over the Prairie Rose ever since you bought that photo card down in Houston. You really should pay more attention to real gals, Gillespie."

Gillespie yanked a card from his pocket and jabbed a finger at it. "The Prairie Rose *is* real. I just met 'er."

His companion smirked. "Yeah. And nearly got gelded in the process."

Snickers broke out in the group.

Gillespie shoved the smirking cowboy. "Shut up, Larson."

Caleb frowned. The Prairie Rose? Who was that, and what did she have to do with Rosalind? He moseyed closer, trying to get a look at the card.

"Tell 'em, Joe," Gillespie called. "You saw her too."

A fellow with a knife in hand a few yards from the main group grumbled, "Leave me be, Gill. If I don't make this next shot, I lose my copy of the Rose."

A throwing contest seemed to be underway, the prize being a sepia-toned card stuck in a crack atop a fence post. Joe's competitor, his knife already embedded in the center of a knothole two inches below the card, turned to face the group, his eyes jerking wide when he spotted Caleb. A similar shock coursed through Caleb. It was one of the hands from the Bar D.

"Take your shot," Thompson groused, stuffing his hands in his trouser pockets and ducking his head back around.

Joe flipped the flat of the blade onto his palm, took aim, and flicked it at the post. It landed with a *thwack* an inch off-center, the handle wagging back and forth.

Thompson wasted no time claiming his prize. He snatched the card from the top of the post, yanked his knife from the wood, then hoofed it in the opposite direction. Caleb had hoped to corner him and ask about the card, but the fellow didn't seem to be in the sharing mood. At least he hadn't given up Caleb's identity, leaving Caleb the opportunity to infiltrate the outer edges of the group. Best not to get too close to the main players. His change of clothes provided only a superficial layer of anonymity.

The cowhand named Larson caught Caleb's eye and nodded. He met Caleb a few feet away from where the core of the group was taking bets on Gillespie's likelihood of cornering the Prairie Rose a second time.

"You local? Don't remember seeing you on the train."

Caleb dipped his head. "Yep. Work on the Bar D with Thompson."

"Ah. The kid seemed to be in a hurry to escape with his prize." Larson chuckled. "Can't say I blame him. Rosie's the kinda woman a man can better appreciate without a crowd pesterin' him."

"You talkin' about that Prairie Rose?" Caleb roughened the texture of his voice and abandoned his usual vocabulary. "Don't see what all the fuss is about. It's just a picture."

Larson shook his head and gave him a pitying glance. "You don't know Rosie." He lifted his head and called to his friend. "Gillespie, let me see that photo card. Our friend here don't believe Rosie's worth all the fuss."

"He will once he gets a gander at her." Gillespie passed the card to the person next to him, who passed it along until it reached Larson.

Larson handed it to Caleb. "See what I mean?"

There, staring up at him with vulnerable eyes and a mysterious, wistful smile was Rosalind. In her underclothes. Hair unbound in riotous waves around her face. A corset framed curves only a husband should see before the photo cut off at her waist. Caleb jerked his gaze away, heat creeping up the back of his neck.

He turned the card over, his only thought to hide the image, but gold lettering engraved along the bottom caught his eye. *Julius Hansom Photography.* Larson didn't seem to appreciate his view being obstructed, though, for he snatched the card back and flipped it over.

Caleb scowled. "Girl's just a kid. Ain't right to be lookin' at her."

There was no denying it was Rosalind, as much as he wished otherwise. Same eyes. Same face. Same smile, only more melancholy. And younger. *Much* younger. Nausea churned in Caleb's gut.

"She was old enough to pose for the picture, weren't she?" Larson said, his voice defensive. He cupped the card in his palm and danced it around. "Pranced around in her underthings for the photographer. Didn't seem to mind *him* lookin'. Had to know others would be lookin' too. Way I figure it, she issued the invitation." He rubbed a thumb along the length of the card, along Rosalind's face, giving the image a full, appreciative gander. "A fella don't have nothin' to feel guilty about if he chooses to answer that invitation."

Caleb wanted to tear the card from Larson's hand and rip it to shreds. But that wouldn't solve the problem. At the moment, he wasn't sure what would.

Chapter Nine

Rosalind only stayed with Constance long enough to reassure the older lady that no harm had come to her despite her red-rimmed eyes and dusty hem. No harm to her physical self, at least. Her heart, on the other hand, had been ravaged.

But a Harvey Girl didn't fall apart when there were customers to serve. She cleaned herself up, splashed water on her face, and did the job she was hired to do. So Rosalind said her good-byes to Mrs. Williams, leaving the widow to enjoy the afternoon and her cakes on the depot bench, then skirted around to the west side of the building and used the kitchen entrance closest to the staircase that led to the boarding rooms.

Once upstairs, she changed out of her soiled clothing and put on a fresh black uniform and white apron. She pulled the pins from her hair, brushed out the tangles caused by her skirmish behind the train, and twisted the tresses into a tight knot, pinning it securely into place. She rubbed a cool, damp cloth over her face and neck, then scrubbed her hands in the basin before checking her appearance in the mirror above the washstand. Not a speck of dust to be found. Her eyes were still red, but she couldn't do anything about that. She'd get through the dinner service, then talk to Mr. Ledbetter about a transfer. He wouldn't like being left short a girl, but Rosalind could recommend a qualified replacement. One of the women she'd worked with in Kansas had talked about wanting to come to Texas. Perhaps the two of them could switch placements. Then, after her current contract expired, Rosalind could put in for a post in Arizona or California. Someplace the Prairie Rose couldn't find her and ruin her life once again.

She turned to leave her room, but the trunk at the end of her bed drew her attention. The photo card she kept as a reminder of her folly lay buried inside. *It* would follow her to California. Rosalind bit her lip as the truth sank into her bruised heart. She'd never be free of the Prairie Rose. Not really. With the mobility of the railroad, no place, no matter how far, could guarantee safety from discovery.

Oh, how she wished she'd never posed for that horrid photograph. She'd thought she was helping her father. He'd been so sick back then. So weak. She'd wanted to ease his suffering, to buy the medicine the druggist had recommended. But they hadn't had the money. Abby had to pour every cent they had back into the bakery to keep it afloat. So when Julius Hansom offered to pay Rosalind a generous sum in exchange for an "artistic" photograph, it seemed like an answer to prayer. In truth, it had been a serpent. The same one who dangled an apple in front of Eve with the promise that she wouldn't die had dangled a camera in front of Rosalind with the promise that no one would ever know.

Am I to be punished forever, Lord?

It wasn't fair. Why could someone like her brother-in-law, whose sins led to a man's death, be forgiven and go on to live a happy life with the woman he loved, while Rosalind's sin kept rearing its ugly head, forcing her to forfeit a life with Caleb?

You promise to make all things new, yet every time I try to escape my past, it rises again to drag me down. If you remove our transgressions as far as the east is from the west, why do mine keep finding me? When is enough, enough? When will I be free?

A frantic rapping on her door startled Rosalind out of her prayer. She jumped forward and opened the door to find Callie on the other side. Her friend's usual cheerful exuberance was nowhere to be found.

"Mr. Ledbetter sent me to fetch you. Hurry. She's causing a dreadful scene." Callie grabbed Rosalind's arm and practically dragged her from the room.

"Who's causing a scene?" Had poor Constance wandered into the restaurant and started rambling about her dead son? She had seemed fairly stable when Rosalind left her on the bench a short time ago, but the mind was a delicate thing. She could have—

"Estella Durrington."

Rosalind stumbled to a halt at the top of the stairs. Callie traveled four steps down the flight before she realized Rosalind had stopped. She craned her neck around, the worry etched into her features causing Rosalind's heart to pound painfully against her ribs.

"She's demanding to see you. She won't say why, but she won't leave until you appear. Mr. Ledbetter tried to escort her into his office, but she refused to budge." Callie climbed two of the stairs and took Rosalind's hand. "I'm sorry, Rosie. I feel like I'm feeding you to the wolves, but if I don't produce you quickly, it'll be both our jobs. The customers are staring, and it's disrupting service. You know how Mr. Ledbetter is about anything disrupting service."

Efficiency and quality were the cornerstones of Fred Harvey's empire. A disruption of either would not be tolerated.

Rosalind nodded and followed Callie into the kitchen. For once, no pots and pans rattled. No dishwater splashed. The silence was eerie. Ominous. Monsieur Dupont gave her a solemn nod as she passed him. She glanced over at Henry's station, but the boy was nowhere to be seen. At least she had one friend who wouldn't bear witness to her demise.

And Caleb? *Please don't let him be here.* He'd hear about the confrontation, she had no doubt, probably from the self-satisfied lips of his mother, but if Rosalind could at least be spared the indignity of being dressed down in front of him, it just might be bearable.

"This way," Callie said, leading her to the outside door. "Mr. Ledbetter doesn't want you behind the lunch counter. He's hoping to minimize the distraction by conducting a quiet side conversation instead of having the two of you bicker over the bar."

That didn't bode well. Rosalind rather liked the thought of having the counter to hide behind, but a quiet discussion would be in her best interest as well. Especially if Mrs. Durrington had come to accuse her of fraternizing with her son—an established Harvey House customer. Usually the staff turned a blind eye to courtship as long as it took place outside of work hours, but if a prominent citizen lodged a complaint . . . well, maybe Mr. Ledbetter would instigate Rosalind's transfer without her having to ask. If he didn't fire her, of course.

The moment Rosalind stepped through the main restaurant door, however, she knew this would be much worse than an accusation of fraternization. For there in Caleb's mother's hand was a photo card that matched the one at the bottom of Rosalind's trunk—the Prairie Rose.

"There she is. The hussy." Estella Durrington stomped over to Rosalind, grabbed her by the arm, and dragged her across the restaurant floor.

"Madam. Please!" Mr. Ledbetter scurried to intercept her, his gaze darting to the customers swiveling their chairs away from the counter to get a better view. Train passengers milled out of line too, apparently less interested in purchasing tickets than in gaping at the drama unraveling behind them. "Whatever your grievance with Miss Kemp, it would be better handled in private."

Mrs. Durrington glared at him. "So you can sweep it under the rug? I think not! The truth has been hidden long enough. It's time to shed some much needed light on the type of establishment you run."

Mr. Ledbetter drew himself up to his full height and tugged on his lapels. "I will have you know that Fred Harvey only operates the finest of establishments. Our food is superb, our service is efficient and friendly, and our staff is beyond reproach."

"Not *this* staff." Mrs. Durrington whipped Rosalind around, throwing her off balance as she careened into the small space between the manager and Caleb's mother. "She's a trollop of the worst sort. And here's the proof." Mrs. Durrington shoved the photo card under Mr. Ledbetter's nose.

The poor man's face turned cherry red as he tried to push the offensive image away from him. "Really, madam." His voice dropped to a horrified murmur. "That is quite inappropriate."

"Precisely." Mrs. Durrington made no effort to lower her voice in the slightest.

This couldn't be happening. Yet it was. Would her penance never end?

"It is *extremely* inappropriate," Mrs. Durrington continued. "Such a person should not be permitted to associate with decent Christian people, luring godly young men and trapping them with false words of love when all she really wants is the security tied to his wealth."

Rosalind stared at a small black spot high up on the whitewashed wall above the ticket counter. Almost to the ceiling. Above the horror. Above the shame.

"This . . . this . . . person could not possibly be Miss Kemp," Mr. Ledbetter stammered. "She's been an exemplary employee for five years. Not even a hint of scandal has been connected to her name during that time. You are mistaken."

"No, sir. You are the one mistaken. Look again." Mrs. Durrington forced the card into his hand.

Rosalind knew what he would see. What anyone would see if they looked closely enough.

"Take your hair down, Miss Kemp." The imperious command echoed through the silent lunchroom.

This couldn't be happening.

"You don't have to," Callie said, coming up alongside her. "She has no right to make demands of you."

Dear sweet Callie. So loyal. Yet even as her friend stood up for her, Mr. Ledbetter began to bend to Mrs. Durrington's will.

"Miss Sanderson," the manager intoned, "please return to the kitchen."

Callie's eyes widened. "But, sir . . ."

Rosalind touched her friend's arm. "It's all right, Callie. Do as he says." She couldn't let Callie get embroiled in this. Besides, there was no point in trying to hide the truth any longer.

As soon as Callie turned to leave, Rosalind raised her hands to her hair.

Caleb's mother's brows arched in surprise at Rosalind's compliance, but then she gave a sharp nod of approval.

Callie had been correct. Rosalind didn't have to do this. Mrs. Durrington's demands didn't hold sway over her. She could run out the door and never come back. But running wouldn't solve her problems this time. The truth had reared its ugly head, and all she could do now was face it with as much dignity as possible. So she removed a hairpin. Then another. Her simple movements held the room in thrall. No one made a sound. No china clinked. No foot shuffled. All was silent.

Once the last pin was out, she dug her fingers into her hair, shaking out the naturally curly tresses and rubbing the sore places on her scalp for a moment before releasing the blond waves to fall around her shoulders.

Then, with trembling fingers, she reached for the clear-glass spectacles she wore and pulled them from her face. She tucked the hairpins and the glasses into her apron pocket, lifted her head, and faced her accuser as the person she most despised— the Prairie Rose.

Chapter Ten

Caleb trudged back to his office in a daze, his heart unwilling to believe the irrefutable evidence his eyes had seen. The woman he loved could never have posed for such a picture. Rosalind was a godly woman. Chaste. Above reproach.

Now, at least. But who had she been before he met her? What kind of woman posed for such a risqué photograph and allowed her likeness to be sold to men? A young one, apparently. The image he'd seen flashed through his mind again. She couldn't have been more than sixteen or seventeen when that photo was taken.

Caleb's step stuttered on the courthouse stairs as he mentally rifled through the facts he'd gathered on Rosalind's past. The loss of her mother when she was a child. The loss of her father at age . . . seventeen. A father who'd suffered heart failure. One who'd been debilitated for months. Rosalind had nursed him while her sister ran the family business. Rosalind had been left unprotected. Vulnerable. No male relative to protect her from someone who might see her beauty and think to take advantage.

Julius Hansom. The name imprinted on the back of the card zinged through Caleb's mental filing system and set his teeth on edge. The photographer should be horsewhipped for taking woeful advantage of one so young.

Yet despite how badly he wanted to mete out some frontier justice upon Hansom, it was Rosalind's betrayal that cut the deepest emotional swath. Logically, he recognized it was unfair to feel betrayed by an action Rosalind committed years before they met, but logic couldn't stem the hurt. A husband should be the only man to see his wife in a state of undress. It was an intimacy reserved for marriage, a special gift a couple gave each other on their wedding night after their union had been blessed by God and family. The idea that countless other men had already seen Rosalind in her underclothes with hair unbound hurt his heart and grated on his pride.

Did he still love her?

Yes. He didn't have to think twice about that answer.

But did he still want to marry her? Could he cherish her without reservation, without holding her past actions against her? Anything less would be unfair to her and would dishonor him.

Caleb carefully pondered the notion, making mental arguments for and against, even though his heart had already decided the case. Sharing a life with Rosalind was worth a few dents in his pride and bruises on his spirit. If forgiveness could buy him a life of love, he'd gladly pay that price and consider it a bargain.

Rosalind had made a mistake. But didn't everyone? He'd certainly made more than his fair share. Yet he'd learned from them, corrected his life's trajectory, and gotten back on track. Rosalind had done the same. She didn't flaunt her beauty or trade on her looks to get ahead. She worked hard, cared for others, and exemplified everything that was modest and admirable. A woman he'd be proud to have share his name.

"Mr. D!"

Caleb blinked, adjusting from an internal focus to an external one. Hank was running up the street toward him, waving his arm above his head. Caleb immediately started back down the courthouse steps.

"Come quick, Mr. D! It's your ma. She aims to take a piece outta Miss Kemp's hide."

Rosalind! Caleb clenched his jaw and sprinted down California, patting Hank's shoulder in thanks as he sped past. The kid tried to keep pace, but Caleb's fresh legs left him behind.

When he reached the depot, Constance Williams gestured to him from the doorway that led to the restaurant. People had piled up behind her in an effort to see inside, but she refused to budge from her place until Caleb reached her.

"Hurry, son," she said as he pushed through the crowd. Her sorrowful eyes met his, and the dread in his gut intensified tenfold.

He stepped deeper into the large anteroom between the lunch counter and the ticket office but froze when he saw Rosalind begin to take down her hair. When the beautiful blond waves lay about her shoulders and halfway down her back, she lifted her chin, her blue eyes glimmering even brighter without spectacles cloaking their shine. She stood tall, ready to accept whatever else his mother chose to dish out.

He prayed fervently for his mother to see what he did—a woman of character owning up to a past mistake with honor and grace—and prayed she would relent and extend mercy.

But it was not to be.

"There's your proof," his mother declared, her voice loud in the unnaturally quiet hall. "I dare you to deny that she is the same woman." She jabbed her finger at a card in the manager's hand, a card Caleb recognized.

Thompson. Caleb bit back a groan. The Bar D hand must have delivered the damning evidence directly to Caleb's mother as soon as he acquired it. He'd probably received a handsome reward for his efforts too.

"I demand you terminate her employment immediately, or I will report this incident to your superiors. If the Fred Harvey organization is the stickler for propriety you claim, I imagine Miss Kemp won't be the only one sacked after I lodge my complaint."

Caleb didn't wait to see what the manager would do. Ledbetter had little choice, after all. Yet Caleb would not be cowed by the woman dictating the scene before him. His stomach a roiling mess, he left the anonymity of the crowd and strode straight up to the trio at the center of the action.

"I'm ashamed of you," he said, his voice low.

He heard Rosalind whimper his name, but as much as he wanted to go to her, he needed to address his mother first.

"As you should be," Estella Durrington proclaimed. "This woman is not fit for decent company. She deceived you, Caleb. Deceived everyone. I'm only glad that I could reveal the truth before things progressed too far."

"You misunderstand, Mother. I'm not ashamed of Rosalind. I'm ashamed of you."

She gasped softly. "Caleb, I—"

"You humiliated a young woman in public. Without a shred of Christian charity or grace."

Her eyes darted around the room, widening as if she only then realized the horrible scene she had created. "I . . . I was trying to protect you. You don't know about her past . . . about the photographs . . ."

"I know enough." Caleb shifted his gaze to Rosalind, but she wouldn't meet his eyes. She had dropped her head and rounded her shoulders. So he moved in front of her and took her hands in his. "I know that we all make mistakes and shouldn't cast stones. I know that I love her with all of my heart and want to build a life with her if she'll have me."

That brought her head up. Tears glistened in her beautiful blue eyes—tears and questions.

"You don't know . . ." She shook her head, the words dying.

He clasped her hands tighter, leaned close, and whispered in a voice only she could hear. "I've seen the card, Rosalind. I can't say that I'm happy about it, but it doesn't define you, nor does it change how I feel."

"But what about your law practice?" she murmured, her eyes downcast again. "I would be a liability. Prestigious clients won't want the lawyer with a scandalous wife handling their business."

He ducked his head until he found her eyes. "Who says I want prestigious clients?"

Her lashes fluttered up, and tiny lines creased the space between her brows.

"I prefer helping those who've been dealt a rough hand in life," he explained. "People who might see their own struggle reflected in the life of a hardworking woman who had the courage to leave her past behind. You'd be an asset in that case." He grinned. "A silent endorsement of my belief in fresh starts."

The lines in her face smoothed just a bit.

Hope surged through Caleb, and his voice gained strength, echoing off the high depot ceiling. "I love you, Rosalind Kemp. *You*. The woman who is kind to lonely old ladies and ornery boys."

A tiny smile peeked onto her face, then widened when Hank led Mrs. Williams out from the crowd, nodding and glaring at anyone who thought to disagree.

"The woman who can decipher coded letters and argue me out of my own opinion."

A delightful blush colored her cheeks.

"The woman who knows how to work hard and work well, who inspires me to be a better man so that I can keep pace with her."

Her fingers tightened around his. "There is no better man than you, Caleb."

His heart gave a leap, followed by a leap of the faith variety. "Then stay with me, Rosalind," he pleaded. "I can't promise it will be easy, but I can promise that I will be by your side through it all."

"So will I!" Constance Williams marched forward and put a hand on Rosalind's arm. "I got a spare room at my place. You can stay with me."

The eavesdropping crowd gasped slightly, knowing the only spare room Constance had belonged to her son, Gordon, the very one she'd refused to believe was truly gone. Until now.

"Count me in too." Hank braced his feet apart and crossed his arms over his chest. "You might be bossy, but you ain't never been mean, and I'm an expert at tryin' a woman's patience. Just ask my ma."

A few chuckles warmed the room as the tension began to break.

A cultured accent echoed from the kitchen doorway. "You have my support too, *mon amie*."

"And mine." Callie squeezed through the kitchen doorway next to the chef, her expression mulish as she glared at Caleb's mother.

Rosalind's gaze darted from one speaker to another, her lips trembling at the love filling a room that minutes ago had held nothing but enmity.

Finally, her attention returned to Caleb, and he made his final argument. "You'll never be free if you keep running, Rosalind. California's not the Promised Land. Not when the people who love you are here. God will give us strength. You'll see. If we stand fast in him, we can overcome anything." He lifted her hands between them, kissed her knuckles, then hugged her fingers to his chest. "Please stay."

Rosalind bit her lip, so many thoughts spinning in her head that they left her dizzy. Caleb had seen the card, he'd witnessed her greatest shame—yet here he stood defending her, defying his mother, and best of all, declaring his love for all to hear.

She didn't deserve such grace, such support, but he lavished it on her anyway. And not only him, but her friends did as well.

Stand fast, he'd said. Those two words rang in her head loudest of all. *Stand fast.* Familiar words. Words her sister had written to her in the first letter she'd received after leaving home to join the Harvey Girls. Words written long ago in another letter—from Paul to the Galatian church.

Stand fast therefore in the liberty wherewith Christ hath made us free, and be not entangled again with the yoke of bondage.

Not twenty minutes ago, she'd cried out to her Lord, demanding to know when she'd be free. The answer had been in her memory all along. Caleb was right. Running wouldn't set her free. It would only further entangle her. True freedom could only be gained by trusting God and standing fast in his strength. Like David facing Goliath. Or Esther standing uninvited before the king.

A daunting prospect, but unlike David and Esther, she didn't have to make her stand alone. She had Caleb—brave, wonderful, forgiving Caleb, who stood by her at this very moment, asking for no explanations or apologies. All he asked was that she stay.

"Rosalind?" Caleb's brown eyes searched hers, an edge of worry infecting his usual confidence. "Will you stay? With me?"

Her heart shouted the answer so loudly, she wondered that the entire room didn't hear it. She managed a jerky nod, then voiced the word she prayed would finally set her free. "Yes."

The smile that lit Caleb's face sent lightning zinging through her, and she swore she felt shackles falling from her soul.

Then everything else fell away too, for Caleb slid his arms

around her waist, lifted her feet straight off the floor, and spun her around with such pure joy that she couldn't help but laugh.

When he finally set her back on the ground, their faces lingered close together for a moment. His gaze fastened on her mouth, and the urge to meet him pulled on her like a needle on thread. Heavens, but she wanted to kiss him. Unfortunately, this wasn't the place nor the time. So she smiled instead and stepped back. "I love you, Caleb Durrington. And I'll stand by your side for all my days."

Applause broke out across the depot, restaurant patrons and train passengers alike joining in the celebration. Never had Rosalind felt so invincible or so filled with hope. And it was all due to the man whose arm lingered at her waist and the God whose promise lingered in her soul, the two of them infusing her with courage, fortitude, and a newfound optimism.

"So you'll marry me?" Caleb asked.

"Yes!"

He tugged her close and planted a quick celebratory kiss on her cheek, his eyes dancing. Yet as he straightened, the joy sobered into something more serious. He released his hold on one of Rosalind's hands and extended his open palm toward the red-faced woman shrinking away to his left.

"Mama?" A world of meaning hung in that single word.

Tears shimmered in Estella Durrington's eyes. She hesitated, her gaze darting from her son to Rosalind. The animosity that had glittered in her expression earlier had dissipated, leaving embarrassment and regret in its place—two emotions Rosalind knew far too well. Caleb's mother might have been hurtful and determined to believe the worst, but she'd been motivated by love for her son. A love Rosalind understood and shared.

So she extended her own hand toward her future mother-in-law, praying that she'd accept the peace offering.

Estella Durrington raised a shaky hand and slipped it into

her son's palm. Rosalind lowered hers, not wanting to embarrass either of them any further, but before her arm dropped more than two inches, Mrs. Durrington's second hand shot out and grabbed hold, latching on tight.

A look passed between them—one that sought forgiveness, that declared loyalty to the man standing beside them and promised to set aside differences to make room for a new relationship.

Rosalind smiled and squeezed Mrs. Durrington's hand. Marrying into this family would certainly pose its challenges, but with Caleb at the center and forgiveness in its foundation, love was sure to flourish.

Epilogue

Caleb carried a laughing Rosalind over the threshold of his no-longer-bachelor residence, kicked the front door closed on the faces of all the noisy well-wishers who'd followed them from the church, and proceeded down the hall.

His bride looked radiant, easily the fairest lady in town, though it was the beauty beaming from her spirit that shone brightest. When he reached the doorway that led to his bedroom, he released her legs so her feet could find the floor but kept an arm wrapped around her waist. He tugged her fully against him the moment she found her footing.

"Caleb!" She giggled as he smashed her close. Her palms pressed against his chest as she braced herself against his enthusiasm. Yet her smile had her blue eyes crinkling at the corners and dancing with delight.

"There's no escape, Mrs. Durrington," Caleb declared in villainous fashion. "You're mine now."

Rosalind grabbed fistfuls of his shirt and raised her chin in challenge. "I'm afraid you're in the same predicament, Mr. Durrington. For now that I have you in my clutches, I have no intention of letting you go. Ever."

He smirked. "I rather like being in your clutches."

"Good."

Her hands loosened their grip on his shirtfront and slid up to his shoulders. Her fingers found their way into the hair at the base of his skull, and electricity danced over his skin as his heart thumped against his ribs. Yes, being in her clutches was fine indeed.

He spread his hands wide on Rosalind's back and lifted her up to meet his kiss. His blood ran hot, but he kept his passion contained, wanting to woo her with gentleness, to adore and cherish her. So he took his time. Nibbled at her lips, laid a trail of soft kisses along her jawline, then over her neck as her head fell back.

"Caleb." She whispered his name, love and desire rich in her voice. His pulse thrummed in response.

He brought his hands up to cup her face. "I love you, Rosalind."

A slow smile curled the corners of her mouth, melting his heart and drawing him in for a deeper taste. He captured her lips in a kiss that held nothing back. He gave all of himself— his passion, his admiration, his love. And she returned the kiss in full measure, twining her arms about his neck and pulling herself up to meet him.

She truly was his. His wife. His partner. His love.

Rosalind slipped away from their kiss, and he relaxed his hold to let her heels return to the floor. Once grounded, she shyly stepped out of his arms. Taking her hand, he nudged the door of his room open and led her inside.

"It was a lovely ceremony, don't you think?" She released his hand, scuttled around the bed dominating the center of the room, and pretended to investigate his desk, running her fingers along the law books stacked haphazardly on the corner.

As much as Caleb wished to investigate a different piece of furniture with her, he followed her lead and gave her a reprieve of conversation. "I enjoyed meeting your sister and brother-in-law, although I worried Abigail and Chef Dupont were going to come to blows over whose cake would be served first."

Rosalind grinned at him over her shoulder. "Thankfully your mother averted disaster by slicing them both at precisely the same time. And inviting guests to try both the lemon and the chocolate was inspired. She even dared Abby and Monsieur Dupont to try each other's cake. By the time they'd finished their slices, they were exchanging recipes and comparing pastry techniques."

Caleb lowered himself onto the edge of the bed, casually crossed an ankle over his knee, and started unlacing his shoe. Rosalind noticed, bit her lip, and wandered over to inspect his wardrobe. Caleb hid a grin. She'd run out of furniture soon enough.

"I'm not sure your brother-in-law likes me much," Caleb said as he pulled the shoe from his foot. "Every time I looked his way today, he was scowling."

"That's just his way." Rosalind turned to face him, leaning back against the closed wardrobe. "Zach adores you. Abby too. You're the man who convinced me to stay in Texas, after all, and in a town only a few hours away from them by train."

He switched legs and reached for his second shoe, but his gaze remained locked on his wife. "I did do that, didn't I?"

She took a step toward him. "Yes." Another step. "You did." Two more steps, and she'd be within grabbing range.

But she came no closer. Just stood in the middle of his floor. Alone.

Well, *that* couldn't be allowed.

Caleb yanked off his second shoe before the laces were fully loosened and joined his wife.

"Do you miss it?" he asked as he ran his hands over the pale pink satin sleeves of the wedding dress her mother and sister had worn before her, the one she had remade with remarkable skill into a confection all her own. "Being a Harvey Girl?"

Her hands found his waist as she shrugged. "Maybe a little. The Harvey organization is like a family. We live together. Work together. Depend on each other. Even though I still see Callie and the other girls at church and around town, it's not the same." She fiddled with the button securing his suspenders. "But I've found a new family. With Constance." Her lashes lowered then slowly lifted, new warmth heating her gaze. "With you."

His grip on her shoulders tightened, and he started to draw her back into his arms, but she spun away, this time finding refuge in his washstand. She adjusted the mirror, tilting it forward so it reflected the bodice of her gown instead of her face.

"God has opened new doors," she said as she ran her fingers along the silver embroidery that accentuated her narrow waist. His fingers itched to trace the same path. "I knew living with a friend would be a gift, but I had no idea that Constance and I shared a love of sewing. I've always been fascinated by fashion and the idea of remaking old gowns into something fresh and new, yet I've never had anyone to discuss designs with. Working with Constance has felt a bit like having a mother again."

Caleb came up behind her and wrapped his arms around her waist, covering her hands with his. "You've brought her back to life, Rosalind. Everyone sees it. She's wearing lighter colors, she smiles and talks and seeks out others instead of shunning them, and I don't think she's been to the depot on a Tuesday since you moved in. The change is nothing short of miraculous."

Rosalind, ever modest, shook her head. "It's just friendship, that's all. And shared interests. Thanks to your mother wearing one of our re-creations and talking us up to everyone she meets, we've actually been turning a tidy profit in the last six weeks with our little sewing endeavors."

Caleb fit his chin over her shoulder and nestled his cheek next to hers. "My wife, the entrepreneur. I'm proud of you."

She turned in his arms. "That's all I want, Caleb. To make you proud. To be worthy of your love."

"You are the best thing that has ever happened to me, Rosalind Durrington, and I'll always be proud that you chose me."

Her lashes curtained her eyes. She'd come a long way from the girl who let a photograph dictate her life, but she still struggled to leave her past completely behind. Perhaps now would be the best time for his surprise, to help her bid the past goodbye once and for all so they could step into their future with nothing entangling them.

Releasing his hold on her waist, he clasped her hand and pulled her toward the bed. "Come here. I have a present for you." He grinned, feeling a bit like a boy preparing to give his favorite teacher a handful of wildflowers.

She smiled back and allowed him to guide her to the side of the bed, where she took a seat. "What is it?"

"You'll see."

He knelt and retrieved the two items he'd stashed beneath the bed. His stomach knotted a bit as he pulled them out into the light. He prayed she'd see the heart in the gift and not be wounded by it.

"Here's the first part." He extended a wooden handle to her.

"A hammer?" She laughed. "Am I supposed to use this to knock sense into that hard head of yours when we disagree?"

Caleb chuckled. "I can think of much more pleasant ways for you to sway me to your way of thinking."

A blush stained her cheeks. Teasing blushes out of her for the next fifty years was going to be a pleasure. Yet as much as he wanted to continue their playful banter, weightier matters needed to be addressed first.

Still on his knees at the bedside, Caleb placed the second gift in her lap, then sought her face. "Open it, love."

The merriment disappeared from her expression as she absorbed the change in him. She untied the string around the flat rectangular box, then pulled off the lid. A frown lined her forehead. "What is it?"

Caleb placed a hand on her knee. "A glass plate negative."

Her hands shaking slightly, she picked it up. The light brought a dark shape into relief. The shape of a young girl with curls around her shoulders and regret in her eyes. She gasped and dropped the plate back into the box. "I—I don't understand."

"Once a negative is destroyed," Caleb explained, "no more copies of the image can be printed."

Her gaze jerked up to his.

Caleb smiled. "Did I ever tell you that my friend David practices law down in Houston?"

She shook her head.

"I paid David a visit about a month ago. Did a little shopping. Turns out Julius Hansom owns a photography studio there. With a side business that caters to men with certain unfortunate tastes." She stiffened at the photographer's name, but Caleb continued on as if he hadn't noticed. "After viewing his collection, I managed to convince him that turning over the Prairie Rose negative would be less painful than having a federal judge open an investigation into his immoral and illegal side venture. Mr. Hansom agreed."

Tears filled her eyes, and she blinked several times to keep them from falling. "Caleb . . . I don't know what to say."

He looked at her, love swelling in his chest. "That's what the hammer's for."

Being a clever woman, it only took a heartbeat for her to

catch his meaning. Her face brightened, and she immediately dropped off the side of the bed and positioned the box on the floor in front of her. Taking the hammer in hand, she held it aloft, paused, and turned to smile at him. He gave her a nod.

She brought the hammer down. Glass shattered. She pounded it again. And again. Until all that was left in the box were unrecognizable shards.

Then she sat back on her heels, laid the hammer down, and clasped Caleb's hand. "The Prairie Rose is dead."

Caleb lifted her hand to his mouth and kissed it. "Long live Rosalind, queen of my heart."

The smile that beamed from her stole his breath—so unfettered and full of love. He helped her to her feet and drew her into his arms. After pushing aside the box that no longer held any power over either of them, Caleb led his bride to the last unexplored furnishing in his room and into their future as husband and wife.

Intrigue
a la Mode

Regina Jennings

Chapter One

EMPORIA, KANSAS
1898

The breakfast rush had ended, and Willow Kentworth had already reset her station. There was nothing to do now except patrol her table and guard against horseflies dying on the starched tablecloth or lilies wilting in the crystal vase. Raised in a household of shabby gentility, Willow wasn't used to such finery. She knew that linens and silver weren't needed for a good meal. The tattered cushions on the chairs at her mother's kitchen table in Joplin were more comfortable than the polished mahogany in the Harvey House dining room. The honeysuckle from their garden wall smelled sweeter than the lilies.

Willow felt her crooked smile emerging as she repositioned a glass. Sour grapes, that was what she was tasting. As if she'd ever have mahogany chairs and china plates. It was just as well to decide now that she didn't need them, she reckoned. No use in cultivating envy, Granny Laura would say to her and her innumerable cousins. Still, her job was important. Controlling every aspect of her table ensured that she kept her job and that her family would get another wire of funds from her. The bread box would be filled, and Mother would get the medicine she needed.

Reaching behind her, Willow felt for the double buttons at the back of her apron, making sure they were still securely fastened. Her puffy sleeves accentuated her slender waist, so she fluffed them once more. Dressed in her Harvey House uniform, she didn't have to apologize for the state of her wardrobe. When she put on the uniform, she was only judged by her performance, and no one could fault her there.

"Stop preening, Willow." Etta Mae scurried by while adjusting the hairnet that held her thick braids. "You look perfect."

No one could fault her besides Etta Mae.

Before Willow could answer, the booming sound of a wooden mallet on bronze set the room abuzz. Outside, a busboy was beating the daylights out of the poor gong. Four miles away. That was how much time they had before the train arrived. Time Willow didn't need, but one could never be too careful when trying to uphold the Harvey Standard.

A telegraph had arrived with news of the next train—thirty-eight passengers for the dining room and eighteen for the lunch counter. On cue, plates of fresh fruit appeared on the serving counter, already counted for the expected guests.

Willow weaved between tables to reach them. Taking two plates at a time, she glided effortlessly in the manner she had learned at the Kansas City employment office. Placing the fruit plates on the table, she frowned at a water spot on a salad fork, but when she rubbed it, she realized it was only the reflection of the crystal glass that had caught her eye.

"Excuse me, ladies." Mrs. Sykes's dulcet voice floated across the dining room, stopping every girl in her tracks. "Remember, we only have twenty minutes to serve our guests. In that time, their experience must be perfect. Whatever cares and concerns you have are of no importance now. The only thing that matters is your customer. Make this moment the best moment of their journey."

Willow fought the urge to smooth back her blond hair. Mrs. Sykes, proudly wearing the black gown of the head waitress, gave some variation of the same speech every meal, and every meal Willow did her best to conform to the Harvey Standard. Whatever new regulations Mrs. Sykes could invent, Willow could match. It was a source of pride for her.

The roar of the train came through the heavy drapes as she carried her last fruit plates to the table. Taking her place against the wall, Willow clasped her hands in front of her and smiled serenely. From the chandeliers to the crystal goblets, the room sparkled. The smell of roasted, milk-fed chicken meant that the main course would soon be on the plates. Everything was ready.

And then the people came.

As usual, the girls in the back of the room offered the first greetings to draw the crowds farther in, keeping the front seats for the latecomers. Willow stayed against the wall until the appropriate number of travelers had passed, and then stepped forward to offer them seats at her table. She took account of her guests, trying to predict what special requests they might have. A young mother pulled out a chair for her little son before collapsing into her own with a baby on her lap. Extra napkins. Willow would bring some on her next pass.

An elderly couple took two seats, but they seemed to be strangers to the mother. Two professional men and a young couple finished out her table.

"Tea, iced tea, coffee, or milk?" Willow asked.

"Iced tea for me, please," the mother said. "A cup of milk for him and, if you don't mind, could I get some milk in the baby bottle? He just emptied it, but we'll need more for the trip."

"Yes, ma'am." Willow took the glass bottle after the mother had removed the nipple, then continued around the table, moving the goblets into the correct positions. The location of the glass told Billie, the other waitress at her table, what drink to fill it with—another of Mr. Harvey's wondrous time-saving techniques. Once she'd finished positioning the glasses, Willow waited with the empty bottle until Billie had finished filling the glasses on the table.

"Can you get this before you put the milk back?" she whispered.

Billie snatched the bottle with a nod. "Don't want a fussy baby. It'll disrupt the whole table."

"Stop it." The mother reached under the table to squeeze the leg of her son while the baby dangled half off her lap. "You're rattling the table." She rolled her eyes at Willow. "I probably should've let him run around the depot platform and skipped dinner. I don't know how he's going to sit still all the way to—"

The horrifying sound of crystal against china set Willow's teeth on edge. The boy had lurched across the table to reach for the lilies and knocked over his glass of milk. Quickly, Willow snatched napkins from an unused table to toss over the spreading tide.

"Mind your dresses," she warned her guests. "I'll go for a towel."

But before she could depart, the mother jumped up and thrust the baby into Willow's arms. Jerking the boy up by the wrist, the mother hissed, "That's the last straw, young man. You're due a whipping."

"But, ma'am . . ." Willow arranged the baby on her hip. "Ma'am, I have to serve. . . ."

But the mother wasn't listening. Yanking her son along, she busted through the front doors and disappeared.

Willow scanned the dining room for help. Mrs. Sykes's face was ashen. This was not the Harvey Standard. The baby hiccupped in her arms.

"Eww," one of the men at the table said.

A warm, wet slime cruised down Willow's hand.

"Oh no. Please, no," she said. The baby had erupted all over the front of her apron and down her hand, even running beneath her sleeve. Willow looked toward the door, but the mother had vanished. Billie was mopping up the spilt milk, having returned with the bottle, but Willow couldn't help with a baby in her arms, much less serve in a soiled apron. "Cover for me," she whispered to Billie.

"For the whole table? And what should we do about the table-cloth? There isn't time—"

"I'll be back." With head held high and baby held at arm's length, Willow glided out of the dining room. She could feel Mrs. Sykes's eyes on her, but she didn't falter. If she could find the mother in a hurry, she could run upstairs and get a fresh apron.

Right outside the doors and in the heat of the steaming engine, the mother knelt before the shamefaced little boy. The lecture must have been going well, but Willow didn't have time for it to reach a natural conclusion. "I'm sorry, but . . ."

The mother took the baby with a frown. "I'd completely for-gotten about Rayland. Good grief. I told my husband I couldn't make this trip without him. Do you have his bottle?"

His bottle? Willow was more concerned about getting up-stairs and into a clean uniform before Billie missed her. "It's on the table inside," she said. "If you'll excuse me."

Willow had started toward the door when a well-dressed woman stepped in her way and blocked her path. Willow might have thought the woman was careless, but then she took a good look and realized the woman wasn't clumsy. She was family.

"Calista York!" Willow grabbed her cousin by the arms. Of all people, Calista was not who she expected to see so far from home. "What are you doing here? Everyone has been wondering where you are." The gown Calista wore was too mature for a young lady her age.

"I heard you went to work for Mr. Harvey," Calista said, "so I came to find you."

"What's wrong?" Willow's stomach turned. "Is it Mother? Granny?"

"They're fine. It's you I'm worried about. You need to find work closer to home. Emporia isn't the place for you."

Her younger cousin had always possessed too much self-confidence, but to drop into Willow's life without an explanation and tell her what to do was preposterous, even for her. "Where have you been?" Willow asked. "Ever since you disappeared from finishing school, your parents have been tied in knots making excuses for you. Have you eloped?"

"You'll be married before me, I'd wager." Calista took Willow by the arm, spun her around, and began to unbutton her dirty apron. "What I'm telling you is that there's danger here. You should leave before you witness something that puts you at risk."

Tidy Emporia with its university more perilous than the corrupt mining town of Joplin? Absurd. Just because there were liquor bottles in the trash bin and on the tracks every morning didn't mean Willow was in danger. Besides, she couldn't resign. She needed the money. And what business was it of her younger cousin's?

"There's been some strange happenings at this station. Go home, Willow. That would be best."

"*Me*, go home? Really, Calista, you have some nerve. As soon as I'm finished serving dinner and the train leaves, we're going to have a talk," Willow said as Calista finished unfastening the soiled apron. "But it's not going to be about my job. It's going to be about you and whatever trouble you've found."

"I can't stay." Calista's mouth crinkled into her pert smile.

"And finding trouble is what I'm good at." She gave Willow a quick kiss on the cheek. "If you won't leave, then keep your eyes open and protect yourself until I see you again."

The only protection Willow needed at that moment was from Mrs. Sykes. If she didn't get back on track, she'd be going home in disgrace, whether she wanted to or not.

Chapter Two

"Whoever heard of a Buchanan working as a waiter?" Marlowe Buchanan lowered his dart while simultaneously raising an eyebrow at his younger brother's appearance.

If one didn't know better, they'd assume that the lowly busboy had erred by wandering into the extravagant private car. His white shirt and white pants fit loosely compared to the dandy's tailored suit, but both men had the same clean-shaven cleft chin and golden-flecked hair, traits they'd inherited from their railroad-baron grandfather. Graham had also inherited his grandfather's taciturn manner, which had allowed the patriarch to surprise the world when he came out of obscurity as a wealthy man.

"The Harvey House doesn't hire waiters, only waitresses," Graham said. "I can't fake being a chef, so busboy is the only avenue left to me. And you're destroying the wallpaper," he added as Marlowe's dart sank into the hand-painted bouquet of orange blossoms adorning the wall of the car.

"And you'll likely destroy more than that, going incognito."

"How else do you propose we uncover the malfeasance? The state officials insist that liquor is being smuggled into Emporia on our trains. They could confiscate our cars if they find it before we do." Graham pulled the dart out of the wall. He walked over to his brother, then, with his back to the dartboard, threw the dart over his shoulder. Turning, he saw the nick in the woodwork and the bent dart lying on the ground. He shrugged. "It was worth a shot."

Marlowe pushed aside the curtain and peered out the window. "You should wait until we hear from Father's detective. What if you're in over your head? This isn't like wooing investors or negotiating rights-of-way."

Faustus Buchanan made good use of both of his attractive, intelligent sons, but Graham wanted a different challenge. Rather than sit in his office looking over manifests and searching for discrepancies on paper, he'd search in person. Over the last year, they'd seen railman after railman along this stretch of track quit. Sometimes it was baggage clerks, sometimes it was freight men, and sometimes it was the employees of the Harvey House at Emporia.

Those who'd walked away from the job were tight-lipped, never disclosing their reasons. When his father had received word that an investigation concerning smuggling on their railroad was pending, the pieces fell together.

"I have a letter of recommendation from the Harvey hiring office," Graham said, "and no one in Emporia knows me. I'm just another employee."

"I'm sure no one will think it odd that a twenty-three-year-old man with aristocratic manners and a patrician accent is working as a busboy. Not the least bit suspicious."

Graham pulled on his white cap. "You underestimate me."

"Actually, if I thought less of you, I'd think you could be mistaken for a common laborer. As it is, you don't stand a chance. Just do me this favor, little brother. When you are discovered, give up the game and wire for help. I imagine there'll be some people who don't appreciate you trying to infiltrate their circle. This isn't the time to go it alone. You have to communicate with us. The telegraph office is at your disposal. Use it."

Graham picked up a ragtag carrying case that he'd bought from a passenger earlier that week. Funny to think that all he needed was inside one valise. He didn't know how long he'd be gone, but he was determined to succeed at the task he'd chosen. He'd persevered through challenging academics, bitter negotiations, and exhausting marathons of paperwork, but how did that compare to the monotony of physical work and routine drudgery? Was he up to the task? There was only one way to find out.

"Thanks for your concern, Marlowe. Don't spare me another thought. I'll wire when I've got it figured out."

His brother followed Graham to the doorway. "In other words, you'll only send for help when you no longer need it." Marlowe rolled his eyes. "One of these days, Graham. One of these days."

~

She was too late. Everywhere around the dining room, men were helping ladies with their chairs, ladies were gathering their bags, and the Harvey Girls were saying their cheerful goodbyes. From the empty plates and satisfied stretches, it looked as if the dinner had been a success . . . all except for the table in the corner.

Mrs. Sykes hadn't said a word. Not yet. Had she seen Willow talking with Calista when she should have been working? The sickness in the pit of Willow's stomach wouldn't go away until she knew. She ducked her head as she returned to her table and found it still lacking dessert.

"But I want to eat my custard." The boy who'd toppled the glass of milk had not been tamed. "You promised we'd get dessert. We can't leave now."

Billie hurried toward them with two plates of dessert. The elderly couple had already given up and were walking away, as was the younger couple. The gentlemen were standing, but from the way they were eying the custard, Willow figured they were willing to fight the boy for one of the plates. Quick as a wink, she grabbed two more plates and rushed to her table just as the train whistle sounded. Ignoring the soiled apron tucked beneath her arm and her drenched sleeve, she slid the custards across the table.

The mother turned up her nose. "A lot of good dessert does us now," she said. "Guess what the next hundred miles of my journey is going to be like." She arranged the baby firmly on her hip before taking the boy by the hand. "Whoever heard of a waitress disappearing for the entirety of the meal?"

Back home, Willow had gone without dessert for whole weeks, but a Harvey customer expected the best. Swallowing her sense of justice, she said, "I apologize if you are displeased with your service. We regret—"

"Is there a problem, ma'am?" It was Mrs. Sykes.

"I'd say. We paid for a meal, complete with dessert, but it wasn't served until the train whistle blew. What kind of service is that?"

Mrs. Sykes's maternal smile showed the disappointment that only a doting mother could have in her favorite child. "We apologize that your experience did not meet the Harvey Standard," she said. "Billie, please carry this kind lady's custards to the train for her."

"But, ma'am, that's china," Billie squeaked.

"Whatever we need to do for the satisfaction of the customer." Mrs. Sykes laced her fingers together. "That's the single priority here."

"Yes, ma'am." Billie pulled her skirt to the side to ease around Willow. The angry mother stuck her nose in the air, gave a huff, and stomped toward the train. Billie followed close behind, playing the hero who'd rescued the situation from Willow's incompetency.

With the last of the customers exiting the dining room, Willow's shoulders dropped. She didn't have to see Mrs. Sykes's gesture to know that she was expected to follow.

She ran her fingers along the soiled tablecloth of her table as she passed. It was time to clean the dining room. Why couldn't she run upstairs, change uniforms, then get back to work? But evidently Mrs. Sykes thought that whatever she had to say was more important than getting the table cleared for the next train.

There was no privacy at the foot of the dormitory staircase, but everyone knew not to linger there when a discussion was taking place.

"Miss Kentworth, how did it happen that your station was shorthanded for the duration of the dinner?"

Willow breathed deeply to steady her racing heart. "First, the boy spilled his milk on the table. While I was attempting to clean the mess, the mother thrust her baby in my arms and took the boy outside. Then the baby erupted on me. Soaked clear through my apron and sleeve. All I could think to do was get the baby back to its mother."

"Surely you thought through the consequences of abandoning your station?" Mrs. Sykes's hair was piled in a soft pillow atop her head. Everything about Mrs. Sykes looked soft beside the precision of her uniform and her voice.

"The consequences didn't matter," Willow said. "I had to rid myself of the child, and serving in a smelly apron is not the Harvey Standard."

"Neither is allowing our customers to get back on a train without the opportunity to enjoy their complete meal. Of the two, I can assure you which will cause the most dissatisfaction."

Mrs. Sykes's advice contradicted the training Willow had received in Kansas City. There, the girls had been reminded again and again of the importance of cleanliness, of presentation, and of professionalism. They'd never been taught what to do when the Harvey Standard of appearances conflicted with the Harvey Standard of service.

"I'll know next time," Willow said. *Please, God, let there be a next time. I don't want to go home, despite Calista's concerns.* "Next time I'll finish serving the meal even if a child is in my arms."

"But that wasn't the only impediment to your work. I noticed that a passenger engaged you in conversation. You claim to have been in a hurry, but it seems you had time—" Mrs. Sykes's mouth went tight, and her brow furrowed. "May I help you?"

Willow turned to see a busboy ambling toward them . . . and the forbidden stairs to the girls' dormitory. He removed his cap to display a haircut that couldn't be done in a kitchen with a pair of shears and a mixing bowl. Judging by his posture and age, he should have advanced far beyond busboy by now. Unless he was a dolt who couldn't tell when he was interrupting a private conversation.

"Yes, ma'am, I'm reporting for work. Are you the head waitress?"

If Mrs. Sykes was as taken aback by his cavalier attitude as Willow was, this young man was in big trouble.

"Pardon me, sir." Mrs. Sykes might look motherly, but it was a mistake to miss the ironclad authority beneath the full bosom and bouffant. "It's not my practice to answer to busboys."

Pure orneriness, if there was such a thing, had Willow fighting back a smile at his shocked expression. But he hadn't learned his lesson. "My apologies, ma'am. I'm looking for someone to answer to myself and thought you might be helpful. If I'm mistaken . . ."

"You are not mistaken. Only the manager outranks me at

this Harvey House, and you are preventing me from a discipline concern at this moment."

"Discipline concern?" For the first time, he looked at Willow. His eyes were direct, intelligent, and not the least bit humble. As fearful as she was over her employment, Willow was even more worried for him. "What seems to be the problem?" he asked.

"Our interview has concluded," Mrs. Sykes said to Willow. "This *busboy* needs to meet the manager immediately."

Willow took one last look at the handsome fellow, certain she'd never see him again. It was a pity. He'd saved her from explaining the unexplainable appearance of her cousin. She wished she could do something in return.

⁂

As usual, Marlowe was right. Pretending to be a busboy wasn't as easy as Graham had thought, and he'd yet to wash a single dish. For years he'd been accustomed to railroad employees answering to him. Even in most Harvey Houses, he was treated with care. The managers knew that all their food and supplies shipped for free on his father's railroad. They knew they could come to him with their concerns and problems. Being left out of a management decision was a new experience for him.

Graham followed the matron as she chugged through the dining room to the kitchen door.

"Please don't go any farther." Her voice sounded as sweet as spun sugar as she allowed the kitchen door to swing closed in his face.

He hadn't fooled the girl. She'd immediately recognized his error in addressing the head waitress. Graham stepped aside as a stout boy rushed into the kitchen with a tray of dirty dishes. He wondered what else the girl had seen while working in Emporia. He'd noticed that she'd snuck away from her station to talk to the young lady who'd arrived on his train. Graham had spent his life on trains. He knew how travelers behaved, and that lady had not behaved like a simple traveler. Over the last few weeks, he'd crossed her path repeatedly between Kansas City and Emporia, but she'd always ducked out of sight when he approached. What was she up to, and how was the Harvey Girl involved? He wouldn't mind talking to the waitress. Someone as observant as she was might be helpful. Someone as beautiful as she was . . .

Graham felt like a churl, not holding the door for the next busboy carrying dishes, but he could tell there was a system and that if he interfered, he'd cause more problems than he'd help. With a sigh, he looked down at his own uniform. Being underdressed was a new experience for him. Next to the uniforms of the ladies, he might as well be decked out in beggar's rags. He had to remember that a busboy's introduction wasn't as coveted as a Buchanan's.

The door swung open again. The head waitress passed serenely by without comment. Graham suspected that she was an excellent worker who brooked no nonsense from her charges. Once this adventure was over, he'd have to look into getting her a bonus. If she fired him, well, that would show even more that she was a good employee.

Behind her came the manager. Perhaps it was his pencil-thin mustache or his too-perfect posture, but Graham had him pegged as a Brit before he ever opened his mouth and proved it with his accent.

"Who am I addressing?" he asked with his mouth tight like he was trying to suppress a yawn.

Luckily, Graham had already planned his alias. "Buck Graham," he said. Better to keep as close to the truth as possible. "I'm reporting for duty from the Kansas City employment office."

The Brit kept his nose elevated as he surveyed Graham from

on high. "Mr. Graham, you've made a poor impression on Mrs. Sykes. I can't imagine what possessed you to interfere with the reprimand of an employee, but I trust you won't do it again."

"Of course not, Mr. . . . ?"

The manager's eyebrow twitched. "It's Mr. Cecil, and in general it behooves lowly busboys to let their superiors introduce themselves when they are ready. Perhaps you've never been in society, but forcing an introduction is bad form."

Actually, he had been in society, but Graham had never had to beg for an introduction before. "I beg your pardon, sir," he said. "This is very different than what I'm used to."

"Quite. Well, you look promising. Mrs. Sykes won't be pleased that I haven't sent you packing, but I'm having difficulty keeping the kitchen staffed, and we are short a busboy at present. There's a stack of dishes and a sink of hot water reserved for your pleasure. Help yourself, Mr. Graham."

Mr. Cecil turned to go, but Graham stepped forward. "I beg your pardon again, sir, but you mentioned that you are losing staff. Why do you think they are leaving?"

If Graham had been given a second chance, he nearly lost it that fast. Mr. Cecil's liver-spotted cheeks drooped in disapproval. "You are not being paid to talk, Mr. Graham. If I wanted a conversation, I could find people infinitely more agreeable to converse with than you."

Fair enough. People quitting, staff resigning, shorthanded kitchens making management edgy—it looked like the problems were just as he suspected, but were they a sign of felonious activity?

Graham adjusted his cap and made his way into the steamy kitchen. He had work to do.

Chapter Three

The gaslights of the saloon across the railroad tracks left a bright halo on the night sky. While cowboys and businessmen alike appreciated the excellent food of the Harvey House, they also appreciated a place to kick up their heels when the day was done, and the fact that alcohol was illegal in Kansas didn't seem to affect their merriment. Willow didn't begrudge the saloon their customers, but she did wish they'd keep their illicit activity on their own property. She'd rather not spend every morning picking up discarded bottles before her breakfast customers arrived. She also resented the late-night ruckus that made sleep impossible. The later the hour, the worse the piano playing and the louder the crowd.

She sat in the thick stone windowsill of the Harvey Girls' dormitory room, her feet braced against the opposite side. Her house dress was a welcome relief after the starch and pomp of her uniform. Selecting a lock of hair, she began the brushing ritual that completed her day. Were her sister and mother doing the same at their house in Joplin? Probably not her mother. While Olive's and Willow's thick blond hair shone, their mother's hair was brittle because of her illness.

And as long as she was thinking about family, what was Calista doing in Emporia? After Aunt Pauline had worked so hard to get her accepted into a respectable finishing school, you'd think Calista would buckle down with her studies and improvements.

But Calista never did what was expected.

"Willow, you have to come in here and watch Etta Mae." Billie held back the curtains that separated Willow from the goings-on inside the common room. "She's imitating that horrid woman from earlier today. She's a perfect mimic."

"I never want to see that customer again," Willow said. "Even in jest."

Even though she could be socializing, Willow preferred being alone with her thoughts. And if she wasn't mistaken, her thoughts were that someone was leaving the warehouse and making their stealthy way toward the Harvey House.

She dropped her feet from the wall and leaned forward, straining her eyes. The light from the saloon made it impossible to see into the shadows, but if the stranger crossed through one of the lit patches . . . there. Wearing the white uniform of the kitchen help, he peered around a wagon parked in the street and then, seeing no one, strolled unabashedly toward her building.

None of them were supposed to be outside after hours. Such guidelines were the only way they could enforce Mr. Harvey's strict non-fraternization rules. Perhaps the men weren't monitored as severely, but breaking curfew would be the end of their employment, no questions or exceptions. Who would be so foolish as to risk it?

Willow couldn't place the man immediately. Jimmy? No, too tall. Maybe Leo? The man was coming toward the door on the bottom floor to gain entrance to the dining room when he saw her. His eyebrow rose as he assessed her. Willow lowered her hairbrush in alarm. It was the new busboy, the one who should have been unemployed by now. What was he thinking?

"The saloon is behind you," she called, "if you're looking for trouble."

"I'm looking for a way back inside, actually." His hands were in his pockets as if he were strolling the grounds after a dinner party. "The door to the men's dormitory must have locked behind me."

"Of course it did." Willow glanced over her shoulder, but the curtain shielded her. The girls in the room across the hall were howling in laughter at Etta Mae's antics and not paying any attention to her. "You won't be able to get back in until morning, and by then it'll be too late."

"That's inconvenient," he remarked. "Could I persuade you to help me out of this pinch?"

"Not for all the gold in Faustus Buchanan's safe," she replied.

His eyes widened in surprise. His mouth quirked like he was trying to find the perfect retort. Willow felt a surge of pride that she'd sparked his interest, but no. He was trouble, and he was on his way out. She couldn't afford to jeopardize her own employment. Her family was relying on her.

Something below her caught his attention. He looked toward the door, then dodged behind the ornamental greenery that flanked the entrance.

Willow could still see him. She could also see Mr. Cecil as he walked outside with Leo. Mr. Cecil stood with his hands against his waist, looking down the track, while Leo jogged to the depot platform. Something was amiss. Willow leaned out the window.

"Excuse me, Mr. Cecil. What's the matter?" she asked.

Crouched behind the greenery, the errant busboy caught her eye. He couldn't plead from that distance without Mr. Cecil hearing him, so he pressed his hands together as if he were begging. Her mouth tightened to hide her smile. He didn't seem the type to have spent much of his life begging.

Mr. Cecil stepped away from the building to see who was speaking to him from above. "We have a midnight train coming through," he said. "Railroad executives who've called ahead for some hot meals to be delivered to their cars. If you're still awake . . ."

"Yes, sir!" Willow hopped off the windowsill, her mind already racing through the steps she needed to get presentable. Taking extra duties often resulted in rewards like free days or promotions. She'd be dressed before Mrs. Sykes made it upstairs to ask for volunteers.

"Excellent," he said. "Leo is getting a head count. I'll wake the chef, and then—"

Her eyes widened as the busboy eased from around the tree and came to stand next to Mr. Cecil. Seeing the movement out of the corner of his eye, Mr. Cecil startled. "Where did you come from?"

"I met you this morning, remember? Buck Graham." He'd managed to position himself between Mr. Cecil and the building, looking for all the world like he'd just stumbled outside behind the manager. "You need help? Is that what you said?"

Willow shook her head in amazement. He had plenty of nerve, and his gamble paid off.

"It'd be good experience for you," Mr. Cecil said. "You just do exactly what Miss Kentworth tells you."

Willow had no time to lose. This was her chance to earn her way back into the head waitress's good graces. She could only pray that the new man didn't get her into more trouble.

⁓

Breaking into the warehouse had been fairly easy. Graham had been around those warehouses since he was carried in his mother's arms, so he knew to look for loose-fitting windows and unlocked doors. But what had changed since he was a boy was the discomfort of squeezing through a half-opened window. He was larger and heavier now. Resting his weight on a splinter-rich window frame wasn't terribly comfortable. And not nearly as picturesque as the young lady perched in the window upstairs.

Graham splashed water on his face and checked his uniform for presentability. His mother would never consider the machine-sewn uniform presentable, but he was after another standard. The Harvey Standard. But the job required more than looking good, and that was where he could fail.

By the time the team was assembled in the kitchen, even the lights at the saloon across the tracks had begun to dim. The town might sleep, but the service here would be just as sharp as if the sun were blazing overhead and they were in the elaborate dining room, or so Mr. Cecil said to the small gathering that consisted of Miss Kentworth, the chef, the baker's boy, and Graham.

"As this isn't a scheduled meal, and considering the short amount of time the chef has to prepare something, he will need extra hands in the kitchen. Instead of individual plated food, we'll deliver platters, along with a stack of plates and silverware. That's where you come in." He pointed to Graham. "You will do the toting for Miss Kentworth and will accompany her on the train back to Emporia when her services are no longer required."

Graham nodded. He'd often had private service in their car but had never considered that the waitstaff was being carried away from their home while he had a leisurely dinner.

Seeing that everyone understood, Mr. Cecil clapped his hands together, and they jumped to work. Except for Graham, who gravitated toward Miss Kentworth. "What do I do now?" he whispered.

Her thick blond hair was pulled back tight, showing a clearly defined widow's peak. "Why did you volunteer if you can't help?" She waited as if his answer determined something for her.

"It was the only way to get back in the building."

"And why did you want to do that?"

"If I didn't get back inside, I'd lose my job."

She shrugged. "This isn't the right job for you. I don't mean you any harm, Mr. Graham, but I don't think being discharged from a job as a busboy will hurt your prospects." She pulled a cart from the wall and rolled it in front of a massive cabinet of dishes. "Load those dishes, and then get six servings of silverware from the chest."

Did she suspect something about him? He turned to the china cabinet before she saw his interest. She had no way of knowing how she caught his eye, but if she were as observant as he surmised, she could be his undoing. With her acuity, she could be someone he relied on, or she could be a threat to his secrets.

~~~~~

The busboy gathered the dishes as she instructed, although clearly he had other things on his mind. What was it about him that made her want to impress him? He was handsome, certainly, but unlike the last busboy, he was thinking about more than the next payday. She'd very much like to know where that thinking was directed. In particular, if he was thinking of her.

And what had he been doing out after curfew?

The ground vibrated under her feet, announcing the arrival of the train. The chef lifted the filets mignons with his tongs and placed them on a silver serving platter. Willow grabbed a carafe and began filling it with coffee from one of the big copper urns. Mr. Cecil paced the dining room until a gentleman pushed his way through the doors.

"Refreshments are prepared?" he asked as he tucked a watch into his vest pocket.

"Yes, sir," Mr. Cecil said, then turned to the kitchen and looked for Willow's acknowledgment.

Willow scanned the cart. She wasn't sure what all the chef had under the covered silver dishes, but it looked like everything was in order. With great deliberation, she turned to Mr. Cecil and gave a slight nod. Seeing her answer, the man from the train spun around and walked away, the hard heels of his custom-made shoes clomping against the floor.

"Follow him," Willow whispered. Mr. Graham bent over the cart and gave it a shove. Willow's jaw clenched at the rattling of the dishes. "Careful. That's not a wheelbarrow full of turnips."

Mr. Cecil held the door open for them as they passed, expressing more gratitude than Mrs. Sykes ever had. "Thank you both. Mr. Sheppard appreciates good service. If you do well, we'll see that you're rewarded."

"Mr. Sheppard, you say?" The busboy slowed as the cart hit the boards of the platform and rattled all the more.

"He's an important man," Willow replied as she steadied the coffee carafe on the cart. She closed the door to the restaurant before continuing her instructions. "As much as possible, stay out of sight, just like you were attempting to do tonight coming back from . . . where were you, again?"

"How are we going to get this cart up on the train?"

"We aren't. The butler will have another cart. We just transfer the things over."

"I didn't think I'd seen this cart on the train before."

"Of course not. They don't serve dinners like this in the general passenger cars." Willow climbed into the private car where the butler was waiting. Piece by piece, Mr. Graham handed up the items until the restaurant's cart was empty. While Mr.

Graham jogged the cart back to Mr. Cecil, Willow pushed the dinner into the kitchen area alone. The train was underway before she had a chance to realize that the busboy hadn't made it back to her. The refreshments were served before she thought to ask herself why that fact left her so disappointed.

Chapter Four

Graham couldn't go in the private car with Milton Sheppard. Not if he wanted to keep his identity hidden from Miss Kentworth and the rest of the workers on this part of the line. Milton, although a generation older than him, had always treated Graham like a peer. If he'd had time to prepare Milton and explain, it might work, but Graham couldn't predict who was accompanying him in the car. Better to stay hidden, which also gave him the opportunity to poke around in places he'd never been welcome before.

After returning the cart to Mr. Cecil, Graham caught the train just as the wheels began to turn. Unaccustomed to having to present a ticket, he was taken aback when a porter stopped him at the steps. Thankfully, the porter corrected himself upon seeing Graham's uniform.

"Sorry, kid. I didn't expect a Harvey House employee this time of night. As usual, your passage is free."

A fortuitous benefit and exactly the sort of advantage he'd hoped for when he'd undertaken this enterprise. With the train picking up speed into the darkness, Graham loitered to visit with the porter. He hadn't been recognized yet, so he might as well take advantage.

"I'm new to Emporia. How often does a midnight train stop here?" he asked.

"Twice a week. It's rare that we pick up anything, though. Usually there's some freight unloaded, and then we're back underway."

"How about passengers? Anybody board the train at this hour?"

"Naw. The depot isn't open late. Only fellas like yourself when we're hauling a tycoon that's got a hankering for midnight vittles."

Looking around the warehouse hadn't been fruitful. No thugs loitering, nothing that looked out of place. Whatever the faults of the warehouse foreman, he ran a tight ship. But this night had unexpectedly given Graham another place in which to snoop.

As Graham Buchanan, he could examine the freight cars anytime he wanted, but he'd hear and see what they wanted the boss's son to hear and see. He hoped his disguise would give him a chance to talk to the men who worked for him instead of just inspecting their work.

He found them inside a luggage car. A lantern swayed from an overhead beam, keeping the poker table illuminated. It was enough light for him to determine that he didn't recognize any of the players. Between his uniform and the lighting, he hoped none of them recognized him.

"Ho there, chap. Didn't see you coming." A man grinned around a glowing cigar—a violation for the working men, but who was Graham to complain?

"I hope I didn't startle you. Just looking to stretch my legs," Graham said.

"And lighten your pockets?" This from an Irishman who had coins equaling his week's wages stacked in front of him.

"Nothing like that. Just wandering around, trying to stay awake before I'm needed in Sheppard's dining room."

"Lucky bloke. Out of Emporia? Which Harvey Girl did they

send this time? Was it the tall sergeant? She's one who could whip me into shape."

Graham paused. Men of his set talked about women—of course they did—but they didn't talk about ladies with men of this class. It wasn't proper. But he wasn't supposed to do what was proper, he was supposed to do what Buck Graham, busboy, would do. He took a deep breath.

"I'm with the pretty blonde. She looks sweet, but you'd better not step out of line with her. She'll claw your eyes out."

The Irishman chuckled. The cigar-sucker wagged his eyebrows. "Sounds like you have firsthand experience."

Graham grinned, thinking about what it would take to fire up Miss Kentworth. "My only offense has been related to how I wash dishes. Whatever experience I have isn't nearly as interesting as you're hoping."

Had that kid just stolen a dollar when the others weren't looking? The rotund boy slipped his hand into his pocket, then said, "If you don't want to join the game . . ."

"No, you go ahead. I'm still getting my feet wet here. Just started this week." Play had resumed, but they were listening. "I hear they've had trouble in Emporia. Sounds like it's been dangerous."

"I've heard that too," said the Irishman. "We talk to the guys at the warehouse when we're unloading, and they say you don't want to be out after dark. There are secret shipments coming in, and it's better not to notice."

"Secret shipments? What's that about?" Graham raised an arm to lean against a stack of crates, trying to look nonchalant.

"How are we supposed to know? Everything we deal in is logged on the register. If it's a secret, it's not coming through our boxcars."

The kid grinned, his chin doubling, then doubling again. "I know why everybody is leaving. It ain't no secret."

Graham took a step closer. "Why is that?"

"It's because of that pretty blond waitress you're with. If she's as cruel as you say . . ."

Graham chuckled. "She's not all vinegar. If you treat her right, she's—"

"Excuse me?" At the voice of the lady in question, all jesting stopped.

Graham could feel her stare drilling into his back. His mouth went dry. How would these men react if they were caught spreading unsavory tales about a lady? Would they feel shame? He sure did, but his act had to continue. Convincing her was vital to his mission.

Despite his inclination, he faced her. "It's about time you showed up," he said. The snickering behind him was insufferable, but he held his course.

"Excuse me?" she repeated.

He had serious concerns that her jaw would hit the ground if it fell any lower. His arm moved to take hers, but he forced it back. Busboys didn't escort waitresses to the kitchen.

"Until next time, fellas," he said.

The smoker winked, and the Irishman whispered something to the boy that had them all rolling. Graham couldn't get her out of there soon enough.

Miss Kentworth hopped neatly onto the next platform, then barged ahead through the car of sleeping people, her words flying over her shoulder. "What made you think you could leave me to do all the work on my own?"

"You said I shouldn't be seen," Graham replied softly, trying not to wake the passengers.

"You should be discreet, not absent. I worked myself frazzled, and then I had to wander the train looking for you. I shouldn't have done that alone."

True. Graham had failed in that regard, especially considering the dangers that were lurking. He moved through the cars, trying to keep pace with her, noticing that she hadn't even asked about the conversation she'd overheard. She kept their interactions professional—about his job, not gossip. Just another thing he admired about her.

"I'm ready to work now. Whatever you tell me to do." They'd reached Sheppard's private car—Graham knew it well. "I'm determined to do better," he said, but instead of walking down the aisle on the left-hand side, Graham turned and pushed open the door to the sitting area.

He heard Miss Kentworth gasp behind him. Sheppard was being helped into his smoking jacket by the valet. He looked up with outrage at being intruded upon, then confusion when he honed in on Graham.

Graham was about to be recognized. What could he say? But before Sheppard could stammer out his name, Miss Kentworth had grabbed him by the arm and dragged him backward.

"I beg your pardon, Mr. Sheppard," she said. "Forgive us. My colleague opened the wrong door." She closed the door in Sheppard's face and spun Graham around. He flattened himself against the paneled wall in the walkway so she could pass, but instead she stopped in front of him, her head tilted up, forehead wrinkled in exasperation. "Are you trying to get us both dismissed? What would possess you to walk in there without permission?"

Graham had never had a lady speak to him like this. There was no pretense. She was so honest, so earnest, so . . . furious. Her brows, just a touch darker than her golden hair, framed flashing eyes. Her anger was exciting. His hands itched to reach out to her, to take her by the waist, but that would ruin everything.

"That's the door you walk in," he said. "I didn't know there was another."

"Have you ever been on a train before?"

"Once or twice."

"Then you should know that you aren't invited into doors that are closed. This door here is for the help. That's the one we use."

He'd never spent much time noticing what the help did, but if they'd all looked like Miss Kentworth, he would have.

She fluffed the sleeves of her dress like she was making a buffer between herself and his foolishness, then moved on to a small service closet. Graham drew a long, steadying breath. What could he do to make amends? To start with, he could do his job.

"Let me get these washed." He started unbuttoning the cuff of his sleeve.

"No," she said. "We only need to load them back on the service tray. Then, at the next Harvey restaurant on the line, we'll leave them dirty and bring back clean ones to replace them. Mr. Harvey is the master of efficiency." She arranged the plates, larger ones on the bottom and the smaller dessert plates and saucers on top.

The service tray crowded the closet, meaning that they couldn't get more than an arm's length away from each other, a situation he could have enjoyed under different circumstances.

"So we'll reach Topeka in another half an hour. Then I suppose we catch the seven o'clock train back in the morning?" He lifted the heavy stack for her and placed it on the tray.

"For someone who doesn't travel on a train much, you know your timetables."

His brother Marlowe often accused him of not communicating enough, but clearly Graham had said too much.

He placed all the silverware on a soiled napkin, wrapped it up, and set it on the tray while she emptied the glasses. It didn't take long to clear the kitchen. Miss Kentworth had adopted

Mr. Harvey's efficiency remarkably well. She wiped down the countertop. When she lifted the window, the cool night air teased the blond strands of hair that had pulled loose in the night. Miss Kentworth lifted the basin of discarded drinks, but Graham stopped her.

"Allow me. If you throw that out the window, it's going to blow back on you."

"Thank you. I should know better. I'm just so tired."

"I'm glad to be of some use."

She pulled the door to the hallway open. He tried not to slosh anything on her when he passed. Their paths crossed and recrossed as she ducked beneath his arm to open the door of the car for him. Now the wind hit him full force. Graham had always enjoyed the exhilaration of standing outside of a speeding train. Being on top of the cars was even more exciting, but he wouldn't share that with Miss Kentworth.

He held the basin over the side railing. The train swayed. Miss Kentworth's balance faltered. To steady herself, she placed her hand against the small of his back. The gesture was unexpected. He tilted the basin. The wind caught it and ripped it from him. It smacked against the car behind them, then disappeared into the darkness.

"It's gone," he said. "I'll pay for it when I get my first wages."

"I'm not sure you'll have a job long enough to afford it," she answered.

⁓

The train rolled into the quiet station of Topeka, belching its white smoke against the dark sky. Willow had done an overnight trip like this before and had been grateful for the company of a familiar busboy to escort her back to Emporia, but nothing about Buck Graham was familiar. He was new, but he gave the sense that he was new in all the wrong ways. That he was new to this life, that he had no life before this one, or at least nothing he was willing to reveal. Willow wanted to know more. What was he hiding?

They disembarked with the dirty dishes in a basin and headed to the Topeka Harvey House. The restaurant had been wired that they were coming, and the manager had left a door unlocked. Willow turned the knob and let them inside the kitchen to deposit the dirty dishes. As soon as their load was delivered, Graham wandered into the darkened dining room.

"Three hours until the return train," Willow said. "I usually wait in the storeroom. You can make a nice seat out of flour bags."

"There are nicer chairs at this table." Graham ran a finger along a salad fork's handle. "Have you ever eaten at a Harvey House? You serve people all day. Have you ever had a meal?"

"I've eaten at the lunch counter when I'm traveling. And of course we get the finest food imaginable while working. A lot finer than anything I ever had at home." Her heart quickened as he turned to her and slid his cap off his head. He pulled out a chair and motioned for her to sit.

She had never sat in the dining room. There'd never been an occasion. But what would it hurt? They could watch for the train from here. She held Mr. Graham's gaze as she moved forward. Willow wasn't accustomed to a man knowing the precise moment to slide her chair forward as she sat, but he did it with surprising grace.

He took the chair opposite her, sitting with perfect posture. "So kind of you to accompany me to dinner, Miss Kentworth."

My, wasn't he putting on airs? She had to admit, the way he used the full tones of each word did leave an impression.

Willow looked at the setting before her, intimately familiar with each piece. She followed the layout of the dinnerware until her eyes traveled back to her partner. "On the contrary, you've shown the kindness by bringing me to the most elegant restaurant in the world."

His smile was kind. "Perhaps the most elegant restaurant in Kansas, but not the world."

"But nicer than anywhere either of us is likely to eat," she said as he took the napkin and spread it over his lap. "Do you mind if I call you Graham?" she asked.

He paused. "Why would you call me that?"

"Mr. Graham sounds too formal, and your first name is too familiar."

"My first name . . . being Buck?"

"That *is* your first name, isn't it?" It didn't fit him. Too abrupt. Graham sounded better.

"But I have no desire to call you Kentworth," he said. "There has to be a better alternative."

"Willow. You may call me Willow."

"It's not too familiar?" He held up a hand. "Don't answer that. I accept and thank you for the privilege."

She looked down at the plate in front of her. "Don't forget," she said, "everything you touch has to be replaced. You're making more work for someone."

His eyes caught hers with a sadness that was unexpected. "Do you count your time by the tasks to be accomplished or by the joy of the moment?"

"Setting a table does not bring joy," she said.

"Then you need another job." He pretended to ladle something into his bowl, then offered her the same. She refused with an upheld hand, so he picked up his soup spoon and pantomimed his first course.

"I'm proud of the work I do," she said. "It pleases me when my table is perfect, but it doesn't bring me joy. Not directly, anyway."

He lifted his empty glass and held it aloft. "Then what joy of yours should we celebrate?"

Willow smoothed the tablecloth. Doing her job made her proud and getting paid was fulfilling, but that wasn't her motivation. "The joy comes after I get paid. I go to the Western Union office with my paycheck, and I give them the address for the wire." The clacking of the telegraph machines, the smell of tar on the new roof of the office, the smile of Mr. Mobley when he saw her enter . . . that was the moment she worked for. That made the late nights and the fight for perfection worth it. "That's when I'm the happiest."

He lowered the glass. "When you place that wire," he said, "who are you thinking of?"

"My family. Mother is sick. Father is a foreman at the ore mine, but there's never enough money for her doctor bills. My sister does the nursing. She's sacrificed so much. More than I have. And then I'm thinking of home. How the bread box my grandpa made won't be empty. How Father will have time for fishing. I think of the linen closet and the smell of the lavender sachet when I open it, and how there'll be blankets enough to keep everyone warm in the winter. All of that. I think of all of that."

Willow folded her hands in her lap. Why had she rambled on? Maybe because she'd never held someone's attention as strongly as she held his at that moment. The moonlight accentuated the hollows of his face, particularly the cleft in his chin and his deep-set eyes.

"No wonder you are so good at your work," he said. "There's love behind it."

His tone made her blush. "God has been good to me. He's given me a lot of people to love." Then, to break the tension, she asked, "How about you?"

Her question took him aback. His spoon rattled against the rim of his soup bowl. "Me? I have people to love, yes, but not someone in particular."

"I wasn't prying," Willow said, now flustered. "I was talking about your job. Do you find joy in washing dishes, or is there a reason behind the labor?"

"Oh." He lowered his spoon and stretched his fingers. "There's family—my parents, my brother. People I work with that I don't want to let down."

"People you work with in Emporia? Do you know someone there?" She breathed easier now that they were on safer ground.

He scraped his knife against the plate, stabbed at the air with his fork, then put it in his mouth. "Delicious. You really should try your dinner. If it's not to your liking, I can send it back to the chef."

Watching him was tantalizing, but he hadn't answered her question. "What is not to my liking is that I told you something personal. Now it's your turn. I know nothing about you."

"That woman I saw you speaking to at the depot, the one who kept you from returning to your table. How do you know her?"

Calista? Her cousin's concerns came back as clear as the crystal goblet on the table before her. "Why? Do you know her?"

"You didn't answer my question."

"You've yet to answer any of mine. What brought you to work in Emporia? Where are you from? And the big question, what were you doing by the warehouse after curfew tonight?"

He studied her for a moment, then raised his napkin to his lips as if wiping off the remains of a delicious meal. "I'm disappointed."

"In what? In me?"

"In myself. I underestimated you, and I underestimated how difficult this job would be. That's not to say that I lack the ability to see it through, but it will take more effort than I expected." His fine words and manners made it impossible to remember that his white busboy uniform wasn't formal dinner dress.

"Washing dishes is harder than you imagined?" she asked.

His eyes crinkled with his smile. Maybe it was the late hour, but the warmth of his gaze made her feel giddy.

"Tenacity. It's a trait I admire greatly," he said.

"Exactly how I feel about honesty." Forgetting that it was all make-believe, she raised an empty glass to her lips while peering at him over the rim.

His smile deepened, but he lowered his eyes. Laying the napkin next to his plate, he stood. "Come. We have a few hours before the train arrives. Let's reset the table, then wait outside. We can watch the sunrise in a bit. It's nearly dawn."

Yes, it was, but Willow was still in the dark.

Chapter Five

Graham lugged another tub of dirty dishes to the kitchen. Pity he couldn't have kept his custom-made Italian leather shoes when he embarked on this adventure. The simple wooden-soled boots that busboys wore made his feet feel like they were crammed into tin cans. Over all, though, the work wasn't too strenuous. His biggest complaint was boredom. The drudgery of gathering dishes, washing dishes, drying dishes, then stacking dishes had him looking for any common diversion. Instead, he'd found the exceptional Willow. Not what he'd expected.

She was as pure and consistent as a bar of gold. Scratch the surface, and you'd find another layer of the same flawless character. In her, he'd found someone he valued, someone he could trust. Or was it too soon to make that determination?

In the two weeks since he'd arrived, he and Willow had grown closer every day. When he'd discovered that her first task in the morning was to gather empty liquor bottles from the tracks and move them out of the customers' view, he was ecstatic for two reasons. First, here was firm evidence that smuggling was taking place in dry Emporia. According to Mr. Cecil, the county sheriff wasn't interested in their concerns, but Graham had to answer to authorities that could confiscate the railroad's property. Disposing of the evidence didn't solve the problem.

Secondly, he was thrilled because it was an opportunity for him to work with Willow. How he loved seeing the early-morning world through her eyes. He was amused by her assessment of the grand houses they walked past as they lugged sacks of bottles to the dump. He was astonished by the stories she told of her raucous extended family. And he adored her honest gaze. In it, he felt real, and he felt that he needed to impress this conscientious, determined woman.

Graham took the kettle of hot water off the stove and added water to his basin. He might trust Willow, but he didn't trust her friend from the depot. He watched for the mysterious lady with every train, although now that he was disguised as a busboy, he had no authority to detain her for questioning. His instinct told him that she was tied to the secret shipments. His instincts also told him that Willow knew more than she was admitting. Two weeks ago, when they'd gone on their overnight excursion, Willow hadn't been forthcoming when Graham asked about the woman. She had offered no information to help him, but maybe Leo would.

Leo punched a loaf of dough on a floured board. It had been two months since Leo had started work at the Harvey House as the baker's boy, but the angry red knot on his cheekbone was a new development.

"What happened?" Graham whispered as Leo folded the dough and punched it again. "Who did that to you?"

"Don't know. I was on the first shift this morning. Got up before the bell rang and went to the warehouse to get another bag of flour. The last thing I remember was wondering whose wagon was pulled up to the loading dock. Munsy found me on the ground when he came along later."

An unknown wagon? Graham had searched the warehouse repeatedly and found nothing, but maybe it was time to try again. "What did Mr. Cecil say?"

"After making sure that my skull wasn't cracked, he asked if anything was missing from the warehouse. The boys checked our inventory, and everything was there. Whatever they were doing, they weren't robbing."

"Or they were, and you interrupted them before they got the wagon loaded."

Leo touched the raw portion of his cheek and winced. "If I saved the company money, you'd think they would let me have the rest of the day off. See if I ever show up for work early again."

But Graham knew where he'd be the next morning.

"I'm not interested in cowboys, with their dusty clothes and forward ways," Etta Mae announced as she spread a clean cloth over her table. "I won't settle for anything less than a railroad man. Sophistication is what I'm after."

Billie rolled her eyes. "Those railroad men are nothing more than glorified butlers. I'd rather have a man who's his own boss, chivalrous and independent. I'll find me a cowboy before the end of the year. See if I don't."

"What about Willow?" Etta Mae asked. "Will anyone ever turn her head, or will she be so busy re-polishing the silverware that she'll never notice a man?"

Willow separated out one of each utensil to set the place before her. "When the right man comes along, I won't care about his profession. It's his character that will win me."

"I hope so," Etta Mae laughed, "because that new busboy will have his heart broken if you want a rich man."

Willow hid her smile and rearranged the silverware even though she'd gotten it perfect the first time. In the mornings before the restaurant opened, she and Graham had found treasured moments alone. He was a purposeful man, and his current fascination seemed to be learning everything about her—that, and learning everything about the railroad and the depot. She shouldn't be surprised. Someone of Graham's intelligence wouldn't be a busboy forever. She'd never met anyone like him, but fraternization meant the loss of her job. For now, their growing relationship had to be kept a secret.

"I don't know what you're talking about," she said. "Which busboy?"

"Etta Mae is talking about the one who never lets you out of his sight," Billie said. "He's handsome enough, especially if you aren't particular about money."

"I'm not going to marry a busboy, no matter how handsome he is." Willow looked up from the table to see the unflappable Buck Graham standing in the doorway.

Etta Mae covered her mouth while Billie ducked her head and scurried out of the dining room. Willow felt heat blooming on her cheeks, but she faced Graham bravely, refusing to give in to girlish antics like her friends. "May I help you?"

His mouth twitched, the only sign that he'd heard more of the conversation than she'd wish. "Yes, ma'am. A cargo train is due, and I need some guidance on what we're to get from the ice car."

"Where's Mr. Cecil?"

"He's occupied."

Etta Mae elbowed Willow. "What's wrong with you? He's asking for your help."

Willow looked around the dining room. They were between meals. The only customers were local cowboys, and Billie had already claimed them. Willow dusted off her hands and in her most matter-of-fact voice said, "I can give you a minute, but just a minute. No more."

Graham bowed his head as she sailed past him and out onto the platform to await the train.

He clasped his hands behind his back and came to stand at her side, watching up the track. "You know, I'm not offended if you think I'm handsome. It's an honest assessment."

He might be laughing, but he wasn't trying to put her at a disadvantage. Her courage grew. "I regret that you didn't hear all of the conversation. The main gist was my assertion that it didn't matter to me what profession my future husband has. Rich or poor, good character is what I find most attractive."

"Unless he's a busboy."

"They were teasing me. I didn't know what else to say."

"And now that I asked for your help, they'll tease you even more," he said. "I hope you can still enjoy my company, because I certainly enjoy yours."

Willow looked up at him. In their short acquaintance, they'd shared a lot with each other. No, that wasn't true. She'd told him a lot, but she knew nothing about him. What was he hiding? A financial failure? A lowly beginning? He needn't have worried. She thought it likely he'd find success in life no matter how humbly he'd begun.

The train roared down the track, making further conversation impossible. This train only had a handful of passengers, and it wasn't a meal time. Willow kept an eye on the few people heading to the restaurant, but she decided she wouldn't be needed and followed Graham to the ice car.

The freight man rolled open the door to the ice car, then waved the waiting wagon forward. Graham followed the freight man as he climbed up into the car, but Willow, ever conscious of keeping her apron clean, waited at the door, where she was greeted with an icy blast of air.

"These barrels here are yours and those blocks of ice," the freight man said, pointing. "Look at the floor markings. Everything in the Emporia section gets unloaded into that wagon and delivered to the ice house."

Graham nodded. "The process seems fairly straightforward. I was curious how it worked."

"Curious?" the freight man said. "Why would a busboy and waitress need to watch us unload? The warehouse men have it well in hand."

The freight man had a point. It wasn't usual for Mr. Cecil to send a busboy to meet the cars. Willow blinked as the thought took form. Had Graham conspired to get her alone? Were their morning talks no longer sufficient? But he seemed more interested in the ice car than he was in her.

The workers rolled the barrels out of the car and into the wagon beds. Cold air rose off them like steam beneath the afternoon sun. Wooden ice cream freezers were packed tightly against each other to lessen their exposure to the elements. Lastly, they separated giant blocks of ice from the sawdust packing and shoved them out of the car. Burlap sacks helped the blocks scoot across the car and into the wagon. Graham watched with a critical eye, but she still had no sense of why he needed her help.

"That's all you get this load," the freight man said as Graham hopped out of the insulated ice car. The freight man rolled the heavy door of the car closed, then climbed aboard the train and disappeared from view.

"Why did I have to be here, again?" Willow asked.

"Because I wanted your company."

"And you feel entitled to my company because . . ."

Something behind her caught Graham's attention. "Look!" he said. "That lady, right there."

Willow could only pray that Mrs. Sykes wasn't looking out of a window as she let Graham drag her toward the depot. As the last passengers were boarding, she saw Calista. The veil of Calista's surah bonnet hid her face, but Willow recognized her, and so did Graham.

"Isn't that the woman you were speaking to my first day here?" Graham asked.

Willow bit her lip. How could she explain Calista and her cockamamie ways when Willow herself didn't understand? While she did her best to satisfy Graham's rabid curiosity about everything from cargo shipments to the bottles in the trash, she grew tired of his refusal to disclose anything about himself. He had his secrets. It was high time that she be allowed a few of her own.

"You never did tell me who she is," Graham said.

"Why is it important?"

For the first time, he seemed unsure of himself. His eyes held hers, but his plea was not what she expected. "It's important because I'm trying to decide whether I can have you in my life."

Her breath caught. She hadn't expected this. Hoped, some-day, but not this soon. And not this demanding.

"You're so full of secrets," she said, "but you won't allow me to have this one?"

"You trust her, but you don't trust me?"

She couldn't help her sharp laugh. "Let's discuss your habit of disappearing from your station, dragging me around chasing wild hares, and avoiding straight answers to any questions."

"Don't do this, Willow. If you understood, you'd help me. I want to trust you, I do, but I can't jeopardize my work."

"Your work as a busboy?" Willow rolled her eyes. "Speaking of jeopardizing work, Mrs. Sykes is going to be livid at my absence. Excuse me."

Over her head, the flag snapped in the wind as she sailed into the restaurant and gathered fruit dishes for her tray. It wasn't fair. If her mother hadn't taken ill, then maybe her family would have more money. Maybe she'd be as independent as Calista. Maybe she could hop on the train and ride away when faced with a conundrum. Maybe a man like Graham would take her seriously instead of yanking her around on foolish errands.

But that wasn't her world, and she had a job to keep.

Chapter Six

Every climb down the drainpipe of the men's dormitory got easier, but it also increased his chances of getting caught. When his feet hit the pavement below his window, Graham dusted off his hands and turned to the dark warehouse. After Leo's attack, the kitchen boys and chefs refused to go to the warehouse alone. Several had placed requests to be moved to other restaurants down the line, which was exactly what Graham was trying to prevent. Their caution meant that no employees were out at night, and that sounded too convenient for anyone who wanted to conduct illicit business. It sounded like the perfect place for Graham to be.

But it wasn't perfect. Tempering his excitement to solve the problems at Emporia was the fear that somehow Willow Kentworth was involved. She'd told him that her family was desperate. She'd told him that she'd do anything to help them. What did that mean? He couldn't believe that she'd do anything against her conscience, but could it be that she was trusting the wrong people?

Graham had begun to imagine what could happen when his mission was over. He'd imagined treating Willow to a nice dinner with actual food this time. He'd imagined the great release of finally telling her something about himself, of finally being honest. He wanted her to know him. He wanted to stop choking down every memory, every experience, and stop giving her nothing in return for the parts of herself that she shared. He didn't want to lose Willow's regard, but he had to put an end to the smuggling, no matter who was involved.

The warehouses lined the tracks, different areas set aside for shipments for local merchants coming in and for produce from the farmers going out. But as far as Graham knew, no farmers were being attacked. No merchants had closed shop. The trouble seemed to swirl around the railroad men, particularly those who had connections with the restaurant. So that was where he was headed again—the Harvey House's warehouse.

A sign hanging by chains creaked in the wind. A tomcat crashed down from the awning and landed right at Graham's feet before bounding away. Graham flexed his fingers to get the feeling back into them. He should've seen that coming. How was he going to protect himself if a cat could dust his toes without warning? Sticking to the shadows when he could, he walked the perimeter of the building but noticed that it was locked up tight this time. Well, he'd sit and watch a spell. The short night would make for a long day, but his livelihood didn't depend on being the best busboy.

It had been an hour when two cowboys wandered across the tracks from the saloon. He needed to suggest to the regulators that they inspect and confiscate the saloon's property instead of his railcars, but they were more interested in squelching the source. At first Graham thought the cowboys' repeated attempts to climb out of the tracks and onto the platform were hindered by their inebriated state, but once their wanderings made it around the building once, they seemed to sober up. No longer stumbling, they consulted a pocket watch by the moonlight, then took out in two different directions with clear intent.

Graham leaned forward. They hadn't seen him. Would they have continued to act drunk if they had? A low rumbling alerted him that the giant warehouse door was being rolled back. He crept forward, his cheap shoes pinching his feet. They were only cowboys, and he'd have the element of surprise. Then again, he wanted to know what was going on. It'd be better not to run them off until he could see what they were up to. The saloon wasn't the only place benefitting from the smuggled goods.

He flattened his back against the depot wall. He glanced at the Harvey House, halfway hoping he'd spot Willow leaning out of her window. No, he didn't want her involved, even though he feared she was already. The same tomcat skedaddled across the road as a light cart pulled by two more men came silently down the street. Each man had the tongue of the cart under his arm and trotted toward the warehouse. They easily spun the cart around and backed it up to the door, taking less time and making less noise than a horse would have. They hefted a heavy box into the cart, then another. They worked in silence, the rasping of the box against the cart's bed and the groan of the axle the only noises. Four men. Confrontation was unadvisable. Especially if Graham didn't want to mess up the handsome face that Willow so admired. But he still wanted to see who they were and where they were going.

He waited until the cart was loaded. Two men disappeared back into the shadows, probably headed toward the saloon to make authentic what they'd been faking before now. The other two pulled the cart away from the warehouse. The going was slower than when the cart was empty, which would give Graham time to follow. He waited until they'd started down the road before he walked after them.

From the corner of his eye he saw a bright light, then nothing.

Etta Mae rolled to the edge of the bed, then sat up and rested her head in her hands. "Why do I have so much energy at night, but when morning comes, I can't manage to get out of bed?"

Willow lay on her back and gripped her blanket as a heaviness settled on her. It had been two days since she and Graham had argued. That didn't mean that he wasn't watching her every time she looked up. And it didn't stop him from placing dishes on her table first, much to the amusement of the other girls. But the imposed distance between them filled her with dread. In the beginning, she'd thought he was a nuisance—that she'd be better off if he went away and let her focus on her job. Now she worried that he'd do exactly that and she'd never see him again. Why was she so confused?

She turned her face away from Etta Mae and toward the open window. Was this how her father felt when marrying her mother? Tuberculosis meant that her mother would never be strong or helpful, but he loved her and had married her anyway. Practical concerns weren't important when measured against their love and his desire to take care of her. And because they put their love before finances, Willow and Olive had had a happy but poor childhood. Because of their love, Willow desperately needed her job and was unwilling to lose it because of the antics of a busboy.

She sat up and hugged her knees to her chest. Today was another day with Graham working at her side but out of reach. What *was* Calista up to? If Willow knew, she would tell Graham—anything to solve this rift between them. As it was, her cousin's erratic behavior had no explanation. Calista was the only person who could clear this up.

Standing, Willow placed both hands on the windowsill. It was time to look for discarded bottles and tidy up the platform. Unlike at Granny Laura's ranch, mornings on the railroad tracks were not spectacular. She missed the ranch. The fields, the cattle, the cousins—that was what she was really homesick for, and seeing Calista made it worse.

The sky lightened in the east. That was the way home, and she'd get to go tomorrow. Because of her late-night work, she'd earned a few days' leave. With train fare free for all Harvey employees, her decision was easy. Some girls preferred to visit their sister restaurants and hotels and see the country, but not Willow. Not this time. With all her confusion, she needed the touchstone of home. She needed to lean on the wisdom of her elders and be reassured that the world hadn't changed just because her heart had.

The tracks stretched out like long arms reaching for her family. *Tomorrow*, she told them. Tomorrow she'd take a ride and clear her head.

With the rising sun, she could see a bump of something down on the tracks. Willow leaned over the windowsill. What was it? Had a cow fallen down there? She looked at the horizon. The morning train came through at 6:15, and it didn't stop in Emporia. If something that big was on the tracks, there'd be a disaster. She reached for her uniform but shook her head. No time. She grabbed Etta Mae's cotton robe, tossed it over her nightgown, and ran down the stairs.

She didn't have time to find Mr. Cecil or Mrs. Sykes for an explanation. She just wanted to make sure her eyes weren't playing tricks on her. She rushed out of the quiet restaurant and to the edge of the platform. Her stomach turned over. It was a man. A man was on the tracks, and the unmistakable rumble of an approaching train echoed in her ear.

But then she realized it wasn't just any man. It was Graham.

"Help!" she yelled, but her voice couldn't be heard that far from the restaurant. She eyed the signal bell at the depot office. They might be able to signal to the train, but it would be a gamble. If she couldn't find the right person soon enough, Graham was doomed. She was his only hope.

Willow dropped off the platform and landed between him and the wall. His face was bloody, and he sprawled cheek-down on one of the rails. She pulled on his arm, but he didn't budge.

"C'mon, c'mon, c'mon," she begged. She knelt and took his chin in her hand, forcing his head up. His eyes opened. "You have to move," she said. "The train is coming."

He was fighting for focus, but then he gave up, and his eyes rolled closed.

"No." She beat on his back. "You gotta move." She looked up to see the terrifying black engine scoop the track under its chin as it raced at them. Graham wasn't moving. She had to do something. Now!

She dropped his head and grabbed his ankles. With one ankle under each arm, she lurched backward. He moved six inches, and his head dropped from the rail onto the gravel beneath the railroad ties. Still not far enough. Another lurch backward, and another, every time moving a little less.

"Please move," she begged. The train was upon them. The whistle from the frightened engineer sounded. One more pull was all she had time for. Graham began to resist, moving his feet to kick her away, but she held on and lunged backward as the train roared over them. Fighting the impulse to cover her ears, instead she gathered him against her, his bloody head on Etta Mae's faded robe, and rolled away from the earsplitting noise.

The ground shook so hard that her heart rattled inside her chest. The heat from the train, the noise, the shaking were overwhelming.

Graham's hands were against her waist, but he wasn't struggling, just moving as if trying to determine where he was. She was shushing him even though neither of them could hear anything. The train wouldn't stop here. Just a few more seconds. Suddenly, with a whoosh, it had passed. The clacking, the ringing bell, and the horn faded. Had the train been sounding its horn the whole time? Her hearing was fractured. Feet appeared as men jumped down. Their mouths were moving, but she couldn't hear. Men from the depot. Mr. Cecil, the manager. The storekeeper. Hands pulling at her, pulling at Graham. His face raised toward hers, questions unanswered. He reached up to touch her face. His hand on her cheek, his thumb pressed against her lips.

And then he was gone.

"He was hit in the head." The doctor pressed again on the back of Graham's skull like he'd never seen a goose egg before.

"Do you have any idea what he was doing on the tracks after curfew?" Mr. Cecil asked.

"I'm a surgeon, not a mind reader," the doctor said. Then, with a pat to Graham's shoulder, he added, "Refrain from strenuous work for the next few days. You can expect a headache and blurred vision, but it'd be a lot worse if that young lady hadn't gotten you away from the track."

Graham nodded and then wished he hadn't when he felt the pain. Knowing that he wasn't thinking clearly, he'd opted to keep his mouth shut rather than risk having his identity revealed. He hadn't fallen on the tracks. He'd been attacked while watching the warehouse, and someone had left him there to die. Someone who might make another attempt on his life when they learned that the last one had failed. So much was foggy, but one thing was clear—Willow Kentworth had saved his life.

"Does he have any family to contact?" the doctor asked.

Cecil nodded. "We sent a telegram to the address in his employee file. What do we do with him until they arrive?"

"Leave him be. He might need help keeping that cut clean, but he'll be back on his feet soon enough."

"He broke curfew," Mr. Cecil was saying. "We'll have to hire someone to take his place."

"They took something from the warehouse." Graham's voice bounced inside his head. "I was outside, and I saw them loading two boxes into a cart."

"Really? Is that your excuse for being out there?" Graham could sense Cecil in front of him, but he didn't feel like opening his eyes. "I'll have the foreman check the warehouse, but if there's nothing missing, you are dismissed."

Graham had nothing left to say. Before Cecil left, the doctor pulled the curtains to darken the room, giving Graham a chance to rest and dream of Willow.

He had no idea how long he'd slept, but when he opened his eyes, his brother was sitting in a chair, kicked back with his legs up on a dresser.

"Do you mean to tell me that this little room is where you've been staying? It's so . . . primitive."

"Good morning, Marlowe."

"It's afternoon, and you wouldn't believe the lies I had to tell to explain why I'm so concerned over a busboy with a headache."

"I doubt your conscience will bother you overmuch."

"True." Marlowe dropped his feet to the floor and leaned forward. "You've lasted longer than I thought you would. They still don't know who you are."

Graham eased up into a sitting position, trying to ignore the pounding in his head. "It won't take them long to figure it out if you keep showing up."

"If it wasn't for me, you wouldn't have a job here anymore. I convinced that Brit to give you another chance, since you nearly died on company property. I also made up a story about your father serving as my tutor when I was little and our family having a fondness for you."

"I hope there's some fondness."

"Don't push your luck. But we've arranged for you to take a trip home to visit this little family of yours."

"Father? Does he want to see me?"

"I'm sure he does, but that's immaterial. It's that Pinkerton agent we hired. Evidently you've nearly blown the cover for the whole operation."

"I did? When? Who's the detective? Is it Leo?"

Marlowe shrugged. "All I know is I'm supposed to give you this message." He pulled a piece of paper from his pocket and held it out to Graham.

Graham unfolded it, but the words blurred. He handed it back. "Read it, please."

"Oh, I get to be involved in this mystery? Very well." Marlowe cleared his throat. "It says, '*Miss Kentworth is going on a trip tomorrow. Accompany her, but don't let anyone in Emporia know.*'"

Willow? He was going with Willow tomorrow? He might recover after all.

"I don't know this Miss Kentworth, but her name seems to have revived you," Marlowe said. "Is there something you should tell me?"

"She's wonderful."

"Does she think the same about you?"

"She thinks I'm a busboy."

"Much below her, then?"

"In every way, except the one you mean. She's a Harvey Girl."

"I see." Marlowe leaned back in his chair. "The one who saved your life?"

"The same. Are you shocked?"

"I'm shocked that she's paying any attention to you if she's as wonderful as you say."

"My head hurts," Graham said. "Are we done?"

"As I said, it's been arranged for you to travel tomorrow, and it sounds like it was at the request of the agent. Whoever he is, he's as tight-lipped as you are. I hope you two can find each other."

Graham covered his face with a pillow. He'd take it easy for the rest of the day, because tomorrow he had a job to do. And even more exciting than meeting the agent was a chance to thank Willow for saving his life.

Chapter Seven

After the pomp and prestige of wearing her starched Harvey Girl uniform, Willow felt plain and nondescript in her normal traveling clothes, a calico gown that she and her mother had sewn together before she left home. But she wasn't going home.

When she wired her father, he'd told her that the family would be gathering at Granny Laura's for the duration of her leave. Grandma's house. That ranch near Joplin was the setting of her best memories—losing her breath when her cousin Finn pushed her on the barn swing, making colorful button necklaces with her cousin Evangelina, and hiding from her parents under Grandma's bed when they were ready to go home. According to her father, the gathering was in honor of her Aunt Pauline visiting from Kansas City. That was another worry. What could Willow say to Aunt Pauline? How could she explain Calista's strange appearances and disappearances in Emporia? Could she go without mentioning their encounter?

Willow shifted in her seat. The omission would feel like deceit. She couldn't bear to hide information from her aunt, but she didn't know what to say either.

She pushed her feet out to stretch her legs but bumped against a lunch pail, nearly turning it over. The farm woman sitting across from her lunged to steady the pail with a look of lazy disapproval at Willow.

"Sorry," she said. If there were a Harvey House on this stretch of track, lunch pails wouldn't be needed. Heading south meant they were at the mercy of whatever dingy kitchen happened to be serving for the twenty minutes it took the freight men to unload the goods, refill with water, and be gone. She'd packed herself a lunch before boarding, but she'd find a less crowded car to eat in.

Willow excused herself as she picked her way through the passenger car. The next car was a private car much like Mr. Sheppard's—the one she and Graham had served on that night. With one hand trailing against the walls to keep her steady, she walked past the paneled privacy doors. The gossip among the staff was that Graham would recover soon, but Mr. Cecil wanted him gone.

What she wouldn't give to see Graham again, healthy and whole. Even better would be if he had an explanation for what he was doing out at night. She wouldn't have believed his claims of a robbery at the warehouse—a complete check had been made, and nothing was missing—except Leo had confided that he'd witnessed the same thing and had also been attacked. But Leo was gone now, and at this rate, Graham wouldn't last long either. As much as she wanted him to stay in Emporia, she couldn't help but think that it wasn't in his best interest to do so.

A door was opening at the end of the corridor. Holding her lunch pail behind her, she swung tighter against the wall and kept her eyes down as she approached. She'd look up to make a polite acknowledgment, dip her head, then—

"Willow?"

Her heart swelled at the sound of his voice. She raised her head. It was him, yet it wasn't. Was she imagining the perfectly tailored suit and the sapphire cravat? "Graham? What are you doing here?"

Instead of answering, he took her by the arm and pulled her into the private room.

She sputtered. "Haven't you learned your lesson about trespassing on trains?" From the potted fern in the corner to the crushed velvet sofa, it was clear that she and Graham didn't belong here. "The owner of this car will be back—look, his tea is still steaming on the desk—and we'll both lose our jobs. Let's go."

But her protests didn't seem to faze him. "You have nothing to worry about, Willow. No one is going to evict us. Have a seat. There's a lot we need to talk about, and maybe some things we can't talk about yet, but I'm looking forward to trying."

Too stunned to flee, she let him escort her to a cushy seat that felt a thousand times better than the bench she'd been riding on. Her lunch pail was forgotten by the door. What had happened to him? How could a busboy wear those clothes so naturally? How could he be so calm after the beating he'd taken? How could he look even more handsome than he had in Emporia?

"You have a lot of questions. Perhaps it'd be best if I started with some answers." He reached for the tea service atop a brass cart and poured the amber liquid into a delicate blue teacup. "This private car belongs to my family, as does the tea service, so please have a cup and don't be concerned that we're trespassing."

Willow's teacup rattled in its saucer. It was no use pretending to understand. She set the tea aside and sat on her trembling hands. "If this is true, if this is yours, why are you pretending to be a busboy?"

"I think I have a natural affinity for it," he said.

"You don't. You're awful. You'd have been replaced by now if it weren't for . . ." If it weren't for someone on the railroad insisting that he stay. She studied the pattern on the thick Oriental rug while the pieces fell into place. His confidence, his manners, how he knew which fork to use when they ate in the empty dining room. He was what Granny Laura would call *quality*, and he'd been lowering himself to her level in an insulting charade. "You still haven't told me why. Why would you work as a busboy when you don't need a job?"

"That's not true. Everyone needs a job. My family believes in the virtue of hard work. It might be a different kind of work than a busboy's, but you'll find no sluggards being cosseted." He took a chair opposite the sofa. "I didn't take this position as a lark. I took it to investigate, and you'd be surprised by what I found."

"Smugglers in the warehouse?" she asked.

"And a woman I admire immensely."

Willow picked up the sofa pillow and hugged it to her chest. "If I'd known what you are, I wouldn't have presumed . . ."

"Presumed what?" He was watching her again with that patient intensity that urged her to share everything.

"I would've been more sensible. How ridiculous I look—talking about you in the dormitory, putting on airs, praying that you would notice me." She wished the pillow was bigger so it hid more of her dress. "I serve people dinner. You . . . I don't know what you do, but I know what you are." She tossed the pillow aside. "Don't worry about me. If I was part of your investigation, I understand. You aren't obligated—"

He left the chair to sit by her on the sofa. "Willow, it's going to take time for you to trust me after what we've been through—time for you to feel confident that you know me—but I believe once you *do* know me, you'll find we have more in common than you might imagine."

When had the train stopped moving? Her pulse jumped when he took her hand.

"Courting as a busboy is not convenient," he said. "I look forward to the freedom allotted me when my mission is finished."

Willow swallowed the lump in her throat. "What's your name?"

"You've been calling me by my name since we met, but Graham is my given name, not my surname."

"I didn't care much for the name Buck," she said. "Graham what?"

His eyes sparkled with orneriness. "You didn't like Buck? And I thought I was being clever. Well, Graham is enough for now. I don't want you to have your head turned and forget your friend the busboy, because he's counting on your company for the foreseeable future."

How was it possible? She should be rejoicing. Graham was safe and healthy—that had been her first concern. And against all odds, he'd found something special in her. But would Graham's world be kind to her? Would a relationship with him take her away from her family?

The train whistle sounded. "We're moving," Willow said. "Where are you going, anyway? How did our busboy get time away?"

"The official story is that I require time at home with my family to recuperate from my injury. In reality, I'm going with you."

"To my grandma's ranch?" Willow dropped against the sofa's back. "Why?"

"I'm not sure, but those are my instructions." He must have noticed her concern. "Don't worry," he said. "I'll be on my best behavior."

Willow took another long look at their joined hands and sighed. He might behave, but she could guarantee that her cousins would not.

Chapter Eight

Willow had looked forward to setting aside the worries of Emporia. She'd get the comforting attention of her grandmother, ease her fears about leaving her mother in her sister's young hands, and maybe, just maybe, gossip with her cousins about the handsome busboy who'd been making eyes at her back in Emporia.

Instead, the handsome busboy wasn't a busboy, and he was with her. There'd be no chance to prepare her family, no chance to explain to them why she was traveling with a man, and she wasn't sure how to warn Graham about the ordeal he would be facing. None of her cousins had yet to show up at the family place with a beau or sweetheart. Any single man showing up with one of the Kentworth cousins would be submitted to a vigorous evaluation, and as luck would have it, she would be the first. She hadn't counted on this complication.

Thankfully, Graham had hired a driver to take them to Granny Laura's ranch so that Willow didn't have to beg a ride from a neighbor. Neighbors were few this far out of town, and Granny's land covered a fair piece of real estate. Graham raised an eyebrow when she stopped the wagon in the middle of the road and asked him to get out.

"We can cut ten minutes off our time if we cut across to that tree." The secret tree was famous in the lore of the cousins. Any secret told while touching the trunk could never be revealed. If you told, the tree would pull up its roots and snatch you out of your bed, never to be seen again. Or that was what her cousin Finn had told them.

"Whatever you say," Graham said.

Willow tried to calm herself while he paid the driver. Her family loved one another. The problem was that they had unique ways of showing that love.

Calista's sister Evangelina was the first to spot them coming through the pasture. She stood between rows of strawberry plants with a basket on her hip. She waved, shaded her eyes to take another look, then shouted toward the barn. Amos jogged out, holding a pitchfork. Willow heard Graham chuckle just before he took her hand.

"What are you doing?" she gasped. "They can see us."

"I want my intentions clear from the beginning," he said.

"No need," Willow answered. "They'll assume your intentions without any word or sign."

But the gesture wasn't lost on Amos. He stabbed the pitchfork into the ground and cupped his mouth to holler at the house.

By the time Willow and Graham had crossed the pasture, the long porch of Granny's house was full of Willow's blood kin, plus a few aunts and uncles who had married into the family.

"Goodness gracious." Graham dropped her hand to adjust his tie. "I feel ill-prepared."

"There's no way to prepare. Just endure. We can catch the train tonight if we survive," she said. "Just keep in mind that the less they know about you, the better."

He laughed again. Really, he didn't understand the risk. One misstatement, and Willow would be teased about it for the rest of her life. She searched the crowd. Corban and Hank were putting their dark heads together, probably debating who should be the first to dunk Graham in the horse trough.

Instead of keeping a low profile as she'd advised, Graham started with a booming announcement.

"Greetings, family of Miss Kentworth," he announced. It was the head injury. That must be why he was acting so recklessly. "I apologize for showing up uninvited, but in my eagerness to meet you, I wasn't able to secure an invitation earlier. My name is Graham Buchanan, and I'm pleased to make your acquaintance."

"Buchanan?" Corban steadied himself on his cousin Hank's flannel-clad shoulder, then straightened his suit. To Willow's untrained eye, it could have been sewn by the same tailor Graham utilized. The York cousins—Corban, Evangelina, and Calista—were city folks who never lacked for money, which was why Willow was surprised to see Corban squirm. "Mr. Graham Buchanan?" Corban stepped out of the family pack and offered his hand. "It's a pleasure to meet you, sir. What brings you to the ranch?"

Willow gaped at Graham in shock. "Did you say Graham *Buchanan*? Why didn't you tell me?"

Before Graham could answer, a silver-haired lady took Corban by his fine collar and moved him aside. She looked Graham over with one sharp, black eyebrow tented. What did Graham think of Granny Laura, wearing her leather chaps and dusty Boss of the Plains hat? More importantly, what did Granny Laura think of Graham?

"I suppose you're one of the railroad family," Granny Laura said.

"Yes, ma'am. Faustus Buchanan is my father."

Granny Laura looked him up and down. "As soon as I'm finished saying howdy to my granddaughter, I want to have a talk with you. What you're charging to ship cattle amounts to nothing less than extortion."

Willow tensed. Biting her lip, she shot a look at Graham, but Graham must have had experience dealing with cattle barons.

"I appreciate your opinion, ma'am," he said. "I'm available to discuss business at your convenience, after you complete your grandmothering."

Granny nodded her approval. The next thing Willow knew, she was getting one of those hugs that was both strong and soft at the same time. With their own mother's health being fragile, her grandmother had been the anchor for Willow and Olive. But Granny was the anchor for all the cousins, and the aunts and uncles. There wasn't a corner of Jasper County that didn't feel her influence. But right now, Willow had what she wanted: love from her grandmother. And she knew everything would be okay. She wasn't alone in her concern for her mother, and she wasn't alone as long as all the people watching from the porch still cared enough to be nosy.

After that it was one long series of introductions—Uncle Bill was out working the farm, but two of his three children, Amos and Maisie, had been given the day off from their chores when the other cousins came to town. Willow was disappointed to hear that her mother had a doctor's appointment in Springfield and her father had taken her, but at least Olive had made it. And then there was Aunt Pauline York, the youngest of Granny Laura's children and mother of Corban, Evangelina, and Calista. Of their second cousins from down the road, only Hank had made it up off their river-bottom farms. Willow feared that Graham would be overwhelmed. He seemed to relish the chaos, however. He might even be learning names.

Aunt Pauline took Willow by the arm, her gathered silk sleeves waving like hankies at a tent meeting. "I'd be remiss not to mention that I'm astonished by your escort. A Buchanan?

Astonished! And I won't fail to tell my brother exactly what a catch you've got on the line."

Willow's ears burned. She could only imagine the pain Graham's were enduring. "I haven't got him on the line, Aunt Pauline. He's not a perch." Despite her aunt's money, she'd been raised right here on Grandma's farm, and no amount of silk could obfuscate her country expressions.

"Have you heard from Calista?" Aunt Pauline asked. "Her last letter said she was nursing a schoolmate who'd had to return home to Emporia. It would've been nice if she had asked for our permission, but what do you expect from a child who runs away from finishing school before she's finished?"

"She told you she was in Emporia?" Willow didn't want to mislead her aunt, but the cousins watched out for one another. "I don't know many of the townspeople—"

"Mother!"

They turned in unison to see Calista approaching.

"You weren't distressing Willow over my absence, were you, Mother?" Calista gave her mother a hug. "I told you that everything is fine."

"How is your friend? You haven't become ill yourself, have you?" Aunt Pauline patted her daughter's forehead and smoothed her unruly brown eyebrows as Calista assured her mother that all was well. But Willow wasn't convinced.

Calista and Graham both here? Finally, Calista could answer for herself and satisfy Graham's curiosity.

Willow spotted Graham across the yard. He'd already noticed Calista, but his reaction was not what Willow expected.

<hr />

"Why did you come here? Are you going to marry Willow?" The young lady asking Graham wore cap sleeves that exposed arms muscled and capable. Her face was as direct as her questions, and if she were anything like her brother, there were more questions coming.

"Maisie, he's not going to marry Willow. We're too poor." If Graham wasn't mistaken, this was Willow's sister, Olive. She had the same fair coloring as Willow.

"Willow isn't poor. She has a good job," Maisie said.

"Corban said a waitress isn't a good job to a man who owns the railroad." Olive snagged Graham's sleeve by the elbow. She rubbed the material between her fingers, chewing on her lip. "That's a fine grain. I reckon he's richer than Uncle Richard."

"Do I pass inspection?" Graham asked.

Instead of answering, the two ladies stood side by side, arms crossed over their chests. One was sturdy, one was slight. One was dark, one was fair, but the resemblance couldn't be denied. He wished he knew what was being communicated silently between the cousins. Or maybe not.

"I agree," Willow's sister said at last. "Let's see what Evangelina says."

Here Graham thought *he* was good at intrigue. Give these ladies a few hours in Emporia, and they'd sniff out the culprits immediately. But then he saw something so ridiculous that he had to laugh. And keep laughing.

The ridiculousness wasn't in the situation. No, it made perfect sense. The ridiculousness was that he hadn't figured it out sooner. For another dark-haired cousin had appeared, and this one he'd seen before.

She had the same widow's peak as the rest of the family and the same lopsided smile—features he now recognized in Willow as a Kentworth trait. With the mysterious lady's appearance, Graham's appreciation for this family soared. If only he had a moment to tell Willow.

Before he could talk to either lady, he was challenged by Hank to arm wrestling and told he was lucky that Finn wasn't there. One of the girls from the well-to-do family told him a story about Willow crying when she learned that the eggs she was eating were baby chickens, and another asked if he had kissed her. The answer to that was no . . . not yet.

A giant bell on the fence sounded, and everyone turned toward the house. An aunt brandished a ladle and swatted two of the young men as they passed.

"Is it safe to subject a man with a recent head injury to this chaos?" he asked as he caught up with Willow.

"You were warned." Despite the scrutiny they were both under, her smile was the most genuine he'd ever seen on her.

"You love it here, don't you?"

"It's home," she said. "Every summer, Olive and I would come here to stay with Granny, along with all the other cousins. Counting one family of second cousins down the road, there's eleven of us separated by only six years."

"Good grief! It must have been a zoo when you all were younger."

"You think it's better now?"

He placed his hand on her back and guided her in. She might not know it, but nosy questions from her cousins had only solidified his intentions. He hadn't known what Willow's family would think, but if they assumed he was her suitor, he was ready to take on the role.

After getting a plate of fried chicken and beets, Graham followed Willow back outside. The older generation had chairs on the porch, the grandma wielding a fly swatter between bites, while the cousins gathered in a shady spot by the barn. He waited for Willow's directions, but when he saw the brunette from the depot standing off by herself, he knew where they were headed.

Without a word of greeting, the brunette looked at him and said, "You can't tell the family. They think I'm caring for a sick schoolmate in Emporia."

"Willow needs to know everything," he told her.

"Missing school to nurse a schoolmate?" Willow rolled her eyes. "Who would believe that?"

"Why not? Olive is missing school for your mother."

Graham sobered. How easy it was to forget the responsibilities Willow carried.

"What are the two of you not telling me?" Willow asked. "Did you know he was going to be here, Calista?"

"She did," Graham answered. "In fact, she arranged the meeting."

"What? How?" Willow asked. "Why would Calista be talking to you?"

The twinkle in Calista's eye challenged him to tell. So he did.

"Your cousin is a Pinkerton detective hired by my family. I didn't realize it until I saw her here, but it all makes sense now. It was important that we meet, and she thought of a place where we'd be unobserved by the criminals in Emporia— Granny Laura's ranch."

"A detective? Calista?" Willow rolled her eyes. "She's my baby cousin. She can't be a Pinkerton."

"Says who?" Calista nearly toppled her plate in indignation. "Well, my parents would say so, but besides them?"

As charming as the cousins were, Graham had too many questions to let them go on. "You wanted to talk to me, so here I am. What have you learned?"

Calista—or Miss York, as he surmised—looked longingly at the potatoes on her plate before answering. "The state agents are correct. Someone is smuggling liquor in on the train. We've found the producer in St. Louis, and we know the saloon in Emporia gets a portion. The missing piece is the middle."

Smuggling alcohol in a dry state could mean good money for someone. Enough for them to kill if their operation was in danger.

"Why don't they bust the saloon?" he asked.

Calista gave her head a tight shake. "It appears the saloon is paying a local permit fee. Nothing short of bribery, but the Emporia police say it's the railroad at fault. They also claim the only evidence of liquor is found at the Harvey House in the mornings."

"Empty bottles dumped there every night. That keeps the attention back on the railroad and away from the saloon. But the heart of the matter is how the shipments are getting there. Who's putting them on the train in the first place?"

"We've gone over the shipment paperwork a dozen times," Calista said.

"Mr. Cecil said there aren't any crates missing," Willow offered. "We've checked."

"Do you trust Mr. Cecil?" Calista asked.

Willow looked to Graham. "I don't have any reason to suspect him or to clear him."

"We'll keep an open mind on him," Graham said. "From the railroad's end, we know the Fred Harvey Company gets all its foodstuff shipped for free, so we're very precise on what's in each shipment. If someone was sneaking in extra crates, we should know it."

"We're talking substantial bulk and weight," Calista said. "Those crates didn't just appear out of thin air. Somewhere there's a record of them."

"Don't you worry," Graham said. "We'll find it."

"I remember your last attempt." Willow reached up and smoothed the back of his head. The gesture was surprisingly intimate and welcome, until he felt the pain of the tender spot and realized she was reminding him of his accident. "Don't forget that you nearly died," she said. "Had I not looked out the window, you'd be a mile long and an eighth of an inch thick right now."

"We can't ignore what's happening," Graham said. "Our property is at stake, but more importantly, they've terrorized our workers. When my employees are assaulted, I'm going to hunt down the people who did it."

"I'll go to St. Louis," Calista said, "and follow a shipment from the distillery to see how it gets on the train. You keep watching from your end. The important thing is to figure out who's falsifying the documents or how they're hauling crates away without it showing up in inventory. Don't force a confrontation. These men are ruthless."

"I wish the two of you weren't involved," Willow said.

Graham was captured in her gaze. He wasn't in a hurry to get another knot on his noggin, but the fact that his injury distressed her gave him more reason for caution.

"Willow, Aunt Laura wants to talk to you." The boy named Hank looked to be around seventeen. His hair was as dark as Willow's was fair, but he had the same widow's peak.

"You'll take care of Graham until I get back?" Willow asked Calista. "I don't trust . . . well, I don't trust any of y'all."

Calista merely smiled. As Willow left, Calista crossed her arms over her chest. "I could warn you again about the viciousness of these smugglers, but that's nothing compared to the danger before you." She cleared her throat before continuing. "I know your type and how they like to impress sweet girls from poor families. While Willow might not have much money, she isn't as vulnerable as you might think. All the money in the world couldn't protect you from her kinfolk if you disgrace her."

Was Miss Calista York threatening him? Yes, she was. And Graham rather enjoyed the challenge. "I desire nothing more than to honor your cousin," he said. "My family is not so far removed from our beginnings that we judge people based on their money. We remember that wealth is no measure of a person's worth or goodness. Miss Kentworth has an abundance of both."

"So you say. You might be my employer, Mr. Buchanan, but don't make the mistake of thinking that gives you privileges with Willow. You have to prove yourself to be admitted into this family, just like any other man."

To tell the truth, her family's protectiveness only raised Willow in his esteem. There must be something special about a lady so loved by her family. And it didn't take a genius to realize that all the harassment and teasing they'd subjected her to was love.

This wouldn't be his last visit to the Kentworth ranch. Of that he was sure.

Chapter Nine

Back at the Harvey House, Willow balanced a tray of ice cream against her shoulder.

Her trip to Granny Laura's hadn't been what she'd expected. Instead of spending time with her mother, she hadn't seen her parents at all. Instead of resting with her family, she'd been thrust into explaining the presence of a man she barely knew. After his consultation with Calista at the ranch, Graham had made his hurried farewells and left Willow to travel back alone the next morning. She understood the necessity. He was an important man on important business. But she did wish that he would invite her into his confidence more. Instead, she was left bombarded with questions by her family about a man whose name she'd only learned hours before.

And now how was she to act? After seeing him as he really was, it felt dishonest to pretend he was a busboy. Graham bewildered her. So charming, so attentive. She admired everything she knew about him. She only wished he would let her know more. If it hadn't been for the coincidence that her cousin worked for his family, she still wouldn't know who he was or why he was in Emporia.

"Excuse me, ma'am?" An adolescent girl pushed her bowl of ice cream to the center of the table. "My ice cream is melted."

Sure enough, the mound of ice cream was half the normal size and mostly hidden by the soupy cream in which it was swimming.

"My apologies," Willow said. "I'll return with another bowl." She plucked the bowl off the table and returned it to the tray.

"Mine is melted as well," said the younger sister of the girl.

Willow scanned the table. Had the ice creams been taken out of the ice house too early? "I'm going to check in the kitchen to see if we can offer you some cake," she said, fearing there might not be enough for her whole table, although some of the guests were slurping up the sweet cream without any concern over whether it was solid.

She glided past several tables of patrons to the kitchen. Graham was at the sink where she expected him with his sleeves rolled and his arms in the sudsy water. Her tray clattered on the metal top of the workstation.

"I need eight desserts for my table," she said to Mrs. Sykes. "The ice cream was melted."

Mrs. Sykes pointed at a cook, who raced to the pie keep. Graham managed a wink while she waited for her tray to be loaded. Her lips tightened. No one was to know that she and Graham were courting, much less that they had traveled together. The only thing she knew to do was put her head down and focus on her work.

By the time the meal was finished and the train had pulled out of the station, Graham had made several attempts to get her attention. Etta Mae had stopped him to ask how he felt and if the knot on his head was going down. He lingered by Willow's station, and even though the conversation was between him and Etta Mae, his eyes never left Willow as she cleared the table.

After he left, Etta Mae fanned her face with a napkin. "My lands, I hope I find a man as crazy about me as Buck is about you."

"He's just friendly," Willow said.

"I wouldn't be so sure about that. Seems to me that he's cautious, but those are the ones who surprise you. You wait and see. Suddenly he'll be professing his love to you, and you won't know where it came from."

Willow suppressed a smile. If only Etta Mae knew that her prediction had already come true.

"Miss Kentworth." Mrs. Sykes had come to her table. "Did you satisfy our customers in regard to their desserts?"

"Yes, ma'am. Instead of going after more ice cream, I served them pecan pie instead. It seemed a quicker solution."

"But not a permanent solution. When you're finished cleaning your station, you should see if all the ice cream is ruined or if we have some to serve for dinner."

"Yes, ma'am."

How could she focus on her tasks when Graham was so near? He'd heard every word, and soon after Mrs. Sykes had gone, he found his chance to speak with her.

"You can't go to the warehouse by yourself. I'm going with you. You'll hear my signal when I'm ready."

Feeling Etta Mae's eyes on her, Willow nodded discreetly, then loaded her stack of dirty plates into Graham's basin. For a lady who never slowed down, never cut corners, and never did anything less than her best, waiting for Graham to finish his kitchen work was excruciating. Her table had been reset with clean linens, goblets, plates, and silverware. She fiddled with the flowers in the vase, knowing that Mrs. Sykes was probably wondering why she hadn't gone to the ice house yet. Finally, at a whistled tune from Graham, she knew he was free to accompany her. Giving the lilies a decisive turn, she untied her apron and headed through the kitchen and out the back door.

"I count myself fortunate." He didn't take her hand but walked so close that his arm brushed against hers. "Even though I can't speak to you as much as I'd wish, you're never far from me."

"It's torture for me," Willow said. "I wish . . . well, I don't want you to think I'm complaining."

Graham turned to face her. "Never be afraid to talk to me," he said. Then, with a smile, he added, "Unless Mrs. Sykes is nearby. Then you might want to wait."

"Maybe it's the situation that prevents you from being forthright, but it puts me at a disadvantage not to know about you. Simple things. Things a lady should know about her man."

"Things like what?"

"Would it have hurt you to tell me you were one of the Buchanans before we got to my grandma's house?"

His eyes slid halfway closed. "I apologize. I was going to tell you, but we never got back on the subject. Besides, just finding out that I wasn't a busboy seemed like enough information at the time."

"No." She was walking faster and faster. "If we're sharing company, sharing our friendship and maybe more, then you don't get to make those decisions for me. I don't like having questions about you. I don't like surprises."

"My apologies. Marlowe has long chided me for not being more forthcoming. It's a bad habit. One I'll have to shed if I expect a lady to trust me." They'd reached the warehouse. Graham held open the small door to the office. "If there's something else you'd like to know . . ."

"My family, my mother. I took this job to help them. If my employment is jeopardized by our relationship, it could cost them."

"Right here, right now," Graham said, "I assume responsibility for any financial hardship that an alliance with me might bring to your family."

"I didn't say anything about an alliance. I meant sneaking off like this with you—"

Willow suddenly realized how quiet the office they'd entered was. The foreman's pen had paused over his ledger book. Two warehouse men standing by the water pail were listening.

"Gentlemen," Graham said, "we've come to get some food out of the ice house."

He'd slipped into his more authoritative voice, too grand for a busboy. And now she knew why it was so easy for him to assume control. But considering that these men could be the ones who left Graham on the tracks to die, she didn't mind if they thought he was condescending.

"Go on through," the foreman said. "Jake, go with them and load whatever they need."

Ignoring the boy following them, Graham said, "I hope your trip home was pleasant, even if it was alone."

"You shouldn't have gotten me a private car. That was excessive."

"I was hoping to make up for my absence. Did it?"

Her cheeks warmed as she ducked her head. "No. I still would've rather had you."

"Oh, love, that's the nicest thing—" He pecked a kiss on her cheek so quickly, she couldn't quite believe it had happened.

The ice house was really a room in the warehouse. Built of thick logs and enforced by plaster, it was tucked into the corner. It made sense to keep it out of the sun, but it also gave it more protection being behind the locked doors of the warehouse, or so Willow had thought until recent events.

Before she opened the latch, she noticed the water seeping out from under the door. Graham didn't seem to notice but was instead sizing up their escort, refusing to go into the little room until the boy went first.

When Willow had been in the ice house before, blocks of ice were stacked to the ceiling and packed in sawdust. This time there were only a few along the opposite wall. As she stepped closer to the blocks, she could feel the cold radiating off them, but it didn't feel cold enough. If the food was supposed to be kept frozen, she'd expect it to be at least as cold as a winter's day. It wasn't.

She lifted a package labeled *mutton*. The butcher paper sagged soggily. "It's thawed," she said, then turned to the boy. "Is this the only cold storage?"

"Yes, ma'am."

"Is it usually this empty?"

The boy's eyes darted to the side. "There's ice. It's not empty."

"Can they serve the meat, or is it ruined?" Graham asked.

"It depends how long it's been thawed. Shipments come daily, so it's probably fresh enough." But having an ice house that couldn't keep the ice frozen meant something was wrong. "This means there won't be ice cream for dessert, though, and we'll soon run out of ice for the tea."

Graham's eyes narrowed. "Stick with me," he said as he strode out of the ice house and into the foreman's office. "Where do you keep your inventory list?" He would have made an intimidating figure had it not been for the white apron he wore.

"Is there a problem?" the foreman asked.

"I'd like to compare what you have with Mr. Cecil's books."

"Listen, kid. I don't answer to busboys. If Mr. Cecil has a question, send him to talk to me."

Everyone in the office waited as Graham weighed his options, but only Willow knew that he had more options than they could imagine. "I'll speak to Mr. Cecil," he said at last. "Your assistance was appreciated."

Willow hoped he didn't hear their snickering at his proper reply. She tried to keep her dignified, Harvey-trained carriage as she kept up with him but soon gave up and jogged a few steps.

"Mr. Cecil will order more ice," she said. "It's an easy fix, but I can't believe they let it get that low."

Graham plowed ahead, single-focused, ready to burst through

the back door to the kitchen, until she caught his sleeve and yanked him to a stop.

"You're doing it again," she said.

"What?" His eyes focused as if seeing her for the first time since they'd entered the warehouse.

"Dragging me along without explaining anything."

"It's only a theory, and that's why I hesitate to share it. I might be wrong."

"I want to know what you're thinking, even if you aren't sure," she said.

"Then here's what I'm thinking. Do blocks of ice go on the inventory list?"

Willow scratched the back of her hand. "A couple that are used for drinks might, but the others are left in the ice house until they melt, so probably not."

"Yet they're the same size as crates. What if our smugglers shipped a few crates instead of ice blocks? They wouldn't show up on the inventory, and until the ice house got warm, no one would notice." He waited for a wagon to pass before he continued. "What we need to do is catch the next shipment coming in and look for extra crates being labeled as ice."

"Don't forget that someone tried to kill you," Willow said. "Your family connections won't help you if you're dead."

"Neither will yours," he said. "I think it's best if I talk to Mr. Cecil alone. You take care of your customers and pretend like you know nothing about the issue. If something happens to me, get on the wire and find Marlowe."

"Why would your brother listen to me?"

"Because he knows I love you."

Willow felt the rush of exhilaration that usually came with the incoming train. A flicker of uncertainty crossed Graham's face. She slid her hand into his, and the tight creases around his eyes eased.

"I love you," he said, his enunciation never more perfect. "Whatever happens in there, I want to be with you. I might not be able to keep this dishwashing job forever, but surely we can find other ways to be together."

She didn't know what to do with the admiration in his eyes. She ducked her head, but she wasn't running away. Instead, she leaned against his arm. "As long as you pull your load," she said. "I can't support another hungry mouth on my salary."

He laughed and kissed her again, this time on the forehead. "Well, now that's settled."

She felt anything but settled. "Be careful," she said. "And if you're wondering, I would wager that my family knows that I love you too."

"I'm glad you got that straightened out before I had to go back to the ranch." His eyes drifted toward her lips, but then he blinked hard. "Gotta go before I forget what I'm about." He opened the door to the kitchen and held it open as she passed.

Work. Customers. It was hard to remember that she had a job to do. All she wanted was to go somewhere quiet and relive the moment over and over. Soon, she promised herself. And there would be more moments to come.

A common man would decide that pursuing his ladylove was more pleasurable than questioning a restaurant manager. A rich man could decide to let someone else do the hard work, and take up the courting immediately. But Graham believed in seeing things through. The same strength of character that meant he wouldn't stop until the smugglers had been caught meant that once the way was free to secure Willow's hand, he'd pursue that just as vigorously.

Mr. Cecil wasn't in the kitchen. The chef scowled at Graham and demanded to know where he'd been.

"At the ice house," Graham responded. "Haven't you noticed that your frozen goods haven't been properly stored?"

From the chef's recital of all the complaints he'd made, Graham didn't think it likely he was involved. Not if he'd called that much attention to the issue. With the chef's permission, Graham headed to Cecil's office.

Mrs. Sykes sat across the desk from Mr. Cecil, her back to the door. "She's the best we have," she said, "but I'm afraid you're right. Ever since he arrived, her attention to detail has suffered. She can't seem to focus when he's around. One of them must go, and I'd hate to lose her."

Graham lowered his head and reminded himself to look like a contrite busboy, not a man in love, hearing how his sweetheart was besotted with him. She couldn't concentrate when he was around? Thank goodness.

"There you are, Graham. We've been discussing your performance." Cecil motioned him inside the office. Mrs. Sykes gave him a sad smile as he entered. "While we regret the accident that befell you," Mr. Cecil said, "it wouldn't have happened had you observed curfew, as is required."

"I paid dearly for that mistake," Graham said. "But I learned something valuable today. The goods shipped in the refrigerated car are not being cared for in the warehouse. The ice house barely has any ice at all."

"That is no longer your concern." Mr. Cecil opened a drawer in the desk and pulled out a check register. "Here are your last wages plus a stipend to get you back home. Please get your things from your room and leave your uniform on the bed."

"Aren't you curious where the ice went?" Graham asked. "You know there are people taking things from the warehouse at night. Here's something that's missing."

"Ice bandits?" Cecil rubbed his domed forehead. "Your account of thieves is not borne out in the record. I checked the inventory. You should've been more concerned about your work in the kitchen, not outside. There's nothing missing from the warehouse."

Nothing missing besides some ice. Miss York had been right. Better to keep up the pretense than announce who he was and have all the bad guys scramble before he had a chance to catch them.

He lowered his head. "If you don't mind, I'd like to bid farewell to my friends."

Mrs. Sykes lifted her hand in warning. "Keep in mind that your friend shows promise here at the Harvey House. I hope you care enough about her future that you won't do anything to hurt her prospects as a waitress."

"I would do nothing to hurt her prospects," he said. Then, with a tap on his forehead, he waltzed out of the office to find her.

Willow had been watching for him. Instead of loading her tray, she lingered by her table, which was precisely set for the four o'clock train. Being dismissed didn't temper his joy at seeing her. The furrows in her brow smoothed at his happy expression.

"Did he listen to you?" she asked.

"Hardly. Mr. Cecil dismissed me. I have to get my things and go."

Her eyes widened. "That's awful."

"My brother was right. I'll never amount to anything." He grinned. "Your cousin was also right. I'm not convinced we can trust anyone here. I'm going to buy a ticket to Kansas City, but I won't get on the train. Instead I'll hide and wait to check out the next shipment that comes in on the refrigerator car. In the meantime, you keep my cover here. If anyone learns what I was up to, they'll bail, and we need to know who all was involved." He noticed Willow's friends had worked their way closer while pretending to count the stemware on the tables.

"They're going to ask me what you said," Willow whispered. "What should I tell them?"

"Tell them I promised to come back and marry you as soon as I find the means to support you."

"That's what you told me? And how did I answer you?"

"Answer the marriage question? Sweetheart, that was settled the moment we laid eyes on each other." He winked. "I'll come back for you soon, and when I do, be ready for a kiss that'll knock you off the rails."

Her eyes lowered, and her lashes fluttered against her cheek. "I'll be waiting."

Why couldn't she walk out the door with him? Turn in her resignation and not return until she was Mrs. Graham Buchanan? But that wasn't the plan, and he was doing his best to keep her informed of what he was doing.

At the depot, Graham wired Marlowe and learned that the night train from Topeka would have a cold shipment on it. All he had to do was sit tight until then. At the saloon across the tracks, Graham hired a private room and changed into a thrifty store-bought suit. It was probably nicer than Buck the busboy would have owned, but not so nice as to attract attention. When he asked for a strong drink at the bar, he was piously reminded that liquor was illegal. He didn't argue but returned to his room and stayed out of the way and out of sight until the refrigerator car pulled into the station that night.

Graham had to take a look before the freight men moved anything. Running to the end of the train from the saloon side with his lantern, he was the first to reach the car. He unlocked the latch and shoved open the rolling door. Shivering inside his thin suit coat, Graham stood among the crates and the sawdust-packed blocks of ice—the perfect hiding place for a crate that could be shipped off the books.

Wishing for gloves, he went to the first stack of ice blocks and swept his hand along the face of the block. His fingers touched ice, bumpy and gritty from the sawdust, but ice. He worked through the car, touching every block, but with each he found the same thing. There were no wooden crates hidden in the sawdust. Nothing disguising itself as a block of ice.

Were the cold goods truly cold enough? Graham set down the lantern and slapped his hands against his legs to work some warmth back into them before reaching across a rack and pressing into one of the ham hocks that lay in a row along the side of the railroad car. It was firm and cold. The canisters carrying ice cream were probably frozen too. No water from melting on this floor. It was cold enough.

He'd bent to pick up his lantern when he saw something strange. Where he'd brushed against the corner of one of the ice blocks, there was a shadow visible inside the glossy exterior. He felt his face scrunch up. What was making that dark spot where the lantern light couldn't come through?

Working quickly, he swept away all the sawdust he could knock from the ice and retreated a few steps so that the blocks were between him and the lantern. Sure enough, there was an unmistakable block within the block of ice. Looking about him, he grabbed a giant pair of ice tongs and chipped away at the corner of the block. He hadn't removed much before the whole face of the ice block shattered and fell to the ground, and a stout, smaller crate was revealed. The ice surrounding the crate was rough, like it had been hewn out to make room, then the face of the block reattached. Graham tried to pry the crate out of the ice, but it was no use. Undoubtedly the smugglers let it melt away, and then they had their prize.

He only wished Willow could have been there to see it. Now he just needed to find a railroad man that he trusted.

The big door of the car rumbled in its tracks, then slammed

closed with a crash. Graham spun around. Why would they close the door? They hadn't unloaded the shipment yet.

He pushed against the door, but it wouldn't budge. Protecting his hands from the cold metal wall, he rammed his shoulder against the door, but it wasn't just stuck, it was locked. Taking the lantern, he held it up to see if there were any release levers on the inside, but there weren't. He was caught. Someone had seen him and trapped him.

What did they have in mind, now that they'd caught him? He could think of too many possibilities, but being unhooked from the train was one that hadn't occurred to him until he heard the other cars leaving without him.

Chapter Ten

"Willow, wake up."

She'd been in a clearing on the side of the mountain with Graham. He was telling her that he loved her. He was holding her hand while feeding her strawberries, talking about melted ice cream, and washing dishes in a tailored suit. She blinked and turned her face away from the lantern that blinded her.

"Who is it?" she asked.

"It's Mrs. Sykes. You have an urgent note from the office down the line."

Willow sat up and rubbed her eyes. She'd rather be basking with Graham in the sun-drenched mountains, but the message sounded foreboding. So was Mrs. Sykes, even in her robe and nightcap. Was it Granny? Mother? Willow prayed everything was alright at home.

She took the unsealed envelope and read its contents.

Our friend has vanished along with the freezer car from Topeka. Search with caution. HIOTW.

Graham was gone? Was that what Calista was saying? The acronym was one they'd used on the ranch whenever one of the cousins was in trouble. Help might be on the way, but Calista was afraid it wouldn't arrive soon enough, or else she wouldn't have contacted Willow.

She turned to see Mrs. Sykes still waiting in the doorway. Reading her thoughts, Mrs. Sykes said, "You know the most grievous offense a Harvey Girl can make is to leave her room at night."

Willow looked at the darkness past her window. Somewhere out there, Graham needed help. There was no time to waste. "I'm sorry," she said. "I don't have a choice."

"You always have a choice," Mrs. Sykes said. Then, with a look at Billie, who was sleeping soundly, she added, "Willow, I don't know what you've gotten yourself into, but my intuition tells me that there's more at stake than I know."

Willow blew out a chestful of anxious air. Mrs. Sykes had always been a smart manager. Why should Willow be surprised she was a smart friend? "Thank you. You won't be disappointed in me."

"Be careful, child. If you're caught, I'll do my best to cover for you." And then she left to let Willow get dressed.

When Willow reached the ground floor, she was surprised to see light coming from beneath the door to the kitchen. Had the cooks already started the baking? She leaned against the swinging door just enough to see in. Strangers. No, wait, they were from the warehouse. She remembered the foreman. And there was Mr. Cecil too. Had Graham finally convinced them that there was illegal activity happening under their noses?

"He's trapped, but we have to be careful how we proceed." Mr. Cecil folded his silk handkerchief and eased it into his breast pocket. "Someone in the company is looking out for him. It's public knowledge that he was dismissed yesterday, so if it can be made to look like he returned for revenge . . . maybe one of your boys acted in self-defense?"

"He should've left like the rest of them," the foreman said. "Especially after being left to die on the tracks. Who would've thought he valued his job as a busboy more than his life?"

"It'll be light soon. We need to get him before the town wakes," Cecil said. "The question is, where do we want to 'find' him?"

Willow couldn't breathe. Her heart hammered in her chest as she floated away from the door. She had to get to Graham first, but where was he? She made it to the front door of the restaurant, and once out the door, she ran toward the depot and the warehouses that lined the tracks.

Cecil had said Graham was trapped. Did they have him in the warehouse? If so, the doors were locked and possibly guarded. She ran around the building, looking for an open window, an unlocked door, some way inside. Then she saw the refrigerated car on the spare track.

Calista had said that the refrigerated car hadn't made it to the next stop. Willow was familiar with the routines of the shipments, but she'd never seen an ice car left in Emporia. The ice cars had urgent shipments for every Harvey House down the line. They couldn't be side-railed.

Looking both ways, she hopped down onto the tracks and ran across the rails until she reached the car. There weren't locks on the ice cars, just a heavy lever to lift out of its traces and swing open. She wedged her hands in the crack and pulled for all she was worth. Immediately the cold air washed over her—so much colder than the ice house had been the day before. The moonlight illuminated crates stacked to the ceiling, but no Graham rushing out to thank her for liberating him.

Her shoulders slumped. She had to find him, and she was running out of time. She spun around and was about to close the door when she heard his voice.

"Willow? Wait!" Graham stepped out from between a stack of ice blocks. His nose and cheeks were red, his fingers curved. "I was hiding, hoping to surprise whoever had locked me in here."

"We have to go. They're coming after you."

"Who?"

"No time. You need to hide. Where can we go?"

"The depot," he said. "I know a secret way to get in."

She took his hand, surprised by how cold it was, and ran with him to the depot. The building was locked tight, but Graham picked up a rock and threw it through the glass of the ticket window.

"You know how to get in?" Her voice shook. "What kind of secret is that?"

"It's railroad property," he said. "They'll forgive me."

He reached between the bars of the window and strained to grab the door handle from the inside. On the outside, Willow wiggled the knob until Graham got the lock released, and then it fell open. They both ran inside, and Graham locked the door behind them.

"Won't they see the broken glass?" she asked.

"We're going to lock ourselves in the telegraph office," he said. "By the time they find us, we will have signaled for help." He held the door to the little office open and turned the lock after she entered. Removing the cover off the dormant telegraph machine, he said, "I don't know the whole alphabet, but I do know how to signal my father's office."

"It was Mr. Cecil," she said as he clacked on the telegraph key. "He and the warehouse foreman are conspirators. I heard him in the kitchen planning your disappearance. He's probably the one who knocked you out last time. He knew you were prying and followed you." She frowned as Graham shivered. "How long were you locked in that car? You must be freezing."

"Come here and warm me up." He turned from the machine and held out his arms.

Willow's feet carried her there without hesitation. After the scare of losing him, she needed the reassurance that he was with her and that his feelings hadn't changed. The cold seeped from his clothes, and she could feel his hands like ice on her back, but she was willing to share her warmth.

"This is perfect," he said. "We just need to move over to the window so we can see who comes to the cold car. That will be important for the inquiry."

With the sun rising, the lone car was visible, as were the two men driving a wagon to it. Willow buried her head in Graham's chest when she saw the pickax that one of the men carried to the door of the car. Graham was warming up, but she felt colder and colder.

"You've saved my life twice now," he said.

"I don't want to talk about it."

"What should we talk about?" He ran his hand over her unbound hair.

"I didn't have time to put it up," she said. "Getting to you was more important. I couldn't fail."

"And you didn't fail. You won. We both won. Now it's time to celebrate."

Willow was on the verge of asking what kind of celebration could take place in a dark office when Graham's cold hand touched her cheek. Then his warm lips met hers, just as he'd promised. And just as he'd promised, his strong, thorough kisses made her feel like she'd jumped the track and was careening through unexplored territory. But she wasn't afraid. She had someone safe with her.

It was the state agents along with a man Graham introduced as his brother who found them in the locked room. By that time, Graham was thoroughly warm, and by that time, Willow wasn't sure she wanted to leave the office after all. She couldn't think of another place she'd rather be.

Epilogue

"Excuse me, ma'am. It appears you've dropped your handkerchief."

Handkerchief? All Willow was carrying was her bride's bouquet as she and Graham made their way to the private railroad car that would be their home for their transcontinental honeymoon. Her trunks, filled with a new trousseau and sentimental items from home, had been loaded for her, but she recognized her cousin's voice and tugged on Graham's arm before he boarded the train.

"Thank you." Willow took the finely embroidered handkerchief, although she'd never seen it before. Noticing several eyes following her cousin, she mimicked the polite disinterest that Calista displayed and kept her words low. "I had hoped to see you before we left. Everyone missed you at the wedding."

"I was at the wedding," Calista said. "You might not have seen me, but I was there, and it was beautiful." She shaded her eyes as she smiled up at Graham. "I want to thank your family for employing me. I hope the agency lived up to its standard."

"Above and beyond." Graham cut Willow a side glance that

set her heart galloping. "I'd say that the result was very satis-
factory."

"Are you headed home?" Willow asked.

"I'm Chicago-bound to get my next assignment. I don't
know what it is yet, but that's how the Pinkerton office prefers
it." Her eyes embraced Willow, even though she didn't move
an inch closer. "Take care, Mrs. Buchanan. Perhaps our paths
will cross, but I might be working in disguise and not be free
to acknowledge you."

"I understand. You be careful."

"What fun would that be?" Calista dipped her head and
strolled across the platform to another train.

"I hope she knows what she's getting into," Willow said as
Graham escorted her into their car.

"Do any of us know what we're getting into?" He dismissed
the steward as they entered their living quarters. Taking her
bouquet, he dropped it in a pitcher of water before joining her
before the picture window. "I came to catch a smuggler. Instead
I caught a wife."

From the window, she could see the Harvey House. Inside,
Billie and Etta Mae would be clearing the tables as the customers boarded the train. They might even be faced with a tall stack
of dishes to handle until they could hire another busboy.

"Don't worry," Graham said. "If you miss the restaurant, we
can always work at this one or another. Maybe tour our way
across the country to see the opening of new Harvey Houses?
We could wash dishes and serve dessert if they're shorthanded."

"That sounds like an adventure." After a childhood of duty
and cares, she couldn't believe the turn her life had taken. But
duties weren't always tiresome, and she'd continue to do her
duty no matter the circumstance. "I'm ready to follow you anywhere," she said.

The train swayed beneath her feet. The restaurant passed

out of view, but Graham was with her. Life with him would be a challenge. Along with her new husband came a new society, new rules, and new expectations.

But Willow was up to the task. Give her a chance, and she'd outperform everyone's expectations. Even her own.

Grand
Encounters

—

Jen Turano

Chapter One

"I know you mentioned you've sworn off gentlemen forever, but Mr. Tall, Dark, and—need I say—Delicious is here again, and, unsurprisingly, he's sitting in your section."

Resisting the urge to look over her shoulder, Miss Myrtle Schermerhorn continued pouring coffee from the large urn into the cup she was holding, ignoring that her hand had begun shaking ever so slightly.

She didn't need to ask who Mr. Tall, Dark, and Delicious was, knowing Miss Ruthanne Hill, her fellow Harvey Girl and friend, had to be speaking about Mr. Jack Daggett.

Mr. Daggett was a frequent guest at El Tovar, and during the five months she'd been working at the hotel, she'd encountered him often, taken completely aback when he began making a habit of sitting in her section whenever he showed up to dine.

That he was tall, dark, and incredibly delicious was not in question.

Standing over six feet tall and possessed of a build that suggested he spent plenty of time engaged in physical labor, he was a man who drew attention like honey drew bees. There

271

was a ruggedness to his features that complemented his large form, and his eyes were a piercing shade of green, filled with an intelligence Myrtle hadn't neglected to notice. His hair was blackest black, occasionally worn longer than was currently fashionable, although that might have simply been because he seemed to travel often around the West, where one couldn't always expect to find the services of a barber.

Mr. Daggett was always formally dressed, wearing a jacket, waistcoat, and a tie no matter how stifling the heat of the day, which Myrtle found somewhat curious. His size suggested he was a man of labor, yet his attire suggested he was something else.

Laborer or not, Mr. Daggett wasn't a talkative man and had barely spoken to her over the past few months except to give her his order and then thank her after he was finished with his meal. With that said, though, there was something about the manner in which he watched her as she served him, something that left her feeling all sorts of fluttery inside, and something that had her reconsidering her vow of swearing off gentlemen forever.

She was not a lady who'd ever drawn such notice from a gentleman before, and even though it left her flustered at times, she found it rather delightful. She also found Mr. Daggett's notice was doing wonders for healing the embarrassment of her broken engagement the year prior, a situation that was responsible for her abandoning New York high society and heading West.

"He's brought someone with him today, someone just as delicious. I think they might be related," Ruthanne said.

Shaking herself from her thoughts, Myrtle set aside the cup that was now filled beyond the brim and dripping everywhere, taking a second to mop up the spill before she lifted her head, finding her friend peering across the dining room.

Ruthanne was all of eighteen years old, five years younger

than Myrtle. She was a lovely young lady with blond hair, a creamy complexion, and blue eyes that always held a touch of mischief. Ruthanne had been vocal from their very first meeting about why she'd joined the Harvey Girls: she wanted a reason to leave her family farm in Ohio, and she was looking for a husband—like many of the Harvey Girls were doing, Myrtle excluded.

Fighting a smile, Myrtle leaned closer to her friend. "You're more than welcome to take my table so you can meet this new man Mr. Daggett has with him."

Ruthanne's eyes widened as she returned her attention to Myrtle. "Goodness, no. Mr. Daggett scares me half to death, what with him being such an intimidating sort. Besides, he doesn't look at me like he looks at you. We Harvey Girls are expected to give our guests a pleasant experience, and his experience today would be more along the lines of *disappointing* if you don't take his order." Her lips curved. "You wouldn't want to disappoint the man now, would you?"

"I try not to disappoint any of the guests I serve at El Tovar."

Ruthanne picked up the cup of coffee she'd poured and leveled a knowing look at Myrtle. "But you don't like any of those other guests the way you like Mr. Daggett, no matter how much you may want to deny it." Not waiting for Myrtle to respond to a statement that was, concerningly, all too true, Ruthanne hurried away.

Myrtle watched as Ruthanne moved to a section situated at the back of the dining room that was a favorite section of the guests. Large windows with spotless glass flanked an enormous stone fireplace and allowed the guests unfettered views of the Grand Canyon. Those views, even with her distracted by pesky thoughts of Mr. Jack Daggett, never failed to take Myrtle's breath away.

There was something mesmerizing about the Grand Canyon.

It was a place Myrtle had never imagined visiting, the starkness and beauty of the vast land at distinct odds from the world she'd grown up in—New York City. In New York, one traveled to Central Park to escape the noise and bustle of everyday life. But in Arizona, one had only to step outside to discover a sense of peace. The varied colors of the canyon lent the area a tranquil air, and the lack of moisture in the air was so different from the humidity that blanketed New York—which she didn't miss in the least.

"Are you done with the coffee urn, Myrtle?"

Realizing that she'd completely forgotten she was supposed to be serving one of her guests a fresh cup of coffee, and that she'd been blocking other Harvey Girls from using the coffee urn in the process, Myrtle pushed her thoughts aside. Turning, she discovered Miss Opal Chapman, an amusing young woman who was always quick to share a laugh or a helping hand, standing behind her, an empty coffee cup in her hand.

"Forgive me, Opal. I fear I was woolgathering."

Opal's green eyes twinkled. "I imagine you were, what with Mr. Daggett showing up for the third time this week and sitting in your section again."

"You've noticed how often Mr. Daggett has dined here this week?"

"'Course I have, as have all the other girls." Opal sent Myrtle a wink. "We think he's sweet on you. We've also taken to marking down on the calendar dates we think he'll finally get up the nerve to ask you to dinner."

"You think he's sweet on me?"

Opal bobbed her head, sending the large white bow attached to her dark hair bobbing as well. "I do. But don't just stand here, chatting with me. Mr. Daggett won't be able to get around to asking you to dinner if you don't go over and talk to him." She moved closer to Myrtle and lowered her voice. "I'd appreciate it if you could speed up his asking a bit. I've chosen today as the day he'll rustle up his nerve, and I wouldn't mind winning the prize we settled on—leaving work an hour early one day, that hour covered by other Harvey Girls."

Having no idea what to say to that, Myrtle sent Opal a weak smile before she picked up the coffee she'd poured and headed across the dining room. Taking a second once she'd delivered the coffee to ascertain that everyone at table five was happy with their meal, she drew in a breath to steady the nerves that had begun to make themselves known. Releasing that breath when she reached Mr. Daggett's table, she summoned up the bright smile Harvey Girls were expected to wear at all times when serving their many guests.

"Good afternoon, Mr. Daggett," she began pleasantly. His head jerked up and his lips twisted into what might have been an attempt at a smile, although she wasn't certain about that, because she'd never seen him smile before. In all honesty, she couldn't help but wonder if he was actually grimacing at her. If he was grimacing, that would certainly imply he wasn't sweet on her at all, which would then reaffirm her decision that men were disconcerting creatures and really not worth the trouble.

"Ah, you must be Miss Schermerhorn," the man sitting beside Mr. Daggett said, drawing her attention. "Jack's told me all about you. I'm his younger brother, Walter. Pleased to meet you at last."

Pulling her gaze from Jack, who was now scowling at his brother, Myrtle tilted her head. "Your brother's told you all about me, Mr. Daggett?"

Walter nodded. "Indeed, but please call me Walter. With you being such good friends with Jack and all, it seems peculiar to be so formal with you."

Knowing she couldn't very well contradict Walter and tell him his brother rarely spoke to her because, well, that would

275

be rude, Myrtle smoothed a hand down the front of her stark-white apron as a flash of heat traveled up her neck to settle on her cheeks.

"You're making her uncomfortable," Jack muttered before he turned his full attention to Myrtle. His green gaze sharpened on her, which sent additional heat crawling up her neck.

When he didn't say anything else and simply continued to stare at her, Myrtle cleared her throat but was spared from having to conjure up something to break the awkward silence when Walter sat forward.

"Sure didn't mean to make you uncomfortable, Myrtle," he began, raking a hand through hair that was as dark as Jack's. "Here I've just finally gotten to meet you, and I'm not making a very good impression by bringing up matters I evidently shouldn't be bringing up." He raked his hand through his hair again. "I imagine all of you Harvey Girls like to keep your personal business personal when you're working, so I'll not say another thing about you and Jack, at least not until you get off work."

Glancing at Jack to see how he was responding to his brother's obviously misguided impression of the type of relationship they shared, she found him buried behind his menu, not paying her or his brother any mind at all.

Finding that less than helpful, she returned her attention to Walter. "Perhaps it might be for the best, Mr. Daggett, if—"

"Walter," he interrupted.

"Walter, then," she repeated, her lips curving. There was something undeniably charming about Walter Daggett, even with his entirely wrong impression of what was between her and his brother. "As I was about to say, I believe I should get your orders, because I wouldn't want you to be late for your train. We at El Tovar pride ourselves on serving four courses in thirty minutes, but that might be difficult to accomplish if

I spend half of that thirty minutes chatting instead of getting your food brought out to you."

"We're not in a hurry today," Walter said, nodding at Jack, who was still buried behind his menu. "Jack and I have decided to stay here for a few weeks. He's teaching me how to do the books, and I convinced him there was no better place to do those books than right here in the Grand Canyon." He caught Myrtle's eye. "Bookkeeping isn't the most exciting part of Daggett Industries, but my mother thinks it's a task I need to learn to help lighten Jack's load, what with how much business has grown the past few years. I imagine he's told you all about that, though, hasn't he?"

"Ah, no. He's not mentioned a word about his business."

Walter's brows drew together. "Haven't the two of you known each other for a good few months now?"

"*Know* each other might be a bit of a stretch," Myrtle admitted.

Jack suddenly lowered his menu, sent his brother a look that could only be described as glowering, then nodded to Myrtle. "I'll have the steak, medium rare, mashed potatoes, the cauliflower in cream sauce, and a cup of coffee to start. Walter will have the same."

Myrtle took the menu he all but thrust her way.

Walter shook his head. "I don't want steak. I'll have the buttered spaghetti with chicken giblets." He handed Myrtle his menu. "I also don't want coffee. A nice lemonade would be far more appealing, because the heat seems extra stifling today, no matter that everyone keeps claiming it's a dry heat here at the Grand Canyon. Apparently that's supposed to mean it's not that hot, but I'm afraid I can't agree with that nonsense."

Myrtle smiled. "I've thought the exact same thing. I'm sure a glass of our delicious lemonade will be just the tonic you need." She turned and hurried for the kitchen before Jack had an opportunity to contradict his brother, something she was certain he was longing to do, given that he'd taken to scowling at Walter again.

Blowing out a breath after she sailed through the kitchen doors, she gave the order to the cook, thanking him before heading right back into the dining room again. After checking on her other tables, she hurried to deliver Jack and Walter their drinks. She was thankful they didn't seem to expect her to engage in conversation with them, although Walter did open his mouth, only to close it a second later when the table gave a suspicious jump, rattling the cup of coffee and glass of lemonade she'd just set down.

"It's turning into a very peculiar sort of day," Myrtle muttered under her breath as she headed across the room again, keeping her smile firmly in place when a guest at table seven stopped her, complaining that his coffee wasn't hot enough. After assuring him that she'd be right back with a fresh cup, she moved to the coffee urn, wishing she'd worn her other pair of work shoes because the ones currently on her feet were beginning to pinch her toes.

"Did you find out anything about the man with Mr. Daggett?" Ruthanne asked, stealing up behind Myrtle.

"Honestly, Ruthanne, you just scared me half to death."

Ruthanne grinned. "Sorry about that, but did you find out anything about that man?"

"He's Mr. Jack Daggett's younger brother, Walter, and unlike his brother, he seems to enjoy talking. He told me that he and his brother intend to stay at El Tovar for a while, apparently so Jack can teach Walter all about bookkeeping that has evidently turned unmanageable because of all the business coming Jack's way, or something to that effect."

"Ah, so they're men of business. What type of business do you imagine they're in?"

"We didn't get that far."

"Did Mr. Jack Daggett ask you to dinner?" Opal Chapman asked, edging her way around Myrtle to get to the coffee urn Myrtle was no longer using.

"Sorry to disappoint you, Opal, but no."

"Pity," Opal muttered before she brightened. "He still has time, though. He could very well get around to it after dessert."

Before Myrtle could respond, Opal dashed away, her black skirt swishing back and forth as she balanced a full cup of coffee perfectly in her hand, not a single drop spilling to the ground even though she was moving at a remarkable rate of speed.

Ruthanne's nose wrinkled as she watched Opal all but sprint across the room. "How does she manage to move so rapidly without ending up with coffee down her front?"

"No idea." Myrtle shook her head. "I tried that last week, and thank goodness it was at the end of my shift, because my attempt at dashing and delivering coffee was not what anyone would deem a success."

"Dashing may not be your specialty, but you're very good with delivering more than one meal at a time, no matter how heavy the plates."

"As are you."

Ruthanne nodded. "True, but that's only because I grew up on a farm and am used to manual labor. I don't get the feeling you did much manual labor in your younger years."

Since Myrtle couldn't argue with that, and nor did she care to disclose that her younger years were spent attending one society event after another—those events hardly preparing her for a position as a Harvey Girl, or any position except being some gentleman's wife—she settled for sending Ruthanne a smile before she headed once again across the dining room.

After delivering the cup of hot coffee to the complaining guest, who didn't even bother to thank her, she checked on another table, then returned to the kitchen, knowing Jack's and Walter's orders would be ready.

She put the plates that were waiting for her on a tray, then moved back into the dining room, serving Jack his steak first, and then Walter his spaghetti.

"Is there anything else you need?" she asked, which had Walter clearing his throat in a rather telling manner that then led to Jack lifting his head and pinning her once again beneath a brilliant green gaze.

"Uh, right then," Jack began. He tugged on his collar as Walter muttered *Get on with it* under his breath.

"You're, ah . . . well . . . " Jack tugged on his collar again, then said something so quickly that Myrtle didn't catch it. She thought he might have mentioned *fetching*, although what he meant by that was a bit of a mystery.

"I'm sorry, I didn't quite catch that. What do you want me to fetch for you?" she asked.

Jack shot a look at Walter, who was smiling in an encouraging way. Jack narrowed his eyes before he returned his attention to Myrtle. He drew in a deep breath, drew in another, then glanced at his plate and nodded, just once. "I don't need you to fetch me anything. I was . . . ah . . . talking about the potatoes. They look very fetching today."

A second later, Walter was on his feet and striding across the room, snorts of laughter following him as Jack's lips twisted once again into what did almost seem to be a smile as he nodded to his potatoes.

Realizing he was waiting for her to make some type of response, Myrtle swallowed the unexpected bubble of amusement rising in her throat. "I suppose the potatoes are looking fetching today. They seem to have a lovely fluffiness about them."

His lips stretched into a genuine smile, one that actually showed some white teeth in the process. "They *do* look fluffy."

Because she had no idea where to take the conversation from there, a circumstance that would have appalled her former decorum instructors, Myrtle gave a bit of a curtsy and turned on her heel, telling Jack she'd check back with him after he had an opportunity to taste his *fetching* potatoes. As she all but raced away, additional amusement bubbled through her, and she barely made it into the kitchen before a laugh escaped her lips.

"Should I take that laugh to mean Mr. Daggett finally found his nerve and asked you out to dinner?"

Myrtle glanced around and found Opal and Ruthanne standing behind her, grins on their faces. Everyone else in the kitchen stopped what they were doing and turned her way, evidently wanting to hear her answer to what had seemingly turned into the question of the day.

Having never experienced the delight of being part of a close-knit group before, even as a member of New York high society, Myrtle suddenly realized that here, on the very rim of the Grand Canyon, she'd finally found her place in the world, one where people accepted her for who she really was, never comparing her to others or forming unrealistic expectations.

Growing up, she'd been included in all the right society events, but she'd never been considered a success, much to her mother's disappointment. Her mother, Cora Schermerhorn, was from one of the oldest New York families and still called herself a Knickerbocker, even though that term was not used much these days by the younger set. Cora, unfortunately, had expected all three of her daughters to take society by storm when they made their debuts. Myrtle's older sister, Helen, had done exactly that, but when Myrtle made her debut, she'd not made much of an impression on the fashionable crowd, a situation that Cora found most distressing, especially since she feared Myrtle's lack of success would affect the debut of the youngest Schermerhorn girl, Eloise. Thankfully, that had not come to pass, since Eloise was a greater sensation than Helen, although neither her older sister's nor younger sister's success in society was enough to move Myrtle from the ranks of the wallflowers and into a more appealing social standing.

Her lack of appeal had never bothered Myrtle much. She'd not entered society for the express purpose of finding a husband, since she'd had an understanding with Mr. Percy Kane for years. That understanding, which was fully supported and encouraged by their parents, centered around the notion they would wed at some point in time. And even though an official announcement had never been made about a formal engagement, everyone within society had known Myrtle and Percy were considered betrothed. That was why society turned their pity Myrtle's way after Percy had the audacity to fall head over heels in love with Miss Vivian Davis, a beautiful young lady who'd been declared the belle of the Season the moment her dainty foot stepped into Mrs. Belmont's first ball of the year.

In all honesty, Myrtle didn't blame Percy for falling in love with Miss Davis. The young lady was charming, graceful, wealthy, and did not enjoy reading—a pastime Myrtle enjoyed to the fullest but that Percy found appalling. Myrtle did, however, blame him for making her the object of whispers behind gloved hands and far too many pitying glances sent her way, that pity directly responsible for why she'd turned her back on—

"So, did he ask you to dinner?" Opal pressed, drawing Myrtle from her less-than-pleasant thoughts about Percy and his lack of gentlemanly behavior.

Smiling at Opal, who was all but bursting with excitement, Myrtle shook her head. "I'm afraid not."

"But he was smiling," Opal pointed out. "No one has ever seen Jack Daggett smile."

"And his brother left the table in an obvious attempt to give the two of you some privacy," Ruthanne added.

"I believe Walter left the table because of a bad case of hysterics, brought about by his brother claiming he found the mashed potatoes to be fetching today."

Ruthanne's nose wrinkled. "That's a strange thing to say about potatoes."

"Quite, and on that note, and before I serve up more disappointment, since nothing Mr. Jack Daggett said to me could be considered an invitation to dine, I really do need to get some pie out to one of my tables, so if you'll excuse me . . ." Myrtle picked up the tray filled with slices of pie and headed out of the kitchen, smiling as Ruthanne called after her not to lose hope and Opal reminded her to try and hurry matters along since she *had* chosen today as the day Jack would ask her out to dine.

After serving the pie to a lovely couple from Chicago who'd brought their two children on an excursion to see the West and had decided to fit in a stop at the Grand Canyon since access to the canyon was now readily accessible through the Santa Fe Railroad, Myrtle moved to Jack and Walter's table, stopping a few feet away when she realized the two men were engaged in an animated exchange.

Jack was shaking his head while Walter was shaking a finger his brother's way, saying something about a "complete disaster" and then following that up with "what were you thinking?" before launching into another bit about "lost your mind."

Deciding to check back with them in a few minutes because it didn't appear to be a conversation that wanted interrupting, Myrtle was just about to turn when Jack looked up, stopped shaking his head, then nodded to his brother, who immediately turned to her and smiled.

"Ah, Myrtle. Been standing there long?" Walter asked, blinking far-too-innocent eyes back at her.

"Not really, although I was contemplating coming back later, since the two of you were speaking so earnestly to each other."

Walter gave a wave of a hand. "We were just discussing, ah . . . the progress being made on the new house Jack is building." He tilted his head. "Jack has mentioned to you that he purchased land in Michigan that overlooks the lake, hasn't he?"

Myrtle looked at Jack, who'd returned to his meal and had just taken a bite of steak. "I can't say that he has," she said, looking back at Walter, who now looked fairly resigned, although the moment he seemed to realize she was watching him, he began smiling again, his look of resignation immediately turning to one of determination.

"Well, that's exactly what he's done, and it's going to be a most impressive residence." Walter's smile widened. "Why, I imagine it'll be finished before Christmas comes this year, or at least it'll be habitable. That means that all that's left for Jack to do now is find a good woman who'll be able to turn that house into a proper home."

"I suppose a wife would be helpful in that regard" was all Myrtle could think to respond.

Walter sent her an expectant look, which left her swallowing.

"And, ah, I imagine your brother won't have much difficulty finding a woman to marry?" she finished somewhat weakly.

Walter sent her a nod of clear approval. "'Course he won't, especially if you hold my brother in the same amount of affection I know he holds for you, which would make his acquiring of a much-needed wife an incredibly easy task to complete."

Chapter Two

The distinct urge to throttle his brother was immediate.

Jack was well aware that Walter was prone to saying whatever popped into his head, but this time he'd gone too far.

He'd all but offered Myrtle a most unusual proposal on Jack's behalf. And even though Walter was apparently under the misimpression that he was being helpful, at thirty-one years old, Jack was perfectly capable of proposing to a woman on his own—not that he'd had much success in figuring out how to let Myrtle know he was interested in courting her.

As it stood now, though, he wouldn't be surprised if Myrtle decided he was completely ridiculous, as well as incompetent, because what woman longed to spend time with a man who needed his younger brother to speak for him?

Given that there was now complete and utter astonishment in Myrtle's eyes, it was evident she'd not been aware she'd garnered his affections. The reason behind that undoubtedly rested with him, because he'd not actually spoken to her much since he'd first laid eyes on her five months ago. That moment was forever etched in his memory, because the second he'd gotten a glimpse of Miss Myrtle Schermerhorn, he'd known she was the woman he'd been waiting for his entire life. He'd also known, though—what with her being the most beautiful woman he'd ever seen—that she was far above his reach.

A beautiful woman such as Myrtle Schermerhorn, who was capable of maintaining her poise even while dealing with the most querulous guests, was hardly likely to be impressed with a man who could claim only an eighth-grade education, even though he was now a self-made man in possession of a more-than-reputable fortune.

She was a woman who drew a man's notice, especially since she had the unusual ability of gliding across a room instead of merely walking across it. And even though Harvey Girls, especially the ones working at El Tovar, were expected to be refined, gracious, and capable at serving their many guests, he'd yet to discover exactly why Myrtle had taken such a menial position.

Being a Harvey Girl was a difficult and demanding job, and though Myrtle had never given him a reason to believe she didn't enjoy the work, it bothered him that she toiled day after day serving others, especially when he had the means to give her a life of luxury—a life where she'd never have to work again. All he needed to do was figure out how to convince her to accept such a life with him.

But since he was failing somewhat spectacularly at convincing her of anything, what with how he seemed incapable of holding an actual conversation with her, he was probably in for a rough time of it, especially after the nonsense Walter had just spouted.

Deciding there was nothing to do but offer an apology for his brother's unfortunate remarks, Jack drew in a breath—a mistake if there ever was one, because he'd forgotten he was in the process of trying to swallow a piece of steak. Air immediately became impossible to come by, and he began pounding his chest, trying to dislodge the steak from his throat.

"Good heavens, Mr. Daggett, are you all right?" Myrtle asked.

As much as he wanted to pretend that he was, Jack was beginning to see stars from lack of air, so he merely shook his head and gave his chest another pound.

"He's choking," he heard her say as she moved to stand behind him. A second after that, she began pummeling his back, something so unexpected that he lurched forward, his face smacking into his plate of mashed potatoes and creamed cauliflower. Thankfully, though, when she hit him again, the steak dislodged, and he pulled blessed air into his lungs. Breathing in another breath, even though doing so left him sputtering because his mouth was buried in potatoes, he raised his head, finding that the entire dining room had gone silent as everyone watched the drama unfold.

Swiping a hand over a face covered in potatoes and dripping cream from the cauliflower, he lifted his gaze, finding Myrtle watching him with wide eyes, her face a delightful shade of pink, probably brought about due to her rigorous pummeling.

"Miss Schermerhorn, what have you done to poor Mr. Daggett?"

Jack shifted his attention from Myrtle to Mr. Gene Eliot, one of the managers at El Tovar, who was currently glaring at Myrtle.

Rising to his feet, Jack took the napkin Myrtle snatched from the table and handed him, and after taking another swipe at his face, he took a step toward Mr. Eliot, who immediately took a step backward.

"Miss Schermerhorn just saved my life, Mr. Eliot, which means you should be commending her. If she hadn't reacted so quickly, I'm convinced I'd now be spread out on the floor, no breath left in my body, which would have then left you with the unfortunate task of cleaning up the mess my death would most certainly have caused."

Mr. Eliot glanced toward Myrtle, then back to Jack. "She saved your life?"

"Indeed. I choked on my steak—although allow me to say that it had nothing to do with the steak, which was delicious. Until I choked on it, that is."

"I suppose that does shed a different light on the matter," Mr. Eliot said before he nodded to Myrtle. "My apologies, Miss Schermerhorn. I'm afraid I jumped to the conclusion that you were accosting Mr. Daggett."

Myrtle quirked a delicate brow Mr. Eliot's way, the quirking drawing attention to brown eyes that some might consider rather ordinary but Jack found nothing of the sort. Myrtle's eyes always seemed, at least to him, to be filled with a sense of excitement as she went about her day serving up meal after meal in the El Tovar dining room. That she could find excitement in such a mundane task and maintain an air of cheerfulness was one of the reasons he'd been drawn back to El Tovar time and time again, even though his traveling to the Grand Canyon on such a frequent basis disrupted the business he'd always so diligently pursued.

That business had begun years ago, when he'd created an unusual concoction to combat the termites eating all the fence posts that kept his family's small herd of cattle corralled. After he'd been forced to dig out one too many posts, he'd begun experimenting with different forms of creosote, adding a variety of different tars to his mixture before he finally added in a bit of zinc to see what would happen. The zinc turned out to be exactly what was needed to repel insects in an effective manner, while the tar in the mixture preserved the wood from the elements.

His family had been struggling financially for years, and because he'd known he'd stumbled onto something that might have value to those involved with the lumber industry as well as the telegraph industry, because so many telegraph poles were needed as the railroads moved west, he'd quit school after finishing the eighth grade and gone on the road, taking his concoction to the timber barons. Because of his unusual size, the timber barons believed they were dealing with a man, not a boy on the verge of manhood, and before Jack knew it, he was selling his product at a rapid rate. Once money began flowing in, he built a factory to produce his creosote in large quantities. He'd amassed a fortune by the time he was twenty-five—one that was now considered one of the greatest fortunes in the West.

"Have I ever given you reason to believe I'm a lady who'd accost a guest dining at El Tovar?" Myrtle demanded, pulling Jack from his thoughts.

Mr. Eliot gave a quick shake of his head. "Can't say that you have."

"Then I'll thank you to remember that in the future, Mr. Eliot, especially if another guest chokes on a meal and I'm forced to take action again." Myrtle turned from Mr. Eliot and winced as she looked Jack over. "I am sorry, Mr. Daggett, about pushing your face into your plate. I imagine I must have taken you by surprise, but do know that I'll pay to have your jacket laundered, since it's now covered with potatoes, which aren't looking nearly as fetching as you apparently once found them."

Ignoring the creamed cauliflower dripping from his chin, Jack shook his head. "You'll do no such thing, Miss Schermerhorn. As I just mentioned, you saved my life. I hope you'll allow me to treat you to a nice dinner, or if that's not to your liking, I'd be honored to escort you around the grounds this evening. The sunset over the canyon is always magnificent, and I would enjoy taking in that view with the woman who just made it possible for me to actually see another sunset."

For a second, Jack thought Myrtle might refuse because she

was looking at him with her mouth slightly agape, but then, to his relief, she nodded, albeit rather slowly.

"That sounds lovely, Mr. Daggett. I quite enjoy seeing the sun set over the canyon. I do hope you won't retreat back to your normal silent self, though, because it will be a much more enjoyable evening if you and I can actually hold a conversation with each other, something we've not had an opportunity to do before now."

"My brother's always been more of a strong, silent type," Walter called out behind him. Jack turned his head and discovered Walter standing next to a Harvey Girl named Miss Ruthanne Hill, a young woman who was currently beaming a bright smile Jack's way, a smile that was accompanied by a discreet nod, as if she was trying to encourage him to . . . well, he had no idea what she was trying to encourage him to do.

Myrtle directed eyes that had begun twinkling at Walter. "That does explain much, but now, if all of you will excuse me, I need to return to work." She nodded to Jack. "My shift is over at six. I could meet you on the front veranda at seven, if that's an acceptable time for us to take our stroll."

Jack caught Mr. Eliot's eye and didn't need to say a word, because the manager immediately turned his attention to Myrtle. "You may end your shift early today, Miss Schermerhorn. You did, after all, save Mr. Daggett's life, and I believe that deserves some manner of reward. Why don't you take off now?"

To Jack's surprise, Myrtle shook her head. "That would cause additional work for other Harvey Girls. I'll finish out my shift, thank you very much, and then"—she smiled at Jack—"I'll meet you at seven."

As Myrtle glided for the kitchen, Jack watched her disappear through the kitchen door, his respect for her increasing by the second.

Her refusal to end her shift early spoke volumes about her

character. That character lent credence to the conclusion he'd been coming to over the past few months, that she was a woman like no other he'd ever known and one he wanted to pursue—or maybe *woo* was a better way to look at it—even though he'd made a complete muddle of matters so far.

Nevertheless, because he was a man who believed in chasing his dreams, and he'd been dreaming about Myrtle a lot these days, he knew it was past time he stopped being ridiculous and got on with the business of trying to convince her he could offer her a life she'd never imagined. Before he did that, though, he needed to get the creamed cauliflower off his face, because no woman would be impressed by a man wearing his supper.

Four hours later, after he'd finally gotten his turn in one of the few bathing chambers El Tovar offered—a situation he had a feeling management would eventually rectify, since so many families were streaming to the hotel to see the wonders of the Grand Canyon—Jack strode into his guest room, unsurprised to find Walter lounging in a wooden rocking chair.

Looking up from the papers he'd been perusing, Walter nodded. "I see you finally got those fetching potatoes off you."

Depositing the towel he'd been using to dry his hair on the back of another chair, Jack released a bit of a grunt. "How did I know you were going to bring up my unfortunate remark about fetching potatoes at your earliest convenience?"

Walter shrugged. "How could I not? I encouraged you to tell Myrtle she was looking fetching today, and the next thing I knew, you were proclaiming your potatoes were fetching instead."

"It was not my finest moment."

"Agreed." Walter smiled. "It was amusing, though, and it

did make me understand exactly why Ma insisted I accompany you here."

Jack sat down in a chair next to his brother. "I thought you accompanied me because you wanted to learn more about doing the books for Daggett Industries."

"If you've forgotten—although I don't how you could, since you're the one who insisted I pursue a formal education—I'm in possession of a college degree. In finance, no less. I could do your books in my sleep."

"So you lied to me about why you wanted to come to El Tovar?"

"*Lied* is such a nasty word. I prefer *stretched the truth*, but only for your own good. Besides, Ma made me, so I really had no choice in the matter."

"Why would she have done that?"

Walter's brows drew together. "How could you not realize that by mentioning Myrtle a few times over the past months, you'd attract Ma's curiosity?"

"I didn't say that much about Myrtle."

"A fair point, but since you've never talked about a woman before at all, the few times you did say something about Myrtle got Ma thinking you might have romantic intentions. That right there is the reason she insisted I travel with you to El Tovar to assess the situation."

"You're here to assess the situation?"

"I am, and good thing, because you're clearly in need of some assistance in the romance department."

"I can do romance without any help."

Walter released a snort. "Romance involves interaction, Jack, something you're woefully inadequate at with Myrtle. She doesn't even know about your work or that you're building a more-than-impressive house in Michigan."

"I didn't want her to come to the conclusion that I'm a braggart."

"I don't believe you need to worry about *that* because she doesn't seem to have been given an opportunity to conclude much of anything about you except that you find potatoes fetching and apparently have a problem eating steak."

"She makes me nervous."

Walter gave a knowing nod. "Because you think she's above your reach."

"She *is* above my reach. She's the most beautiful woman I've ever seen and has this air of refinement about her that one doesn't normally find in a waitress. She also has the most glorious way of gliding across a room. I could watch her walk for hours and must admit I've done just that over the past few months."

"You really think she's the most beautiful woman you've ever seen?"

"Without question. She has an understated beauty that I'm sure many overlook, but her face is very expressive and suggests she's a lady who is captivated with life and all the adventures it has to offer. And while some might find her hair to be a normal shade of brown, I can't help but feel the most unusual urge to study it closer, especially to see if the red I think I noticed in it a time or two when she's walked past a window is really red or just a figment of my imagination."

"You might want to refrain from doing that until the two of you become better acquainted. She might not know what to make of you suddenly inspecting her hair with any intensity."

"Think she'd notice if I slipped on the spectacles I occasionally use for reading to get a closer look at it?"

"Probably, particularly if she hasn't seen you wearing spectacles before."

"Perhaps I should take a book with me next time I dine, which would allow me the perfect excuse to let her see me with spectacles." Jack smiled. "Did I mention that I've often seen Myrtle holding a book when she's heading off to take a break?"

Walter returned the smile. "You have not, but how delightful to learn Myrtle is a reader. You can use your love of books as a common interest and discuss them with her when you take that stroll this evening."

"I don't imagine she reads the same books I do. She doesn't strike me as the type to enjoy *Dracula* or *The Time Machine*."

"You never know, she might. But if you're worried about that, why don't you bring up that new book our younger sister was talking about last week—*The House of Mirth* by Edith Wharton? Sadie said it revolved around New York high society, and I've yet to meet a woman who isn't interested in high society or who doesn't secretly long to join it—our sister included."

"That does explain why Sadie's been so determined to enroll in a finishing school." Jack shook his head. "I've told her that our family isn't cultured enough to be accepted into society, but she's still determined to get herself invited into Chicago society, which is why she's been pestering me to build a house there."

"I think Chicago society would be only too willing to have our family join their ranks, given the vast fortune you've made over the years. New York society, on the other hand, which Sadie tells me is *the* society of choice, wouldn't be keen to open its doors to us, because we're definitely considered upstart members of the newly rich."

Jack nodded before he frowned. "Do you think Myrtle has dreams of entering society? She's refined enough to impress even the most critical of society members, even with her taking on a position as a Harvey Girl."

"I know this is probably a ridiculous question, seeing as how you've rarely talked to her, but have you asked her why she decided to become a Harvey Girl?"

"I haven't, but I would think she's done so because she needed to earn a wage."

To Jack's surprise, Walter shook his head. "I don't think that's the only reason."

"Why not?"

"Because I had a lovely chat with Miss Ruthanne Hill after you left. I moved to Ruthanne's section, you see, to get out of Myrtle's way because she was cleaning up the mess you made, and—"

"Myrtle had to clean up the mess I made?" Jack interrupted.

"She had help from a busboy, but yes, she did clean up all the potatoes strewn about the table."

"I should have stayed and assisted her."

"She wouldn't have appreciated that, nor would she have agreed to your assistance. But getting back to why she's a Harvey Girl, Ruthanne told me something I think might be of interest to you."

"What?"

"Myrtle apparently suffered a broken engagement almost a year ago, and even though Ruthanne said Myrtle doesn't say much about that unfortunate situation, it seems to me as if that broken engagement might be behind Myrtle's decision to become a Harvey Girl."

"What man in his right mind would break off an engagement with a lady like Myrtle?"

"I have no idea, but perhaps that dastardly business is also why Myrtle told Ruthanne that she's made a vow to swear off men forever."

Jack blinked. "That might make any attempt at wooing somewhat tricky."

"Except that Ruthanne—who is a very delightful young woman, by the way, and one who agreed to take a stroll with *me* later this evening—told me she thinks Myrtle's had a change of heart about that because of you."

Jack's lips curved. "You don't say."

"I do say, and I think now is the point in the conversation where you thank me for opening the door to that courtship you've been hoping to pursue with Myrtle."

"You're mad if you think I'm going to thank you after you extended Myrtle what amounted to nothing less than a very peculiar secondhand proposal."

"One she didn't get an opportunity to accept because you ruined the moment by choking."

"Thus giving her a much-needed excuse to avoid the topic altogether."

Walter tilted his head. "You'll need to broach that topic again with her—and the sooner the better. Can't very well leave a marriage proposal up in the air like that."

"I didn't propose marriage to her—you did. Maybe *you* should broach it with her, tell her you completely took leave of your senses for a moment or something to that effect."

"Or you can use my proposal as a perfect opening to allow her to know you're interested in wooing her."

"Or allow her to understand that my family is a bit deranged so she'll realize what she might be getting into before I broach the topic of wooing."

"Myrtle won't have a problem fitting in with our family. She seems to be a most sensible sort, and you know Ma will adore her after she discovers she saved your life today."

With that, Walter got up from his chair, snatching up the papers he'd been looking over. "But now, if you'll excuse me, I'll get out of your way so you can get ready for what I'm sure will be an interesting evening." He nodded to the freestanding wardrobe. "I'd wear the pinstripe trousers and jacket, paired with that embroidered waistcoat Sadie brought back for you from Chicago. It's very fashionable, or at least it is according to Sadie."

It took all of fifteen minutes for Jack to make himself presentable in the clothes his brother had recommended, and after he checked his appearance for what felt like the hundredth time in the long mirror attached to the back of the door, he was fairly confident he was sufficiently groomed. The waistcoat his sister had purchased for him was far more embellished than he was used to, but it did give him a somewhat dapper air, and if that impressed Myrtle, well, he was going to have to remember to thank his sister.

Striding out the front door, he glanced around, nodding to a few of the guests, who nodded back as they sat in chairs on the large veranda.

Disappointment was swift when he couldn't find Myrtle, but then he looked out onto the grounds and spotted her surrounded by railroad men, who were evidently waiting to board the last train of the day.

Even though she was smiling, there was something about the smile that suggested she wasn't appreciating the attention the men were giving her. That was proven a blink of an eye later when she began walking backward to get away from them, her escape blocked when a man suddenly stepped forward and had the audacity to take hold of her arm.

His temper flowed freely as Jack strode down the steps, set his sights on the man Myrtle was trying to shake off, and felt his hands clench into fists.

Chapter Three

Calling herself every sort of fool for wandering into the midst of railroad men who were evidently passing the time before the last train left for the day, Myrtle tried to shake free from the hand wrapped firmly around her arm.

"I'll thank you to release me, sir," she demanded, her words merely earning her a grin from the man holding her, the distinct smell of whiskey wafting from his breath the moment he opened his mouth.

"Now, there's no need to be like that. I'm a fun man, and me and the rest of the boys enjoy spending time with attractive women such as yourself. I bet you're a Harvey Girl, and everyone knows you Harvey Girls like to have fun as well."

"You're mistaken," she bit out as she tried to tug her arm free. When he tightened his grip and leaned closer to her, Myrtle had had quite enough. Drawing back her free arm, she let it fly, the book she'd brought with her to pass the time until Jack arrived connecting soundly with the man's nose.

A howl of rage erupted from him as he stumbled backward, but then he found his balance and narrowed his eyes at her. Swiping a hand over a nose now bleeding profusely, he raised his fist, exactly as if he was about to strike her.

Bracing herself, she closed her eyes and drew in a breath,

holding it for what seemed like forever as she waited for a blow that didn't come. Opening her eyes when she ran out of air, she blinked and then blinked again at the sight before her.

Jack was standing directly in front of her, and he held on to the man who'd been accosting her by the scruff of his neck. He wasn't saying a single word, but his eyes were flashing with fury.

"Mr. Daggett," the man said in a voice that had risen a good octave since the last time Myrtle had heard him speak. "What are you doing here, sir?"

"I think a better question would be what are *you* doing?" Jack countered in a deadly tone that had the man turning an interesting shade of red, although that might have been a result of how Jack was holding him around the neck.

"I didn't mean no harm, sir. She's just a Harvey Girl, and—"

"She's not just a Harvey Girl. She's a lady, as are all the Harvey Girls," Jack interrupted. "You'll apologize to her, and then you'll get yourself on that train over there. You then need to steer clear of El Tovar, because I won't be held responsible for what happens to you if I see you around here again."

The man shot a nervous look at Myrtle, then looked at Jack, who arched a brow. The man turned back to Myrtle again. "Apologies, ma'am. I didn't mean nothin' by it, was just tryin' to be friendly. There was no need for you to break my nose."

"She had every reason to break your nose, and that wasn't a good enough apology. Try again," Jack said.

The man licked his lips, swiped a hand over a nose that was still dribbling blood, then nodded at Myrtle. "I beg your pardon for touchin' you and beg your pardon for not mindin' my manners."

Myrtle inclined her head. "Apology accepted, but do know that we Harvey Girls do not appreciate uncouth men. If you'd ever like to impress a Harvey Girl in the future, you might want to brush up on those manners of yours."

As the man nodded, Jack released him, and after scooping up his hat from the ground, the man turned and fled in the direction of the train, the other railroad men racing after him.

Jack waited until the men disappeared onto the train before he moved to where she'd dropped her book. He picked it up, dusted it off, then handed it back to her.

"Are you all right?" he asked.

She nodded. "I'm fine. Annoyed with myself for forgetting how rowdy the railroad men can be this time of day, but fine all the same." She caught his eye. "Thank you for coming to my rescue."

"I wanted to tear him limb from limb."

"That would have been a sight, but with so many families around, I'm thankful you weren't forced to resort to that. Frankly, I think you won the battle the moment he recognized you."

Jack shrugged, then surprised her when he took her arm. "I travel on trains often, so I'm a known figure to the railroad men. I readily admit I've often used my size and reputation to settle disputes that are far too common." He smiled. "Men do seem to enjoy throwing themselves into fights. I've gotten remarkably adept over the years of knowing how to end fights with relatively little blood spilled." He gave her arm a pat. "But speaking of blood, I do think you broke his nose."

She winced. "That was quite unintentional, and I almost regret it." She held up the book in her hand. "It seems somewhat fitting, though, that *Dracula* would be behind all the blood spilled."

Jack pulled her into motion. "You're reading *Dracula*?"

"For the third time. It's a riveting tale, although I probably wouldn't be reading it again if I had other books to read. El Tovar does offer its guests a small library, but I've read almost everything available and am currently waiting for some books to arrive that I ordered over a month ago."

To Myrtle's delight, Jack surprised her by launching into a discussion about books—those he'd read, those they had in common, *Dracula* being one of them, and books he was looking forward to reading in the future. His ability to converse so easily on the subject took her completely aback, especially since he'd barely spoken to her over the months they'd known each other.

"My younger sister, Sadie, is currently reading a book by Edith Wharton. Perhaps you've read it as well—*The House of Mirth*?"

It took a great deal of effort to suppress a shudder. The truth, of course, was that she'd read *The House of Mirth*, but Myrtle had found it beyond depressing. Rumor had it that the author had based her characters on members of the New York Four Hundred—the cream of society. As she'd been reading the book, Myrtle had recognized many of the characters as society members she actually knew. One of those characters greatly resembled her distant relative, Caroline Astor, a woman Myrtle was only slightly acquainted with because Caroline, being in her late seventies, currently spent her days locked away in her Fifth Avenue mansion. Caroline, or so they said, was now a shell of the woman who'd once been considered the queen of society and was no longer capable of mingling with the New York Four Hundred, which she'd been responsible for creating along with the social arbiter of that day, the late Mr. Ward McAllister.

"Should I take your silence to mean you've not read Edith Wharton's book?" Jack asked, pulling Myrtle back to the conversation at hand.

Even though she'd not been hiding the fact she'd once been a member of New York high society—although she'd never actually told anyone at El Tovar the details of her past—Myrtle had the uncanny suspicion that Jack wouldn't be pleased to discover she'd spent years mingling with the elite of the country.

Jack seemed to be a complicated man, and if she wasn't mistaken, he possessed some measure of wealth. She wouldn't be surprised to learn he'd earned that wealth on his own, but it had been her experience that self-made men were somewhat touchy when it came to matters of high society. New York society was filled with the most snobbish people in the country, ones who believed that the *nouveau riche* were not cultured enough to enter their hallowed circles. Myrtle knew from gossip she'd been privy to over the years that the nouveau riche were prone to dislike the established rich, probably because of the abuse they suffered whenever they had the audacity to try to become accepted into the highest societal circles.

"I have read the book, Mr. Daggett, but I didn't particularly care for it," she settled on saying after she realized Jack was waiting for her to answer what should have been a fairly simple question.

"Since you did save my life, do you think you'd feel comfortable calling me Jack?"

Myrtle's knees immediately turned wobbly. "I suppose I could do that, but only if you agree to call me Myrtle—although not when I'm working, of course. Mr. Eliot might take issue with that, and I would hate to get terminated from my position as a Harvey Girl."

Jack stopped walking, glanced around, then drew her over to a stone bench that afforded a wonderful view of the canyon. Helping her take a seat, he sat down beside her, studying her for a long moment before he tilted his head. "I'm curious as to why you decided to become a Harvey Girl."

The casual way he posed the question left her frowning. "Why do I get the distinct feeling you might already know the answer to that?"

"Because you probably saw Walter chatting with Miss Ruthanne Hill?"

She blew out a breath. "That would explain why Walter kept throwing guilty looks my way every time I passed by him in Ruthanne's section." Myrtle shook her head. "And here I was, thinking he looked guilty because he'd abandoned my section and was having Ruthanne bring him slice after slice of pie instead of me. Frankly, I was going to ask if your brother had come down with a stomachache after consuming so much pie, since he didn't join us for our stroll this evening."

"Walter eats like a horse, and I've never known him to come down with a stomachache. But because you've brought him into the conversation, I should probably take a moment to try to explain the completely unacceptable statement he made to you before the whole choking incident."

"The one where he all but proposed for you?"

"So you did pick up on that. I was hoping you might have misinterpreted what he'd been trying to say."

Myrtle grinned. "That would have been tricky, since he was pretty determined to make sure I knew you were in the market for a wife."

"He was wrong for speaking for me. In his defense, though, he'd apparently concluded I was making a muddle of everything with you and decided to take matters into his own hands and blurt out that bit about me being ready to settle down."

Anticipation licked its way up her spine, mixed with a sense of curiosity, because she'd never spoken with a man about marriage before—Percy not really counting since theirs had certainly not been a normal relationship. Setting her book on her lap, she struggled for something to say in return, finally settling on the only question that sprang to mind. "*Have* you been looking for a wife long?"

"Truth be told, I've not given the thought of taking a wife much thought at all. That is, not until recently."

"*How* recently?"

303

Jack took off his hat, placed it beside him, then raked a hand through his hair. "Perhaps it would be for the best to return to the subject of books."

"Because you're not comfortable discussing how recently you decided to turn your attention to finding a wife?"

"I'm not really comfortable discussing much with you, but I'm sure you've noticed that by now."

Myrtle smiled. "You seem to be growing more comfortable holding a conversation with me this evening."

He raked his hand through his hair again and sent her a rueful grin. "Since this day has served up one embarrassing moment after another, I suppose there's no reason to stop now." He caught her eye. "So, to answer your question, all I have to say is this."

When he suddenly stopped talking and began watching her far too intently, quite like he'd done often over the past few months, Myrtle pressed her lips together to keep from smiling but finally felt compelled to speak after a full minute passed and Jack remained mute.

"Have you lost the thread of our conversation, Jack?"

He blew out a breath. "I haven't lost the thread of our conversation. I just don't know how to phrase what I want to say."

"I've always found that simply spitting it out in these types of situations is best."

"Sound advice to be sure." He caught her eye. "I've taken a shine to you, Myrtle. In fact, I'm, ah, well, smitten with you."

Of anything she'd been expecting Jack to say, that had not been it. "You're . . . smitten . . . with *me*?"

"Guilty, and that's why I've been thinking about taking on a wife."

Myrtle's mouth dropped open. "You didn't just propose to me, did you?"

Jack rubbed a hand over his face. "This courting business

is far more difficult than I expected, but no, that wasn't a proposal, although I do hope that doesn't disappoint you. I assure you, I'm certain if I ever do extend you a real proposal, I'll make an attempt—or I imagine I would—to do a better job of it."

A sigh of relief escaped her. "You haven't disappointed me. I just wanted to make sure I wasn't about to offend you by telling you I think it's too soon to discuss much of consequence between us."

Jack grinned. "Thank goodness. I was afraid I was going to have to tell Walter I'd made a complete mess of matters *again*, and there's no telling how he might react to something like that." His grin faded. "But with that settled, allow me to redirect the conversation to something we touched upon a few minutes ago: the reason you became a Harvey Girl. Walter told *me* that Ruthanne told *him* that you came west because of a broken engagement."

Myrtle refused a groan. "She probably wanted Walter to tell you about my broken engagement so you'd understand why I've vowed to swear off men forever."

"She did make a point of mentioning that to Walter."

"Did she also mention that I might have recently been reconsidering that vow?"

What appeared to be male satisfaction flickered through Jack's eyes. "She might have touched upon that idea as well. Is it true?"

"Don't be smug. It doesn't suit you. But yes, I have been reconsidering it."

His lips curved into a smile before he suddenly sobered. "What happened with your fiancé?"

"He fell in love with someone else."

"Then he's a fool, because you're the most beautiful lady I've ever seen."

Never in her life had anyone proclaimed her beautiful, and that those words had been spoken by a man who was one of the most masculine men she'd ever met brought tears to her eyes and robbed her of anything remotely intelligent to say in return.

"Have I said something to upset you?" Jack asked, moving closer to her on the bench as he actually took hold of her hand and gave it a squeeze.

"No one has ever called me beautiful," she returned in a voice no louder than a whisper.

"Then you've been surrounding yourself with the wrong sorts, because you *are* the most beautiful woman I've ever seen. And before you argue with that, know that I'm very well traveled. I've seen many ladies, but none of them compare to you."

Myrtle dashed a gloved hand over a tear that had fallen from her eye. "Those are some of the nicest words I've ever heard."

Jack frowned. "Didn't your ex-fiancé extend you compliments?"

"Percy and I weren't officially engaged, although we'd shared an understanding for years that we'd eventually marry, something both of our parents wanted to see happen. In all honesty, though, and with the distance my position as a Harvey Girl has given me, I've come to realize that Percy didn't suit me in the least. He was often short with me, didn't appreciate that I enjoy books, and hated my name because some people referred to me as Myrtle the Turtle because my head is often buried in one book or another." She smiled as a bit of temper flashed through his eyes. "There's no need to be offended on my account, though. I've always found the nickname to be ridiculous because turtles don't read books, but it bothered Percy, which is why he began calling me Mertie instead of Myrtle, since Mertie doesn't rhyme with turtle."

"I have the strongest urge to run this Percy down. Have a bit of a chat with him. But just so you know, I think Myrtle is a lovely name."

For a second, Myrtle had the distinct desire to throw herself into his arms, or better yet, kiss him, but luckily sanity quickly returned, which left her settling on giving his arm a good pat.

"You're very kind, Jack, but there's no need for you to intervene on my behalf with Percy."

"You could still tell me where he lives."

"You're also apparently a bit tenacious. Percy, since I have the sneaking suspicion you'll keep asking, lives in New York, where I'm from, but I don't want you to track him down. That would lend him the impression I'm still bothered about him abandoning me for another lady. The fact of the matter is, I stopped caring and thinking about Percy months ago. He's probably happily married by now to his Miss Davis, and at this point, I wish him well and am actually thankful he jilted me, because if he hadn't, I wouldn't have come west."

"So you *did* take up a position as a Harvey Girl because of your broken engagement."

Myrtle turned her attention to the canyon. The ragged rocks, brilliant colors, and an endless sky still seemed foreign to a woman used to living amongst tall buildings, and left her slightly awestruck as she considered Jack's statement. Turning back to him, she frowned. "In all honesty, taking on a position as a Harvey Girl was more of a way to escape the gossips than a desire to distance myself from Percy."

"Did you live in New York City?"

"I did, and while it's an enormous city, you'd be surprised at how small it can seem at times. Word spread quickly about Percy taking up with Miss Davis, and I soon found myself the object of pitying looks and whispers about spinsterhood." She smiled. "I'm twenty-three, you see, an age considered by many to be firmly on the shelf. My mother was distraught about my new situation and began hinting that she was going to take aggressive steps to find me a husband. After learning that, I decided I needed to seek out some counsel about the matter, which is how I found myself sitting in Grace Church, speaking with Reverend Jonathon Mayhew about what to do with my life from that point forward."

Jack frowned. "I've been to New York City and have actually visited Grace Church. From what I saw there, it was a church that was attended by a lot of well-heeled patrons."

"It *is* one of New York society's favorite churches, but not everyone who patronizes Grace Church is of the society set."

Realizing she'd just been given the perfect opening to disclose that she'd once been a member of high society, Myrtle opened her mouth but closed it again when Jack somewhat absently picked up her hand and sent her a smile that caused her pulse to begin racing.

"I suppose churches *do* cater to a wide variety of patrons, although the churches I normally frequent are incredibly small and more often than not held in the railroad workers' camps out in the middle of nowhere."

"I wouldn't mind attending a church like that. It would definitely lend a certain atmosphere to the sermon."

"Indeed it does. But returning to Grace Church, may I assume Reverend Mayhew lent you some valuable advice?"

She smiled. "Frankly, he was somewhat vague, saying I needed to pray about the matter and then follow the directions God would most assuredly send me. I thought my time with Reverend Mayhew hadn't been well spent, until I left the church and stopped to buy a newspaper from a boy who was trying to unload his last copy of the *New York Herald*."

"And that boy had something to do with you becoming a Harvey Girl?"

She laughed. "No, but the newspaper he sold me had an advertisement about the Harvey Girls. It occurred to me that God might have sent me in the direction of that newspaper boy because the moment I saw the advertisement, I knew I was meant to turn my back on the gossips in New York City and find my way west."

"And you came directly to El Tovar because of that advertisement?"

"I went to Chicago first, where I was interviewed and given a bit of training." She grinned. "Frankly, I needed more than a *bit* of training. I'd never worked in service, you see, and learning how to pour the perfect cup of coffee was far harder to master than I thought. I also had to learn how to carry food on a tray without dropping it on an unsuspecting guest, as well as get accustomed to being on my feet all day, but I won't bore you with a laundry list of what my initial training involved. When I was done with my training, though, I was convinced I was going to be sent off to one of the more obscure Harvey locations, but to my delight, I was told management had decided I would fit in well as a Harvey Girl at El Tovar." She leaned forward. "Apparently my proficiency with proper etiquette impressed them, which is why they sent me to work in what is known as one of the more desirable Harvey Houses."

"And your mother was fine with you taking on a position that sees you working such long hours and serving customers?"

"Not at all. Mother was furious and threatened to cut off all contact with me as well as any financial support if I went through with my plan. She made good on that promise after she realized I was heading west despite her protests, which is why I'm thankful to have a position at El Tovar. I'm also thankful that Mr. Eliot told me just the other day that he'd be happy to extend another contract to me once my six-month contract is up in about a month."

Jack's gaze sharpened on her face. "Your contract is up in a month?"

"It is, and I'm perfectly content to sign another one. The

Harvey Company demands its girls sign contracts, mostly as a way to keep an eye on us and have us abide by their rules. I haven't found those rules too bothersome, although I do wish we weren't held responsible for keeping our aprons and bibs starched, ironed, and pristine. It takes me a good hour every night to get them looking shipshape, and I'll be the first to admit I'm not the most proficient with an iron yet."

"You have to iron your own aprons?"

"We do, but we're not responsible for laundering our work clothes, just ironing and starching the aprons. They send our clothing out to be cleaned because they expect Harvey Girls to project a certain image, and nothing could ruin that image more than Harvey Girls wearing clothing that has been improperly laundered."

"But aren't you tired after working your long shifts? You must find it daunting to then have to see to the task of your aprons."

"Most certainly, but I enjoy my work as a Harvey Girl. I never imagined myself as a waitress, but there's something fulfilling in knowing I do my job well, and there's also the bonus of getting to meet so many new people every day." She smiled and blew out a breath. "But enough about me. Tell me about you and that business Walter mentioned, as well as that house you're building in Michigan."

"I don't really like talking about myself."

"And isn't that too bad, since I'm curious to learn everything about you? Especially what type of business you're involved with that sees you traveling around the country so much."

Jack rose to his feet, helped her to her feet as well, then took her arm and started strolling down the path that bordered the rim of the canyon. As they strolled, he began to tell her all about how he'd come up with a resin that was in much demand, apparently warming up to the idea of speaking about himself because his tone took on a distinct trace of enthusiasm. After he finished telling her how he'd gone about selling that resin to more and more businesses, he told her about the factory he'd built in Michigan to produce the amount of creosote he needed to fulfill orders, explaining that he'd settled on Michigan for the location of the factory because that state still produced a large percentage of lumber for the country, even though the lumber industry was in the process of moving farther west.

After that, he turned to the subject of his family, telling her that he'd built a house for his parents and younger sister, Sadie, but that Walter lived in his own house, as did Jack's two other brothers, both of whom were younger than Jack, but older than Walter. A hint of wariness suddenly settled in his eyes as Jack stopped walking and turned to face her.

"All of my brothers have gone on to pursue formal educations and earn college degrees, but I feel compelled to disclose that I don't have a degree. In fact, I only finished the eighth grade and am not proud of the fact I'm an uneducated man."

"Forgive me for being blunt, but I find it ridiculous that you'd be ashamed of your lack of formal education." Myrtle reached out and took his hand, evidently surprising him with that action, because his eyes widened. "You may not have a formal degree, but I know men who pursued degrees who didn't amount to much. You, on the other hand, have enjoyed what sounds like remarkable success, and you also seem to be well read, which means you're not illiterate. Add in the notion that you're providing for your entire family, and I'd say you have more than enough reason to be incredibly proud of all of your accomplishments." She gave his hand a squeeze.

For the longest time, Jack simply stared at her. Then his lips curved into an honest-to-goodness smile, one that took her breath away, as he lifted her hand and placed a kiss on it.

"I believe I've just realized that you're even more beautiful on the inside than you are on the outside, Myrtle. And while we did agree that it was far too early to discuss anything of consequence between us, I'm afraid I'm going to break that agreement."

Myrtle blinked. "You are?"

His smile widened. "Indeed. Because, you see, I seem to be notoriously horrible at matters concerning you, so to avoid any misunderstandings, I need to ask you something."

"You do?"

"Yes, and that something is this." He paused for a moment but only because he gave her fingers another kiss. "I would be humbled and incredibly grateful if you would allow me to court you."

"You want to court me?"

"In all honesty, I want more than . . . well, best not to get myself into trouble by moving too quickly, but yes, I would like to court you."

It took all of a second to nod, and then, after she found her fingers being kissed again, it took all of another second to completely abandon her vow of swearing off men forever, because somehow, and she wasn't exactly certain how, Mr. Jack Daggett, the most intriguing man she'd ever met, was courting her.

Chapter Four

Myrtle smoothed a last wrinkle from the fanciest dress she'd brought with her from New York and then rehung it in her wardrobe, stepping back to look the gown over once more before she went about getting ready for the dance El Tovar was hosting that evening.

Thankfully, the dining room had closed early that day because a dinner would be served at the dance. That made it possible for Myrtle, as well as the other El Tovar Harvey Girls, to take their time getting ready, time she appreciated because she wanted to look her best when Jack arrived to escort her that evening.

During the month since he'd asked to begin courting her, she'd spent every spare moment with him. When she wasn't working, she enjoyed hiking with Jack into the canyon, accompanied more often than not by Walter and Ruthanne, who seemed to be enjoying their time together as well.

When they weren't hiking around the canyon in the split skirts Myrtle and Ruthanne had purchased from the small store in the hotel, she and Jack spent their time reading on the veranda, or if they wanted a setting not filled with tourists, they took their books and settled down in the shade of the few scant trees surrounding El Tovar.

Thankfully, Jack had abandoned his practice of not being able to speak in her presence and now seemed to be trying to make up for the months he'd been all but mute. They discussed everything under the sun, and he'd even admitted that he'd begun stopping at El Tovar so often not because of business matters but because he liked watching her.

When he said things like that, Myrtle always felt all sorts of fluttery inside. She knew she was becoming more than smitten with him, although he'd not broached the subject of marriage again, even though he had urged her to hold off signing a new contract to continue working as a Harvey Girl. He'd not elaborated on why he wanted her to hold off, merely brushing aside her question with some vague response of never knowing what possibilities the future might hold.

A knock on her door pulled her abruptly from her thoughts. Walking across the room, she opened the door and found Ruthanne standing on the other side, smiling back at her.

"Walter and Jack have just arrived on the afternoon train," Ruthanne began. "Thought you'd like to know so you wouldn't worry they'd been delayed and would miss the dance."

Over the past few weeks, Jack and Walter had left El Tovar three times because of matters of business, but they were never gone more than four days in a row, which was a relief to Myrtle. She missed Jack somewhat dreadfully while he was away, clear proof that she was far more than smitten with—

"And there you go again, getting all dreamy-eyed at the mention of your Jack."

Heat began crawling up Myrtle's neck, heat that wasn't caused by the scorching warmth of the day. Returning the grin Ruthanne was sending her, she waved a hand in front of her face, hoping to cool it just a touch. "Since I can't currently see my eyes, I'll have to take your word for it. But before I turn even redder than I'm certain I am at the moment, allow me to artfully redirect the conversation to something less embarrassing. Have you got the dress you're wearing tonight ironed and ready to go?"

Ruthanne's grin didn't falter as she nodded and stepped into Myrtle's room, heading directly for the wardrobe and letting out a whistle when she caught sight of Myrtle's dress. "That's some dress you've got there, and it doesn't look homemade like mine. Is it store-bought? Or better yet, where did you buy it? And for goodness' sake, if you did purchase it, how did you manage to afford it, since it looks expensive?"

Myrtle was hesitant to admit that her dress had come from the House of Worth in Paris, or explain that it wasn't what anyone in New York would consider appropriate to wear to a dance since it was, in actuality, a dress more suited for the theater. She settled for a shrug. "I suppose it was somewhat pricey, but my mother bought it for me." She smiled. "She's since cut me off and hasn't spoken to me or sent me so much as a single letter since I decided to join the Harvey Girls."

Ruthanne looked at the dress, then back at Myrtle and frowned. "You've not said much about your family, although I was under the impression they're not struggling financially. Now, however, what with the quality of your dress, I'm beginning to wonder if your parents aren't incredibly wealthy."

"Since they've cut me off, that doesn't really matter these days."

"It might matter to Jack."

Myrtle's brow furrowed. "You really think so?"

Ruthanne nodded. "Growing up on a farm, I was surrounded by farmhands, the majority of them men." Her eyes twinkled. "That gave me quite the education about the way men think, especially because I might have—as in, I did—overhear many a manly conversation when I eavesdropped behind hay bales or whatever was available to conceal me."

"You eavesdropped on the farmhands?"

"'Course I did. I thought the information I could glean by doing so would aid me someday in understanding a potential husband, which is why I feel confident now to lend you some advice." Ruthanne caught Myrtle's eye. "Men don't care for women keeping secrets from them, and I don't think Jack's an exception to that. If you grew up in a wealthy household, you have to tell Jack, and the sooner the better."

Myrtle shoved aside the silk chemise and stockings she'd set on a chair and sat down. "I've gotten the distinct feeling that Jack might be sensitive when it comes to things like society, so I didn't want to discourage him from courting me by telling him the awful truth about my family."

Ruthanne didn't bother to shove aside the books sitting on another chair, plopping down directly on top of them as her eyes grew wide. "You're from *society*?"

Blowing out a breath as she realized what she'd inadvertently revealed, Myrtle nodded. "I'm afraid so, but do know that I was never a member of the New York fashionable set."

Ruthanne began twirling a stray strand of her golden hair around her finger. "I once read in a magazine that New York society ladies enjoy buying their clothing in Paris. Is that where your dress came from?"

"Are you going to stop being friends with me if I admit that it did?"

"Of course not, but have you *been* to Paris?"

"Every spring since I was ten, although I missed the trip this year since I came west instead."

Ruthanne leaned forward, ignoring that the action sent one of Myrtle's books tumbling to the ground. "You left New York and gave up what sounds to be a most impressive lifestyle to become a *Harvey Girl*?"

"Best decision I've ever made."

"Why would you say that?"

"Because I'm happy here. I love my job, I love interacting with all the guests who stream through El Tovar every day, and I love . . . "

"Jack?" Ruthanne finished for her when Myrtle faltered. "You love Jack?"

Myrtle released a sigh. "I suppose I do."

"You're going to have to tell him."

"I can't tell him I love him. That would be far too forward. Call me old-fashioned, but I believe it's the man's job to declare his love first."

Ruthanne rolled her eyes. "I didn't mean tell him you love him, I meant tell him about your past and that you come from a New York society family."

"What if he doesn't like hearing that, and what if he decides he no longer wants anything to do with me?"

"Have you not seen how he looks at you? Granted, he might be a touch put out with you for keeping that information from him, but I highly doubt he'll abandon you like that ex-fiancé of yours did. Jack cares about you, and he deserves to know the truth."

Myrtle bit her lip. "You're right, of course, I suppose I really should tell him." She drew in a breath and nodded. "I'll tell him tonight, but after the dance. I'm not about to ruin the first opportunity I'll have to dance with Jack by making him cross with me."

"Don't blame you for that," Ruthanne said. "With that settled, I have to start getting ready. Think you'll still have time to help me with my hair?"

"Certainly, but you remember that I'm only good with the Gibson Girl style, don't you?"

"I love the Gibson Girl. But just out of curiosity, did you ever do your hair before you left New York?"

"Will you be annoyed with me if I say I used to have my own personal lady's maid?"

Ruthanne rolled her eyes. "How in the world were you able to adapt to a life in service as a Harvey Girl after growing up in the lap of luxury?"

Myrtle smiled. "It wasn't easy at first. I had no idea how to do most of the tasks we're expected to do on a daily basis. Learning how to carry a tray filled with food was a feat I wasn't certain I'd be able to master, not with how my arms took to shaking every time I picked one up. I eventually built up some strength, though, which allowed me to carry the trays more easily—and more gracefully, I must add. I've yet to figure out how to keep my feet from aching every day after standing for so many hours." She shook her head. "I thought I was accustomed to aching feet, what with how often my feet were stuffed into uncomfortable dancing slippers. However, there's a distinct difference between having aching feet from dancing and aching feet from doing a hard day's work. When you're attending a ball, you can choose to sit out a set and take off your slippers. I'm fairly certain management wouldn't be very understanding if I tried doing that during one of my shifts."

"Agreed," Ruthanne said, leaning forward. "But how did you learn to deal with surly guests? I don't imagine members of society ever treated you as some of our guests do."

Myrtle shrugged. "As I mentioned, I was never one of the fashionable set. So while society believes it's not good form to be blatantly rude, many in society were beyond adept at leveling cruel remarks my way, done so with a smile on their faces and malice in their eyes."

Ruthanne frowned. "It's no wonder you wanted to leave New York."

"Indeed, and now, having met Jack, I know I made the right decision. But speaking of Jack, we both need to get ready for the dance."

"Too right we do." Ruthanne rose from the chair, sent Myrtle a smile, and hurried from the room, shutting the door firmly behind her.

Moving to a small table where she kept a hand mirror and her hairpins, Myrtle pulled up a chair next to it and took a seat. As she went about the daunting task of styling her hair in a Gibson Girl, which was not an easy feat to accomplish on her own, she couldn't help but wish she still *did* retain the services of her lady's maid. Her former maid had been an expert at styling hair and might have been able to turn Myrtle, at least for one night, into the beauty Jack always claimed he found her to be.

Chapter Five

"Do you still have the ring?"

Jack finished knotting his tie, then stepped away from the mirror, frowning at Walter, who was pacing around the room. His pacing suggested he was more nervous than Jack was, even though Jack was the one planning on proposing that night.

Fishing into his pocket, he withdrew a small box. "Of course I still have the ring, and you don't need to continue asking me that every five minutes. I'm not going to lose it, not after we went all the way to Chicago to purchase it."

"Think Myrtle will know how special a Tiffany ring is?"

"She's from New York. Of course she'll know. But you didn't mention to Ruthanne that we were going to Chicago, did you? I told Myrtle you and I were off on a matter of business, but I didn't mention that business centered around buying her an engagement ring."

Walter gave a roll of his eyes. "While I completely adore Ruthanne, I'm fully aware that she's incapable of keeping a secret, which is why I didn't say anything about Chicago. And because I don't want anything to go wrong with this night, I'm determined to make sure you don't lose that ring. It wouldn't be much of a moment if you ask Myrtle to marry you and then discover you've left the ring behind."

"I'm not going to forget the ring."

"So you keep saying, but that doesn't mean I'm going to stop pestering you about it."

"You're very annoying."

"That's because I'm your younger brother. Annoying comes with the territory."

Unable to argue with that logic, Jack returned his attention to the mirror, pulling down the brightly colored waistcoat he'd purchased in Chicago, the purchase prompted after Myrtle had remarked a time or two about how much she liked his embroidered waistcoat, the one he'd been wearing when he'd asked permission to court her. After readjusting his tie, even though it was still perfectly in place, he turned to Walter and frowned.

"Are you sure I shouldn't have made an effort to seek out Myrtle's father and asked for his blessing before I ask Myrtle to marry me?"

Walter edged around Jack and began fiddling with his own tie. "I told you, there isn't time for those types of gestures. Ruthanne told me that Myrtle's contract with El Tovar and the Harvey Girls was up yesterday. The only reason Mr. Eliot hasn't pressured her to sign a new one yet is because he's been busy with preparations for the dance tonight. You mark my words, though, Mr. Eliot isn't a man to neglect something like a contract for long, nor will he want to lose someone like Myrtle. The guests love her, she's a hard worker who doesn't complain, and she's not an employee any employer wants to say good-bye to. That means if you go off to seek out Mr. Schermerhorn's blessing, by the time you get back, Myrtle will have undoubtedly signed another contract, and then you'll need to wait six whole months before you'll be able to marry her."

"I don't want to wait six months."

"Then you'll need to forgo asking her father's permission. Besides, since Myrtle and her parents are apparently estranged,

Myrtle might not want you to seek out her parents. Perhaps they're really horrible people, and she doesn't want you to discover that just yet."

"I don't even know what her father does."

"Maybe he's a shady sort."

"I don't think a shady sort could have raised a daughter like Myrtle."

"Good point." Walter smiled. "Ruthanne's father is a farmer, and she's told me he's a very nice man, but she just didn't want to stay on the family farm." His smile turned into a grin. "I was relieved to hear that, because I will need to meet him at some point, since I intend to marry his daughter."

"You're thinking about marrying Ruthanne?"

Walter nodded. "'Course I am, but I'm not in any hurry to propose. Ruthanne, unlike Myrtle, still has two months on her contract, so I have time to figure out how to pull off a spectacular proposal, one she'll never forget."

Panic immediately surged through Jack's veins. "I haven't planned a spectacular proposal for Myrtle. I was simply going to pull her aside at the end of the evening and ask her under the moonlight."

"Since you're less than adept in the romance department, that *is* a spectacular proposal, and I bet Myrtle will love it and cherish the moment forever. And with that said, shall we go and collect the ladies? We're supposed to meet them at the foot of the staircase in less than ten minutes."

Nodding, Jack turned and walked out of his room, Walter falling into step beside him. After reaching the first floor, Jack stood beside the staircase the Harvey Girls always used, anticipation flowing freely as he considered the night ahead.

He'd never thought he'd meet a woman like Myrtle, let alone ask someone so delightful to marry him. But she truly seemed to enjoy his company, laughed often whenever they were together, and he was confident the affection he felt for her was returned . . . although if he was mistaken about that, the night might not go off as planned.

"There they are, coming down the stairs."

Pushing his newfound anxiety aside, Jack lifted his head, his eyes widening as he got his first glimpse of Myrtle.

He'd always thought she was the most beautiful woman he'd ever seen, but tonight, dressed in a delectable green gown, her hair pulled up on top of her head with little wispy bits teasing her cheeks, she was more beautiful than ever. As a matter of fact, the word *beautiful* didn't seem to do her justice. Perhaps lovely or—

"Jack," Myrtle said, interrupting his musing as she beamed a smile at him and came to a stop at the foot of the stairs. "You're looking exceptionally dashing this evening."

"Stunning" was his less-than-eloquent reply to that.

Myrtle's eyes twinkled. "Are you suggesting you prefer the word *stunning* over *dashing*, or have you reverted back to the time when you tossed single words my way and expected me to know exactly what you meant?"

His lips began to curve. "No, I don't want you to use *stunning* over *dashing* in regard to my appearance, and yes, I did for a moment revert back to my former ways. In my defense, though, you are beyond stunning this evening, and you stole the very breath from me."

"Nicely done," he heard Walter say as his brother took Ruthanne's arm and strolled away, telling Ruthanne she looked stunning as well, which had Ruthanne laughing as she informed Walter that *stunning* had already been put to good use that evening, so he had to try harder.

"They make a delightful couple," Myrtle said as Jack brought her gloved hand to his lips and kissed it.

"And what of us? Do you believe we make a delightful couple as well?"

"I suppose we do, at that."

Returning the smile she sent him, Jack tucked her hand into the crook of his arm and began moving with her through El Tovar, making his way outside, where the dance was to be held that evening.

He drew her to a stop at the edge of a wooden dance floor that had been built for the night's festivities and glanced around, taking in the sight of old-fashioned lanterns hanging on hooks and tables draped in white linen.

He nodded to where members of the band that had been hired for the evening's entertainment were already assembled. "It looks like they're almost ready to begin."

Myrtle nodded, but then she frowned and caught his eye. "I never thought to ask, but do you enjoy dancing?"

"I'm not that light on my feet, but I do know how to dance. Took lessons a few years back with my little sister." He smiled. "Sadie decided she needed someone to practice her steps with, and I thought it wouldn't be bad to learn. I'm glad I took those lessons now because I won't need you to take over the lead."

Myrtle returned his smile. "I'm sure you'll do just fine, but I am capable of leading and did so numerous times when my younger sister, Eloise, was preparing to make . . ."

"Preparing to make what?" he pressed when she didn't finish her sentence.

Before she could answer him, the band began playing, and the next thing he knew, he was in the very middle of the dance floor, Myrtle in his arms. Any lingering questions about what she'd not finished telling him were forgotten the second they began to waltz.

It quickly became evident that Myrtle had waltzed more than a few times, moving across the floor with such grace that he found himself not paying attention to his own steps, which had him treading somewhat heavily on her foot. "Sorry about that."

She waved his apology aside. "Happens all the time."

As they continued to waltz, Jack found himself wondering how often Myrtle's feet had been trampled during a dance, and then wondered where she'd been doing that dancing in the first place. Deciding that would be a great topic for conversation after the music ended, he pulled her closer to him, that closeness allowing him to enjoy the subtle perfume she'd dabbed on her neck. To his regret, the music soon came to an end, the guests broke into a polite round of applause, and just as he was about to ask Myrtle if she wanted to dance the next dance with him as well, she suddenly stiffened right as someone tapped him on the shoulder.

"Excuse me," a man drawled from behind him in what could only be considered a cultured tone of voice. "I believe the rest of Mertie's dances are meant to be mine."

Turning, Jack narrowed his eyes at a slender man with thinning blond hair who was dressed in what was clearly an expensive suit. "And you would be . . . ?"

The man puffed out his chest. "I'm Mertie's fiancé, of course—or at least I will be after we clear up a small misunderstanding we have between us."

Chapter Six

As Jack glowered at Mr. Percy Kane, the man who'd left her for Miss Vivian Davis, Myrtle felt the enjoyment she'd just experienced over sharing a first dance with Jack disappear into thin air.

Why Percy would think she'd welcome him with open arms was quite beyond her, but when he crooked a finger, quite as if she were some type of dog who would immediately obey his summons, she lifted her chin, crossed her arms over her chest, and refused to move so much as an inch. "What are you doing here?"

Percy blinked and lowered his hand. "I've come to make amends."

"Over the *slight* misunderstanding you just mentioned to Jack?"

"Who?"

She nodded to Jack, who looked more than intimidating, especially considering his hands were clenched and a vein had begun throbbing on his forehead. "Jack, or rather, Mr. Jack Daggett, my *suitor*."

Percy frowned. "You can't very well have a suitor and a fiancé at the same time, Mertie."

"Her name is Myrtle," Jack said before Myrtle had an opportunity to respond. "You'd be wise to remember that from this point forward."

Percy drew himself up, even though doing so still made him a good six inches shorter than Jack. "You dare threaten me, Mr. Daggett? Do you have any idea who I am?"

"I'm thinking you must be the man who left Myrtle for another woman, which, if you ask me, constitutes more than a mere misunderstanding. I would think it's definitely along the lines of a very grave mistake that I don't believe you'll be able to fix."

"I'm Mr. Percy Kane of the New York Kane family," Percy began, ignoring everything Jack had just said. "We're one of the oldest and most respected families in New York. Mertie, or rather Myrtle, and I have been promised to each other since before she left for finishing school and I left to study in England." He looked Jack up and down before he released a sniff. "I doubt you can claim the same impressive pedigree."

When Jack stiffened, Myrtle stepped forward, hoping to defuse a situation that was rapidly getting out of hand. "Perhaps we should take this conversation somewhere more private. If the two of you have neglected to remember, we're at a dance, an event that's supposed to be enjoyable, not hostile."

Unwilling to allow either man an opportunity to argue with her, she took hold of Jack's arm and tugged him from the dance floor, Percy immediately falling into step with her as she charged away from the guests.

Not stopping until she rounded the corner of El Tovar, she all but shoved Jack onto one of the stone benches where they'd spent many an enjoyable evening, taking a seat beside him as Percy remained standing, watching Myrtle closely.

"You look different," Percy suddenly said, his gaze traveling the length of her.

"I've lost some weight," she returned, knowing that if she

ignored his statement, Percy would launch into the reasons he thought she looked different, pontificating on and on about the matter until he figured it out. She'd always tolerated his pontifications in the past, but tonight she had no patience for that, or for that matter, for Percy.

"It suits you," Percy said, sending her a smile she knew he thought was charming, but at the moment she found it anything but.

"When did you get here?" she demanded.

Percy gave a wave of his hand. "A few hours ago."

"And you thought to wait until I was dancing before making your presence known?"

"I fell asleep in my room. It was a very tiring train ride to this desolate place, and I was exhausted once I finally got here."

"But why are you here? Don't tell me it's because you're desperate to make amends. The last we spoke, you were more than clear about your lack of affection for me, stating, in case you've forgotten, that I was a good sort, but not the type of woman you'd ever be able to love—not like you loved Miss Vivian Davis."

"Vivian and I decided we didn't suit."

"Why?"

Percy shot a look at Jack, then returned his attention to Myrtle. "I don't believe there's any need to get into that in front of a stranger."

"Jack's not a stranger to me."

"Right, because he's your *suitor.*"

"He is."

Percy waved that aside. "What type of man would want to call on a woman who spends her time as a waitress?"

"I'm not a waitress. I'm a Harvey Girl."

"Same thing. You do know that your mother has had to go to extreme measures to keep this little adventure of yours quiet, don't you? She's been telling everyone that you went away to enjoy the hot springs in Colorado, but we won't be able to keep your Harvey Girl status quiet forever if you continue on in your ridiculous position."

"I'm not giving up my position as a Harvey Girl."

"I'm sure you'll reconsider that attitude once you think about how your little act of rebellion will affect our future children. Do you think they'll enjoy whispers about a mother who spent a year serving coffee and mopping up spills?"

"There'll never be any future children between us, Percy, because I'll never marry you. With that said, I have every confidence in stating that your trip to El Tovar has been a complete waste of your time."

Percy jerked his head in Jack's direction. "Is that because you intend to marry him?"

Myrtle chanced a glance at Jack and found him watching her closely. There was something unfamiliar lingering in his eyes as he watched her, something she was very much afraid might be disappointment. Drawing in a deep breath and not allowing herself to dwell on that just yet, she released the breath and looked back at Percy. "Jack and I haven't discussed definite plans to marry yet, but that has nothing to do with you. I'll never marry you."

"Your parents want you to marry me."

"I doubt that, not after what happened at Mrs. Oelrichs's ball at the end of the summer Season last year in Newport—one where, if you'll recall, you made a grand production out of announcing to everyone that you and Miss Davis were engaged." Her lips thinned. "You didn't even afford me the courtesy of telling me, your supposed fiancée, that you were marrying someone else. Because of that, I can't believe my parents are still keen to see the two of us married, even if they did once want exactly that."

"Who do you think encouraged me to come fetch you or gave me directions to locate you in the first place?"

"Do not say my mother told you where to find me."

"She did, and speaking of your mother, I have a letter from her to give you, one you're certainly going to want to read at your earliest convenience."

Before Myrtle could respond to that, Jack was suddenly on his feet, frowning not at Percy but at her.

"We need to talk, Myrtle."

Percy nodded. "Good idea, Mr. Daggett. The sooner the two of you break things off, the sooner Myrtle can begin packing her belongings to return to New York with me."

"I'm not going back with you."

"I imagine you will after you read your mother's letter. Did I mention she's already reinstated your trust fund and that she told me to tell you that you can once again access your bank account?"

Rubbing a hand over a forehead that was beginning to throb, Myrtle looked at Jack, who was now watching her not with disappointment in his eyes but disbelief.

"Perhaps we *should* go have that talk," she suggested, albeit reluctantly, since there was little doubt the conversation between them was going to be anything but pleasant.

"Lead the way," Jack said shortly, thrusting an arm out for her, which proved that, even though he seemed to be struggling to maintain his temper, he was still a true gentleman at heart, unlike Percy, who hadn't even bothered to seek her out when he'd first arrived at El Tovar and had apparently felt there was nothing wrong with once again ambushing her in front of a crowd.

Taking Jack's arm and walking with him across the lawn, Myrtle increased her pace, wanting to get far away from Percy as quickly as possible. She stopped beside a scraggly tree and released Jack's arm, wincing when he crossed his arms over his chest and leveled a cool eye on her.

"I'm listening" were the first words out of his mouth.

"I'm not sure where to begin."

"Why don't you start with the part about how you're evidently a member of New York society, or better yet, explain to me why you didn't bother to tell me important details about your past. Didn't you think I'd eventually learn the truth?"

"Well, yes, and I was actually going to tell you all about my past later tonight. I simply didn't want to ruin the earlier part of our evening by disclosing truths I knew you weren't going to enjoy hearing."

"I think your Percy managed to sufficiently ruin the evening for us."

"He's not my Percy, and I'm not going back to New York with him."

Jack let out a grunt. "You would have me believe that you're perfectly content to continue as a Harvey Girl after learning your mother is willing to reinstate your finances? Your improved financial state will obviously allow you to return to enjoying not one, but two social Seasons a year, one of those Seasons being in Newport."

Myrtle winced. "You picked up on the Newport reference?"

"Where Percy disclosed he was engaged to another woman? Yes. And do know, even with me being an uneducated man and not a member of any society, I know how exclusive Newport is. Why, I even know that the summer residences everyone refers to as 'cottages' are nothing of the sort, since they're, in actuality, mansions."

He began pacing back and forth, mumbling under his breath words she didn't fully catch, although she did hear him say something about being a fool and "should have known better."

Stopping a moment later, he lifted his head. "Does your family live on Fifth Avenue in New York?"

She refused another wince. "They do, but before you begin firing more questions about my time in New York, or anything about my involvement with high society, allow me to simply state that I was never embraced by that society. I certainly was never what anyone could consider fashionable. In all honesty, I was nothing more than a wallflower."

"While it's confusing to me how you could have earned the label of wallflower, I don't understand why you didn't tell me all this before tonight. You've had plenty of time to do so over the past few weeks, and yet you said nothing."

"Which, in hindsight, was very wrong of me." Myrtle shook her head. "Ruthanne encouraged me to disclose all the details about my past to you, and I must say she was certainly right that failure to do so at my earliest convenience would cause trouble between us."

Jack's gaze sharpened. "You told Ruthanne about who you really are?"

"I haven't been hiding my identity, Jack. I merely didn't divulge details about my unfortunate family and their social circumstances."

"Shall I assume your family possesses more than an adequate fortune?"

Myrtle bit her lip. "I'm afraid so. My great-grandfather made his original wealth in real estate, buying up land surrounding New York City before it became the most progressive city in the country. My grandfather and father have only added to that fortune with their business opportunities."

"You're *old* money?"

"About as old as you can get, but if we could return to the matter of me disclosing the truth to Ruthanne," Myrtle hurried to continue because Jack was now looking rather furious, "I only told her the full truth tonight after she grew suspicious about the dress I'm wearing."

"Why would she be suspicious about your dress?"

"Because it's a very expensive dress that came from Paris."

"You've been to Paris?"

"This is probably not going to endear me to you, but yes. I used to travel there every spring to select a new wardrobe for the Seasons in Newport and New York."

"You're right, that disclosure doesn't endear you to me at all."

"And that's exactly why it took me so long to work up the nerve to tell you about my family."

"You didn't tell me. Percy did."

There was something quite maddening about trying to reason with an angry man. Taking a deep breath, Myrtle released it and took a step closer to Jack, who immediately took a large step backward. She pretended she didn't notice. "But I was *planning* on telling you. If you don't believe me, you can ask Ruthanne. She'll vouch for me."

"Whether or not you were planning to tell me tonight is really beside the point. As I've already mentioned, we've spent a great deal of time together, but not once did you mention anything about New York society, except for . . . " Jack tilted his head. "You did mention to me that you didn't care for *The House of Mirth*. I also recall my sister saying Edith Wharton's characters were inspired by real New York society members." He frowned. "Those characters wouldn't have been inspired by anyone you know, would they? That would explain why you wouldn't care for that particular book, if those characters were shown in a bad light."

"One of them might have reminded me of a distant aunt."

"And that aunt would be?"

"Caroline Astor, whose maiden name was Schermerhorn."

"You're related to Caroline Astor?"

"You've heard of her?"

"I may have grown up in the country, Myrtle, but I've traveled extensively over the years. Of course I've heard of Caroline Astor, along with the whole Astor family." He rubbed a hand over his face. "You're not related to the Vanderbilt or Rockefeller families as well, are you?"

"I've got a few Vanderbilt cousins, and my father's sister is a member of the Rockefeller family."

Jack threw up his hands and stalked a few feet away from her, stopping and turning back a second later. "This changes everything."

"I don't see why it should. I left my life in New York behind when I joined the Harvey Girls—left my fortune behind too. As far as I'm concerned, I'm merely Myrtle, a Harvey Girl, and a woman who has been fortunate enough to learn she was never meant to live in high society."

"You'll come to miss that life at some point."

"I won't, not if you'll forgive me and—" She stopped talking, realizing she'd almost said too much.

"You'll eventually come to resent my lack of education and lack of proper manners if we were to continue on together," Jack said quietly, the resignation in his tone all but breaking Myrtle's heart because it suggested he'd already made up his mind that they would *not* be continuing on together.

Her vision turned blurry with unshed tears, and unwilling to allow Jack to see those tears, she stepped into the shadow the tree afforded from the lantern light, swiping a hand over her eyes before she lifted her chin.

"Do you think so little of me that you truly believe that?" she asked.

"I don't know what to think of you, but I do know that we come from two different worlds, and yours is not a world I'd ever fit into. With that said, I think you should return to New York."

"And what will you return to?" she whispered.

"My business, of course. I've neglected it of late, and it's past time I rectify that."

Myrtle drew in a deep breath. "So we're ending our courtship?"

Jack regarded her for a long moment before he nodded. "I think that would be for the best."

Without saying another word, he strode away, disappearing into the darkness of the night.

Chapter Seven

"You're a very difficult man to run to ground."

Lifting his head from the contract he'd been working on, Jack pulled off his spectacles and narrowed his eyes at Walter, who was winding his way through the small tables at the outdoor café directly across from the Palmer House in Chicago, where Jack had taken a room. Following directly behind Walter was Ruthanne, and directly behind her was another Harvey Girl, Opal Chapman, if he remembered correctly.

Jack stood up and shook Walter's hand, then nodded to Ruthanne and Opal as Walter pulled two additional chairs up to the table and helped the women get settled. After they'd taken their seats, Jack sat down again, Walter taking a chair beside him.

"What are you doing in Chicago?"

"I already told you," Walter said. "We've been trying to run you down, and we've had quite the time doing that, since we've had to trek across the country."

"It's been an adventure," Ruthanne added. "One where I got to meet your mother, Jack. She's a lovely woman and wanted me to tell you that even though you've apparently made a complete mess of things with Myrtle, she's confident you'll put all of what she called 'that nasty business' to rights in the end."

"You met my mother?"

Ruthanne smiled. "I have, and again, she's a lovely woman."

Jack frowned. "But why have you come with Walter to run me down? Won't you and Opal be in trouble for missing your shifts at El Tovar?"

Ruthanne waved that aside. "Walter arranged everything. He convinced Mr. Eliot to allow Opal and me to take a few of our vacation days, even though they certainly weren't planned. I do think Walter might have slipped Mr. Eliot some money to convince him to allow us the time off."

"I'm here as Ruthanne's chaperone," Opal said, fanning herself with a menu. "It would have been a big scandal if she'd taken off with Walter without one, what with them not being married and all." She smiled. "I saw it as my Christian duty to volunteer to accompany them."

Ruthanne released a snort. "You volunteered because Walter offered you a tidy sum to come with us."

Opal's smile turned into a grin. "Well, there is that, but God would have expected me to volunteer even without the money Walter gave me." Her grin faded ever so slightly. "I was worried, though, that I wouldn't have a job to return to after this adventure is over once it became clear that our time away from El Tovar was going to be longer than expected. Mr. Eliot isn't known for his understanding nature, even if he did agree to allow us to take a few vacation days without notice."

Jack frowned. "You're worried you're going to be fired?"

Opal's grin returned. "I *was* worried. But when your brother learned I have a talent for organization and typing, he offered me a job at Daggett Industries as a secretary." She nodded toward Ruthanne. "Ruthanne's been offered a job as well, although I don't imagine she'll need to take it, not since Walter got up his gumption and asked her to marry him."

Jack caught Walter's eye. "You and Ruthanne are engaged?"

Walter nodded. "We are, but I've yet to get her a ring, since we've been occupied with trying to find you."

After telling Ruthanne congratulations, and then kissing her on the cheek and giving Walter a hefty pat on the back, Jack turned to Opal. "You're not overly distressed, are you, about giving up your position as a Harvey Girl?"

Opal shook her head. "'Course not. My dear grandma told me time after time that God presents us with unexpected opportunities in life, ones that can lead us in directions we never imagined. I thoroughly enjoyed my time as a Harvey Girl, but I can't say I'll miss being on my feet all day. I'm looking forward to renting myself a nice room in the vicinity of your factory." She sent Jack an unexpected wink. "I'm also looking forward to meeting some of those fine young men who work in your factory and who your brother promised to introduce me to."

For the first time since he'd parted ways with Myrtle, Jack felt his lips curve. "Which means you might not be employed as one of Daggett Industries' secretaries for long."

As Opal beamed in delight at that idea, Jack turned back to Walter. "Returning to the reason all of you are here—why have you been searching for me, and how did you figure out I'd be in Chicago?"

Walter picked up a menu from the table. "Ma suggested we look for you here after we learned you'd not gone home to Michigan."

"Why did you think I went home to Michigan?"

"You always go home when something's bothering you, and I knew losing Myrtle bothered you."

"I didn't lose Myrtle. She left me."

"She did *not* leave you."

Jack shook his head. "I beg to differ. When I returned to El

Tovar the morning after the dance to speak with her, after I'd had a long night under the stars to settle my thoughts, I found she'd already left. She certainly didn't hesitate about taking my suggestion to return to New York after I told her that's where she belonged, amongst the socially elite."

"Which you should have never told her," Walter argued. "But why did you sleep outside when you had a perfectly good room to stay in at El Tovar?"

"I needed to think, and there's no better place to think than under the stars in the middle of nowhere with no people around. Gives a man a new perspective on things and also allows him an opportunity to have a long chat with God with no interruptions."

Ruthanne tilted her head. "And did God bring you to any conclusions about what you were discussing with Him?"

Jack rubbed a hand over his face. "I thought He did, but after I returned to tell Myrtle I might have overreacted, I discovered she'd taken the first train out that morning—and with Percy, no less. That left me with nothing but to conclude that God hadn't wanted me to make amends with Myrtle after all. So that's that, and I'll just continue on as I have before, without Myrtle."

Ruthanne leaned across the table. "Myrtle didn't go back with Percy because she decided she belonged in New York. She only left El Tovar because Percy gave her a letter from her mother that explained how she has been suffering from a heart ailment that might very well see her dying soon."

Jack blinked. "Her mother's dying?"

"According to the letter she sent Myrtle, yes."

"No wonder she left, but . . ." He turned to Walter. "Why did you leave El Tovar before speaking with me?"

Walter shrugged. "I thought you'd already left for Michigan. That's why Ruthanne, Opal, and I hopped on the next available train, hoping to catch up with you so that Ruthanne could tell you about Myrtle's mother, and—"

"You wanted me to know Myrtle hadn't left El Tovar because she wanted to marry Percy?"

Walter nodded. "I did, but I also wanted you to hear directly from Ruthanne what she overheard from Percy after you left the dance . . . and after Percy enjoyed a bit too much whiskey." Walter shook his head. "Unfortunately, I was mistaken about where you'd gone, so that's why it's taken us five days to track you down."

"You said Ma pointed you toward Chicago?"

"Knowing how upset you must have been about Myrtle, she thought you might have come to Chicago to return the ring. She guessed you wouldn't want to keep a reminder of what might have been and was now never going to be, since you made a complete disaster of things when you turned your back on Myrtle."

"I didn't turn my back on her."

Ruthanne cleared her throat. "Myrtle told me you ended your courtship."

"Well, yes, I did."

"That's turning your back on her." Ruthanne settled into her chair. "I'm sure she'd be annoyed with me for telling you this, but she was very remorseful about not disclosing the truth about her past to you earlier, and she was very distraught when I spoke with her later that night."

Jack frowned. "She didn't seem overly distraught to me."

"Myrtle doesn't like pity, Jack," Ruthanne argued. "She wouldn't have allowed you to see her cry, but that's exactly what she was doing when I found her."

Something unpleasant began to churn through him. The thought of Myrtle crying was appalling to him, and that he'd been the reason she was crying . . .

"Tell him what you overheard Percy saying," Walter said.

"It's a fairly sordid tale and might require some coffee first so I'll do it justice," Ruthanne said.

"Forgive me, ladies." Jack raised a hand, which had a waitress hurrying their way. "I've completely neglected my manners. Of course you should have coffee first."

"And a nice plate of cakes might be nice as well," Opal said, grinning as she peered over the menu once she'd stopped fanning herself with it. "And I wouldn't be opposed to some cucumber sandwiches, which I've always wanted to try."

It took a good few minutes to place their order for coffee, cakes, and sandwiches, and by the time their waitress left, one whom Opal felt was very proficient at her job, another few minutes had passed. They were quickly served their coffee, and after Ruthanne had a few sips of hers, she sat back and pinned Jack with a stern eye. "You've been an idiot."

Jack blinked. "That's what you overheard Percy saying? That I'm an idiot?"

Ruthanne waved that aside. "'Course not, it's just something I've been wanting to say to you."

It was difficult to suppress a grin. "Duly noted, but why do you believe I'm an idiot?"

"Because you ended your courtship with Myrtle the second you learned she comes from a wealthy family. Why did you do that?"

Jack rubbed a hand over his face. "The most important thing I could offer Myrtle was a life of luxury and access to the fortune I possess. Learning she came from wealth left me believing that I didn't have anything else of worth to offer her."

"You *are* an idiot," Ruthanne returned with a shake of her head. "*You* are all that Myrtle wanted, not your wealth, and you've done her a disservice by believing otherwise."

Something that felt a bit like hope began to swirl through

his veins. "If what you say is true, then clearly I *am* an idiot. And, with that out of the way, tell me what you overheard Percy say and how you managed to overhear him in the first place."

Ruthanne took another sip of her coffee. "Well, after I talked to Myrtle for a good hour once you left the dance, I returned to see if I could help clean up, and that's when I discovered Percy chatting away with some man from Nebraska. Both of them were well into their cups by then, but when I heard Percy tell the man that he wasn't interested in Myrtle in a romantic way, I knew I needed to hear more. I crawled underneath a table that was directly next to where Percy was sitting—and no, he never spotted me—and I spent the next hour getting quite the earful about why he suddenly decided to try to make amends with her."

"Why do I get the distinct feeling I'm not going to like what you have to say next?" Jack asked.

"Because you obviously realized, as did all of us who met him, that Percy is a despicable man. I overheard him say he hates Myrtle's name, doesn't think she's even remotely attractive, although he was pleased she'd lost some weight since the last time he'd seen her, and—this is the worst part of what I overheard—he came to fetch her back to New York because he needs to convince her to marry him because he needs her fortune."

"What?"

"He's broke," Ruthanne said. "His family apparently embraces a lifestyle that exceeds their means, although Percy was evidently unaware of how dismal their financial situation had become. He also neglected to realize that the reason his parents had been pushing him to marry Myrtle over the years was because of their dire financial state, nor did he understand how desperately his family wanted to get their hands on the money that would come with Myrtle once a wedding took place."

"Percy ended things with Myrtle almost a year ago," Jack said slowly. "Why come back for her now?"

Ruthanne's lips thinned. "Because he only recently discovered that Miss Vivian Davis, the woman he announced he was marrying at that ball last year, doesn't possess the fortune he was led to believe she did."

Jack tilted his head. "And did this Vivian Davis also discover that Percy didn't have the fortune I'm guessing she thought *he* had?"

"She did, which is why she tossed him over for a wealthy industrialist, apparently breaking Percy's heart in the process—at least according to what I overheard Percy say, although I have doubts that man has a heart."

For a long moment, Jack let everything Ruthanne had disclosed turn in his mind before he looked to Walter. "I have to go after her. Percy sounds like a desperate man, and desperate men are prone to desperate measures."

Walter didn't hesitate to nod. "I'll go with you, of course."

As the waitress returned with their food, everyone settled into eating their meal, until Walter set aside his sandwich and frowned at Jack. "Do you need any help figuring out how you're going to go about apologizing to Myrtle once we get to New York?"

Jack paused, a cucumber sandwich halfway to his mouth. "I think I can figure that out on my own. I'll tell her I'm sorry, and—"

"You're going to have to do better than that," Ruthanne interrupted. "Perhaps you should extend her that apology on bended knee, or better yet, tell her you took leave of your senses when you told her she belonged in New York."

"I suppose I could tell her that, if you think it might help."

He lowered his sandwich. "But in my defense, she did lie to me about several issues."

Walter shook his head. "She didn't lie, Jack. She merely neglected to disclose everything to you. In fairness to Myrtle, even though the two of you had known each other for months, you only started talking to the woman mere weeks ago, which really didn't allow her much time to divulge everything."

"And she really *was* planning on telling you the whole unvarnished truth about her past," Ruthanne added. "But then Percy showed up and ruined her plans."

"I have made a disaster of this, haven't I?" Jack blew out a breath. "I still can't help but wonder, though, why Myrtle would want to be with me in the first place. She grew up in high society, surrounded by culture. I grew up on a small farm in Michigan and have no formal education."

"She doesn't care that you're not from high society, and from what you told me, she definitely doesn't care about that lack of education. She only cares about you," Walter said. "Deep in your heart, you know that."

"What if she's decided she doesn't want anything else to do with me since I was the one to break up our courtship?"

A ghost of a smile played around the corners of Walter's mouth. "Then, knowing Myrtle, she'll tell you exactly that. Ruthanne and I, however, are fairly confident she'll give you a second chance if you ask."

Jack picked up his coffee and took a sip, thinking through what his brother had said. If he was honest with himself, he did want a second chance with Myrtle, but he *had* made a mess of the matter. She'd suffered rejection before when Percy abandoned her, and yet even knowing that, he'd done exactly the same thing, undoubtedly damaging any affection she held for him in the process.

"You love her, Jack, you know you do," Walter said, interrupting Jack's thoughts.

And that right there was nothing less than the truth.

He loved her. He was miserable without her, which meant . . .

"I need to get to New York as soon as possible," he said, setting aside his cup of coffee.

Ruthanne, oddly enough, shook her head. "She's not in New York. Percy was going to escort her to Newport, where her mother is staying."

Opal, who'd been relishing everything the waitress had brought her, set down her fork on a now-empty plate and nodded to Ruthanne. "You forgot to tell him what Percy has planned for the last ball of the Newport social Season."

"I didn't forget. I just didn't want to completely overwhelm him." Ruthanne caught Jack's eye. "Are you feeling overwhelmed, or are you ready for more?"

"Might as well tell me all of it."

Ruthanne nodded. "Well, the last of it is this—Percy's planning on making a big announcement at the ball, telling everyone that he and Myrtle have repaired their relationship and that they'll be getting married as soon as possible."

"Don't you think, with Myrtle's mother being so ill, that Myrtle probably won't be up for attending any balls?"

"I don't think it'll matter to Percy if she's there or not," Ruthanne said. "From what I overheard, Percy thinks if he makes a public announcement, then Myrtle will give in and agree to marry him, if only to spare herself and her family additional embarrassment."

Pushing back his chair, Jack rose to his feet. "Then I guess all that's left for us to do is get to Newport before Percy has the opportunity to put his plan into motion."

Walter got to his feet as Ruthanne and Opal did the same. "You still have that ring?"

Jack nodded. "Curiously enough, every time I headed to Tiffany's, I couldn't seem to make myself actually walk into the store to return it."

Ruthanne immediately looked smug. "Which proves you're in love with Myrtle. Let's hope you'll not mess up when you get around to telling her that, and that you'll need that ring after all."

Chapter Eight

"I cannot believe you sent a letter with Percy, claiming you were dying, when obviously you're the picture of perfect health."

Myrtle's mother, Cora Schermerhorn, readjusted the diamond necklace that drew attention to her lovely neck before she leveled cool eyes on Myrtle, who was sitting on the opposite seat of their carriage.

"I don't understand why you find that hard to believe, Myrtle. You've been more than difficult over the last year. I knew there was a distinct possibility you wouldn't return east with Percy if I didn't take drastic measures."

"I *wouldn't* have returned because, if you've forgotten, Percy threw me over for another woman, making me the laughing-stock of society."

"He feels very badly about that now."

"Eloise told me he only changed his mind about me because he's desperate for money."

Cora blinked. "How did Eloise come by that information?"

"Your youngest daughter is very good at eavesdropping, Mother. I'm sure she overhead that nasty bit of news at one of the many society events she's decided she no longer enjoys attending."

"It is troubling how difficult you and Eloise have turned of late. Thank goodness Helen is not causing me any trouble."

"Helen has always been the model of a proper society lady, Mother. But getting back to Percy, did you know his family was suffering from severe financial difficulties?"

Cora looked out the window. "I might have known the Kanes are not currently flush with cash."

"And yet you're still determined to see me married off to Percy because . . . ?"

Cora pulled her attention from the lovely view of the ocean and frowned. "Alice and Colman Kane have been great friends of mine for years. They're from some of the oldest families in New York. I can't merely sit back and watch them suffer through such hardships when your extremely large dowry will set them up nicely again."

"Father could simply extend them a loan."

Cora pursed her lips before she shook her head. "I suggested that to him, but your father has a few doubts regarding how adept Colman and Percy are at actually making money. Their original fortune, if you didn't know, came from Colman's father, and before that, his grandfather. *Your* father seems to believe he would never see a loan repaid, which is why he refused to consider my suggestion."

"But Father's fine with me marrying Percy, even though he's refused to extend Percy's family a loan?"

"Your father is unaware that Percy's come to his senses and longs to marry you again."

"Which is comforting to be sure, but what's less comforting is knowing that you apparently have no qualms bartering me off so that your friends can continue living a lifestyle they've not been able to afford for years."

Cora didn't so much as flinch. "You're a confirmed spinster, Myrtle. If you don't marry Percy, you'll spend the rest of your life alone, and what woman wants to do that?" She frowned as she took a long second to look Myrtle over. "I will admit, though, that your time away certainly seems to have agreed with you. You now have a most lovely figure, and the loss of weight has done wonders for bringing out the bone structure in your face."

"Losing weight is remarkably easy when you're on your feet all day, lugging around heavy trays filled with—"

Cora lifted a hand, stopping Myrtle mid-sentence. "You know I find talk of your time as a waitress to be most distressing. I'll thank you never to broach the subject again, and do be certain not to let it slip out tonight at Tessie Oelrichs's famed last ball of the Newport Season. I've told everyone you were taking the waters in Colorado, and I'll thank you to stick to that story."

"There's nothing disgraceful about earning an honest day's pay for an honest day's work. There was absolutely nothing wrong with me accepting a position as a Harvey Girl."

"There was everything wrong with it. You're a Schermerhorn. We don't serve anyone, and we certainly don't traipse off to the wilds of the Grand Canyon in order to take up a lowly position."

"The Grand Canyon is spectacular, Mother, and I wouldn't be opposed to going back there after I get matters settled with Percy once and for all."

"There's no society in Arizona."

"True, but I was given an opportunity to experience what I've come to think of as grand encounters with people I never would have met if I'd stayed in the small world of New York high society. Those people were kind, intriguing, and . . ." She stopped talking as an image of Jack flashed to mind, that image forcing her to swallow the word *delicious*, because that was hardly a word her mother would enjoy hearing come out of her daughter's mouth, and it would undoubtedly lead to questions Myrtle wasn't ready to answer.

She hated that she'd had to leave El Tovar without seeing Jack again and doing a better job of explaining to him why she'd withheld her past from him for so long. Granted, she didn't really have much more to say to him on the matter, but she would have been willing to try anything if only to see if they might possibly still have a chance together, because . . .

She loved him, desperately so, and she didn't want to return to society and didn't want to marry any other man, especially Percy.

"Oh, look, we're almost to Rosecliff," Cora exclaimed, pulling Myrtle from her thoughts.

Sitting forward to look out the carriage window, Myrtle set her sights on the large cottage sitting in front of the ocean. A row of carriages, along with quite a few automobiles, already lined the crushed seashell drive. She sat back. "Why didn't we take Father's automobile tonight? I thought you preferred being driven around over using a carriage these days."

"Your father's using the automobile right now, trying to locate Eloise, who, if you failed to notice, is not currently with us, even though I specifically told her I wanted her to be here tonight because this particular ball will mark your triumphant return to society."

"How do you figure that?"

"Because it's where Percy will publicly make amends for all the trouble he caused you last year."

"What?"

Cora waved the question aside and suddenly began fumbling with the evening bag lying beside her, pulling out what seemed to be a clipping from a newspaper and thrusting it at Myrtle.

"That right there is a sign to me that this is to be your night of triumph."

Myrtle unfolded the piece of paper and frowned. Turning it over, she scanned what appeared to be a random article about boating, then turned it over again, her brows drawing together as she looked at an advertisement from Tiffany's, one that had the word *hope* scrawled in large print right beneath a drawing of a diamond ring. "I'm afraid I'm at a bit of a loss as to why you want me to see this," she finally said.

"That's my sign from God. And I'm certain it's a more accurate sign from God than the one you mentioned *you* thought you got from Him when you saw that advertisement for the Harvey Girls."

Myrtle lifted her head. "You believe an advertisement from Tiffany's is a sign from God that means . . . what exactly?"

"It means you're meant to accept Percy's proposal this evening, if that's what he's intending to do, and I'm meant to feel a sense of hope because that word is written under the ring."

Myrtle narrowed her eyes at her mother. "First off, Percy better not be proposing to me tonight, because I was very firm when I told him I wasn't interested in marrying him. Secondly, since his family apparently doesn't have any money, I doubt he can afford to present me with a ring from Tiffany's."

"I didn't think about that," Cora admitted before she smiled. "But if he does propose, even if he doesn't give you a ring from Tiffany's, do know that I'll buy you that ring if that's what you've got your heart set on."

"I haven't said a thing about a ring from Tiffany's. You're the one who pulled out this advertisement from the newspaper."

Ignoring that, Cora readjusted her diamond necklace again before she nodded to Myrtle as the carriage came to a stop. "Remember, dear, this is your night. Don't ruin it, and please at least try to look like you're enjoying yourself."

Myrtle opened her mouth to argue with that bit of nonsense, but before she could voice a single argument, the carriage door opened and her mother disappeared through it, leaving a whiff of expensive perfume behind.

Knowing there was nothing to do but follow her mother, since there was no telling what Percy might do if she decided not to attend the ball, Myrtle accepted the hand of a member of the Oelrichs's staff and stepped from the carriage. Marching her way toward the front door of Rosecliff, one of the most extravagant homes in Newport, she joined a throng of guests waiting in the receiving line. It took less than a minute for the whispers to begin. Fans were soon brought out to hide wagging tongues, but curiously enough, the gossip that was obviously spreading about her didn't bother Myrtle in the least.

She sent Mrs. Belmont, the previous Mrs. Vanderbilt, a nod when she caught that lady gawking at her, then swept her way into Rosecliff, presenting Mr. and Mrs. Oelrichs with a curtsy and pleasant greeting before she headed for the ballroom, keeping her head high.

"Mertie, there you are," Percy called out the moment she entered the ballroom, his refusal to use her given name sending temper crawling through her.

"You need to stop calling me Mertie. And if you don't, I'm giving you fair warning that you're not going to like what I'll do to you the next time I hear you use that ridiculous nickname," she said, not bothering to lower her voice.

"You're acting quite unlike your usual self, and I have to tell you, I'm not enjoying this new you." Percy stepped closer and took hold of her hand, his eyes narrowing when she tugged her hand from his.

"What's wrong with you?" he demanded, grabbing hold of her hand again, which she immediately tried to get back.

A bit of a tug-of-war erupted between them, something that left her grinning when she won the battle in the end. Crossing her arms over her chest, which effectively made it all but impossible for him to go after her hand again, she arched a brow. "Why would you think something's wrong with me?"

"You're behaving in a very un-Myrtle-like fashion."

"Thank you, but perhaps I wouldn't be forced to behave that way if my own mother hadn't lied to get me back here and if you hadn't lied to me about why you wanted to resume what was never a proper relationship between us in the first place."

"I didn't lie to you."

"You certainly didn't bother to tell me that you only tracked me down at El Tovar because you're in desperate need of my fortune."

Percy blinked and then actually ran a hand through his thinning blond hair, misplacing several strands in the process. "Who told you that?"

"My sister, although how Eloise found out is a mystery. However, with that said, do know that I have no intention of marrying you, and—" Myrtle stopped talking when she caught sight of Miss Vivian Davis, the lady Percy had thrown Myrtle over for a year ago. That Vivian seemed to be heading Myrtle's way was clear cause for concern, as was the fact that Percy was turning a remarkable shade of purple, probably because Vivian was on the arm of a large man by the name of Mr. Curtis Sinclair. Mr. Sinclair was a wealthy industrialist Myrtle knew only slightly, but he was a man clearly smitten with Vivian, since he was looking a bit dazed as he kept his attention on her face.

"Miss Schermerhorn," Vivian all but gushed, stopping directly in front of Myrtle. "How lovely to see you returned to the fold." She nodded to Percy. "Mr. Kane."

"Vivian," Percy bit out, his use of her given name drawing Mr. Sinclair's immediate attention. Percy, however, didn't notice Mr. Sinclair glaring at him because his attention was settled squarely on the woman who'd broken his heart. He'd made that odd admission to Myrtle during one of the many peculiar conversations they'd shared on the long train ride to New York, even though he'd been trying his hardest to convince Myrtle to take him back.

Vivian turned from Percy and smiled brightly at Myrtle. "I simply have to say that you're looking marvelous, Miss Schermerhorn. Taking the waters in Colorado certainly agreed with you. And, with that said, I wanted to make certain that you're not still cross with me about what happened last summer."

Finding it almost surreal that she was standing with the two people who'd been responsible for her rapid departure from society, Myrtle tilted her head, trying to think of something to say to that, smiling as the perfect response sprang to mind.

"I'm not cross with you at all, Miss Davis. In all honesty, what happened last summer allowed me to enjoy all manner of grand encounters with people I'd never have met if I'd stayed in New York. Those encounters, I'm delighted to say, showed me the world in an entirely different perspective. For that, I thank you, so we'll let bygones be bygones, if it's all the same to you. But now, if you'll excuse me, I'm off to find some refreshments."

Not bothering to wait and see if Vivian had anything else to say, Myrtle walked away, stopping to accept a glass of wine from one of the many servers. Having no desire to engage in idle chitchat with anyone, she strolled through the open French doorways that led from the ballroom to the back courtyard, not stopping until she reached a stone wall that separated the grounds from the cliffs leading down to the sea.

Lifting her face to the breeze that was blowing off the ocean, she closed her eyes and allowed her thoughts to drift, wondering what she was going to do next with her life.

She'd been considering returning to El Tovar, but because Jack would no longer be stopping there to see her, she knew it would never be the same. Taking a sip of wine as the orchestra began to play in the ballroom, she pushed aside her troubling thoughts as the music soothed away some of the turmoil she'd been feeling of late.

How long she simply listened to the music, she had no idea, but her sense of peace suddenly evaporated when her mother dashed across the courtyard, calling Myrtle's name.

"Ah, there you are, my dear," Cora said, drawing in a few raspy breaths as she came to a stop in front of Myrtle. "I've been searching for you everywhere."

Trepidation was immediate. "Why?"

"Because Percy's just told me he's about to make an announcement in front of everyone, and I didn't want you to miss what will surely be a moment you'll never want to forget."

Chapter Nine

"Does anyone else find it curious that a minute after our rented cab breaks a wheel, Myrtle's father and sister just happen to drive past us, graciously stopping to see if we need assistance?" Ruthanne asked from where she was squished up against the window of the automobile they were currently racing down the road in, trying to get to a Newport ball as quickly as possible.

"I think that's what's known as divine intervention," Eloise Schermerhorn said, turning to smile at Ruthanne from her position in the middle seat of the automobile driven by a chauffeur who'd told Jack his name was Duncan. "I was already supposed to be at the ball, you see, but decided on impulse to take a trip to the Newport Casino earlier." She glanced at her father, Mr. James Schermerhorn, who sat beside her. "I needed to talk to Daddy about what I'd learned about Percy, but Mother was being annoyingly difficult, always swooping in whenever I managed to get Daddy alone. That's why I snuck out to the casino, leaving word with our butler about where I was going, knowing Mother would send Daddy to fetch me when she realized I might miss the ball."

"You could have simply told me you needed a private word," James said dryly.

"But then we wouldn't have run across Jack, Walter, Ruthanne, and Opal," Eloise pointed out. She glanced at Jack, who was squished between Opal and Walter in the back seat. "Myrtle's told me all about you, and may I say that I'm delighted you've decided to come after my sister. She's very fond of you."

Jack blinked. "She told you that?"

"Indeed, and I hope you realize she wouldn't have left matters with you as she did if Mother hadn't insisted Percy deliver that ridiculous letter, stating that she was at her last prayers."

"You didn't tell me anything about your mother sending a letter to Myrtle," James said.

"I haven't had time to tell you everything, Daddy. It took you forever to come fetch me from the casino, and because we're on a tight schedule, I thought it was more important to tell you about how Percy's intending on making a grand announcement at the ball tonight."

"One he apparently believes will cause Myrtle to accept his proposal because he intends to do it in front of Newport society, if I understand you correctly," James added with a shake of his head. "I really cannot believe your mother neglected to mention that Percy has decided marriage to Myrtle is his only option to save his family from financial ruin, something your mother must have known I wouldn't agree to and certainly wouldn't give my blessing to. What *could* she have been thinking?"

Eloise shrugged. "Mother longs for the time when society was different, Daddy. She misses the exclusivity of old society, and because the Kanes have been a part of New York society forever, I believe Mother thinks that if she's able to help them maintain their social position, she'll be able to hang onto at least a bit of the society she's always loved."

"A ridiculous notion, to be sure," James said. "It's the twentieth century. Of course things are changing. If I had any idea Cora was intending to use Myrtle's dowry to get the Kanes out of a financial disaster of their own making, I would have gotten rid of Myrtle's dowry with a stroke of a pen."

Jack tried to sit forward, then abandoned that when he realized he was firmly wedged between Opal and Walter. "Mr. Schermerhorn, Myrtle told me that you and your wife cut her off from her finances when she decided to become a Harvey Girl."

James leaned over the back of the seat and frowned. "I did nothing of the sort. Myrtle's my daughter, and while I was a little wary about her picking up and moving out west, I think that move was exactly what she needed. She seems more confident in herself now, more self-assured. But there was no need for her to believe she had to take a job as a Harvey Girl. She always had access to her trust fund."

"She has a trust fund?" Ruthanne asked.

"She does."

"She also seems to have a dowry," Opal added, her eyes wide as she kept gazing around the large automobile. She'd admitted to Jack in a whisper when they'd first driven off that she'd never been in an automobile before and found it somewhat terrifying.

"Speaking of Myrtle's dowry," James said, catching Jack's eye, "am I to understand that you've rushed to Newport because you want to make amends with my daughter and then ask her to marry you?"

Jack rubbed a hand over his face. "I'm not sure she'll have me, sir. I did break off our courtship after Percy showed up, which I'm convinced hurt Myrtle and left her disappointed with me."

"He only did that, though, Mr. Schermerhorn," Ruthanne added, "because Myrtle was withholding some of the details of her past. She didn't mention anything about growing up in society, nor how much money she had." She smiled. "Not that I blame her, mind you, since Jack didn't take the news about her fortune well. I think Myrtle will forgive him, though, seeing as how she loves him."

James shot a look at Jack, then returned his attention to Ruthanne. "You think my daughter loves him?"

Ruthanne nodded. "Most definitely."

"And what of you, Mr. Daggett?" James asked, turning a stern look on Jack. "Do you return that love?"

"I do, sir." Jack blew out a breath. "And with that said, I would like to ask for your blessing before I ask Myrtle to marry me, but do know that I'll understand if you're not yet comfortable giving it to me."

"Can you provide her with a happy life?"

"I'm somewhat well off, Mr. Schermerhorn. My business, Daggett Industries, is rather profitable."

"I know who you are, Jack, as well as about your business," James surprised him by saying. "I'm heavily invested in the telephone industry, where your name and the products you supply are well known. I'm aware of how successful you've been, and how you can provide for Myrtle. But that's not what I asked you. I asked if you can provide her with a happy life."

Jack took a moment to allow the question to settle.

While it was clear Myrtle had no need of his fortune since she already possessed one, he was beginning to hope that she might have need of him, because she seemed to enjoy his company, and he'd been told she'd been distraught after he'd parted ways with her. That suggested she truly did care about him, and perhaps once she learned he loved her, that would provide her with the happy life her father was questioning him about.

He sent James a nod. "I believe I can."

James returned the nod. "Then you have my blessing. But further talk about other details will need to wait, because we're almost to Rosecliff."

Everyone leaned left as the car took that moment to turn,

then a minute later, it stopped in front of a grand courtyard. After Duncan opened the door and James got out, everyone else followed, practically falling from the automobile, since they'd been so squished inside it.

"You ready for this?" Walter asked, gesturing to the large mansion in front of them.

"Ready as I'll ever be."

"Just remember, everyone in there is really no different than us. A bit snobbier, perhaps, but at the end of the day, we're all just people trying to get through this extraordinary thing called life."

Unfortunately, the butler manning the front door was definitely of the belief that Jack and Walter were different, because he took one look at their less-than-formal attire and shook his head. "I'm sorry, but I can't let the two of you pass. Mrs. Oelrichs has strict rules about what her guests are allowed to wear, and tonight you can only gain entrance if you're wearing formal wear—and by that I mean black jacket, black trousers, white shirt and collar, white tie, and white waistcoat."

James stepped forward. "I'm sure Mrs. Oelrichs would allow you to make an exception just this one time, since we've got a bit of an emergency we need to handle inside."

"Mrs. Oelrichs made me turn away Mr. Leer last month because he'd forgotten his tie, and she's fast friends with him." The butler shook his head. "I'm sorry, sir, but I really can't make an exception."

"I'll be right back," Eloise said, and even though she was not dressed in an evening gown, the butler inclined his head to her after she sent him a sweet smile and dashed through the door.

"Perhaps I should go make certain Percy hasn't done anything yet," James said, moving for the front door and disappearing through it, leaving Jack and Walter behind.

Jack glanced back to the far end of the courtyard, where

Ruthanne and Opal had insisted on staying, both of them proclaiming they would not be comfortable going inside since they were dressed in plain skirts and blouses. He smiled when he noticed they'd begun strolling casually toward the side of the house, obviously looking for another way inside for Jack. Unfortunately, they were stopped a second later by a uniformed guard. He immediately took hold of their arms and began ushering them down the drive, which sent Walter sprinting after them, telling Jack over his shoulder he'd be back in a trice.

"I found a solution," Eloise suddenly called, drawing Jack's attention as she dashed out of the house, pulling a very large man with her. That man, Jack was amused to discover, seemed to be about his size and was dressed in the formal attire the butler had told him was needed to gain entrance to the ball.

"Jack, this is Mr. Howard Van Alen, a dear friend of mine who has graciously agreed to loan you the use of his clothing as well as the use of his personal invitation to this event on the chance the butler might demand one of those from you next. Howard, this is Mr. Jack Daggett, a most desperate gentleman at the moment and the man I'm convinced will soon be my brother-in-law."

Mr. Van Alen grinned. "Pleasure, Mr. Daggett, but do know that I'm not actually being overly gracious. Eloise promised me a game of tennis tomorrow if I'd lend her some assistance, and I've been trying to get her to agree to a match all summer."

"Enough of the pleasantries," Eloise barked, nodding toward some large bushes. "You two can switch clothes behind those."

It took less than five minutes to change, and even though Jack couldn't help but think his life had turned very peculiar of late, anticipation was flowing through him, as was a great sense of hope.

Thanking Mr. Van Alen again, Jack headed for the door, bracing himself as the butler looked him over, then looked over

Chapter Ten

As Percy gave a bow and the applause died down, Myrtle, even though she was more furious than she'd been in a very long time, couldn't help feeling a little curious about what Percy intended to say.

She'd been more than upfront with him about her unwillingness to marry him, but even though she'd been so vocal, it seemed as if Percy thought he could force her into accepting his proposal merely by announcing his intentions in front of society.

Her grip on the book she'd snatched from a table, a hefty tome of poems that had clearly been left out as more of a decorative piece than anything anyone would care to read, tightened as Percy cleared his throat.

"I must first thank our lovely hostess this evening, the incomparable Tessie Oelrichs, for inviting all of us to what has become the most anticipated ball of the Newport Season," Percy began, his words eliciting another round of applause. After he inclined his head to Mrs. Oelrichs, he smiled before he gestured to Myrtle, which made everyone look her way. "As many of you may recall, my dear Mertie—"

"It's Myrtle," someone called out. Someone who sounded remarkably like Ruthanne.

Myrtle craned her neck and peered around, but she didn't spot Ruthanne in the crowd, although it was highly unlikely Ruthanne would be in Newport, what with it being so very far away from—

"Yes, quite right," Percy said, his smile dimming before he hitched it firmly back into place. "As I was saying, most of you, I'm sure, remember that Myrtle and I ran into some difficulties last year at this very ball, but I'm pleased to report that we've enjoyed a reconciliation of late, and . . ."

As Percy continued on with his speech, Myrtle saw her father making his way to the front of the room. His appearance left her smiling, but because Percy was her problem and one she knew she needed to deal with, Myrtle caught her father's eye, shook her head, then strode forward, the crowd drawing in a collective breath when she reached Percy's side and gave him a bit of a wallop with the book of poetry she was holding.

It immediately became clear that she had walloped him a bit too hard, since Percy went careening backward, his feet flying out from under him. He remained flat on his back on the highly polished floor, blinking owlishly up at her as she peered down at him.

"Sorry about that," she said, offering him a hand, which he ignored as he all but jumped to his feet.

"Myrtle can be a little too enthusiastic with the loving taps she enjoys giving me."

She couldn't help herself—she hit him again, harder than the first time, although Percy seemed to be more prepared for her attack, because even though he stumbled, he didn't lose his feet. However, the glare he sent her after he regained his balance spoke volumes.

"What are you doing?" he demanded in a voice no louder than a whisper.

"Trying to knock some sense into you, since clearly yours has gone missing."

Murmurs began running rampant throughout the ballroom.

"You're embarrassing yourself," Percy hissed.

"No, Percy, I'm not. *You're* embarrassing both of us. I'm merely trying to stop you from making a complete cake of yourself, but since that doesn't seem to be working . . ." She spun around and faced the crowd of guests, who were pressing closer.

"Percy and I have not reconciled, nor will we be reconciling in the future. I don't love him and he doesn't love me. Although, now that I think about it, he does have very nice manners when he sets his mind to it, plays a mean game of tennis, can sit a horse with ease, and comes from one of the most established families in the city."

"Why are you telling everyone that?" Percy muttered.

Myrtle gestured to the crowd. "Because I know this ballroom is filled with ladies who just adore matchmaking. And to those ladies, I say this—if you know any eligible ladies who have verified fortunes who may be interested in attaching themselves to one of the oldest families in the city, send them Percy's way. He's available because, again, I won't be marrying him."

Streaks of red stained Percy's cheeks. "Stop it."

Myrtle shook her head. "I won't stop it, Percy, because I've had quite enough." She lifted her chin as she gestured to the crowd again, many of whom were gazing back at her with their mouths agape. "I'm through with the gossip, the pettiness, and the intrigues. I'm also through with the attitude of superiority that we in society seem so keen to embrace merely because of our ancestry or how much money our grandfathers made in the past."

Her chin lifted another notch. "As Percy so charmingly reminded you, he and I did have some difficulties last year, brought about when he abandoned me for another lady. If that unpleasant surprise wasn't bad enough, all the whispers and pity many of you in this very room sent my way after I was jilted . . . well, it made my unfortunate situation almost unbearable. I didn't want to be pitied, but now, in hindsight, I can only thank the good Lord above for that experience, because it gave me the strength to abandon the only world I'd ever known and enter into one I never imagined existed."

She glanced at her mother, who looked horrified, and sent her a small smile before she continued. "My mother does not want me to tell you this, but I've spent the last several months working as a Harvey Girl."

That announcement sent additional murmurs sweeping through the room, murmurs that didn't bother her at all. She gave an airy wave of her hand. "Yes, yes, quite shocking, I know. But you see, being a Harvey Girl allowed me to find myself, and it also allowed me to meet people from all walks of life and realize that not everyone cares about what dress to wear, or who the right people are to spend time with, or . . . well, I could go on and on, but this is a ball, after all.

"What I want to say most of all is this: Because I left New York, I met a man I fell deeply in love with, but I made a mess of that because I was hesitant to tell him who I truly was—or rather, what type of world I came from—worried he might be intimidated by my illustrious family and lifestyle." She drew in a breath and slowly released it. "I've since come to realize something of great importance. The real reason I didn't tell him the truth about my past life was because I'm ashamed of the world I grew up in. I'm ashamed of our selfishness, our materialistic desires, and mostly, I'm ashamed of how we treat one another. Jack Daggett, the man I love with all my heart, is honorable, kind, intelligent, and, I must add, incredibly handsome, and while I denied his claim that he wouldn't fit into my world, he was right. He's far too good for the likes of us."

Dashing away a tear that had escaped her eye, Myrtle nodded. "That's all I have to say, so if you'll excuse me, I'm off to find my Mr. Daggett and make amends."

"You don't need to go very far to find me. I'm right here."

Myrtle dropped the book she was still clutching as the crowd parted, and then . . . Jack was striding toward her, looking more than delicious in formal evening attire, his gaze never wavering from hers.

"Who in the world is that?" Myrtle heard her mother ask.

"It's Jack, Mother. Jack Daggett, the gentleman Myrtle just announced to one and all that she loves," Eloise called from the other side of the room.

"What are you doing here?" Myrtle asked when Jack drew to a stop directly in front of her.

He smiled as his eyes began to twinkle. "I came to tell you that Percy wants to marry you because he needs your money."

If his eyes hadn't been twinkling so much, she might have been disappointed with what he'd just said, but she had a feeling he wasn't done quite yet.

She nodded. "My sister, thankfully, already told me that."

He smiled. "I've met your sister. She's delightful. But returning to the matter of Percy, I was hoping to take care of him for you, but you did a wonderful job of that all on your own." He took hold of her shoulders and turned her around, which allowed her to witness Percy bolt out the door that led to the back courtyard and disappear from sight.

"I guess he didn't want to stay to see what happens next," she said, turning around again.

"I'm sure you're right, just as I'm sure he'll eventually land on his feet again, especially since you told every lady in the crowd that he's eligible and actively seeking a wife."

"Least I could do, since my parents are good friends with his parents."

"Yes, well, you're kinder than I would have been with him, though you did tell everyone you find me to be a kind man."

"You are, although you can occasionally be grumpy."

"Guilty as charged, and allow me to apologize most profusely to you for reacting so poorly when I heard the truth about your past. That was not well done of me. I did a grave disservice to you, and I can only hope you'll be able to forgive me."

"Of course I do. I was more in the wrong than—"

Jack placed a finger over her lips. "You certainly have nothing to apologize about. But since you're evidently willing to forgive me, allow us to set that aside and move forward to something a bit more pleasant. You said you love me."

"I must admit that I do."

"Well, I'm going to pretend that I didn't hear you bellow out to everyone that you love me, so that when I tell you I love you, we can always claim that I said the words first."

Myrtle's knees turned all sorts of wobbly, so wobbly in fact that she had to reach out and take hold of Jack's arm to steady herself. When she felt capable of standing on her own, she gave a wave of her hand. "How lovely, although . . . am I to understand that you love me?"

Jack blew out a breath. "I swore to my brother that I was going to do this properly this time, but I'm afraid my nerves are getting the better of me, since I'm not off to a stellar start."

"You seem to be doing fine to me," Myrtle said with a smile.

"Then allow me to continue in that direction and simply say this—I love you, Miss Myrtle Schermerhorn, and . . ." A second later, he was down on one knee as a collective sigh rang out from all the ladies in attendance. He reached into his pocket, frowned, then froze. "Honestly, Walter warned me this could happen, and yet I didn't believe him."

"What happened?" Myrtle asked.

"He's missing the ring because he had to exchange clothes with Mr. Van Alen and forgot to take this little box out of his pocket."

Looking up, Myrtle found Walter trying to make his way into the room, the Oelrichs's butler trying his very best to stop him from doing that by holding on to one of Walter's legs. He was pulled along on the floor as Walter staggered forward.

"Mr. Burlington, do release the poor man, because everyone is waiting with bated breath to see how this plays out," Mrs. Oelrichs called. The butler let go of Walter, who immediately strode forward and handed Jack a small box, one that was a distinctive shade of blue. The sight of it left Myrtle a bit breathless.

"I knew you were going to have trouble with this," Walter said to his brother before he turned his charming smile on Myrtle. "It's lovely to see you again, Myrtle. Ruthanne and Opal are waiting outside. I couldn't get them past the butler, but that was Ruthanne correcting Percy about your name. She had to resort to yelling through an open window."

"I thought I heard her voice."

"I'm sure you and Ruthanne will have much to talk about, what with—"

"Don't you think this might be able to wait until a more appropriate time, Walter?" Jack asked, still down on one knee and looking rather amused.

"Oh, yes, right. You're in the middle of . . . I'll just wait over there," Walter said. He strode across the room, earning himself more than a few appreciative glances from the ladies, something Ruthanne was probably not going to appreciate. But then again, Daggett men were dashing sorts.

"Where was I?" Jack asked.

"You said you love me, then said *and* . . ."

"Right, *and* . . ." Jack looked up, caught her eye, then flipped open the lid of the little blue box, revealing a beautiful diamond ring from none other than Tiffany's.

Myrtle sucked in a deep breath. "Hold that thought. I'll be right back."

As Jack's mouth dropped open, Myrtle sent him a grin, then dashed over to her mother. "I need to see that newspaper clipping."

"Now?" Cora asked.

"It's important."

Cora fished the clipping from her evening bag, then glanced at it, glanced at the box Jack was still holding up, then looked back at Myrtle. "Do not tell me that's the same ring."

"I think it is." Taking the clipping from her mother, she raced back to Jack, looked at the advertisement, looked at the ring, then smiled. "Just as I thought. Another message from God, and this one letting me know that hope is alive and well in our world."

"Should I assume that's another sign you found in a newspaper, just like the one you received about joining the Harvey Girls?" Jack asked.

"Indeed, but no need to delve into the matter right now." She tucked the advertisement into the bodice of her gown, knowing she would keep it forever. "Now, to remind you, you were at *and*."

"I know." He smiled a smile that left her wobbly at the knees again. "To recap, since it's been some time now since I started this, I love you, and I would be the luckiest man alive if you would agree to become my wife."

Blinking away tears that threatened to blind her, Myrtle managed a nod as she stuck out her hand. "Consider yourself lucky then, my darling Jack, because I would love nothing more than to marry you."

After stripping the glove off her hand so the ring would fit properly, Jack slipped it onto her finger, drew her close, told her he loved her again, and then . . . he kissed her.

Tracie Peterson is the bestselling, award-winning author of more than 100 novels. Tracie also teaches writing workshops at a variety of conferences on subjects such as inspirational romance and historical research. She and her family live in Montana. Learn more at www.traciepeterson.com.

Christy Award finalist and winner of the ACFW Carol Award, HOLT Medallion, and Inspirational Reader's Choice Award, bestselling author **Karen Witemeyer** writes historical romances because she believes the world needs more happily-ever-afters. She is an avid cross-stitcher and shower singer, and she bakes a mean apple cobbler. Karen makes her home in Abilene, Texas, with her husband and three children. To learn more about Karen and her books and to sign up for her free newsletter featuring special giveaways and behind-the-scenes information, please visit www.karenwitemeyer.com.

Regina Jennings is a graduate of Oklahoma Baptist University with a degree in English and a minor in history. She's the winner of the National Readers' Choice Award, a two-time Golden Quill finalist, and a finalist for the Oklahoma Book of the Year Award. Regina has worked at the *Mustang News* and at First Baptist Church of Mustang, along with time at the Oklahoma National Stockyards and various livestock shows. She lives outside of Oklahoma City with her husband and four children and can be found online at www.reginajennings.com.

Jen Turano, a *USA Today* bestselling author, is a graduate of the University of Akron with a degree in clothing and textiles. She is a member of ACFW and RWA. She lives in a suburb of Denver, Colorado. Visit her website at www.jenturano.com.

Sign Up for Authors' Newsletters!

Keep up to date with latest news on book releases and events by signing up for their email lists at:

traciepeterson.com

karenwitemeyer.com

reginajennings.com

jenturano.com

More from the Authors

Only while trick riding can Ella Fleming forget the truth about who she really is—the daughter of a murderer. Phillip DeShazer buries the guilt he feels for his father's death in work and drink, and his guilt continues to grow the more Ella Fleming comes to his rescue. Will they be able to overcome their pasts and trust God to guide their futures?

What Comes My Way by Tracie Peterson
BROOKSTONE BRIDES #3
traciepeterson.com

Fleeing her past, naturalist Tayler Hale accepts a position at the popular Curry Hotel in Alaska. There she must work with Thomas Smith, who calls the hotel home. As Thomas struggles to get used to the idea of a female naturalist, unexpected guests and trouble arrive at the Curry. They'll have to band together to face the danger that follows.

Under the Midnight Sun by Tracie Peterson and Kimberley Woodhouse, THE HEART OF ALASKA #3
traciepeterson.com; kimberleywoodhouse.com

After being railroaded by the city council, Abby needs a man's name on her bakery's deed, and a man she can control—not the stoic lumberman Zacharias, who always seems to exude silent confidence. She can't even control her pulse when she's around him. But as trust grows between them, she finds she wants more than his rescue. She wants his heart.

More Than Words Can Say by Karen Witemeyer
karenwitemeyer.com

⬦BETHANYHOUSE

You May Also Like . . .

Caroline Adams returns to Indian Territory craving adventure after tiring of society life. When she comes across swaggering outlaw Frisco Smith, his plan to obtain property in the Unassigned Lands sparks her own dreams for the future. When the land rush begins, they find themselves battling over a claim—and both dig in their heels.

The Major's Daughter by Regina Jennings
THE FORT RENO SERIES #3
reginajennings.com

As part of a bargain with her wealthy grandmother, Poppy Garrison accepts an unusual proposition to participate in the New York social Season. Forced to travel to America to help his cousin find an heiress to wed, bachelor Reginald Blackburn is asked to give Poppy etiquette lessons, and he swiftly discovers he may be in for much more than he bargained for.

Diamond in the Rough by Jen Turano
AMERICAN HEIRESSES #2
jenturano.com

Regency England, late 1800s New York, and 1920s Maine come alive in this romantic and inspiring novella collection from three acclaimed, award-winning Christian historical fiction authors! Includes Kristi Ann Hunter's "A Search for Refuge," Elizabeth Camden's "Summer of Dreams," and Amanda Dykes's "Up from the Sea."

Love at Last by Kristi Ann Hunter, Elizabeth Camden, and Amanda Dykes
kristiannhunter.com; elizabethcamden.com; amandadykes.com

◊ BETHANYHOUSE